CATACLYSM

An 11:34 Novel

MJ DelConte

Scrawny Llama Press

ISBNs: 978-1-954628-00-7 (Amazon eBook),
978-1-954628-03-8 (Amazon paperback),
978-1-954628-02-1 (Draft2Digital),
978-1-954628-04-5 (Google Play)

*To my wife, Melissa, for helping me realize
my dream.*

CONTENTS

PROLOGUE

I believe in God, the Father Almighty. Maker of heaven and earth.

And in Jesus Christ, His only Son, our Lord, who was conceived by the Holy Spirit, born of the Virgin Mary, suffered under Pontius Pilate, died, and was buried. He descended into hell. The third day, He rose again from the dead. He ascended into heaven and sits at the right hand of God the Father Almighty.

From thence He will come to judge the living and the dead.

— The Apostles' Creed

ACT 1: IN THE BEGINNING

1 - RECOVERY

December 20, 2015: Philadelphia, Pennsylvania

The sun was a full hour away from rising, but the sky would brighten well before sunrise, which gave them a narrow window to complete their mission while it was still dark. It was a few minutes before six in the morning, and traffic was nonexistent. The holidays were around the corner, which meant people were on vacation. Or they had stayed out late to shop or attend parties. Or they worked nine-to-fives and were still asleep. Whatever the reason, the lack of traffic meant the twin shiny black SUVs could speed down the main avenues in an area of Philadelphia that wasn't quite seedy but not far from it. Holiday decorations added cheer to the otherwise-worn street-facing façades: colorful Christmas lights, menorahs, even an occasional decorated tree. Given the hour, there was no pedestrian traffic, riffraff, or police. Surveillance monitored the whereabouts of patrol cars, but it was quiet, likely due to shift changes. The operation was intended to be a textbook in-and-out. No witnesses. No cops. No news. Quieter than a whisper. Remaining anonymous was of utmost importance to their organization.

The original plan to acquire their target had been nixed when they lost contact with their field operative. Ten minutes later, the plan was altered, to the chagrin of the Executive, who sat quietly in the modified seating of the rear SUV, his eyes losing none of their intensity. A bulletproof vest covered a long-sleeve black sweater. At his side was a Glock 21, a .45-caliber pistol he swore by because it was not only formidable but also noticeably lightweight.

Across from him sat three men, all ex-military, covered head to toe with black bulletproof armor and tactical gear, which they had triple-checked upon entering the SUV. Now they waited, faces impassive, heading into a hot situation. Been there, done it. The Executive knew they had laid their lives on the line countless times in the Middle East.

Life after the military is a crapshoot for soldiers returning home. Some luck out and find jobs or go back to school; some are as physically and emotionally war-torn as the villages they had defended. Still others find themselves wanting more, but no longer desire to serve their country. Not necessarily out of lack of patriotism. Everyone has a reason when they choose to leave a job. Some may be burned out from workplace politics, sheer boredom, or the day-to-day grind. Some seek improved benefits, better pay, or career advancement. Whatever the reason, it occurs with the men and women in the military. They check out when they have had their fill. And a few fortunate specialists seeking a position where they can keep their toe in the water find the Executive.

The Executive rigorously vets each person and hires only the best of the best. After they laid their lives on the line for the betterment of the world, he believes they have earned it. Those who survive the hiring process are not only paid handsomely but become members of the family. Newly hired personnel receive private quarters, full life and medical benefits, and all meals paid. In return, the Executive expects them to be ready at a moment's notice and perform at a level of professionalism and competence commensurate with the lofty standards expected from them by their countries.

After achieving a business degree abroad at Yale, the Executive had returned to England and stood by his father's side. His father had built a stock investment empire. The youngster was not naïve; he watched and learned. But it was not his passion, and his father knew it. One day, his father let him in on a secret: it hadn't been his ambition either. He was merely funding his son's foray into stopping the Apocalypse. When his father passed away, the Executive sold off enough stock to lose the majority share. He did retain a hearty percentage, to protect his father's investment and to continue financing his new endeavor. It's always a good idea to have a back-up plan.

His father had hired good people to build his

investment firm. He sought out the best of the best and paid them generously for their tireless and relentless dedication. Similarly, the Executive needed support — strong, like-minded men and women whose passion rivaled his own. He used the same strict vetting process his father executed with tremendous success. Flawless precision and effective enforcement were paramount traits. The execution of those traits was a technical, immutable skill that required a hammer and an anvil that would be used to shape the future. Those under his employ would call him the Executive.

One advantage he counted on with former military was that if anyone got out of line, there was always peer pressure. After that, the group captains would take charge. In his time running the organization, the Executive never had a single dispute reach his desk.

"Approaching first target." The female voice over the headset spoke with an equal measure of silkiness and placidity.

They had reached the point of no return. The Executive nodded to the captain sitting across from him. The captain answered, "Copy that."

There was a four-way stop at the intersection, but neither SUV slowed. The first SUV turned left while the rear SUV continued down the avenue. The streets were a conglomeration of patchwork and potholes, but at least they were dry and free of snow and ice.

"Police patrol, east, six blocks, heading south,"

came the silky voice over the headsets.

They were traveling north.

Ten seconds later, the female voice spoke again. "Team Alpha, fifteen seconds." Then, "Team Delta, thirty seconds."

The first SUV braked hard, and three men from the Alpha Team leaped out armed with HK MP5 suppressed submachine guns. They moved down the dark alley like phantoms. They unlatched a gate to a simple metal fence, entered the backyard of a three-story building, and glided up the exterior steps all the way to the top floor. They pushed a four-digit code into a dimly lit keypad. A click of the lock broke the silence. Easing the door open, they slipped into the building.

The second SUV approached its destination. Duplexes, one indistinguishable from the next, lined both sides of the street. Every building was addressed using blocky numbers, each faded by weather and age. The SUV parked in front of one such building. Three armed men and the Executive sprang out the back and hurried down a narrow, cracked sidewalk. Their target lived on the second floor. They ascended creaky, weather-worn stairs by straddling the wooden handrail to minimize noise. They reached a simple door with several small panes of glass in it. One of the men stepped forward and tried the door handle. Locked. An unsecured door might put an entirely different spin on the matter. He punched through the glass nearest the door handle, then reached in and unlocked the door. He gave the door a firm shove but found it chained. A chained door added to the suspicion that their quarry was safe and sound. Unsavory characters requiring rapid egress do not usually take the time to lock and chain a door first. The next obstacle would typically include guns or dogs. They knew their target owned neither.

"Sir, we have acquired the first target. However, our agent is down. I repeat, Manning is down."

They remained silent, waiting for the go signal from the Executive. He motioned them to move in. With their flashlights clicked on and weapons pointed, the three men entered, followed by the Executive, his Glock at his side. They proceeded into the small apartment and reached a doorway on the left. The captain and the Executive entered the bedroom. One of the men stood near the threshold watching the entrance while the last man searched the rest of the flat, returning moments later to give the all-clear. The captain and the Executive each hovered over one side of a snoring figure, clearly a sound sleeper, on the twin-size bed. The Executive gave the man a vigorous shake and he snuffled awake. He sat up, taking a moment to shake the cobwebs from his head, which the Executive obliged. The man gained full alertness when he saw the captain's weapon, and he froze, eyes squinting against the harsh beam of the flashlight but fixed on the barrel aimed at his forehead.

The Executive said, "Harvey Mitchell. I am the Executive." The man jerked slightly, having not realized that a second person stood at his bedside. He turned to face the Executive, whose stalwart form in the glow of the flashlight cast something more akin to that of a reaper. "We spoke briefly yesterday. Agent Manning works for me. I need you to get dressed and gather the evidence we discussed."

It was all coming back to Harvey now, the sleepy haze lifting, supplanted by the shattered remnants of a bad dream. The puzzle pieces quickly locked into place, and recognition set in. "Sir?"

"I need you to move right this second. We need to leave immediately."

Harvey swung the sheets off himself. Wearing only boxers, he stepped across the cold floor to an open closet. Harvey reached for a shirt, took a huge whiff, then threw it back into the jumbled mass of clothes covering the closet floor. The next shirt passed the whiff test. He yanked on crumpled jeans from the pile without smelling them. Forgoing socks, he tied the laces of a clean pair of sneakers. He put on his jacket, also picked up from the floor, and zipped it up, then retrieved a small, heavy-duty cardboard box atop a wire shelf in the closet.

"Take it," he said, pushing the box into the Executive's chest. "It has caused me nothing but trouble."

The Executive took the proffered box, and they hastily exited the building, racing down the middle of the creaky stairs, turning a corner, and running across the sidewalk.

When they reached the front of the building, the Executive announced, "Target two acquired. Alpha Team, meet at Rendezvous Point Charlie."

The Alpha Team leader acknowledged the message.

Harvey Mitchell and the Delta Team crammed into the back of the SUV and the driver sped off. A block away, feeling the exultation of a successful mission, the soldiers fist-bumped one another, encouraging Harvey and the Executive to join in. The Executive sighed and gave a reassuring nod to Harvey, who appeared to be riding high on adrenaline.

The captain gave Harvey a friendly shoulder bump. Harvey looked his way, unsure what to think or say to the man, but he relented, slumping down into the seat. Maybe it was all over. Harvey couldn't help but wonder why there was so much fuss over him and his box. He had seen its contents and considered burning it long ago, even after his father made him swear to contact the Executive. His father had told him the Executive would know what to do with the box. In the waning moments of his life, he gripped Harvey's forearm with a god-like vise, and he pleaded, voice barely audible, with words squeezed from constricted lungs huffing their last breaths. Harvey agreed, the grip relaxed, and alarms rang out from the machines surrounding his father's bed.

In the days that followed, Harvey assumed his father had grown mad — until strange, unexplainable things began to happen. Items around his apartment changed places. Cabinet doors opened of their own accord. After returning home one day, he found his bed a foot away from the wall. At first, he kidded with himself by chalking it all up to the paranormal. Maybe his dad had returned for a visit. It stopped being a laughing matter when Harvey started noticing a burly guy, one he did not recognize from his neighborhood. The guy always seemed to be stretching. But the guy appeared to be more vigilant about Harvey and the environs than his hamstrings. He saw the same musclehead at the grocery store sifting through an assortment of discounted paperback romance novels, inspecting mops, and reading cat food labels. He caught him walking on the other side of the same street peering into a windowed storefront adorned in pink neon signs boasting nail, hair, and spa treatments. Then, after stuffing a load of clothes in a washer at the corner laundromat, he saw the same guy through the plate-glass window, standing on the opposite street corner, watching. It came to a head when a car with heavily tinted windows sped past, inches from striking Harvey, after he put his foot in a crosswalk a few blocks from his apartment. He was sure he'd seen the same car parked in the lot where he worked. The incidents were far too many to be coincidental.

That was when he followed through on the promise he'd made to his father. He had no idea who the Executive was or what he could do for him. Since then, the Executive had told him a lot of stuff that seemed so outlandish that it could only happen in a movie. Then he met Chad Manning, a field operative for the Executive, who swore to protect him. But from what or from whom?

That was three days ago. Yesterday afternoon, Chad Manning had called him. The field operative was babbling, talking gibberish. Harvey panicked, trying to make out the instructions. He shouted at Chad to stop. Then, like a priest at a sermon, in words spoken clearly and concisely, Chad asked him for the location of his box. Per his father's wishes, Harvey had kept it locked away in a safe deposit box at his bank. Chad told Harvey to retrieve the box, lock himself in his apartment, and await further instructions. He was not permitted to leave no matter what.

Soon after, he received a call from the Executive. A plan was in play to transport him and his box out of Philadelphia. He, too, instructed Harvey to retrieve the box. Everything else would be left behind, and Harvey was never to return. No one, at any time, actually said he was in any danger. In retrospect, that was probably a wise idea.

That night, he could not fall asleep. He waited for another call or a knock at the door, but neither came. Still, he waited, trying to stave off sleep. At some point, in the crooked-numbers hours of the morning, eyes unable to stay open, he succumbed, until awakened by the man who had shoulder-bumped him and the man sitting across from him who called himself the Executive.

He stifled a yawn as he sat amid a group of men who dressed and carried themselves like Navy

SEALs. He knew little of the military. What he did know was that these guys and the weapons they carried were terrifying. Grimacing, he glared at the box. What was the big deal with it, anyway? It was just a bunch of dumb pictures. Some of them were black, some looked undeveloped.. His father had been a hotshot journalist and photographer. Harvey skimmed the accompanying notebook, but the details inside made no sense to him. How had his father known the Executive? Why were these guys treating the situation as if his life was at stake? So many unanswered questions zipped through his mind. *All because of this damned box!* The soldier next to him said, "It's all over, Harvey. We're good to go. You have nothing to fear anymore."

A loud crack rippled through the silence of the neighborhood like a meteor striking land. The rear window shattered at the same time Harvey's face exploded into a red mist. His headless body sagged forward. Arterial blood spurted, at first striking the roof several times with a wet splat before coating the interior and those sitting across from him, until his corpse settled onto the floor, blood flowing into the labyrinth of grooves in the rubber floor mats. In those first moments, no one heard the cry for help.

Chaos followed. The vehicle swerved, tires screeching. Someone shouted orders to the driver: "Drive! Drive!"

A flashlight clicked on, a hand obscuring the light to lessen the risk of being targeted by the sniper.

"I'm hit."

The muffled light moved onto the Executive, who was desperately clutching his left leg. He groaned weakly. The man with the flashlight pushed the Executive back into the seat to assess the damage. The light revealed a gruesome wound pooling with blood. It was impossible to determine how deep it went. The thigh muscle was exposed and shredded from one side to the other. There was no way to know if the femoral artery was compromised.

The experienced driver needed no one to tell him what to do. He swerved all over the road to avoid giving the sniper a clean second opportunity. A second shot struck the vehicle with a *bang*. Tires screeched as the vehicle veered down a narrow side street, fending off any other possible attempts from the sniper. The SUV reached a thoroughfare and raced down the patchy road at eighty miles an hour.

Two men tended to the Executive, applying a tourniquet to the wounded leg to stanch the bleeding. They tightened the tourniquet with such an abrupt jerk that the Executive saw the pain flash white-hot and he cried out. They laid the Executive flat across the bench seat and elevated his wounded leg.

Despite the gravity of the moment, the third soldier remained equable. *Been there, done it.* "Shots fired. Target Harvey Mitchell is down. We need medical to be ready at Rendezvous Point Charlie. The Executive sustained a gunshot wound to his left leg."

There was brief hesitation in the response before the female voice, with a note of concern, asked, "How bad is it?"

The captain gazed at him, unblinking.

"We need medical to be ready at Rendezvous Point Charlie," the soldier repeated, his tone less firm.

The female voice responded, "Roger that. Medical is standing by at Rendezvous Point Charlie. Do you have the package?"

The soldier answered, "Affirmative. The package is secure."

The sky grew brighter with every passing moment. The two vehicles reunited along their way to Philadelphia International Airport. They reached an open hangar where a private jet idled. A woman wearing a pewter-colored parka stood nearby. The SUV with the Executive skidded to a stop. The two soldiers tending to the Executive eased him out of the vehicle. The Executive murmured something to the captain, who dropped back to retrieve the box from the SUV before climbing aboard the plane. The captain waited for the three soldiers from Alpha Team to climb aboard before latching the door. While the drivers parked the vehicles in the hangar, the jet taxied toward the main runway. By the time they received clearance to take off, the Executive had an IV inserted in his arm and a pint of blood squeezed into his vein. A second pint was administered before the wheels left the ground. They leveled off at thirty-five thousand feet.

At the rear of the plane, her back to the soldiers, the woman quietly worked to repair the damaged artery, occasionally speaking into a microphoned headset. Mounted overhead was a high-resolution camera situated up and over at a slight angle from the injured leg. The soldiers busied themselves by cleaning their weapons and tidying up their gear. The woman stifled a curse. Unable to contain themselves, the soldiers stole sheepish glances in the way children do after being scolded by their parents or a teacher.

They flew above clouds, an endless sea of floating white cotton balls. Occasional breaks provided a glimpse of the shadowed terrain below, the earth a rippled bevy of ridges covered by a blanket of white.

After a time, the conversation intensified, her words spoken in a clipped, excited tone. Her movements became increasingly frantic. She cursed after an alarm sounded. She rubbed her forehead with the back of her wrist, avoiding contact with the blood dripping from her gloved hands. She shouted into the headset, "I'm trying!" The outburst garnered the attention of the six soldiers, their gear suddenly forgotten. Another alarm chimed. She listened attentively while a calm, commanding voice instructed her to compose herself. She took a breath and went back to work. The femoral artery had been nicked, but not severed. How he remained alive was beyond her comprehension. The swift action of the soldiers probably saved his life. She stitched the artery.

"I repaired the femoral artery. I think he is going to be okay."

Alarms pierced the cabin. Red lights flashed across a console. The Executive went into V-fib. She checked for a pulse and found none.

"Shit, shit, shit! No, no. No!"

Once she established that his airway was clear, she reached for the defibrillator paddles and flipped a switch. After a moment, she yelled, "Clear!" The rhythm did not change. She switched to 360 joules and repeated. Still no pulse. She started CPR. After two minutes, she administered one milligram of epinephrine. She began CPR again. One of the monitors beeped, and the chorus of alarms fell silent. Some of the lights still flashed. She read the monitor and placed her fingers on his neck to check for a pulse. She gasped. "He's alive!" she shouted. She remained busy for several minutes. She located the fifty-caliber slug and removed it. The bloody mushroom-shaped slug landed in a metal pan with a clank. She did her best to patch the wound, but it was like looking at shredded beef. She closed her eyes, breathed in, and after holding it for several seconds, slowly exhaled.

After collecting herself again, she answered a question over the headset: "I'm fine. I don't know what more I can do here. His leg is…" She swallowed hard. "He is stabilized for now. His fate rests on your team."

She listened once more. "Roger that."

A few hours later, the plane landed at an undisclosed location, where a surgical team awaited them. Beside shattering a window and turning a man's head into a Slurpee, the high-powered slug had done considerable damage to the Executive's left leg. The medical equipment in the jet sufficed for general injuries, even minor surgery, if it came to it, but the gunshot wound proved to be too severe and required far more extensive medical attention. The collective heads were less than optimistic about his chances of survival through the night, let alone their transoceanic return trip to Switzerland.

The jet parked in front of a small white structure built of corrugated metal. The building had seen better days. Its paint job had faded long ago and rust set in around the seams. Weeds prospered around the structure and amid cracks in the asphalt.

Outside the open hangar door waited a medical team sporting blue scrubs and latex gloves. They stretchered the Executive into the hangar. A small, olive-skinned woman in scrubs stood in the center of the hangar threshold glaring at them, her eyes daring anyone to attempt to enter. No one challenged her. She removed a small, dark gray remote control from her pocket and held it up for all to see. She clicked an oval orange button, and in response, the massive doors on each side slowly rolled closed. The woman, along with the soldiers, stared for many moments at the closed door. She pulled off her bloodstained latex gloves and dropped them to the ground. After rubbing her eyes, she strode towards an adjacent corrugated metal structure. The white paint had faded long ago, and rust was visible in swaths along the exterior. At the far end of the building was a 360-degree observation tower. She pulled open the glass door and entered.

The soldiers remained standing outside the hangar. Nary a word was spoken, but the same thoughts rattled around their minds. The fate of the organization rested with that man. If he died, what would they do? Where would they go? But such questions paled in comparison to their loyalty and respect for the Executive. The man had a code, one from which he never strayed. He carried himself honorably and treated every single member of the organization as if he or she were the most important person on the team.

Furthermore, he had not yet completed his mission, a mission they all wanted to see through to the end. Or die trying. Harvey Mitchell and the box were considered mission critical. They had a job to do, and every single one of them would have gladly eaten that bullet if it meant drawing one step closer to completing their mission.

Instead, they felt an overwhelming sense of failure.

They had found field operative Chad Manning splattered all over his rented apartment. Manning had been tasked with keeping an eye on Harvey until the extraction could be coordinated.

Harvey's call to the Executive escalated the priority of the mission. He said someone had been inside his apartment, but it did not appear anything was taken. He claimed he had a close call crossing a street, but he could not be sure, since Philly drivers were notoriously aggressive. He had retrieved the box as instructed by Manning and the Executive. He also let the Executive know about his last communication from Manning. The field agent sounded afraid, according to Harvey. The Executive assured him that he and his team were on their way. He was told to stay in his apartment and lock his door.

The Executive received a call from Manning minutes after Harvey did. The Executive answered but heard only the throaty, gurgling sounds issued during a strangling. There was an audible thump after the gurgling ceased, and the call disconnected.

When the soldiers arrived at Manning's apartment, they found a body. The killer had smashed Manning's head into a pile of goop. Bloody boot prints painted the floors and walls of the flat.

Now the six soldiers stood in front of a metal building in the middle of God-knows-where, guarding it out of duty. It was the first time in a long time that any of them were unsure. Unsure what to do. Unsure of themselves. Unsure of the Executive. Unsure of their organization's future.

Their boss was unlucky, but not as much as Harvey Mitchell. The man lost his head. If it were not for the rear windshield and Harvey Mitchell, who knows what would have become of the Executive. All they knew for sure was that stowed safely in the jet was a mysterious box the Executive said might save the world.

2 - THE OFFER

1445 BC: Mount Sinai Peninsula

A bearded man leaned against his staff as he aimed his full attention at the deep, resonating voice speaking to him. The voice instructed Moses to erect a tabernacle on the first day of each month. At a faraway distance, another — Lucifer — watched and listened, sitting cross-legged on a rocky ledge, elbows on knees and both fists under his chin. A gleam in his unblinking eyes, he brimmed with curiosity. The booming voice instructed that within a tent shielded by curtains was to be an altar made of gold. Behind this altar, He commanded, should be the Ark of the Covenant, the chest containing the stone tablets of the Ten Commandments.

After agreeing, Moses bowed and took his leave.

"A good man is Moses," Lucifer spoke casually. There was no one around him, but Lucifer's words were not intended to be heard by man. "He would walk into a lake of lava if you so instructed."

The booming voice that instructed Moses was soft, reserved. "Yes, Lucifer, a good man is Moses."

"Indeed," said Lucifer. Lucifer continued to watch, saying nothing more, even as night fell.

Immortals were not impervious to time, but they could manipulate it. Lucifer allowed time to slip at an accelerated pace so he could more quickly watch Moses and his followers do as they were instructed. As the sun plunged toward the horizon, the sky flared with fiery crimson before giving way to a satiny violet.

With a twinge of impatience with Lucifer's dramatics, the deep voice asked, "What brings you to me this day, Lucifer?"

"Blunt and to the point, I see." Time returned to its standard pace. "Well, it has been a long time since we last spoke, you and I. I should think it would please you to—"

The Lord interrupted. "I have lived a long, long time. I have created and wiped out many existences, each time starting out with a blueprint for creation, improving upon it with each iteration. Once I was ready, I began building it. With this iteration, on the first day, I created light. On the second day, I created heaven. On the third day, I created earth, sea, and plants. On the fourth, I created the universe and all of its stars, moons, and planets. On the fifth day, I added life that could fly above the water and swim underneath its surface. On the sixth day, I created the creatures that walk the earth, including man. On the final day, I invoked free will, randomness, and changeability. This put my creation into motion, enabling the effectuation of life — and death — to occur without intervention. It allowed this iteration to thrive. Birthing. Living. Dying. Expanding. Contracting. The invocation allowed me to relax, watch, and wait. Though I liked this iteration of creation best, I am growing weary of it once again. It is only a matter of time before I begin anew. The existence of creation is governed by the fall of my fist. All I need to do is lower my fist upon it and it will cease to exist." The Lord sighed. It was many moments before he spoke again. When he did, the ground rumbled, unsettling silt and small stones with each passing syllable. "My patience runs lean, Lucifer. While I consider the fate of this iteration of creation, I have little tolerance for your wanton depravity. Speak your desires or hold your forked tongue until the end of time."

"Ah, yes, well, let me start by saying I come bearing good tidings. And with them, an offer."

Silence hung in the air while Lucifer waited for a response. When none came, he continued. "I wish to offer my services to you and for the good of mankind once more. It has been millennia since we last conspired — what was it?" Lucifer tapped a ringed finger against his chin, feigning deep contemplation. As if roused by the recollection of lost memory, he said, "Ah yes, it was a test of faith, one we employed upon that poor soul, Job. He did himself and all men a great deed."

The final spoken words echoed along the sacred landscape. Clouds built up on one side of the mountain and shadows stretched across the width of the valley.

When the Lord spoke, He said, "Man proved himself fortunate, thanks to the everlasting faithfulness of Job. Since that time, man has grown both wiser and in population. Man needs good leaders, leaders like Moses. Free will leads idle minds to corruption, for the time for leadership has never been greater. Men require someone through whom I will speak."

"How true, Father," Lucifer chuckled. "Sometimes, it amazes me how we think alike. So it is on this day I present you with an offer. Not quite the burnt remains of cattle or goats as you sought from men, mind you, but something of greater significance."

A moment passed before the Lord spoke. "What is this offer?"

"These people who follow are thirsty for your affection, but they carry an uncertainty with them like a long walk through a desert searching for an oasis beyond the next dune. Some, like Moses, carry enough of you in their hearts that if it were water, it would be enough to fill rivers, lakes, and seas to their brims with enough left over to quench the thirst of every man and beast for eons.

"I question not the direction of Moses or his followers. Some men are not believers. They doubt your very existence. And then there are those who have not received your word."

"My word will spread."

"And what of those who choose not to believe?"

"Not all people follow in the steps of the righteous, true. It is the actions they take when events unfold before them that define their true nature," replied the Lord.

"Yes, yes. True are your words," said Lucifer, "However, even in your presence man remains split as to whom he serves. Many men have forsaken thee. Dare I say 'Golden Fleece'? I fear the waters they sip from cupped hands are impure. Corruption soils their souls. They sate themselves with glut, greed, and lust. And here among them are you and those you command, men like Moses. Yet so many others are not so inclined to believe or to follow. Their darkened hearts repel that which is good and pure. Those men sidle from the light into the darkness, toward me, and that darkness grows at a dizzying pace. Does this not disturb thee?"

"And what would you have me do, Lucifer? Lower my fist and smite their miserable existence over some who do not believe?"

Lucifer returned to tapping his chin with a finger, contemplating. "Hmm, that would be a sight to behold. However, I am sure we can agree on something a little less offensive. I offer something worthy of both demesnes." Lucifer's tone became that of silk. "I offer thee the issuance of another test."

The land cooled as night seeped into the valley. Then the sun rose, chasing away the vestiges of nocturnal activity. The sun crossed the sky, and night returned. Entire conversations between immortals varied in time as it suited them. In the perception of man, they might be instantaneous or stretch for hundreds of years. The conversation carried on as time sped up.

"Why?" the Lord eventually asked. Seasons passed before He replied. "To what end?"

"They questioned you. Mankind questions you still. You present them with gift after gift, and they return your love by killing and stealing and adulterating. This, even after you displayed a show of wrath for all time and cleansed the earth of its impurity. What will it take to make them understand? To believe? To love? To care? You unleash the plague upon those who dare defy you, and for those who boldly claim their obedience, fractures remain visible in their hearts. If I can see the murkiness that stains their souls, I know you must. When will it end? How much more are you willing to sacrifice? What will it take before you see the truth in my words? I do not doubt you will grow weary over this creation once more. I came here selflessly. My presence is not for my benefit. I believe you need my help."

"You believe they will rebel as they have in past iterations?" the Lord asked, curiously. Lucifer had fallen from the grace of Heaven, but there was a reason the Fallen One created and held dominion over Hell.

"They already have. Look down upon them

from your Throne." His words carried a tinge of heat. Lucifer loathed betrayal. The Lord knew it was one of the great hypocrisies surrounding Lucifer. Lucifer had seen betrayal for what it was. Given what he had done, perhaps it took a hard lesson in reality and eons to understand, but the Lord remained guarded. Lucifer continued his rant. "Some fear you and will heed anything someone with a voice deems to be your words, which are to be incontestable. Heavenly words spouted to control weak-minded fools. They have an inner voice, your voice, the voice of conscience, one that aims them down the golden path, but they are deaf to it. For they would not step forward to help those in need. They would not spread your word because their tongues have wilted dry with rot. Their children and their children's offspring would be devoid of the knowledge you desire all to know, to share.

"I have as much contempt for them as those whose tongues waggle just to be waggled. They are flies that could annoy the dead. They speak words, but they do it for the need to gain, not to sacrifice. They use slick words that benefit them, not those of the common good. Their vanity drives their obsessive need for selfish passions.

"When someone bigger, stronger, and louder comes along, he will become their leader. If he walks a path not aligned with yours, he will sin greater than all who walked before him, and they will permit him to do so. He will leave a wake of the oppressed and the dead, rising above you and your precious Commandments in the eyes of those he leads. He will not have a single worry for retaliation, for he will stand before an army at his sides and back. They will be his fist when he opts to rest his voice and punch his enemies."

"That is possible," the Lord said.

"It is inevitable."

"It is up to them to walk the path of the righteous."

"Not if they are made to see the light."

"You cannot force them to see. They must see with their own eyes."

Lucifer gritted his teeth, hissing out his frustration.

The land darkened, as it had hundreds of times throughout their conversation. A crescent moon crossed the sky, along with a few shooting stars, before giving way to the rise of a new day. The sun rose like an angry giant in the desert, feeding on long shadows until it was sated. After filling its belly, the sun fell lazily toward the horizon. Little lights twinkled in their infinite abundance of sterling beauty, while another crescent moon arced across the cloudless sky.

Old seasons ended and new ones began. Mortal years whisked by until, finally, there came a response from Mount Sinai.

"What is this test you propose?"

The flow of time ebbed. A man tossed a fish from his boat to another man on the shore of the Nile River. The fish hovered in the air from the fisherman's fingertips as it began to arc, inching toward the awaiting man. Before the fish completed its journey, Lucifer laid out his plan.

"Perhaps I shall call upon you once more, Lucifer. I find your idea undeniably aggressive, and yet I am bemused to find it equally intriguing. I acknowledge this would be more merciful than ruination." There was a note of satisfaction in the booming voice. Then the Lord added, "You are right about one thing, Lucifer. We cannot make them see the light. In place of light, men could be challenged with that of a new test, one that brushes away their infantile blindness. Make them wash away the very sin they cast. This test of yours is intriguing, indeed. I must give it due consideration."

As the fish reached the fingertips of the man on the shore, the flow of time returned to normal. Mingled with the whispers of the wind came the Lord's words: "A test... one where mankind, at last, sees with their own eyes."

3 - THE MEETING

April 3, AD 33: Golgotha, Jerusalem

The night stretched across the land like a cat after a long nap, and a gentle wind cooled the arid desert, carrying particles of dust and small grains of sand. A patrolling guard covered his face to fend off the flying grit. Not long after, the wind died. Then, as abruptly as it had left, the wind blew hard and brought with it an unusual wintery payload of chilled air and low-flying, sideways-blown snow.

The Messiah strained to lift his head in response to the strange energy feeding the unusual weather. Moving his head depleted what little strength remained. The chill air curled around his limbs and torso, and it made its way into his lungs. A torrent of energy spilled forward from his chest, and he gasped. There was something curious about the air. It made him stir with life. His body spasmed, and his fingertips twitched. It seemed like a lifetime since he had felt anything. His forehead tickled, but he couldn't make his fingers scratch the itch.

The Messiah took in a few deep breaths of the cold air. A nagging prickle replaced the itchiness circling his forehead. Life was seeping back into his body. The prickle morphed into a thousand mosquito bites. A flood of unbearable, white-hot pain replaced the numbness in his useless and unmoving limbs. Eyelids, crusted over with sweat, dirt, and blood, flashed open. His mouth sucked in the icy air until his chest was ready to explode. His chest heaved, and the pain went away, dissipating as if it had never really existed. His sight returned with full clarity. He looked from his hands and feet to the ground beneath him. *Am I dead?* The thought registered as clear as any rational thought he ever had. He looked around. He was suspended high above the ground. *Is this a hallucination?* It was possible. He reached out with his mind. No one else was there. He was alone and free of pain, not even a cramp from being in the same position for... *How long have I been here?* His eyes moved in all directions, assessing his plight. He remembered the sun and the unforgettable drive of those iron nails through his flesh and bone, through his hands and feet. He screamed from the agony of it all. He was lifted in the air to bake under the merciless sun. Then came the flies, relentless and unabated.

As he searched his mind for answers, he knew only that there was no brutal sun, no flies bit, and he was not in pain. In some strange way, he was relaxed, accepting of the next phase of his being. He hoped death was near, and he was crossing over.

Yet something made him suspicious that this was not death. The nighttime sky showcased millions of dazzling stars. Snow drifted across the ground. *Snow without clouds?* He exhaled and saw the warm vapor escape his lips. The temperature grew increasingly colder. He sensed it, but did not feel warm or cold.

Injuries sustained by crucifixion killed most men in hours, and hours had already passed. He hung there with closed eyes as his mind wandered over the day's events. Word had spread, and people came to witness and pray. Soldiers barricaded the area surrounding his crucifix. Even as they guarded the perimeter, some prayed in the safety of their minds. Others jeered at the very man who fed the hungry, healed the afflicted, and turned water to wine. There was a sign affixed above his head that read "King of the Jews" for all to see. He could hear their voices in his head, a blend of sorrow and rage mixed with confusion and doubt. *If you are the Son of God*, they mocked, *how can you save so many people but not yourself? Where is the martyr's God now?* He recalled it all.

Jesus opened his eyes, allowing them to roam the landscape, but they could not penetrate the darkness of night. Gifted or not, he was still a man. The light from the near-new moon and the stars cast vague shadows across an already dark landscape. He guided his eyes in the direction of the first distinct sound, which came from his left. The cadence of scrunching sand drew steadily closer and more pronounced.

Jesus spotted a figure moving in his direction, though it was too dark to see who it was. But while he could not quite make out everything, his sight seemed… better. He heard footsteps in the sand far sooner than he rightly should have. His aural senses were crisp and clear. Since he had begun breathing in the icy air, everything about him felt different. Perhaps different was too vague. Improved might be a more apt description.

The silhouette stopped several paces away from his crucifix and appeared to assess the situation. The figure turned its back to Jesus. The man wore a lustrous hooded cloak that cast a silken reflection in the moonlight. Next, he raised his arms. As he did so, dozens of long poles rose out of the sand in a jagged W pattern covering a half-circle to the front of the cross. The figure turned, its arms still raised, before dropping them downward dramatically. An eruption of bright sparks ignited the tops of the poles. Blue flames jetted out of the poles before the fire died down to torch-sized flames. The poles morphed, too. They now appeared to be black, metallic roses standing stiff and straight. The fire from the tops of the flower-shaped poles provided ample light for Jesus to see clearly. The person pulled his cowl back. The eyes of the man were solid black with white points more brilliant than the sun. Recognition was instantaneous.

"Lucifer!" Jesus shouted.

"Yes." Lucifer bowed with practiced eloquence, arm crossed in front of his belly, bending forward, maintaining the graceful pose for a glorious moment before tracing the same poetic movement in reverse. "Me."

"At the hour of my death! Have you come to gloat?"

"Why, Jesus." Lucifer's tongue carried an unusual but polite accent, one from the future and closely related to Scottish. Jesus had heard that the future could be seen but not foretold because it was always in flux. "I am hurt by your accusation."

"Why would you come here, now of all times, if not to gloat, heathen?"

"Before the Messiah leaves this place of wretchedness and despair," Lucifer said, brushing flakes of snow from his shoulder, "and before you leave those who have forsaken you to sit at the side of the Father Almighty, I wished to talk. A friendly chat, if you will."

"A chat? Your lecherous tongue befouls the very words thou speweth forth and the air we breathe. I shall play no part in your lechery."

"Lechery?" Lucifer considered the insult, then rocked back and forth with a hearty laugh.

"I do not wish to be fodder for your enjoyment, Lucifer. Speak and be gone. I wish to perish *alone* in the peaceful veil of night."

Lucifer grinned widely, displaying a set of sparkling white teeth that gleamed with an unnatural brightness. He stepped a few paces away, pulling the cloak from his torso and allowing it to fall to the ground. The cloak never truly touched the ground. The ground simply swallowed it until it was no more. Lucifer returned to his position before Jesus, busying himself with personal grooming. Jesus watched with utter contempt. Lucifer adjusted his bowtie and brushed the rounded shoulders, cuffed sleeves, and tapered breasts of his cream-colored tuxedo. A pair of matching tails dangled from the fancy suit. He took a moment to gently pat at his pleated pants, which matched the color of the tuxedo. Lucifer wore a pair of shiny camel-colored boots that might have worked in another time. They were an eccentric feature, but they provided a tremendous amount of comfort as well as functionality, all of which, in Lucifer's opinion, was paramount.

Jesus abhorred this ridiculous fashion show, but he could do nothing to prevent it. He watched with mounting contempt. Knowing that Lucifer was gimmicky, he kept his guard up, though there was little he could do from his perch.

"Ah, that's better." Lucifer's accent had changed yet again. Though Jesus did not know it, this one was cultured and snooty, but sophisticated and aware. "Out of respect to you, Messiah, I dressed for this very special occasion."

Jesus eyed Lucifer warily before responding.

"Respect?" Jesus scoffed. "Truly you jest. While I remain crucified, you entertain yourself with fire and…" He wanted to point using his hands, but instead jabbed with his chin. "And these strange robes with which you clothe yourself. Such foolishness! Have you no boundaries for vanity?"

"No." Lucifer shrugged. "Perhaps not."

Seeing Jesus's evident scorn, Lucifer chuckled. "I mean no disrespect. Please calm yourself."

"Why? You have appeared before me on this eve of my death. You restored me of my life at the time of death's knock on the door. You speak using strange tongues, twisted and disguised. You came from shadow and stand before me now in shadow. I ask once more and then sealed forever my lips shall become. Why have you come to witness my final hour, Lucifer?"

Lucifer regarded Jesus for several seconds before relenting. The tuxedo limply fell from his body, disappearing into the sand. Lucifer donned the dark robe again.

"I see. Like Father, like Son. You are cautious. Indeed, I could remove you from your current plight, but it would come at the greatest cost. Man attempts to kill His Son a second time. Lucifer saves His Son, wiping a fair number of good and evil men from existence, a big no-no in His opinion. The repercussions of my actions would be catastrophic. I foresee Him laying the foundation of a great war between Heaven and Hell. Mankind would be obliterated. It would be—"

"No," Jesus interrupted, tiring of Lucifer's endless babble. Jesus had no intention of betraying his Father.

"No?" Lucifer spread out his hands in confusion. "I'm sorry. I do not understand. I have asked nothing of you. For a second time, I am wounded by your lack of trust in me. It has me at a perilous disadvantage." Lucifer chuckled, but it sounded forced. "I do not want a holy war. My day will come, as sure as I stand before you, Son of God. As such, my dear Jesus, you will remain crucified until your mortal self lives no more. Your immortal self will rise. It is then that you will truly see for the first time. It will change your perspective about the existence of man. It might change your perspective about me."

Jesus snorted.

"My perspective will not be altered by you. Babies are born innocent, free of sin. Babies are harmless and dependent. As they mature, they use their minds. They learn the difference between right and wrong. They think. They choose. When a man chooses and acts upon his choice, that action determines the character of that man. No man is free of sin, but they choose the path they walk, a journey that can be influenced, something you can control. You have been known to interfere."

"It is true, men choose and men sin. I do none of that for them. My control has limits. I test their faith, a power I have been granted to use at my discretion by your Father." Jesus raised an eyebrow. "Oh yes, He is quite supportive of the Test of Faith."

Jesus's face reddened. "Heathen! You speak foul!"

Lucifer expected this, and said, "Before your time, it began with a man named Job. Since your Father did not have you to speak on His behalf, He had His word carried by those deemed worthy. To keep humanity from falling into a bottomless chasm of sin, He came to me."

Jesus scoffed.

"You wanted the <u>truth</u>, and I speak true. I may deceive from time to time, but I am no liar."

Jesus said nothing.

Lucifer conjured an apple and a small piece of cloth. As Lucifer spoke, he worked the cloth over the apple, though it needed no cleaning or polishing.

"Those whom He chose had limits and countless obstacles. Time worked against Him, in part due to mortal man's limited existence, and He began to see the improbable task laid out before them. His desire to cleanse the world of sin became a task fraught with greater impossibility than probability." Lucifer bit into the apple, savoring its sweetness, before finishing. "Finding no other solution, your Father came to me, and an arrangement was made."

The shocked expression on Jesus's face did not escape Lucifer. Jesus may have been mortal, but he had abilities now that extended beyond mortality. Everything Lucifer said rang white with the purity of truth. Though Jesus was not sure how he knew that, there was something in him that actively accepted what Lucifer said. For the first time, Jesus noticed Lucifer was not speaking garrulously in some strange tongue. There was a notable edge of seriousness in his words.

Lucifer finished the conjured apple. He lifted the core into the air, and it disintegrated into ash. Lucifer dabbed at his face with the cloth, then lifted it into the air before it, too, disintegrated into ash. As Jesus watched the charade with the apple and the cloth, he gathered Lucifer had an ulterior motive all along.

Jesus sighed. "What do you want of me, Lucifer?"

Answering with a brilliant smile, Lucifer said, "I seek a new arrangement."

4 - LUCIFER'S CONTRACT

April 3, AD 33: Golgotha, Jerusalem

T he bright blue light diminished when the staked poles sank into the sand. Lucifer walked away in the direction from which he had come. Jesus felt the cold embrace him once more, and he exhaled his last breath.

A booming voice he had heard so often before spoke to him following death's embrace:

My Son, I implore you to heed my words, for they will be the last your mortal self will hear. Mankind has forsaken me. I gave them heaven and earth. I gave them a warm sun, a bright moon, and rivers and oceans and mountains. A world filled with land to cultivate. Animals to provide clothing, food, and aid. Plants to provide medicine, shelter, and sustenance. They chose to walk a different path. A path of injustice, believing in false gods, and filling their empty hearts with mindless needs such as gold and lust. I tried. Over and over I tried. I shook the world. I sent floods. Still, they chose folly and frivolity over righteousness and love and belief. Before you, I sent them a man, one of their own, who spoke unto them the words from my voice. Moses presented the Ten Commandments, a gift incarnate and the guiding laws for peace and love. Despite the words etched in stone, they still carried doubt in their hearts. Then, I gave them you. A son, born of a virgin, a miracle child. And they have forsaken you, too. You will leave their world a martyr, a savior, a healer, a carpenter, and so much more. You were a man with mettle. You leave a world feasting on peace, with its eyes set on chaos for its next meal. Soon, you will be a god, and sit at my side. You can no longer be with them, and must rule from Heaven's Throne. It is a difficult road for you, Son, as you will soon mold men and shape their world. You were one of them. Spent a life among them. And you leave with experience at being at their side. You will harness a power greater than you have ever known and an awesome responsibility you must come to bear.

Lucifer once served me. I had entrusted my once-beloved fallen angel to test mankind. I had asked Lucifer to prove to me that men were faithful, to prove unto me they were worthy of creation. Stories have been told and retold of Job's faith. His test was scribed and will be a testament to the foundation of faith for all time. Lucifer did the requisite deed even if those involved had to suffer. The test was a difficult decision for me and a necessary one. Time has passed, and Job's tale, though sad, proves to be a valuable lesson for man. Not for all, I am afraid, for man has fallen deeper into sin.

When Moses was my voice, it was Lucifer who sought me. It would seem even Lucifer had taken notice of the corruption of souls descending into Hell to be en-

slaved as his servants. He had an idea, one I gave due consideration. As much as it is a burden, it is also a gift I present to you. This honor as an immortal will become your first decision, your first task. One that could shake the pillars of creation itself. I insist you give the gift similar consideration as I have given it. Remember, Son, this decision is a fork in the road that will change the path mankind walks.

Be wary of Lucifer's treachery, be purposeful of mind, walk shoulder to shoulder with righteousness, always have faith, and believe in yourself.

I love you, Son, and await your arrival.

Jesus opened his immortal eyes, though his physical eyes were already open. He had tapped into something beyond mortal comprehension. It was as if the gateway to the universe had unlocked, and, as massive iron gates swung outward, a brilliant light greeted him, blinding at first. His immortal eyes quickly adjusted. The light enveloped him, lifting him high. It carried him past the twin gates. He was inside.

Not inside a place, in a physical sense. He was everything, everywhere, and everything and everywhere became him. He watched the universe unfold. Time sped beyond the scope of the speed of light. His mind traveled from one corner of the universe to the next. The sensation threatened to expel him from his physical body. His mind swam in the tides of power and energy that created the universe. In that revelation, he had changed — was still changing. The great light dimmed, flowing more steadily now. His physical eyes no longer saw, because his immortal mind allowed him to see and feel without the need for mortal eyes and mortal flesh. Following his metamorphosis, he stretched and writhed until he was free from his human cocoon and the crucifix. The immortal Jesus floated from the mortal Jesus. Then, something below garnered His attention. The cloaked figure returned. For the first time, he saw Lucifer with eyes that were not human. He saw Lucifer, truly.

"How do you feel?" asked Lucifer.

"My body buzzes. There is a strange burn flowing up and down my arms and legs, from my belly to my forehead. I feel… different. Neither stronger or weaker, nor living or dead. I float, but I have no wings with which to fly. I see things I have never seen before. I see… I can see you, Lucifer."

"Your immortality fills you. I have felt the throes of newly minted immortality. The very same now fill you. How interesting! I have never witnessed it happen to another. The sensation will soon pass. Your mortal body followed the normal course of biology and died. The fire you sense within your new self is your immortality burning away the last vestiges of its mortal bondage."

Jesus spun around and faced himself. Not a reflection. He took a final glance at his lifeless human body. He felt neither anger nor remorse.

Sensing his agitation, Lucifer said, "The buzz you feel is your immortality protecting you during this transition. You would not survive it otherwise."

Jesus lifted his arms to look them over, feeling the electrical surge coursing through his limbs. Lucifer added, "That's Purity you sense buzzing about. It is a Blessing bestowed unto you by your Father. While in my presence, it prevents you from transforming into one of my minions. It will soon pass."

Jesus studied his hands, turning them over. He watched as burning embers of golden ash fell away — the last remnants of mortality — drifting away toward the swirl of snow and sand on the desert floor. What was left was the corporeal glow of his immortal self.

"Come." Lucifer passed through space. Jesus followed, leaving the desert behind.

Jesus found himself floating near a room resembling a cabin belonging to a king. Along the back length of the room stood a massive fireplace. A fire blazed away in the hearth, but it seemed a waste since it provided no heat. Polished onyx pillars stood at every corner. The floor and the fireplace appeared to be constructed of the same glossy black stone. Outside the room was infinite darkness. Lucifer stood near the edge of the room and beckoned Jesus over. Jesus floated gently down until he sensed himself touching the floor. The room seemed to contain light, but, other than faux fire, there was no source. Lucifer went to the fireplace and stoked the fire with a poker that appeared in his hand. He stared at the fire for a few moments. Sensing his guest's disdain for the theatrics, he raised his hand and waggled his fingers. Behind him, out of the stone floor, rose a table so thick and sturdy, it would surely last a thousand years if properly maintained. Rising next were two matching chairs at each end of the table. In the center of the long table, a bowl appeared. In it were shiny red apples.

Jesus recognized the source of the fruit and cast a frown at Lucifer.

"You can't blame me for trying." Lucifer chuckled, and the bowl disappeared. He moved to the far end of the table. "Please sit," he said, extending an arm out in invitation.

Jesus pulled a chair out and sat. Lucifer did likewise.

"I would like to know your idea," Jesus said.

"Ah, the direct approach. To the point." Lucifer smiled. "Just like your Father." Lucifer considered but resisted the urge to change his clothes, and he remained cloaked. The cloak blended with the stone. Its edges shimmered in the firelight. "It is a test, really."

"What kind of test?" Jesus asked.

"Not just a test. *The Test.* We shall delve into a man's soul to determine his worthiness."

"Worthiness," Jesus repeated flatly. "How?"

"Surely you know. Your Father spoke to you after I left, did He not?" Jesus squinted suspiciously at Lucifer. "Well of course He did." Lucifer relaxed further by crossing one leg over the other and resting a ringed hand atop his knee. He continued, "Your Father gave man an incredible gift. He created them, gave them life, souls. He constructed a universe for man to use to learn and explore. He gave him a planet complete with everything man needs to sustain himself and life in general. How has man repaid him? How has man conducted himself? Your Father asked them only to follow a few simple rules along the way. Instead of appreciation, their perverse exhibitions have sown the seeds of the foulest corruption in their very souls."

Lucifer stood and stepped thoughtfully toward the hearth.

"As generations passed, they became more and more comfortable with their acts of depravity. It has become a normal component of their existence. Each generation loses something of value from the previous one. In its place is emptiness, one they fill with sin."

Lucifer turned to face Jesus. He held a finger in the air to make a point.

"They choose to fill that emptiness themselves. I play no part in that. Man reeks of sin, as if they bathe in it. I swear their putridness permeates the walls of Hell. The days leading up to your execution were foulest. That wretchedness, I heard, infiltrated the Gates of Heaven, polluting the air of angels and archangels all the way to His Throne. We all witnessed your demise. Heaven quaked when the first nail drove through your flesh. Do you know when Heaven last quaked?"

Jesus shook his head, not knowing the answer.

"Neither do I. Some say it was when I left, but I

truly do not know. Heaven was not the only place to feel Father's pain."

Jesus asked, "Hell, too?"

Lucifer nodded. "He came to me and told me you were the heir to mankind, that you would be making the decisions regarding their future. Or." Lucifer tilted his head. "Their demise." He turned back to the fire, staring at the roaring flame. The logs in the fire popped, though there was no rational reason for them to do so, since there was no air or heat. Jesus wondered if any of this was real. Lucifer so excelled at deception that Jesus wondered if he could tell the difference between what was real and what was not. "Long before He created you, I approached Him. There was skepticism in His voice about the future of man. I noticed that His love for humanity lacked the fervor it once held. It was the first time I began to believe He was preparing to lay waste to the world of man. It seemed irrational to me, so I formulated ideas, approaching Him with the one I hoped would be acceptable in His eyes. He needed time to think it over, which confirmed my suspicion, and I watched mountains grow, rivers erode, and landscapes change, and still, I waited." Lucifer strolled over to the fireplace and stared into the fire. "The keys to the kingdom have been handed down from Father to Son. Mankind cannot continue to travel down this path, as it will only lead to their demise. It is you who must be the wind in their sails and forcibly alter their course."

Jesus cast a rueful look at his transparent

hands. There was a lot to process within such a short time — a time in which he had crossed over some spiritual rift and became immortal. He considered he would face challenges of unparalleled magnitude. The words his Father spoke rang in his ears. *Be wary of Lucifer's treachery, be purposeful of mind, walk shoulder to shoulder with righteousness, always have faith, and believe in yourself.* He had no difficulty in readily accepting the challenge, but disappointing his Father was something he wished to avoid. He may be new at this, but failure was not an option. He considered this for a moment. His Father had given him an assignment, one that left him with the choice to allow mankind to live on or smite them all. Saving them, he wondered, was implied. It was his first test. The one thing that stood in the way: Lucifer. His Father warned him of the potential for betrayal. It would be easy to avoid the unpleasantness of working with Lucifer by just saying no and smiting everyone. Jesus was not accustomed to taking the easy way out. People were generally pretty good. He knew this. He lived with them. Ate with them. Walked among them. He was one of them. People who chose a path of sin still had goodness in them, even if sometimes it was buried deep.

"I must choose whether mankind lives or dies?"

"Precisely."

Jesus shook his head. "I will not be their destroyer. They live."

That was the first significant hurdle. Relieved,

Lucifer continued, "Then you must act now. Force them to see with their own eyes."

"How?"

"I wish to help you choose their path."

"You mentioned something before, a test of finality. My Father also mentioned this when He last spoke to me. Is this the path you wish to discuss?"

"Yes."

"Tell me about this test."

Lucifer faced Jesus.

"It was a test of faith to be sure man was faithful. Your Father questioned this virtue in man. I tested a man."

"Job?" Jesus asked.

"Job," Lucifer said, turning back to the fireplace. "It was a Test of Faith. I'll not bore you to tears. The short version is your Father and I tested man, and man passed. It was effective. Unto you, I propose the issuance of a new test. A test not for a single man but for all men, one that tests their fortitude, one that determines where their love and desire for the gift of life lies. Their very lives and those around them should be placed in mental and physical peril to test their will to survive. If they have inner strength and resolute faith and can withstand a test challenging body and soul, they will prevent their annihilation."

Jesus sat back to consider this idea. He could not allow mankind to fall, but he also needed to be mindful that this was the first important task given to him by his Father. He was about to speak, but held up a finger to withdraw the thought. Lucifer patiently waited. Jesus found every conceivable question came to one resounding conclusion: Man walked the crumbling edge of a precipice. How would Jesus pull mankind back to safety? Having no other alternative, Jesus resigned to the notion that he had to trust Lucifer.

Asked Jesus, "What do we call this test?"

Jesus could not see the broad, toothy smile stretching unnaturally wide on his counterpart. "The Test of Mettle," Lucifer purred, and Jesus felt the first pang of regret.

5 - SHAPING METTLE

Saturday, April 4, AD 33: Hell

"**B**efore we progress," Jesus said, "we will have rules policed by both sides. Can we agree that these rules are to be strictly followed?"

"Absolutely," answered Lucifer, still standing by the hearth. "And to be certain all rules are abided, I propose a covenant, similar to the one your Father and I did for the Test of Faith. I imagine it would put your mind at ease about a great many concerns you have. Covenants are a promise made to man. For the Test of Faith covenant, we used Job's blood, taken while he slept.

"For the Test of Mettle covenant, we will use your blood. I took the liberty of filling this inkpot with your blood during the time we spoke."

Jesus said, "Which is why you could not wait an hour longer."

Lucifer smiled. "Naturally."

"I felt no pain," Jesus recollected. "You took my pain away."

"It would undoubtedly befoul your eyes in the judgment of me had I strode up to you, slashed you open, and filled the inkpot. I don't believe you would be quite so amiable toward me now."

"I suppose not. So you did it discreetly while we spoke?"

"I did."

"Thank you for your discretion."

Lucifer crossed his arm over his abdomen and carefully bowed. It was not done with the same gimcrackery on display in the desert. Jesus knew this was an act performed with absolute sincerity, even if done with Lucifer's casual use of dramatics.

Be wary of Lucifer's treachery, be purposeful of mind, walk shoulder to shoulder with righteousness, always have faith, and believe in yourself.

"Fine, then. A contract written in my blood, transcending the Faith Covenant, using the last living drops of blood of the mortal Messiah to forge a union between Heaven and Hell. Let us discuss the terms and compose our new covenant."

Lucifer placed the blood-filled inkpot atop the table next to Jesus. He removed a roll of heavy parchment from within the breast of his cloak and put it next to the inkpot. He dug into the breast of his cloak once more. His tongue stabbed the air as he poked around. "Aha! Found the little bugger," Lucifer exclaimed. From his breast pocket, he retrieved a raven's feather.

With the feather near his lips, he instructed it to write the words to the new covenant using the inkpot and parchment on the table. It fell to his palm, and he blew his breath upon the feather lightly. It floated toward Jesus. Jesus plucked the feather from the air and spoke the same words. The feather, the inkpot, and the parchment glowed brilliantly for a second before disappearing from the room.

The immortality of Jesus continued to fill him with a wealth of information. He knew the parchment would carry not every spoken word, but those they agreed upon to make law.

"I will begin," Jesus said as Lucifer sat at the other end of the table. "Who are we testing? You said you wished to test all men. I disagree. I wish only to test those whose body and mind are able. To test a toddler would be unimaginable and preposterous, for they are undeveloped, unprepared, and unsullied by sin."

"A point I will not argue. I would like to test any person who has reached manhood and feels fit — mind, body, and soul."

Jesus added, "There is to be no testing the weak, weary, or dying regardless of how healthy they believe themselves to be. They have suffered enough already and cannot be given an equally reasonable chance to succeed."

"What if they recover?" Lucifer asked.

"If their mind, body, and spirit are as able as all other healthy men, then candidates they become. Otherwise, they are to remain untouched."

"Agreed," Lucifer said.

"I believe your minions would serve well to perform these tests," Jesus said. The lines along Lucifer's forehead rose. He had not expected this to be suggested, let alone recommended. "From time to time, Heaven holds the right to exchange a demon for an angel. I prefer your minions to be used, and do not see much need for angels to be involved, provided these rules are followed unequivocally. Your minions have a knack for dark spaces, creating chaos, discomfort, and pain." Jesus watched Lucifer carefully. Lucifer clasped his hands before him and could not help shed a slight smile. *Pride*, thought Jesus, and inside his mind, he rolled his eyes. That smile would be short-lived. Jesus continued, "They are not to show up at any given time, to torture, kill, rape, or devour everyone in their path. They must be focused on a target, one of your choosing."

"You cannot be serious." Fingernails as black as night extended from each of Lucifer's fingertips and dug grooves into the seemingly indestructible table. "I would think it impossible should the man of my choosing be guarded by thirty soldiers."

Jesus considered this, and said, "You raise a valid point. However, there are a great many men from whom to choose. I would expect you to choose your target wisely. Perhaps your targets should be less shielded if you are unable to focus on them." Lucifer frowned. Jesus considered his recent travails. "Conversely, I have seen those sick with power and corruption, for they do not dare travel alone. Those who travel by their side often share the same convictions. Though your minions must focus on a single target, anyone who walks alongside the target may also be tested, as long as they meet the rules of this covenant."

Lucifer's nails retracted from the gashes on the table. He casually brushed the wood shavings onto the floor. A hand went up, but before he could speak, Jesus continued, "When you tested Job's faith, you and your minions were not seen." Immortality had proven useful by supplying information about the Test of Faith. "All acts occurred naturally, even if there was a supernatural element or a feeling of coincidence to it. I wish to employ the same concept here. Your minions are not to be seen. If they are seen, they return immediately to your domain, and the test is ended without further repercussion."

Lucifer retorted, "I would like my minions to have an opportunity to use deception without prejudice. Let us say they shape-change into some other visible form. I would prefer their interactions to go uninterrupted even if witnessed. If we are testing man, after all, I require some latitude."

"Deceit," Jesus drawled. "You used this well previously. And you are right. You deserve some latitude, that I will grant you."

"Splendid!"

Jesus thought Lucifer might spring from his chair to sing and dance.

"With limitations," added Jesus.

If Lucifer had intended to call forth party balloons, then they would have popped, their limp strings falling to the floor.

"Limitations," Lucifer repeated flatly.

"First, you may be viewed by the eyes of man in another form and continue the test without abatement. If they look upon a cloaked figure but see a demon in shadow, then the test ends." Jesus held up a hand when Lucifer tried to interject. To quash any further disruptions, he added, "I will also grant you this. Man is blind, and we wish for him to see the light. Therefore, sighting a demon is not enough to end the test. A mere glance will not be enough. Man must face his demon with mind, body, and soul. Only then will he truly see."

Lucifer said nothing.

Jesus continued to speak.

"If man lacks clarity due to fear, then he lacks conviction. If man lacks conviction, then he lacks mettle. Man must face that which tests him and do so with absolute certainty and courage. For if man does so, he passes the test and may walk the road my Father had paved for them."

"What if one of those thirty soldiers looks upon my one demon in shadow and sees a demon?" Lucifer asked.

"The test ends, Lucifer. It matters not to me who fails. If one passes, then the test ends. It is you who must employ care with whom you test and those men who surround those being tested. All it takes is one who views a demon with mind, body, and soul." Jesus leaned forward in his chair; his voice lowered, but his tone was unmistakably serious. "I wish to make this rule perfectly clear, Lucifer. You are responsible for your minions. You. If the demon is not up to the task, then perhaps you should alter your plans. But, make no mistake, if your minions choose not to follow the rules, you — and you alone — will be held accountable. There will be repercussions. Let us not make war over a breached covenant. Agreed?"

An almost inaudible growl reverberated. Jesus not only heard it, but he sensed the vibrations ripple along the floor and in his chair.

Jesus asked again, this time sternly: "Agreed?"

"Agreed." Spittle shot through gritted teeth of a false smile.

"Good," Jesus said. "Next, you will not set your forces out in mass."

"What if there are thirty—" Lucifer started.

"I care not, Lucifer."

The near subsonic rumbling set the furniture in motion. The fire in the hearth erupted as if an accelerant had been tossed in.

Jesus waited for the growling to cease. When it did not, Jesus pressed the issue.

"You will not cover the hills, valleys, and mountains with your minions. Do you honestly believe I would allow brigades of your minions to run loose and freely among men for as long as you saw fit?"

"What do you propose, dear Jesus?" Spittle shot through needle-sharp teeth. This time, the spittle hissed when it struck the table, sending great puffs of smoke into the air. Smooth holes were visible on the table after the smoke dissipated. The spittle passed through the table and melted holes in the floor.

Jesus decided to change tactics. He said, "You disagree? Fine. I would like to hear your proposal."

"What?" Lucifer stammered, clearly off guard. The furniture ceased vibrating. He took a moment to consider what might be viable, even if it leaned slightly in his favor, but he made it sound like he was giving Jesus the deal of the century. "I guess we could give them a year of their time. The test with Job lasted far longer. I would think a year would be more than adequate to perform a test."

"How many demons would you use?" Jesus asked.

"I would leave that open for evaluation," Lucifer answered. He could not believe his good fortune. Not wishing to overplay his hand, he said, "Yes, open for evaluation. You never know how many may be associated with the target."

Jesus scratched his chin and asked, "Which is how many? Surely a leader as great as you would know such a thing."

This was going very well. Better than expected.

"It would depend on the number of men being tested."

"I am sure it would," Jesus said. "Ten to one? Fifty to one? A thousand to one? How many?

"Twenty," Lucifer blurted.

Jesus howled. "Twenty minions for a year!" This was followed by a burst of gut-busting laughter. Somewhere in the middle, he cried out, "Is that all?" Lucifer joined in, even if his laughter carried a note of nervousness. Jesus wiped tears from his eyes. Lucifer played along, dabbing at his eyes with a handkerchief that suddenly appeared in his hand. Jesus could not resist, coughing out, "To test but a single man? Are you mad? Oh dear, Lucifer, I am barely immortal, but I have not lost my sensibility. To think I would have the mettle of one man tested by twenty demons to determine his worthiness!" All embers of humor evaporated. "I think not."

"But…" If ever the Lord of Hell had blushed, then Jesus could say he made it happen.

"No, Lucifer. I thought I made myself quite clear. I will not have scores of your minions covering the hills chasing after but a single man or his followers," Jesus explained. "Your minions vary in size, strength, rank, and power. I think it fair to have their stay measured by that. You are the strongest and rank highest in your domain. Since deception is high on your list, then let's consider performing the Test of Mettle at night, when it is dark, when you will have the advantage. With you being the most powerful, I think you should last until sunrise the next day. A lowly chaos demon ranking low in your order, I would think, should not carry the same power as his master. Showing you up might prove unwise and rather embarrassing."

Lucifer growled in defiance at first, but Jesus

finished by playing into Lucifer's vanity. He could barely argue with having one of his lowliest of minions possessing the same power as he or being awarded the same longevity. Still, one night was barely enough time to do much of anything. His lips curled, baring his teeth. If he had a full night, then what time did his minions have? The more the idea stewed, the angrier he became. His eyes sizzled with fury. "I do not like having so little time. It is not feasible to perform a Test of Mettle in a fraction of one night."

"I disagree. I believe you can, but you will need to work smarter and use your resources wisely. If it does not work as intended, then perhaps we can alter the covenant. As of right now, I do not believe you need more time. Your minions are to work at night only."

Brilliant blue flame burst from the hearth and a ring of blue flame encircled them.

"ONLY ONE NIGHT?"

Lucifer's face was obscured by the roiling clouds of smoke discharged by the table melting onto the floor; the blazing white pinpoints in his eyes were quite visible. They would have cut through the pyroclastic plume of an erupting volcano. Lucifer stood, and at the same moment, his chair flew into the black stone wall, exploding into a green flame that crawled up and over the wall. Lucifer hunched over, retreating a few steps from the table. There were ominous popping and bone-snapping sounds. His hands stretched and reformed into a diabolical set of sharp, onyx claws. He threw his head back and roared.

Jesus remained placid, hands folded behind his head. He witnessed the entire spectacle of Lucifer's tantrum through smoke and flame. When the surrounding inferno subsided, Lucifer had returned to his less sinister human form. The table had been horribly damaged. Any normal floor carrying the holes now present under the once-magnificent table would have collapsed under the weight of the massive table. This was not a mortal place, and things here did not follow mortal physics. Lucifer, Jesus noted, was seated on another chair at the table.

"Are you limiting me to the use of one minion?" Lucifer calmly asked. "I would find it more agreeable if I am allowed to use multiple minions if I am to operate within a small window of time in which to perform a test."

"Perhaps, and, if you do, I am insisting you use a rule of proportion. It will be based on the number of minions used, along with their combined power. The combined power of two minions will be reduced by half, three to a third, and so on, if equally powered demons are deployed. Whenever they use deceit, their power wanes in conjunction with the amount of power used. The greater the act of deceit, the more power they use, which reduces the amount of time to perform the Test of Mettle."

Through dangerously gritted teeth, Lucifer answered, "Agreed."

"I do not," Jesus said.

Lucifer's stood up, sending his chair toppling over backward. "What? This is insanity! You just created the rule!" Fury returned to his eyes. Flames ruptured outside the hearth and blue flame crawled up the wall like a breach in a dam.

"I am not yet satisfied. I want to clarify this rule, even if it bears repeating. The more strength and power your minions use during the test, the more time shall be taken from them. This is arguably the most important rule of all. It will force your minions to police themselves, instead of being unpredictable avalanches of destruction."

The floor of the room vibrated once more. The blue flame shifted to a green flame.

"If you do not control your temper, dear Lucifer, I will see fit to leave and end these negotiations."

Lucifer walked over to his chair, lifted it as high as he could with a single hand, and smashed it into the floor. The chair exploded into a million fragments, every one melting into nothingness. He retreated away from the table, down the length of the long room, and stepped from the floor out into the ocean of nothingness. Vicious spikes ran along the curvature of his back. Jesus waited until Lucifer had sufficiently calmed down. When he returned to the table, his spikes had retracted. All that remained were the white pinpoints of his eyes.

"I apologize for my temperament. This test was my idea, and I feel I have no say in it." He motioned to the table. "Allow me." Jesus motioned a hand as if casually swatting a fly. The table melted into the floor. He raised his hands and waggled his fingers, and another table rose from the damaged floor. Jesus closed his eyes and sighed. The floor repaired itself and the flames engulfing the wall were extinguished.

Lucifer waggled his fingers. Up rose a new chair. Lucifer twirled and his attire changed. He gave his new tuxedo lapels a solid tug before seating himself. He folded his hands and rested them on the table. The room returned to the way it had looked when they first arrived.

Jesus sighed. "It is your test, Lucifer. It is yours to oversee. It will be a tremendous responsibility. But it is I who must be the voice of reason. When we adjourn, *we* will have an agreed-upon covenant."

A moment passed before Lucifer spoke in a tone that was barely audible. "I do not agree with one night."

"I do not agree with one test," Jesus said.

Lucifer raised an eyebrow in question.

"You heard me true. I believe any man may be tested up to three times, provided he has not passed a Test of Mettle. A demon may not confront anyone who passes the Test of Mettle. They will be shielded by Heaven, immune to all."

"Agreed," Lucifer said. He genuinely liked this idea of multiple tests. "Anything else?"

"Yes. Your minions are not there for the benefit of slaughter. Death, I imagine, will occur, but I want your minions restrained. They may be physical, but I do not want them freely killing with their hands, claws, or whatever demon parts they have. Let us agree that man shall suffer no death through physical contact with your minions. I will not condone outright slaughter. This is a test of *man's* mettle. Your minions must be prepared to use their wits and cunning. Not rely on overpowering brute force. I will be observant. I pray you will be, too."

There were thousands of ways to kill a man, Lucifer knew. He had even invented quite a few along the way, but that would go against the very essence of the test. Or would it? He needed to be creative. It was his test, after all, and Jesus had said as much. He would lose face if he could not make it work. He would see to it. The contract did not seem so bad in retrospect. He would ensure that his minions followed the rules.

"I have questions," Lucifer said. "If we are to test man, how are they to know of the test?"

"The test ends when the minion is out of energy, something we established. You will police those being tested, watch over the minions, and pull them back when their time is up. They should be made to feel time pull them as that time draws to a close."

"Okay," Lucifer said. "You mentioned someone of my stature would last through sunrise. When do we begin the test?"

"That is a good question, one I have been mulling over." Wanting to hear Lucifer's opinion, Jesus asked, "When do you believe the test should begin?"

Lucifer had an idea. The parchment, inkpot,

and feather reappeared on the table. His eyes fell upon the raven's feather scratching on the parchment. Next to it was the inkpot filled with Jesus's blood. It was as brilliant as it was apropos.

His eyes remained on the inkpot for a long moment before he answered. "Why not begin the test at the time of your death? It was at night, near the start of a new day."

Jesus nodded. "I like that. Agreed."

Lucifer beamed.

"Now the last order of business is to communicate to man," Jesus said. "Because you are charged with the oversight of minions, I will oversee this. I wish to create a physical location for the documentation of every single test. If we test man, the encounter will be documented and stored. This temple of tests will be known as the Repository. One of my archangels shall act as the will and voice of the Repository. It will be a living repository, immortal and all-knowing."

Lucifer nodded. "Creative."

"Thank you," Jesus said. "It is important that man sees the light. We will use parchment. Scrolls would be best. When man views the scrolls, the Repository will translate. When men read what the Repository narrates unto them, I believe their eyes will be sufficiently opened."

"Agreed," said Lucifer. "Where would you like to locate the Repository?"

"Everywhere, anywhere, as anything. The Repository will choose," Jesus answered.

Lucifer asked, "When do we commence the first test?"

Jesus considered this for a moment. "We will create a hall within the Repository that leads to the library. It will contain warnings to any who defile the temple with their presence. Any mortal who crosses the seal leading into the library will commence the Test of Mettle. This will be deemed their final chance to thwart sin."

"So, we tempt them?" Lucifer purred. "Ooh, I like it."

Jesus shook his head. "No immortal is to interfere. Man must make the choice uninhibited. Turn and leave, or cross the seal and commit the Final Sin."

Lucifer was working up a froth. Frisky hands that were not his own appeared and roamed all over his human form. His eyes rolled back, and his head lolled in a heightened state of euphoria. They were beginning to discuss the punishment, and Lucifer was getting off on it. Witnessing it firsthand was unsettling, but Jesus maintained his composure and cleared his throat. The hands slid down below the tabletop, and Lucifer stiffened. It was an odd sight to watch eyelids fall over the pinpoints of white.

Lucifer coughed, asked, "How long shall mankind endure the Test of Mettle?"

Disgusted, Jesus would have vomited bile if he were in his mortal skin. Instead, he again cleared his throat. Somehow he managed to respond. "A millennium." Lucifer moaned, and Jesus felt a wave of nausea ripple through him in undulating waves, each wave crashing into him like a stone wall. His vision blurred, and he saw Lucifer in true form. They were not in the room with the wood table and the single wall with the stone hearth — they were in a fiery pit filled with minions and humans. He watched the enslaved souls of men and women being tortured. Another massive wave struck Jesus. He shook his head and found himself sitting again at the table across from Lucifer, who was calling out to him in a voice so distant it was barely audible. Everything seemed so fuzzy. Another ripple crashed him, and Jesus grabbed the arms of the chair, preparing to fall backward. The chair never moved.

"Jesus?" Lucifer called out. Jesus heard the compassion in his voice. The Lord of Hell was concerned, and rose from his chair. Jesus saw no sign of the disembodied hands. Whatever vision had pulsed through him was gone.

Before Lucifer rounded the table, Jesus patted the air. "I am fine."

"Are you?"

Jesus narrowed his eyes while Lucifer retook his seat, never taking his eyes off Jesus, studying him intently. Something had just happened, but Jesus was unable to recall what it was.

Lucifer carried on with buttery smoothness. "After one millennium, they will be mine."

After one millennium. The words echoed in his mind, trying to jostle loose a memory. He recalled speaking the words, but was it he who spoke?

He needed to concentrate harder. Be in total control. Maybe whatever happened had been a fluke. Or maybe Lucifer was up to one of his tricks.

Jesus brushed away the remaining cobwebs. Firmly, he said, "They must be given an opportunity to rise above the Test of Mettle. Those who open their eyes should be afforded the opportunity to rise in the name of love, sacrifice, and commitment. A final test. Those who see it through with open eyes will conquer the Test of Mettle, thereby terminating the covenant."

They spoke at length to tidy up the new covenant. With all terms negotiated, they signed the parchment using the raven's feather and Jesus's blood from the inkpot.

This covenant represented only the second such agreement made between Heaven and Hell. This time, it did not focus on a single marked man. This time, all spiritually, physically, and mentally able men were targeted.

Jesus departed Hell and returned to the world of man. He awoke in the cave where his flesh-and-blood body was being stored.

ACT 2: THE TESTS OF METTLE

6 - ANNIE'S ENCOUNTER

Annie tried to suppress her scream by biting her lower lip, but this was too good. She stifled it as best she could. She sunk her nails into her husband's flesh. He blissfully groaned, crossing the finish line with his beautiful wife, reveling in the glow of their romantic interlude. Annie, on top, breathed heavily, beads of sweat leaving trails along her taut, smooth skin. The windows on the second floor of their home were wide open, but with no wind, it did little to cool the house. It did permit Annie to lay out several candles without fear they would be blown out. She found his hand and intertwined her fingers with his.

"Eight years." Her throat was hoarse and cracked. She moved his hand up to her damp breasts. She gave his hand a playful squeeze. She loved his hands. They were his best feature. His hands were calloused, large as mitts, and as powerful as the paws of a grizzly bear. Yet surprisingly she found them to be as soft as cotton. He stood over six-foot, and the candles did a grand job of showing off his sculpted muscles. He spent much of his time working his fields and his machines. When the weather was less than cooperative, he could be found tinkering in his shop.

Goose bumps erupted along her spine, and she rolled on top of him and tightly embraced him with one of her powerful hugs. "Can you believe it? Eight years."

He worked to slow his breathing, she could tell, but it did nothing to stop her from hugging him more tightly.

"Happy anniversary," he said. Annie responded with a moan of utter content.

Their bodies remained glued together for several minutes. After his breathing calmed, she slid off and stretched her naked form. She bent forward to pick up her crumpled pink robe from the floor.

"Yummy," he mumbled.

Her lips gave way to a naughty smile. She turned back and found he had one eye open. She slipped on her robe, leaving it untied. She hunched over and kissed him on the forehead, breasts dangling in full view.

"Don't be long." The threshold of sleep caused his words to slur.

"I won't. Get some sleep."

Annie usually had a burst of energy following sex. She did not want the remains of their anniversary celebration to sit overnight. After blowing out the candles, she opened their bedroom door and tippy-toed out, leaving the door ajar. Her tiny frame floated down the carpeted hallway, a simple nightlight helping her efforts. She reached her son's bedroom door and carefully pushed it open. He was sound asleep, hugging a little blue blanket clutched in a single fist, while his outstretched thumb rested just outside his lips. It was strange to think her little munchkin would be starting school next year. She watched her little boy sleep, feeling joy ooze from every cranny of her soul. Satisfied, she pulled the doorknob, leaving it open a crack before taking light, bouncy steps down the stairway. When her feet reached the wood floor, Annie palmed the top of the polished banister — maybe it was the kid in her, but she enjoyed the cool smoothness of the wood — as she turned and walked alongside the railing toward the kitchen. Unlike the soft carpet upstairs, the wood floor creaked with every step until she reached the tiled kitchen floor.

Before reaching the kitchen, Annie stopped at an old grandfather clock. It was as tall as her husband and much older than him. The clock was a family heirloom given to them by his grandfather shortly before he passed away. It was hand-crafted and over a hundred years old. Because it had been well kept, the heirloom remained in remarkable shape. She opened the door and pulled one of the handled cords, winding the clock for another few days. The brass pendulum swung back and forth as the gears ticked away with each passing second. Annie began closing the door, then startled when the grandfather clock chimed once. *Darn creepy old clock!* She did not care for its constant ticks, clicks, and chimes. She had always wondered if the clock was haunted, because it was old and gave her the odd feeling that it was watching. Just like now, the thing had a knack for chiming anytime she went near it, which often left her on the wrong end of a start. She peered through the pane of glass in the door. The clock face read eleven thirty. She knew it was just doing what it was designed to do, but that did little to comfort her.

She flipped a light switch on the wall and allowed her eyes a moment to adjust to the brightness before stepping into the kitchen. The kitchen had been recently wallpapered with a sunny floral pattern to give it a pleasant, homey aesthetic. This was her domain, and she kept it clean and sparsely decorated. Simple wood cabinetry stood in one corner next to the walk-in pantry, which was tucked under the stairs. Sunny yellow curtains outlined a double-paned, rectangular window over a double-basin sink. The sink was mounted in the middle of a long countertop. Atop the counter was a single-slot toaster and a woodblock for knives. To the left of the counter was the back door. In the center of the kitchen sat a square dining table, stained dark, with four matching chairs. The smell of grilled meat lingered deliciously in the air.

Annie moved the remaining dishes and silverware from the table to the sink. She placed the glass cover on the cake and moved it to the countertop. Knowing her husband and son, the cake would not survive beyond tomorrow. She twisted the hot and cold knobs at the sink and placed a stopper in the bottom of the left sink basin. She added dish soap to the running water until bubbles filled the basin before piling the dirty dishes in to soak. Annie swiveled the spigot to the right basin and soaked a sponge. She looked outside, squinting from the loud glare from the reflective window. She could make out the single light outside the barn, but the reflective light made it all but impossible to see the crops, tractors, or their old Ford pickup truck.

Annie reached into the hot soapy water and pulled out a serrated knife. She began to wash it carefully with the sponge. A breath of warm air puffed on the nape of her neck. Then another. A coy smile spread across her lips and goose bumps flashed down her spine. She cocked her head to the side as another puff of warmth slithered across her sensitive skin. Her husband had been playful all day. She was pleasantly surprised he still had the energy to carry on this late. She craned her neck to the side and glanced up at the picture window. Half hoping to see his naked body in the reflection, she instead saw a dark and grotesque reptilian form standing behind her. The thing was wide and thick with muscle, and its skin varied with shades of green. It had a shuddersome bat-like face and stood more than a full head taller than her. She froze, hoping her eyes were playing tricks on her. But the thing opened its mouth, revealing white, feral teeth that glowed like pointy specters within a blood-red mouth. Soulless red-glowing eyes locked directly with hers. Annie's hand began to shake, nearly causing her to lose her grip on the knife. She squeezed the knife's hilt, then whipped around with her elbow cocked, the steel blade murderously pointed forward.

Standing there was her little boy, his blue blanket clutched in one hand and dragged along the floor behind him. His other hand was wiping at the sleep in his eyes; his yawning mouth made a big, round O. Annie saw no sharp, feral teeth. She saw no green lizard skin. She saw no red-glowing eyes or grotesque head. Every tense muscle in her body shook with the ache of adrenaline overload. Annie coughed, gasping out a breath at her near-fatal act. Quickly bringing the knife down, she released it into the basin of soapy water behind her. She blinked back the teardrops cresting around her eyelids, working to regain her breath.

The little boy rubbed away at his sleepy eyes. She barely heard his tiny, hoarse voice. "Mommy, I'm thirsty."

Annie stammered. She stared helplessly at her son, not registering his simple request for water. What kind of mother was she? She had nearly butchered her little boy. Her mind overloaded, flooding with too many awful what-ifs to process. A tear trickled down her cheek. She needed to cry or scream or both. The little boy did not look up, probably because of the bright light, and continued to rub his eyes. She turned back to the sink in ragged jerks. Her mind worked feverishly to chronicle what had just happened. There in the brume of her thoughts, she heard her boy speak. He'd said "water" and "thirsty." She tried to reply with the word "okay," but it came out as an indecipherable gurgle.

She reached for one of the dinner glasses, trying in vain to get her muscles to heed her command. She needed to wash the glass first, before putting water in it, she chastised herself. She dipped it into the soapy water and began scrubbing it with enough force to degrease an engine. She put it under the still-running water to rinse away the remaining suds.

"Thirsty," the voice behind her repeated. That single word came across as inelegant and raspy and labored, not in the timbre of a sleepy little boy. Then, in a menacing, gravelly tone, it added, "Thirsty for your blood."

The glass slipped from her hands and shattered in the sink. She gripped the front of the sink, squeezing her eyes shut for several rapid heartbeats. When she could muster the courage, she turned slowly, moving at an agonizing pace. She waited for the inevitable attack, half expecting her last memory to be of that monstrosity in the reflection with the fangs and the reptilian skin. The pit in her stomach sank like an anchor in the ocean. The back of her soapy hand covered her mouth, and a shaky breath escaped from between her trembling fingers.

Nothing was there. No little boy with a blue blanket. No horrible creature. She was alone in the kitchen, swathed in the bright light and sunny wall-paper. She stood motionless as the onset of a sob turned into wracking waves of an uncontrolled cry. She tried to scream, but it passed through tear-stained fingers as nothing more than silent agony. A warm trickle ran down her inner thigh, pooling on the wood floor at her feet. She hurt all over, as if she'd stepped outside into the face of a fierce blizzard while the wind flayed off layer after layer of her bare skin. Her eyelids grew heavy, and she wanted nothing more than to close them. She fought half-heartedly to keep them open. When her eyes closed, the creature appeared in her mind's eye, vivid and alien. She squeezed her eyelids tighter. Images of the thing flashed past. She whimpered, wanting it to stop. And it did.

The final image was of the creature standing in front of her.

As she raised her head to get a better look at it, the creature reached out for her. She jerked back and turned away, but her legs would not move. As if there were a magnet strapped to her back, she felt herself sliding backwards toward the creature. She grabbed the sink basin. She pulled with all her might until she could look out the window. In the reflection, the creature stood. It reached out and gently wrapped its clawed fingers around her shoulder. She could feel the strength in each of those fingers. She remained still, watching. It pulled her into its embrace, wrapping its leathery hands around her waist. The clawed fingers burned her skin as they slithered across it. Red-glowing eyes peered into her tearful brown ones. She wanted to scream, but she could not remember how. The creature gripped her waist and pulled her tightly against it. Its clawed hands came around to the flat of her stomach, untied her robe, and allowed it to drop to the floor. The demon's fingers snaked their way from her belly button towards her ribs, then upward. She tried to turn her head, but those red-glowing eyes found hers in the reflection. A huge hand traveled over her breast and cupped it firmly. The creature's other hand repeated the foul act on her other breast. She shuddered in disgust. Then she watched as her hands rose of their own volition, caressing the demon's hands. It smiled widely at her, displaying those awful teeth. She felt the rise of bile and forced it back down.

At that moment, she was able to momentarily resist the demon. Her eyes traveled downward toward the floor. There, she saw a familiar pair of boots. She peered into the window again. Her husband stood behind her. His strong hands, firm but not nearly as gentle as she knew them to be, held her in a tight embrace. Eyebrows furrowed, she looked at him through the reflection in the window. Her husband stared back, but there was no mistaking the red glow in place of his eyes. The bile rose fiercely once more. She spun to shove him away but found herself alone in the kitchen. She glanced around the kitchen, then into the window at the reflection. She realized she was still wearing her robe. Stealing a look at the floor, she frowned at the source of the warm puddle surrounding her feet. She looked toward the window again. After confirming she was alone in the kitchen, Annie switched off the running water, frowning once more. There was broken glass in the sink. She reached to pick up one of the shards of glass.

CLANG!

She jerked at the chime of the grandfather clock, and yelped, not just from the momentary scare, but also from a sharp pain in her hand.

CLANG!

She spun around to glare at the indignant clock.

CLANG!

She felt a warm trickle on her finger. Upon inspection, a glass shard had gashed her fingertip.

CLANG!

She reached for a cotton towel and tightly wrapped her finger in it.

CLANG!

Blood seeped through the towel.

CLANG!

"I'm thirsty." She heard the innocent-boy words spoken again, coming from every direction at once. She was alone.

CLANG!

She pulled the towel off to check her finger. Blood leaked from the clean slit in her skin. Droplets of blood fell from her wounded finger and mixed with the urine on the floor.

CLANG!

"Thirsty for your blood!" The hostility of the words filled her with dread.

CLANG!

Instead of fear, anger consumed her.

CLANG!

How dare this thing come into her house and turn her upside down emotionally. She stepped out of the puddle of urine. Not to mention the embarrassment of trying to explain why she peed on the floor. She rewrapped the towel tightly around her finger.

CLANG!

She considered retrieving the knife from the sink, but then remembered how she had nearly killed her son with it.

CLANG!

Her son! Her eyes went wide. She bolted toward the staircase, grabbing the banister to aid her 180-degree turn up the stairs, taking them two at a time.

From a dark corner in the living room, glowing red eyes watched her ascend the stairs. The creature stepped toward the staircase, but then an intense tug made the demon wobble. The creature was being called back to Hell. Its end was nigh.

Annie reached the top of the stairs, breathing hard. The door to her son's bedroom was ajar, the way she had left it earlier. Her maternal instincts were in full flight. She whipped open the door, holding the doorknob firmly to keep it from smashing into the wall. She hovered over a small bed.

The creature placed a clawed hand on the banister. The tug pulled harder.

The little boy slept soundly on his back. His outstretched thumb rested on his bottom lip while his other tiny hand gripped his blue blanket. She tilted her head and watched his chest rise and fall. He twitched. She watched her little boy smile. Whatever was happening in his dream, she sensed him having a good time there.

Annie let a long breath escape. Her son was safe. She continued to study her little boy while questions arose in her mind. She wanted to revisit the events that had occurred minutes before.

Was that a hallucination? Or was it just a dream? Was that creature a ghost? Is my house haunted?

A hand reached from behind her and gripped her shoulder. Annie screamed. Her son started awake from his place of joy.

"Annie! Annie! It's okay. It's me." A pair of strong hands spun her around. "It's okay. It's just me."

Before her husband could say another word, she embraced him in a viselike hug and began sobbing uncontrollably into his bare muscular chest. He put his arms around her to console her. He was about to ask what happened, but she dug deeper into his chest and wept.

No one witnessed the shadow in the hallway slide away from the doorway, nor did they hear the sizeable peal caused by the door to Hell closing behind the demon. All that remained of the demon's visit was an odorless cloud, which dissipated into nothingness long before Annie and her husband made their way to the kitchen to greet the new day.

7 - DEMON PRESERVE

February 1, 2007: Mansfield, Ohio, United States

"**W**inky Back? Wasn't he some kind of composer?"

"Come on, Chuck. We went over this. Wenckebach is the doctor who discovered a common form of arrhythmia. Arrhythmias are a type of heart block."

"Jeee-zus!" Chuck squeezed his eyes shut. "I can't take any more of this. I'm a goddamn truck driver. Not some Winky Binky heart guy."

Melinda looked up from her book for the first time since she had sat down to study after arriving home from work. She still wore her drab blue scrubs provided by the hospital.

"Honey, we've been doing this for damn near three hours. I want to spend time with you, not these dusty old medical books."

Melinda earmarked the page she was on and closed her study book. She had purchased it new a few months ago, and already the corners were curled, the spine was lined and cracked, and the front and back covers were marred with several bends, creases, and food stains. Dozens of pages were earmarked. Countless sticky notes limply hung out of the book and served as reminders of areas she needed to firm up her knowledge on. The handwriting on some of them was smudged and illegible.

"I can't. Up 'til now, I've been riding someone's coattails. I told you last week. And the week before that. If I don't pass, I don't work. I want to be an ER nurse. Besides, if I don't work, I don't get paid. That kind of puts a monkey wrench into our wedding plans, doesn't it?"

Chuck threw his hands up in frustration, muttering a string of profanities through gritted teeth. He booted a pillow across the living room into the mundane kitchenette. After he exhausted all the good cuss words, his shoulders slumped.

Feeling her own pent-up frustration, Melinda sympathized. "I can't tell you how much I appreciate all the help and support you've provided. You've been wonderful."

The frustration etched on Chuck's face morphed into something resembling the Cheshire cat. As he sashayed toward his beloved, Melinda was unable to suppress a warm smile. She adored his boyish charm. Her fiancé was a real trouper, spending all his free time over the past few months studying with her. Just as Melinda was about to rebuke him, Chuck hunched down and nibbled on her nape. His touch sent a prickling wave of goose bumps down her spine. Unable to resist, she tilted her head askance, giving Chuck unfettered access to her neck, in which he indulged. For a few precious moments, Melinda let her guard down. She had been studying for weeks and had had no free time. She had failed her previous ACLS examination by a hair. According to hospital policy, after two failures they had to terminate her. If Melinda wanted to stay employed, she needed to study. No sex, no dates, no television — all of which added up to one very displeased fiancé. She could indulge for just a little bit, though, right?

Her head rolled as Chuck worked her erogenous areas. Her hand began to lose its hold of the thick medical book. Chuck's hand caressed her bare left arm down to her wrist. His fingers found the bottom of her hospital smock and tugged it up to expose a white Victoria's Secret bra. His deft hands collaborated to unclasp the front of it. Melinda enjoyed the moment, because he was having a rough go at it. This particular bra hooked in the back, Melinda knew, but she said nothing, enjoying the tension it created between it and her partner. His increasing agitation turned her on even more. She wanted nothing more than to rip his clothes off and take him right there. Chuck's lips stopped working Melinda's neck. His hands worked more furiously to undo the missing front clasp. Just as it seemed he had reached his limit with the bra, the book slid from Melinda's hand hard onto the floor. She sat upright, causing Chuck to stumble backward.

Pulling her shirt down firmly and recapturing her breath, she conceded. "No, Chuck, I can't do this.

I have to study. I'm sorry, sweetie. I just can't. Not now."

Chuck released a heavy, pent-up sigh. "Come on, Melinda. I ain't gonna see you for a week. I told you. Tomorrow I gotta pick up my trailer and haul ass to Illinois. I won't get back 'til next Friday. You know how it is with me workin' more hours and taking more loads when I can. Guys been gettin' laid off left and right 'cause of the economy. I ain't complainin'. It seems I'm never around anymore. When I am, I wanna spend time with you."

"So move in."

The words carried an edge to them, sharper than Melinda intended.

"Christ, Melinda! How many times are we gonna frickin' go over this? I can't leave 'cause of my lease. It's up in May. If I leave now, I gotta pay some damn fees. For now, I have to stay put. It's only a few more months."

"Whatever," she said. "Look, if you want to spend time with me, stay the night. But, like I said, I need to study."

"But—"

"The test is in three days."

"But—"

"Three. Days. After I pass and you get back…" Her face softened, and a sly smile appeared. "I'll dress up nice and sexy for you, take you out, and then you can have me any way you want. I promise."

"But—"

"If you're staying the night, then you better

find something to do to keep yourself occupied."

Chuck grabbed his winter coat before slamming the apartment door behind him. He stepped away from the apartment complex and gagged. An Arctic front had swooped down from Canada, swept over the Great Lakes, and covered the region in six inches of snow, after which the temperature plummeted to zero during the day. He had no clue what the temperature was now, but his body shivered as he yanked his arms into the coat sleeves. He pulled the zipper up to his Adam's apple, plucked a wool cap out of a pocket, and yanked it down over his frozen ears. From the other pocket came a pair of gloves. He blew warm air into each of them before tugging them on.

Chuck blinked furiously. His nose started running, causing him to sniffle, before he made it halfway to his car. Holy crap, it was cold!

Rust would have been an adequate description of the car's color at the DMV. He just hoped the bucket of bolts would start. He and Melinda were saving every penny they could. Buying a car, new or even used, was not in their budget, and neither were the repairs this car desperately needed. He hoped it would make it through the summer. By that time, after things settled down, they could figure something out together.

Chuck bit the fingers of his glove and pulled his hand free. He dug into his pocket and pulled his keys out. He managed to slide the key in on the first try, turned the lock, and pulled the creaky door open. He plopped into the bucket seat and nearly sprang up just as fast. The vinyl seat felt as if it had been converted into a block of ice. Cussing at the cold, Chuck turned amid the cramped quarters to retrieve an old newspaper from the refuse littering the floor and back seat. He spread it underneath him with his exposed hand and eased himself onto the crinkling paper. He pulled the glove back on and scratched at the windshield to remove the frozen mist. He created a small circle in the cracked windshield — the crack was spreading wider every day — and peered through it across the dimly lit parking lot to the warm glow emanating from Melinda's windows. He strongly considered hanging out for the night, but the cold seemed to carry less bite than getting rejected. They hadn't had sex in weeks. Stupid Winky Back, or whatever his name was. He jammed his key into the ignition. The car made two pitiful attempts to turn over before resorting to a short burst of rapid ticking. After that, it did absolutely nothing. None of the usual idiot lights illuminated.

"Are you kidding me? Goddamn piece of worthless Winky Binky shit!"

He kicked open the creaky door, slid off the crinkling newspapers, and slammed the door shut extra hard in retaliation. He rubbed his gloved hands together and nestled them into his coat pockets. Chuck arched up and down on his cowboy boots. He enjoyed the comfort, especially when trucking. They were not, however, designed for long walks, let alone slippery winter conditions. At least they kept his feet warm — for now.

Chuck's apartment had a one-car garage attached to a short driveway. Next door lived an elderly widow whose husband passed away years ago. She did not know how to drive; her husband, she once said, drove her everywhere, including batty. She had asked Chuck if he would park his truck in her driveway when he was in town because it made her feel safer having strangers think a big, burly trucker lived there instead of a frail old lady. Tonight, his truck was keeping her safe.

The problem he now faced was distance. His apartment was five miles away if he walked the bicycle path along the highway circling the forest preserve sandwiched between Melinda's apartment and his. It was a little over two miles if he cut through the preserve along its main trail. The bitter cold made the decision reasonably obvious.

After a brisk half-mile peregrination with several slips and near-falls, Chuck reached the main trail to the forest preserve. Snow partially covered a brown sign stipulating the hours of access to the public. White letters denoted the preserve was open at sunrise and closed at dusk. As of this moment, Chuck could care less if the frickin' park was open or not. He was upset with Melinda. Maybe deep down, he knew it was not her fault. Or maybe it was. He was too cold to argue.

A gust of bitter wind reminded him that he was freezing his ass off in the middle of the frickin' night, adding to his ire. His Toyota POS refused to run. The boots he wore afforded him little traction, and had already put him dangerously close to kissing the asphalt with his ass too many times to count. Overhead, a single street light provided hardly enough illumination to read the park signs. He glanced at the sign once more. Or maybe it did. He read the park hours and gave the sign a two-handed bird. Leaning into the jaws of the harsh gale, Chuck trekked into the park.

There were no lights along the trail. Stars in the sky glittered, and the moon floated near the horizon, providing minimal visibility. He was trespassing, he supposed, so it was probably to his advantage no one would see him. The only sounds were the wind and the clomping of his cowboy boots on the snow-free pavement. At least the path was relatively free of ice and snow. Chuck continued into the teeth of an unrelenting, driving wind. The skin on his face felt like someone had run a power sander across it. Tired of swiping at his raw nose, Chuck thumbed one nostril closed, leaned toward the side of the trail, and blew hard. After doing the other side, he wiped his nose with a gloved hand. He pulled the zipper down, plunged his burning face into its accumulated warmth, then yanked the zipper up just over his nose. The winterized coat did an excellent job of repelling the wind and keeping him toasty. Bitter cold hunted for exposed areas to bite into. His jeans failed miserably to deter this kind of weather. He had to keep his legs moving, keep his muscles working, words that had always seemed clichéd to Chuck, but now he understood. This was dangerous life-and-death stuff here, and though he was doing his best not to get noticed in the park after it had closed, a little voice in his mind kind of wished someone would catch him. Sitting in the back of a warm police car as he was transported to a warm police station was a comforting thought. Another voice — the one known for reasoning — pointed out he had no money to post bail or pay a fine, which meant he would sit in that nice, warm jail cell until well after he was expected to show up for work in the morning. With layoffs in full swing, they were looking for any excuse to give the axe to current employees. Having no idea what car repairs might run him, he also had a wedding to consider. It was time to man up. He swore into his coat and plodded deeper into the preserve. He occasionally gazed up at the skeletal arms of the trees. Their hungry, bony fingers reached out, alive in the wind, ready to snatch him up when he least expected and swallow him whole. It did not take long before he felt suffocated and, admittedly, scared. To hell with falling — he picked up the pace.

Chuck remembered the last time he was at the preserve. He and Melinda walked this very trail during a beautiful fall day, the last truly warm one Ohio had for the year. It was late in the morning, and the sun worked its magic. Right now he could almost feel Melinda's hand holding onto his. Her hands were flirty that day, and her smile was wicked. She suddenly pulled him through a thicket of bushes. When he squeezed out the other side, she planted an unexpected kiss on him that nearly put him on his ass. She pulled her shirt off, exposing her perfect breasts. To his surprise, she was not wearing a bra. Chuck had been stymied by her wont to take flirty playfulness to brazen, naked, outdoor sex. Instead of being Mr. Confidence, he gawked like a wide-eyed teenage boy seeing boobs for the first time. Then Melinda unzipped her jean shorts and let them drop to the ground. No panties either. Chuck swallowed, and her wicked smile turned absolutely villainous.

He missed that sexually charged feral side of hers something fierce. It scared the piss out of him at times, like it had on that fall day. That was the last time she let loose.

A gale of wind caused him to wince, vaporizing the steamy memory. Then the wind simply ceased. Still leaning into the gust, Chuck tried to shift his weight, but it was too late. He managed to dislodge his gloved hands from his pockets in time to brace his fall.

"Goddamn weather!"

His voice echoed off the trees, capturing his attention. The trees stood deathly still. Nothing moved. Chuck smacked the pavement with the flats of his gloved hands before standing up. He looked around nervously, fully expecting the wind to sucker punch him at any moment, but it never came.

Aloud he said, "What the hell is going on?"

His voice echoed amid the trees, and he almost wished he hadn't spoken. He felt isolated, yet some primordial ember sparked in the back of his brain, passed down hundreds of generations, harnessing the power to heighten instincts. Its primeval warning was clearly received: *RUN!* Instead of heeding the warning repeating over and over in his mind, Chuck stood stock-still. After the trees stopped dancing in the wind, their skeletal arms arced high overhead, motionless. Even the trees seemed afraid to move.

A twig snapped to his left, causing Chuck to flinch. A series of quick, heavy footsteps crackled upon exposed dead, dry leaves and crunched across patches of snow and ice. Chuck remained still, not daring to breathe. He rubbed the side of his neck, where his carotid artery pulsed painfully. Thanks to all that studying with Melinda, he knew where it was and what it was called. Chuck squinted, trying to espy anything within the interior of the forest. The only things in his field of sight were the naked trees and the moonlight peeking through an endless canopy of branches, giving the ground a violet, shadowy pall.

Another twig cracked some distance ahead. Perhaps it was a spooked animal, like a deer or raccoon.

He listened carefully. To his chagrin, he heard a loud grunt. It was followed by a sizzle in the air, which terminated when a stone roughly the size of a basketball bounced a few feet to his left, leaving a white, powdery mark on the asphalt.

Deer, my ass, he thought. Slipping as he turned, Chuck regained his footing and hauled ass. His toes and heels hurt with each step. Boots were not designed for running. Pain or not, a jolt of adrenaline got him moving in a hurry.

A tree standing on the left side of the trail toppled across the asphalt fifty feet ahead of him. Chuck skidded clumsily along the frozen surface; his arms windmilled to maintain his balance.

Chuck took a few steps back, surveying the trail before him. It was silent. The wind had not returned.

"Hey!" Chuck tried to keep his voice steady and crude, but it crackled with fear. "This ain't funny. I'm getting tired of this bullshit."

A wild, phlegmatic laugh filled the air, coinciding with more movement in the forest, this time to his right. Whatever it was, it was circling him at inhuman speed. He followed the sound, and it struck him that no person could maneuver through the shadowy domain of the moonlit forest. His fear cemented his feet to the ground. No *person* could move like that. If this was not a person, then what was it?

Chuck was not a religious devotee. The last time he saw the inside of a church was his baptism. God crept into his mind. He could use the Big Guy right about now. He considered praying but didn't know any prayers; none of the good ones, anyway. Fear had never engulfed him like this. Oh sure, he was scared of stupid kid stuff growing up. But what kid wasn't? He was a tried-and-true, nose-to-the-grindstone, beeline to the state line, pedal to the metal, goddamn trucker. He drove all hours of the day in all sorts of weather in all kinds of towns, cities, and neighborhoods. He parked his rig in faraway places and alongside unfamiliar roads just to catch a few zees. He regularly shrugged at the things most people feared.

Until now.

Something was being dragged across the ground to his immediate right. He squinted into the trees. He could almost make out a dark form. He blinked, and it was gone. He heard a whimper in that direction. A *human* whimper.

"Hello? Who's there?"

The whimper intensified. Someone was out there, suffering. Probably because of whatever was putting the fear of God into him.

Time to man up. Chuck pushed his fear aside and entered the forest, traversing the rabble of scrawny trees as quickly as he could. The ground was frozen hard, pitted and uneven. Moving with caution, he tripped over exposed tree roots and slipped on icy patches, cussing with gritted teeth each time he did so. The fury roiling within helped keep his fear at a healthy distance. He came upon a narrow opening in the trees. Peering through the slit, he could make out the form of a person lying on the ground. The person sounded female, and she sobbed.

"Hello?" Chuck called out.

"Hello?" she choked out. Her voice was weak, almost breathless. "Please help."

"I can see you," Chuck called out. "Keep talking. I'm looking for a way in."

"I — I'm hurt. Please help me." Her voice weakened.

Saplings clustered tightly together here. Chuck looked right, then left, to locate an opening wide enough to squeeze through. He hurried along the wall of saplings until he located a gash. He slipped through barely flexible saplings into a modest clearing. He searched where he was sure he had spotted the woman lying — only no one was here.

"Hello?" There was no answer. Chuck squatted to inspect the ground where he'd seen the woman, but he found no trace of anyone ever having been there. No footprints, no blood, no evidence of a physical presence.

He stood up straight, trying to make sense of all this. First, it was the thing with the insane laughter moving at light speed. Next, it was trees toppling over. Then, massive boulders were tossed in his direction, landing in uncomfortable proximity to him.

A thought struck him. Maybe this whole thing was a wild game. And there was probably more than one jackass out there playing him. It made him see red. He prepared to let them know he was onto them, and he was not going to put up with their shit.

"Is this some kind of..." Staring, he spotted something hanging from a branch amid the gazillion trees surrounding him. He finished meekly, "...

sick joke?"

At first glance, it appeared to be an article of clothing, like a jacket. Chuck checked left and right before treading carefully toward the object.

Halfway there, he called out, "Hello?" The forest responded with silence.

Smooth, round stones threatened to put him on his ass again. Chuck cussed as he carefully closed the distance. He was now twenty feet away. Fifteen feet.

He inspected the ground, maneuvering around an outcropping of stones. Ten feet. At an arm's length away, he snatched the object. It came away without hindrance. He spun around to survey the area around him. The forest remained calm. He moved to an opening in the trees where moonlight trickled through. To his horror, he held a hospital smock with an embossed ER logo and the name of the hospital stitched on the breast. It was too dark to read the letters. His breath caught when a waft of perfume captured his attention. Trembling, he held it close to his nose and breathed in the scent.

"Melinda!" he shouted. "Oh, Christ, Melinda! Where are you?"

No response.

"Dammit, Melinda! Talk to me! Where are you? I'll find you."

A gurgled laugh came from behind him. Twirling around, he thought he caught a glimpse of a shadowy figure standing in the trees, watching him.

"You son of a bitch! I'll fucking kill you!"

Chuck scuttled over the slick stones and knotted surface. He came to the spot where he'd seen the shadow, but there was nothing except, every which way he turned, trees. He found himself staring into the forest, getting sucked into its murky vortex. The utter silence resumed. Chuck felt himself being swallowed by the gloom. He spun in circles, seeing nothing but trees, trees everywhere, and he fell on his back. Overwhelmed by trees dancing in his vision, he clamped his eyes shut. After several moments, Chuck reopened his eyes and saw twinkling dots of light. Stars. The dizziness subsided, as did his temporary claustrophobia. He figured he was somewhere in the middle of the forest preserve chasing rogue shadows, laughter resembling drowning victims, Melinda, and presumably a homicidal maniac. Perhaps the wisest thing to do would be to seek help. How would he do that from the middle of the preserve? He spent a great deal of time on the road. Besides them being costly, he had no need for a cell phone because his rig had communication equipment.

Twigs snapped somewhere to his right. He needed to get the hell out of this godforsaken forest. He would make his way to safety by, first, heading to Melinda's apartment. He did not know what to make of the strangeness, but one thing remained certain in his mind: he would not rest until he knew Melinda was okay. Maybe his mind was playing tricks on him in the forest. He recalled the hospital smock.

Was it even real, he wondered. He thought back to the woman in the clearing. *Was she real?* He decided to return to Melinda's apartment, perhaps flag down a driver along the way. He scolded himself for using the wedding as an excuse not to purchase a cell phone. It would have been a lifesaver.

Chuck squeezed through a V-shaped tree, hopped over a rock half embedded in the ground, and sidled through a pair of leafless, waist-high bushes. He zigged through a dozen trees and zagged through another dozen. He pressed on, but after several minutes, he stopped to catch his breath. Where was the frickin' trail?

Leaves crackled from somewhere behind Chuck. He turned to look but was shoved hard in the back. He lost his balance, catching the toe of his boot in an unseen rut hidden by a patch of snow. He worked to stay upright, taking three long, uncontrolled strides before his forehead struck the trunk of a tree with a thud, followed by a blinding white flash.

Chuck strained to move, his limbs stiff from the cold. He gradually rose to his knees with his face pressed against the raw bark of the tree he'd smacked. A mental fog made it difficult to think. When the mist began to subside, he wondered if he had been unconscious. He rubbed at his elbows. He remembered running, then being hit hard in the back. It gave him no comfort to know he had been lying on the ground for God knows how long with something wishing to do him harm. When the last of the fog lifted, his head began to pound. He placed his hand against it, and it came away wet and warm. *Not a good sign*, he thought. He rose unsteadily, hugging the tree with both arms for balance. The urge to barf came and went. He turned so that his back could rest against the tree.

He looked skyward, but the stars did little except contribute to his dizziness. He lowered his eyes to the ground, his body moving forward. He regained his balance, then fell back against the tree. His balance was for shit. He would just wait it out until he felt better before moving.

A rustling sound snapped his attention like a bear trap. He was not quite sure where it came from. The left, maybe? What could it be? He just stood and listened to the noise. Whatever it was, it did nothing to disguise its location. Maybe it no longer cared, since he was injured. It could probably take him now without much of a fight. Chuck needed to buy himself some time. He pushed himself off the tree and staggered to the right, away from the rustling sound.

His mental faculties had returned to normal, like a rebooted computer. Something was stalking him, he figured. It had tricked him into entering the forest. Then there was the matter of Melinda and her hospital smock. And the crying woman who vanished into thin air, leaving not a single trace. The shadows and the unbelievable speed of whatever was out there. Without realizing it, Chuck moved with more urgency now, his steps becoming more determined and less wobbly. Nausea and dizziness had subsided, thankfully, but the ache in his noggin was less forgiving. A large stone crashed through the treetops. This one was heavy enough to snap off inch-thick branches. It thumped to the ground a mere eight feet away.

"What do you want with me?" Chuck cried out. "Who are you? Show yourself, you fucking coward!"

A thick, putrid laugh borne of lungs dripping with brimstone and malice echoed in the woods. Unable to locate its source, Chuck felt ire heating his belly once more. He was tired of this charade. And that laugh — that godawful laugh — was driving him mad.

"You coward! Stop dicking around with sticks and stones. Come fight me like a real man!"

Chuck figured whatever was out there was toying with him, and he knew his only recourse was to get out of this forest preserve and find help. He expected no response to his threat, but from behind, a gravelly voice hissed in response.

"I'm no man," it said.

Chuck felt the impact before he could react. He was airborne for fifteen feet, driving through a line of saplings. The saplings snapped, as did Chuck's collarbone. His left side bounced off the frozen ground, knocking the wind from his lungs. He groaned aloud. The pain seemed to radiate everywhere. He would have rolled over if not for the blinding pain coming from his shoulder. Something deep inside had Chuck moving. He gasped from the shockwave of pain he received by getting himself to his feet. He was trying to catch his breath when, from behind, came the crunch of leaves and snow. He was unable to react. Something zipped by, and, as it did, it whipped him across the back with a long, thin branch. Chuck yelped and staggered forward. He caught a tree with the inside of his arm to save himself from eating the hard ground again. Inertia spun him around the circumference of the tree.

Chuck panted hard. If delirium had not claimed him by now, then unconsciousness surely would. The pain was becoming unbearable. He wanted to curl up in a ball and go to sleep, but he shook away those thoughts. He was still awake and still alive. He also knew that falling now would mean falling for the final time. He had to stay upright. He had to remain strong for Melinda. His ribs protested with each breath. They were probably bruised, broken, or both. His head and shoulder pain were equally intense. Spots danced before his eyes, so he closed them. He needed a minute. Leaning all of his weight against a tree now, and using his good arm for support, he thought of Melinda, with her beautiful face and her bright smile. She worked hard and never quit. Failure was not in her vocabulary. She had pushed through adversity all her life. She once told him she was born with a heart defect and required an operation when she was four or five. Then there was the speech impediment she couldn't quite overcome until her teen years, and the relentless teasing she endured because of it. Or the time she was struck in a crosswalk by a senior hit-and-run driver. Luckily, she came away with only a few scratches, but the bicycle at her side was not so lucky. The old-timer fled the scene before anyone could note the make of the car or catch a glimpse of the license plate. Chuck witnessed it, jumped out of his Toyota POS, and helped her to her feet. It was how they met. They fell in love. She was perfect in every way. He was a flawed asshole, but somehow she saw past his defects. She confessed she wanted a life with a man whose brash exterior was nothing more than a thin, fragile candy coating covering a gooey, mushy side he kept hidden. What would she think of his candy ass now?

"Please don't hurt me," a distressed feminine voice cried out. It may have sounded like Melinda, but it did not belong to Melinda. He knew it was part of the game he was now a reluctant player in.

Chuck chuckled. Somehow, this was not real. It was ridiculous. This whole fucking thing was one great big sham, and it bolstered his amusement into a gut-splitting, knee-slapping fit of laughter. It hurt to laugh, but it would be more painful not to laugh.

"You don't have her, you dumb son of a bitch!" Tears carved lines down his dirty cheeks as he cackled. "You ain't got her!"

Something big flew by his ear with enough force that he felt its breeze on his face. An unnatural howl filled the air. Perhaps it was dismayed by the fact that it had missed. Chuck did not wait to find out. He hauled ass, weaving through trees that began to thin, until the toe of his boot clipped something that sent him sprawling forward. He danced across a patch of ice before his cowboy boots shot out from under him, and he landed square on his ass. He realized he was sitting on asphalt. The trail! He whipped his head around in each direction. In one direction, the path was dark. In the other, he saw the streetlight marking the entrance of the forest preserve. Chuck sprang to his feet and ran toward the light.

Behind him, he heard the trees lining the trail snapping. The demon found the same patch of ice and slid across the trail. It crashed into the trees and shrubbery on the opposite side of the trail. Chuck heard another unnatural howl. It was not human, nor did it sound like any animal he had ever heard. It spurred him on. He had only one hundred feet to go, but the clacking sound behind him grew increasingly louder as the enraged demon closed the distance. Chuck felt a strain in his right calf. He had reached the limit of his physical endurance. He half jogged and half limped until he reached the entrance. He had exhausted everything in his tank. If this was the way it was going to end, then he would do it facing whatever hunted him. He spun around. Two sets of eyes met. At that exact moment, Chuck faced his demon, sending the high-ranking minion back to Hell. The immediate opening and closing of the portal triggered a powerful blast of air, forcing Chuck to stagger back a few steps.

An enormous, dense cloud, generated by the portal, enveloped him. He had instinctively clamped his eyes shut to protect them from the concussion of the blast. Chuck opened his eyes immediately afterward. He saw the thing wink out of existence before again closing his eyes. All around him were whorls of vapor. He never saw it, but he was pretty damn sure the thing was history. Maybe it blew up. Chuck felt a wave of elation.

"You lost mother—"

The winter wind returned in full force. It caught Chuck by surprise. His tired, aching body staggered back several steps before he was able to regain his balance. The remains of the cloud lit up brightly before the winter wind blew it away. His head turned suddenly to the sight of a wide, steel body and headlights. The brakes of the semi-tractor trailer locked. Chuck's body was ejected ninety feet from where he stood into a tree along the side of a highway, his body broken, his life gone.

The distraught trucker related to the police what he had witnessed. From a distance, he saw a single cloud — fog, maybe — drift from the forest preserve across the empty highway. He thought nothing of it at first until he saw a shadow in the cloud. Then, oddly, the cloud suddenly dissipated, revealing a lone man standing in the middle of his lane. How can a cloud just leave a man in the middle of the road like that? At fifty-five miles per hour, pulling twenty-two tons on eighteen wheels, the driver was incapable of avoiding the man.

On the morning of Groundhog Day, shortly after midnight, and for the second time in a half-hour, a trucker believed he saw a shadow.

8 - THE HORROR
IN AMITYVILLE

October 31, 2010: Amityville, New York, United States

T he truck passed a sign at the edge of town. It read:

Welcome to Amityville
Incorporated in 1894

The passenger turned the black knob on the Pioneer sound system counterclockwise. AC/DC's "Thunderstruck" was jamming in the spacious confines of the truck through its many high-end speakers and subwoofers. Two of the passengers worked in the back of the truck while enjoying the tunes. One chewed on a pencil while blogging about the last show of the season, and his counterpart peered through magnifying goggles and tested a box that was overflowing with wires and packed with specialized power cells. Both turned their attention to the front of the truck when the audio ebbed.

"We're here," the passenger in the cab announced. Then he turned the knob past its previous setting on the audio dial. The two rear passengers cheered and high-fived one another. The driver stole a glance at the team member riding shotgun. The passenger was now rubbing his hands on his jeans with more strokes and greater frequency. The driver refocused his attention on the road ahead, his smile broadening. The truck motored down the highway this late Halloween morning.

A few blocks later, the truck turned into a parking lot, passing an ornate sign built with smooth, round sand-colored stones mortared together and surrounding a dark gray slab of slate. Engraved in the center, in white, were the words Amityville Realty. Only two cars were present in the spacious lot designed for ten times that. Perhaps they had more employees who were out selling houses. Or maybe they were trying to present optimism to potential buyers and sellers who entered their premises. The driver parked lengthwise across three angled slots. A minute later, the crew of four was outside, stretching the last leg of the journey from their stiff bodies. A woman spotted the truck through the large windowpane at the front of the building. She tapped on the glass. When she got their attention, she held up a finger, informing them she would be just a minute.

The driver wore sunglasses but shielded his eyes as he peered up at the overcast sky. He blew into his hands, then said, "It's frickin' cold. What's our weather look like tonight?"

The blogger answered, "Cold. Possible flurries. In the twenties. No rain, thankfully."

"I gotta piss," moaned the technician. He danced stiffly, his hands and arms tucked into the sleeves of his lab coat. A cold front was blowing through the northeast. The evening forecast called for clear skies, an icy wind, and a sharp drop in temperature.

They squirmed two minutes longer, until the approach of heels clicking on pavement summoned their attention. The woman from the window wore a pressed white button-down blouse with a peach coat and skirt. Even her shoes were peach. Her arms crossed over her chest tightly.

"Good morning, gentlemen. I'm Wendy Titus of Amityville Realty. Welcome to Amityville." Her pleasant tone seemed unaffected by the current weather conditions. Her smile and sparkling personality amplified that warmth. "How was the drive?"

"Fine, thanks for asking." The driver pointed to the technician, who was arching his feet up and down. "Mind if Nano-Bladder uses the facilities?"

She chuckled. "Sure. Go in through the front, third door on the left, just after the water cooler."

"Thanks," said the technician, and he skittered away.

"By the way, I'm Matt Depone, lead investigator of Ghost Rustlers," the driver said, offering his hand. She shook it. Her handshake was firm and professional but displayed a trace of feminine softness. He pointed at the blogger. "This is my brother Jay, lead investigator." They shook hands. "And this is Devry Little, investigator and all-around chickenshit. He hates ghosts."

"Man, what is wrong with you?" the front passenger scolded. He shook her hand and added, "Who likes ghosts anyway?"

The woman chuckled. "Right?" she mused.

She turned her attention to the truck and gasped at the paint job along the right flank.

"Wow!" Her tone was genuine, shedding its professional edge. "Oh my God! That is impressive!"

The entire rear panel displayed a desert scene of a cowboy on a horse, with an extended length of rope tied from the saddle horn to a ghost and a demon. The ghost cast a woeful look as it floated a few feet above the terrain. The demon was short and angry-red with bright green glowing eyes. It had a long tail ending in a spade. In a huff of rebelliousness, it pouted over being captured. Its back was turned; its arms and legs were crossed. The childish demon allowed itself to be dragged over the terrain. Small round clumps of cacti stuck like pincushions to its rump and legs. Mountains could be seen in the distance. At the upper rear of the truck was the bottom right quarter of a brilliant full moon, its craters clearly visible. Adding to the illusion of depth was a coyote sitting atop an outcrop of rock howling at the moon. *Ghost Rustlers — Paranormal Experts* was painted under the mural. Below that, in a slightly smaller font, read *We Specialize in Demon Removal.*

"It helps to have sponsors. It's a converted GM delivery truck purchased new before this season. It's fully decked out to carry all of our electronics, has its own power source — solar, of course — and acts as our central command. Our technician, Fritz 'Nano-Bladder' Jones, who you met ever so briefly, keeps all of our equipment armed and alive. He's the best in the business. But I think next season we're going to ask about upgrading our truck to include a bathroom."

Fritz half jogged back to the group.

"Ah, much better. Thanks," Fritz said, tucking his shirt into his pants.

Matt sighed.

"Well, it's getting a bit nippy out here. Here is the key so you can get started."

"Thank you, Mrs. Titus," said Matt, taking the key. "You still dropping by tomorrow morning at sunrise?"

"Yes, I am. Do you have the address and directions to the house?"

"I do, 108 Ocean Avenue. Satellite internet in the truck, so we got access to MapQuest to help us find our way."

"Well, just give me a call if you have any issues at the house, then," Wendy said.

"Excellent." Matt shook her hand. "Well, I think we're good to go. I guess we'll see you tomorrow morning."

"Only if the boogeyman doesn't get you first," she joked.

The men piled into their seats inside the truck. Matt turned the key, the music resumed at a volume comparable with most rock concerts, and they were off to 108 Ocean Avenue, the most famous haunted house in the world.

With Jay directing the effort, they successfully backed the truck into the driveway. The rear doors burst open, and Fritz gawked at the house. The three-story Dutch Colonial was larger than life. The exterior was covered with a sunny yellow siding. The balconies and trim were painted white, as were the windowpanes. After several renovations over the years, it looked nothing like the spooky house from the movies.

Devry walked up from the passenger side of the truck and placed a hand on the open door.

Fritz said, "There she is."

"Yeah, it's a whole lot creepier in person than to see it on television or the Net."

Fritz rolled his eyes.

A sharp smack on the rear door sent Devry darting toward the lawn, and he tripped over a protruding tree root near the driveway. His butt took the full brunt of the fall. He found Matt smirking at him. Matt had taken a detour around the front of the truck to scare him when he was not looking. Again.

"Goddamn it, Matt. That shit ain't funny no more."

"Sure it is."

"Chickenshit," Jay said to Devry, smacking him on the back of the head as he passed. "It's just too easy, and easy never, ever gets old."

"Besides," Matt said, "since when do paranormal investigators fear the ghosties?"

Devry sighed. "Guys, I told you. It was the case in Montgomery. It felt like there was something alone with me in that basement, trying to take control of me. It touched me."

"Yeah, yeah, yeah," Jay mocked. "We heard this bullshit like fifty times. Devry almost got possessed; Devry got touched. After the way you told that story to those girls in Toledo last night, it sounded like you were damn near gang-raped by Casper and Pac-Man's four ghosts."

Fritz lit a cigarette, sucked the end bright red, exhaled, and added, "You know how many ghosts there are?" He held up one finger, a knobby digit with a dirty, chewed fingernail. "One. Me."

Devry scowled. "Yeah, whatever."

Matt said, "Sounds scientific to me. Jay, let's add that quote to the website."

"You got it, boss," Jay answered.

There was an awkward moment of silence as Devry studied their faces, seeing that, perhaps, they were being candid. Devry frowned. Unable to help themselves, they burst into a chorus of hearty laughter. He settled his gaze askance, squeezing his lips as tight as he could. His face burned with a mix of anger and shame.

"Aw, c'mon, Dev. We're just fucking with you."

Matt stepped forward and slapped Devry on the shoulder. "Lighten up, bud. Really."

Matt turned his attention away from Devry and nodded up to Fritz.

"All right. Quick meeting, fellas. Fritz, I see you're still working on the SunCell packs. Give me good news, my man."

Fritz eyed Matt, cigarette dangling from his lips. His face remained empty, and he said nothing. The optimism drained from Matt's face.

"Dude, are you friggin' kidding me? What's wrong with it now?"

"What isn't? I tore cells four and five apart. We knew there was a critical failure somewhere between the solar panels mounted on the roof down to the SunCells. I disassembled 'em and the solar panels, testing every inch of the system I possibly could on the meters. There is no problem with conductivity. I put the solar panels back together and mounted 'em again. I plugged in the SunCells, and still no juice after a full day in the sun, which implies the solar panels are bad. But that ain't all. I think SunCells four and five are bad, too. I took all five of our leftover SunCells off the panels and plugged 'em in at the hotel yesterday. They charged for eight uninterrupted hours. There is five percent in cell four and three percent in cell five. They're toast. Cells one, two, and three are fully charged."

"Ouch," said Jay.

Matt gave Fritz a deer-in-the-headlights look.

Fritz opened his hands to give Jay the floor.

"I told you to read up on it, bro. If I got it right, in the end, SunCells are big batteries mounted in the truck that our gear can plug into to charge their internal SunPack batteries. Because all our gear is specifically tailored to operate with SunPacks, we need working SunCells to keep them charged. Fritz can plug the SunCells directly into an electrical outlet. He plugged each of our five SunCells into an outlet last night. Only three charged; two are dead. Right now, the SunPack batteries in the equipment are charged but will only run up to four hours. That's not enough to run our shit overnight. Three working cells means twelve hours. Central has a computer — PC, monitor, keyboard, mouse — which takes two SunCells. Overnight for us lasts about six to eight hours. That means the PC will not make it through the night, and we have exactly one SunCell with four hours' worth of juice to charge all of our remaining gear. SunCells are needed for the cameras, the two-ways, the flashlights, the special effects — all of our stuff. After the gear with built-in SunPacks runs dry after four hours, then we have a single SunCell to charge them, which means four hours of juice to divide up among all of our gear, which ain't gonna last. It's bad enough we somehow made it through this season without upgrades or extra equipment, but it was never in the budget. So we had to make do. That means tonight we will be short two extra SunCells to power our gear."

Fritz chimed in, "Don't forget we have to account for four fixed cams: two infrareds and two thermals. They run from the start of each operation to the end. Plus, each has its own recorder. They tend to run two to three hours before needing to recharge. Remember the half dozen spares we had at the top of the season? Well, I used 'em to replace defective cells we accumulated from last season and the start of this season. Remember that freak fest we did in Missouri? We lost three cells that night. None of them was budgeted to be replaced. So, these last three live SunCells are all that's left."

The guys had wondered why the studio never budgeted for this. After all, the studio went all-in with the plans for their new and improved truck with its state-of-the-art eco-friendly equipment. It made no sense why their equipment could not be upgraded. Their show was doing well. Multiple networks were interested enough to inquire about the rights to rebroadcast it. Since Matt was seemingly always indisposed, busy with big business, Jay was the pipeline to express grievances.

"What? Why did no one tell me?" Matt was dumbfounded.

Fritz threw up his hands in frustration. Jay placed a hand on his brother's shoulder and looked him dead in the eyes. "We did, multiple times, but it's neither here nor there. Look at this house, bro," he said, changing the subject. "Tell me we can't make history here tonight with what we got."

Matt gritted his teeth. He wanted to argue, but what was the point? "Okay," he conceded. "So what you're telling me is we don't have enough power to run our gear tonight?" To punctuate that fact, he muttered, "Tonight of all nights."

"That's what we're telling you," Jay answered.

"Shit," Matt said. "Where does this leave us?"

"Pretty much screwed," Fritz said. "All that sweet stuff we were gonna add to the show is shelved. Worse, I had our effects charging on four and five. No juice, no special effects."

"Shit," Matt repeated. Fritz and Jay waited while Matt chewed at his fingernails to mull over what technically should have been a priority weeks ago. What Matt did not share with them was that there were rumors about possibly changing the show's date/time slot, which he argued against, or even canceling the show altogether, which shelved the arguments. No one but Matt knew what was going on in the minds of the studio's executives from one week to the next. He shielded the others from that. Sure, he messed around with the ladies. Who didn't? But he never did drugs. Did he want fame and glory? In the end, isn't that kind of the goal? Then the Amityville house went on the market, and the opportunity presented itself to Matt at the last minute. He made a few calls and, miraculously, was awarded the opportunity to close the season with the most famous haunted house in the world at center stage. He had let the guys know two days ago, but the surprise backfired. They had no time to prepare. Plus there was a major equipment problem he ignored. The guys had their suspicions: women, drugs, power — the usual things that tended to follow glory hounds from the shadows. Matt had dropped the ball big time, and the guys knew it. Worse yet, Matt knew they knew it.

Jay was his brother, after all, and he always had Matt's back. Jay said, "Matt, Central Command will be dark except for the recorders. Someone will have to stay behind to monitor them, the SunCell levels, and the charging of the SunPacks. It's gonna be essentials only tonight, just like in the old days."

"Damn it! Amityville is *the* place. Our once-in-a-lifetime opportunity, and it's fucked up right from the start." Matt shook his head. "What else can possibly go wrong?"

A sinister organ ringtone played in Matt's pocket. He pulled out his iPhone.

Before Matt answered the call, Jay said, "Tell Jack the Ripper he owes us twenty bucks for getting here first."

Matt nodded in affirmation. "We're at the house. You owe us twenty bucks, Rip. Where are you?"

Matt rubbed his forehead while he listened. Finally, he heaved a great big sigh, and said, "Yeah, okay, got it. Jack, you and Lana be safe, okay? We'll catch up with you guys next week."

Matt tucked his cell phone into his pocket. There was a mixed bag of anger and defeat in his eyes. He paced back and forth, thinking.

"They can't make it," Matt finally said. "A trucker dropped some pipe on I-80, jackknifed, and created a big mess. They were part of a small pileup in the middle of Nowhere, Pennsylvania. Nothing around for miles. They have some things to tie up with the state police. They're both a little battered and bruised, but they are okay. Outside of that, our SUV is totaled, and Lana and Jack can't make it. That leaves us four."

"Well, there goes the eye candy and the demonologist," Fritz said.

No one saw Devry sneak up right behind Fritz. With his mouth behind Fritz's left ear, he said, with a little extra snap, "Jack is not eye candy."

Fritz startled. He reeled on Devry, shoving him back a few steps. "C'mon, dude! It's not funny."

Devry sneered. "You know what they say about paybacks, Fritzy."

Over the next two hours, the four members of the Ghost Rustlers team carried padded equipment cases and cable reels into the house. They set up audio and video equipment, taking precautionary steps for safety like running cable against the wall and taping wires to avoid tripping. After basic special effects were set up, they tested their cameras, electromagnetic frequency readers, electronic voice recorders, and the recording devices in the truck.

Once finished, they pulled bottles of spring water from a cooler in the truck. As they drank quietly, two cars slowed and parked along the sidewalk in front of the house. A woman exited the first car while a withered man parked the second, got out, and walked a few steps behind her. The man had a bright pink scalp, thin silvery-gray hair, and a face lined by wrinkles and splotched with age spots. Slightly stooped, he ambled gingerly. The woman was short, dark-haired, plump, and possessed no discerning limitation when applying makeup. Each of the woman's fingers were adorned with at least one ring. Her dress was a deep violet and decorated with swirls of silver and gold. It was fashioned to showcase an excessive amount of cleavage. A golden cable held a charm, also made of gold, which wedged itself into her ample bosom. The hefty charm had been molded into an equilateral triangle with two closed eyes atop the base of the triangle. The Seeing Eye, whose iris was made of pure silver, was mounted on top of the closed eyes and extended beyond the boundaries of the triangle.

She spoke first. "I take it you are the Ghost Rustlers."

Though it was not a question, Matt answered, "We are."

"Hi. I'm Margie Applegate, psychic with the Third Eye."

Matt's eyes fell upon the charm. After a few awkward seconds, the older man cleared his throat and introduced himself.

"Hello, I am Gabriel Hoffman, a historian from the celebrated American Museum of Natural History and resident expert in all things Amityville. Looks like I arrived a little early for our three o'clock interview. I was excited about our meeting. I hope that isn't a problem."

"Actually, your timing is perfect," Matt said.

"We just finished setting up our gear."

After they finished greeting one another, they moved to the warmer confines of the house.

* * * * *

Six people stood in the living room on the first floor. Devry and Fritz had their backs to the windows, and they each rested a soft, whirring camera on their shoulders as they recorded. One camera focused on Matt; the other recorded the historian.

"So, what can you tell me about the house itself?" Matt asked.

"Well," said Gabriel, "it's a Dutch Colonial house that has five bedrooms and three and a half bathrooms. It went on the market in May. There was an asking price of one-point-one-five million dollars by its owners. The house, of course, has had its share of owners over the years and has changed in appearance dramatically. It looks much different than it did when it became the center of attention in the mid-seventies. The address of this house was changed from 112 to 108 Ocean Avenue some years ago to deflect attention. You have to figure the people that lived here at the time simply grew tired of the history buffs, horror chasers, fanatics, lunatics, and trespassers. I spoke with some of the neighbors some ten, fifteen years ago. One of them told me about some nuts who camped out in his backyard just to be near the house."

"Wow. It's gotta be disturbing to wake up, look

out your window, and see a tent with people sleeping there. I think it's legal to shoot trespassers in some states."

"Maybe." Gabriel chuckled. "But as we know, everything about this house began back in the seventies when the DeFeo family lived here. Some say Ron DeFeo Senior was an abusive father and husband. I don't know if that is true, to be honest. Some say the murders were because of the abuse. Others seem to think the evidence painted a supernatural picture."

"Like what?" Matt asked.

"The murders took place on November 13, 1974, between three and three thirty in the morning. The movie twisted this and suggested the evil would awake at exactly three fifteen in the morning."

"Maybe it wears a watch." Matt laughed. "What do you think? Do you believe spirits can tell time? Maybe ghosts don an ethereal Rolex."

"I'm not much of a ghost expert," Gabriel said, "but I have a tough time believing anything supernatural performing an act at a predetermined time. Let's just say I've been around a long, long time, and I've never met a ghost who kept a date."

"You said something about the evidence. Why was this viewed differently by some investigators?" Matt asked.

Gabriel said, "Well, you have to keep in mind that Ron Junior was the only one who survived, and his fingerprints were all over the rifle, which was identified and proven to be the killer's weapon. Police initially took him into protective custody, arrested him later, and eventually threw the book at him, giving him six life sentences.

"But because of the alleged abuse, some believed the relationship between Ron Junior and his sister Dawn had turned incestuous. No one ever proved that. However, some think Dawn killed her parents and siblings while they were in their beds — they think that because Ron was high on drugs, he couldn't have performed the act. But when he came out of his stupor, he saw the bodies. In his grief and anger, he retaliated by shooting Dawn while she slept in her bed. They found gunpowder residue on her nightgown, suggesting she fired the rifle at some point."

"So he took the rap. Meantime, you got a recipe for that type of negative energy to bake in this house," Matt said. "But, Gabriel, here is what I don't understand. If I were to fire that rifle — or any rifle — right here, right now, in the middle of the day, how many people would hear it?"

"Everyone, probably," Gabriel said. "I imagine a shot from a rifle could easily be heard for four or five blocks."

"But we're talking three in the morning. It's quieter at that hour, right? The telephone switchboards had to light up."

"Nope," Gabriel said. "Only one neighbor claims to have heard it and called it in. It's still one of the great mysteries of this house. And that mystery is right up there with how the family members did not react to a rifle shot in their house in the middle of the night."

"Man, I'm getting goose bumps just thinking about that." Matt pulled his shirt sleeves up. "Dev, get a shot of my arm. Holy crap, look at that. That's just nuts. Do you guys feel anything? I feel like, off, or something."

"Dude, it got cold over here when you said that," Fritz said. "I felt air just rush by. I thought it was air passing through a vent or something. But there's no vent anywhere on this side of the room. And the window is on the other side."

Devry added, "I thought I saw something from the corner of my eye. It's pretty bright in here, so I dunno if I saw Fritz or something else. But I got goose bumps too."

"That's just whack," Matt exclaimed. "All right, whatever's in this house," Matt shouted to no one in particular, "we know you're here. We're coming for you later tonight. If you can tell time, you best check your watches. The rustling begins at midnight."

Jay bounded into the room.

"Guys, something just happened to Margie. She almost passed out."

Everyone funneled out of the living room and circled the main floor until they reached the kitchen. Margie was pressed against the cabinetry, fanning her face with a folded piece of paper. Jay led the group into the kitchen.

"Margie," Jay said, "you okay? Can you describe what you felt?"

Margie fanned harder, trying to summon the words. Her eyes closed, and her head drooped. Folds from her neck skin puffed out. The fan stopped in mid-flight. She moaned, and her head lolled to one side. She jerked twice, and her eyes shot open. Rising until she stood on her tippy-toes, she flailed wildly at her neck. She made awful gurgling sounds as if some invisible hand choked her. Drool ran down the side of her chin. Her eyes darted around urgently as her face turned as purple as a plum.

Jay moved forward to assist, but Matt blocked him with a forearm. "Not yet."

After several seconds, the gurgling stopped, and Margie no longer thrashed. She descended until her feet were flat. Her head slowly turned to Matt and Jay.

"This house belongs to me," she growled. Her voice was nothing like they'd heard earlier; it now carried a rough, sinister edge. "You do not belong. Leave now. LEAVE NOW OR DIE!"

She slumped down to the floor with her back against the counter. Jay moved past Matt to help her. The cameras were still rolling. Jay blocked Margie from their view as he assisted her to her feet. Suddenly, she shoved Jay back, ran to the sink, and threw up in the basin. The pungent odor forced them to wrinkle their noses. Gabriel pulled a white handkerchief from his pocket and covered his nose and mouth.

Matt pumped a tattooed fist in the air and shouted, "Is that right? You think you can scare us? Chase us out of here? Ain't gonna happen! I'm not scared of you. It's you who's gonna run! We got a little Halloween surprise for your sorry ass."

"That's right," Jay added with equal enthusiasm. "We've whooped ghosts left and right all over this great nation. What makes you think you're any different?"

There was a thud in the house from one of the floors above.

"Did you hear that?" Matt asked. They listened intently for a few seconds.

"Do it again, if you're such a badass!" Jay yelled out.

The house remained silent for several seconds.

"Really? That's all you got? You ain't so tough," Jay called.

Matt turned his attention to Gabriel, who stood last in the line of people to enter the kitchen. He swallowed hard after returning the handkerchief to his pocket. Unsure what he might face in the next room, he began rubbing his hands together and fidgeting as if preparing to flee.

"Gabriel," Matt said, stepping toward the man. "Shall we resume our conversation after being so rudely interrupted?"

"Sure, uh…" Gabriel twisted his hands, eventually placing them in his pockets. "The, uh, Lutz family moved into this house in December of 1976.

They ran out twenty-eight days later, citing something sinister in the house." Gabriel couldn't help but look straight up. His face strained with unwanted anticipation, like something evil would strike him down because he stated the truth. His hands moved from his pockets. Fear fed a steady shake into his fingers. "G-George couldn't keep warm. Kathy had problems with flies in a couple of the rooms upstairs."

"Flies?" Matt asked. "Wait a minute. It's December. Wintertime. Where the hell are the flies coming from? They can't be coming from outside. They couldn't survive the cold, right?"

"My expertise is not with insects." Gabriel wiped at the sweat beading on his forehead. "But I think everyone pretty much agrees flies cannot survive the cold, especially during winter in a place like Amityville. There have been all sorts of arguments, including one being that the flies infested the house because of the killings. You know, blood and corpses."

"But the killings were in November. Kind of hard to convince me November is a warm month in New York and a good month for flies to reproduce, Mr. Hoffman."

"I agree. Let's not forget the Lutzes moving in two whole years later. What were the flies feeding on during that time? How were they reproducing? I guess one can make the argument that they could have found a way into the house during warmer seasons. But swarms of flies, as she contended?"

"Another mystery, for sure," Matt said.

As if on cue, they heard buzzing somewhere in the house. It was uncharacteristically loud. A fly landed on Margie's face. She did not flinch. It ran in a semi-circle and flew off. Another fly landed on a cabinet. Two more landed near each other on the countertop. Soon, hundreds more buzzed around the kitchen. The group swatted at the pesky insects. Then the droning ceased. As quickly as they'd come, the flies were gone. They listened intently, but the house stayed quiet. All of them remained still and speechless, waiting for an explanation. Matt mouthed *What the hell was that?* at Jay. Jay shrugged.

"Another mystery, for sure," Matt drawled. Then he returned to Gabriel. The man was wheezing slightly, and his hands were clasped tightly together against his belly. Trying to regain normality, Matt continued, "We get some very poor performances by the spirits wherever we go. Don't pay them any mind, Gabriel." The historian no longer appeared willing and eager. Matt disregarded it, and said, "So the Lutzes experience strange things in the house and are scared out. Soon after, a book by Jay Anson hits the shelves and is an instant bestseller. Then a movie. Doesn't this kind of taint their story to some degree?"

Gabriel saw Matt staring at him. "What?" *Who was Jay Anson? What book? Who were these people?* His head hurt. He took a few deep breaths before it all rushed painfully back to him. He wobbled. Matt placed a hand on his bony shoulder to steady him.

"Gabriel, are you okay?" Matt asked.

"Yeah. Yeah, I'm fine." He took one more deep breath and asked if Matt would repeat the question. Matt did, knowing this was first-rate stuff. Gabriel said, "First thing any rational person says is that it was planned and the Lutzes did it for the money. Many people will argue that point — except more things occurred later on, and they were documented."

"What? You're kidding," Matt said. "Like what?"

"Back in March of 1976, two months after the Lutz family fled — now, mind you, this is well before the book and movie — a team of parapsychologists and psychics inspected the house."

Matt asked, "When you say 'inspected,' you mean what?"

"They went to areas of the house where certain events took place and felt things, emotional and physical. One guy was purported to have grabbed his chest, sensing where one of the shootings took place.

"Then, in January of 1977, another team came here. This time, they brought a medium, a woman, to use her body as a conduit to speak with the entity or entities. Her voice dropped a few octaves, and a Native American Indian chief spoke through her. He was displeased having his sacred land — a burial ground, if I recall — having been desecrated by this house."

"That's creepy," Jay said.

"That's not all," Gabriel continued. "A camera was taking pictures on the second-floor landing. It was pointing at the top of the staircase and a few of the doorways. They set it to take a picture every few minutes or so. Well, they caught something. Something no one can explain. They snapped a picture of a little boy with green-glowing eyes peeking out of one of the bedrooms. The picture was as clear as you standing next to me now."

"No way!" Matt said.

"And that picture was taken around two in the morning. No one brought any children with them. There were no children present. And if you look at the pictures, you see adults coming and going throughout the house. It was a busy place. Someone would surely have seen a child, or admitted one was here. But they didn't.

"I heard about another picture that supposedly shows a man atop a horse in the picture's background."

"The Indian chief," Matt and Jay said simultaneously.

"We certainly have our work cut out here, Mr. Hoffman. Thank you so much for your time," said Matt. "If Margie were feeling up to it, we'd take her with us during our investigation tonight. Right now, I'm not feeling too optimistic about that." He waited a few seconds, then said, "Cut."

The noses of the video cameras lowered and powered off.

A few minutes later, Devry and Matt were outside with Gabriel, shaking hands and thanking him once more.

Inside, Jay thanked Margie for being a terrific sport. Jay handed her a folded white envelope as they shook hands. She slipped it into one of the cups of her ample bosom. Fritz descended the stairs holding a bowling ball.

"Just a damn shame you're too ill to join us tonight," Fritz said to the woman.

"Yeah, I know." One side of her thick red lipstick crooked up into a half-smile. Her penciled-in eyebrows stretched up, and her makeup puckered in a pouty face. "Darn."

"Remember the agreement?" Fritz pleaded.

She squeezed his cheek. "You've nothing to worry about, sweetie. I've done this before. I know the drill. Gabe doesn't know a thing." Her lips curled into a devilish smile. "I thought for sure he was gonna piss himself when that thing hit the floor. Well, ta-ta for now, and good luck with the chase. I can't wait to see it on TV."

Fritz and Jay watched her weave around some trick-or-treaters as she made her way to her car. A small group of young children and their moms — one was dressed like a cat, another like a witch, a third dressed like a she-devil — stopped along the sidewalk to admire the truck in the driveway.

"Fritz," Jay finally said, "that was genius, man. Pure genius. I had no idea. I think you even got Matt. I don't think any of us knew you set up the flies."

Fritz turned to regard Jay.

"I didn't."

＊ ＊ ＊ ＊ ＊

Four men sat on the barren floor of what was considered to be the living room, each against one of the room's walls. Located in the middle of the room on the floor was their only light source: a newly purchased Duracell-powered lantern Fritz had picked up from a local Home Depot late in the afternoon. The house was dark and lifeless. Outside, the wind blew steadily. Matt watched Fritz, who sat across from him, nibbling on pizza crust. A pair of stacked pizza boxes stood next to the lantern.

"Another gourmet dinner." Matt belched. His head tilted in thought for a moment before adding, "Weird that no flies showed up for the pizza, huh?"

Jay and Fritz shared a look but said nothing. Fritz tossed the unfinished pizza crust on top of one of the pizza boxes.

"What time is it?" Matt asked.

Fritz pressed a button along the side of his watch. The display glowed with turquoise luminescence. "Eleven twenty-two," Fritz said as his watch went dark.

"Before we clean up and get started," Matt said, "let's discuss the game plan. No Jack. No Lana. That means we can't cover the house and the grounds with our normal crew. We usually have two pairs investigating, one at Central Command and one covering the effects. We've been short before, but our gear helped cover the loss of manpower. We find ourselves short on both tonight. So let's concentrate on what we do have and be the professionals we are. We know the house has a history, but it's still just a house. I don't buy any of the bullshit hype surrounding it. Every time someone dies in a building, their ghost haunts the place for all eternity, and someone claims to have seen or heard them. I've never seen a ghost before. You know I don't believe in them." He looked Devry's way. "Right, Dev?" Devry squirmed uncomfortably under Matt's glare. "So there is no reason for you to believe in them. Fritz, tell me about the special effects you set up."

"Like I said before, nothing too special. Got the ball drop upstairs in the bedroom where the kid was seen. That one worked out pretty good earlier. As you know, these babies are my design and run on triple-A batteries. I activate the remote in my pocket, and the ball drops onto a towel, making a big bang. That historian dude nearly shit himself earlier with that gag."

The team shared a laugh.

He continued, "Got flour traps set up. One is in front of the first-floor stairs. That one is for show. Another is along the second-floor landing in front of the bathroom at the top of the stairs. The third is on the third-floor landing. I put remote-powered fans in the doorways, out of sight of the cameras. Hit the button on the remote, and it's showtime for the infrareds. I mounted squealers at the bottom of the stairs in the basement and on the topmost step of each floor. So watch where you walk. That's pretty much it."

"Squealers?" Matt asked. The others also showed they had no clue what squealers were.

"Squealers," Fritz repeated, hoping the word would trigger their memory, but he was awarded with more uncomfortable silence. Sighing, he said, "They're motion sensors that run on trip-As, not SunPacks. I boxed them up and saved 'em in case we ever wanted to use 'em again. Don't you guys remember? We used 'em before we got all pro-environment. Squeal louder 'n hell when they're tripped. Lasts ten seconds, then resets." Then with a little zeal, he added, "Great for establishing spiritual movement in areas we are not in, if you know what I mean."

"Oh yeah," Jay said. After a moment to consider this, he asked, "We called them squealers?"

"Well," Fritz admitted, "that's what I called 'em."

Jay shrugged.

Matt slapped Fritz on the back. "Outstanding job, as always, Fritz."

"Hey, Matt," Jay said. "We still need someone to stay in the truck to monitor the gear."

Matt frowned. "That's right. So that leaves three of us. I want two in the house and one outside. The trick-or-treaters are long gone, and it's colder than a witch's tit outside. Fritz, you're our tech. I need you to man the truck. Report anything that goes bad over the radio."

"Roger Dodger," he answered with a salute. "But the range is sketchy with these remotes. I'll need someone to relieve me so I can be indoors to activate them."

"Better yet, give them to Jay. Give him the show-and-tell. Jay, I want you to do a thorough check of the grounds, including the boathouse out back. I'll take the second and third floors. Dev, you get the basement and first floor."

Devry sighed.

"Chickenshit," Fritz teased. He handed a pair of small pocket remotes to Jay, then turned his attention to Matt. "Gotta make a quick detour first."

"Go upstairs," Jay said. "I kinda killed the one down here, and it ain't flushing."

"Damn it, Jay. That's just nasty," Matt said.

"Sorry. I had to go."

Fritz flipped on his flashlight and bounded up the stairs, taking two at a time and intentionally landing on the topmost step. It triggered the motion detector, which made a high-pitched squeal with alternating tones.

"That was me," he yelled out, as was protocol, before entering the bathroom across the landing at the top of the stairs. He locked the door behind him. Fritz aimed the flashlight at the mirror to improve the overall illumination. Dancing in front of the commode, he unbuttoned his jeans and yanked the zipper down. When the stream commenced, Fritz responded with a heavy sigh of relief. Behind him, he heard the innocent giggle of a small boy. Some reflexive muscle clamped shut, causing the flow of urine to stop abruptly.

Fritz stood still, listening for a bit, before calling out, "Hello?"

Maybe one of the guys was messing with him. Probably Devry with his lame paybacks. The whole team could add practical joker to their resumes. Even Devry had a great sense of humor, once upon a time. Fritz surrendered to an inward chuckle. They almost had him. "Yeah, that's real original, fellas." Fritz returned his focus to the business at hand. He resumed peeing. Something caught his attention as he zipped his pants. He watched a few flies buzzing around the mirror. "What the..." He stared in stark disbelief. "I don't get it. How the hell are you guys getting into the house?"

The lock on the door clicked. He swiveled around and watched the knob. It jiggled, rotated, and the door opened a few, creaky inches. *Give a man some privacy, guys!* He yanked the door open all the way and stepped out into the hall in hopes of catching the jokester. No one was there. He searched the second-floor landing. Nothing. The infrared camera was pointed in his direction. Perhaps it had captured someone. Or something. That final thought unsettled him.

"G-guys?" He choked out the words; they hardly registered louder than a whisper. "Who's there?"

A boy giggled in response. Footsteps padded faintly overhead on the third floor. A frosty shiver ran up his legs and spine. None of the guys would dare risk fucking up tonight. This was the real deal. Fritz stumbled into the bathroom to retrieve his flashlight, but it clicked off as he reached for it. He yanked his hand back as if the flashlight were freshly removed from a hot oven. His consternation was acknowledged by another boyish giggle. He snatched the flashlight from the vanity and clicked the power button, swallowing hard after it flipped on in one try. Somewhere deep within, he wanted to convince himself there was an explanation for this. *Just a coincidence*, he thought, trying mightily to do just that. He walked across the second-floor landing toward the third-floor stairs. The squealer on the third floor activated. He turned and high-tailed it down the stairs, setting off the second-floor squealer. As Fritz leaped over the flour trap at the bottom of the stairs, Jay walked out of the foyer, on his way to the boathouse. Fritz slammed into Jay, causing Jay to stumble. Fritz opened the front door in one adrenaline-filled jerk and was out of the house.

"Dude, what the hell is wrong with you?" Jay yelled, rubbing his shoulder. He glanced up the stairs, annoyed by the squealers. As he did, he thought he saw a shadow move back out of view. *Was that a... small boy?*

"Hello?" Jay called out. The squealing from the third floor stopped. "Is someone there?"

He stepped across the flour trap to the base of the stairs, craning his neck to gain a better look at the second-floor landing. The squealer at the top of the stairs stopped chirping.

"Boo!"

Jay nearly jumped out of his sneakers and turned to see Matt behind him.

"You bastard!" he said, and he punched Matt in the shoulder. "Goddamn it, Matt! You scared the shit out of me!"

Matt laughed, and Jay joined in.

"What's up?" Matt asked. His smile faded with Jay's response.

"I dunno. Fritz got freaked out. He nearly dislocated my shoulder running outta here like his hair was on fire."

Puzzled by this, he asked, "Fritz freaked out?" Fritz was a rock. Nothing scared him. He was always the one skulking around in the dark. Fritz was the one who kept everyone else on their toes lest you become the target of one of his pranks. Trying to keep his tone light, he added, "Maybe he saw a spider."

"Who knows? Devry's been skittish since Montgomery, and now it seems so is our special effects guy."

"I need this to be solid, bro." Matt was deadly serious. Amityville was the season finale of their widely popular television series. Their contract was up, and the cable station had a new executive to oversee content. Even with their solid ratings in the books, he balked at extending their contract and refused to finance equipment upgrades or repairs. They worked exceptionally hard all season long, but it was Amityville that was going to make or break a new deal. Tonight, they were shorthanded, their gear could not be relied upon, and Matt needed everyone focused, especially his brother. "Your head on straight?"

"No worries there, big bro. I'm good."

"Great. It's around eleven thirty. About time we get this investigation started. Be careful out there."

Jay, his shoulder smarting, switched on his camera. As he walked past the truck, Jay gave the metal wall a hearty slap.

"Asshole," he rebuked. Retaliation complete, he checked his watch, strapped on a headlamp, flipped on the camera, and spoke aloud.

"This is Jay. It's 11:31 at night on Halloween, and I'm outside the Amityville house, walking toward the boathouse."

The steady wind fed the waves that sloshed noisily inside the boathouse and viciously slapped the shoreline. The camera lens was dotted with a salty mist. Jay turned on his headlamp. Light instantly filled the area in front of the boathouse. He kept the camera running, reached into a pouch around his waist, and extracted a smooth cloth to wipe the lens. As he cleared the lens, a loud crash came from inside the boathouse, followed by a deafening growl.

"What the hell was that?" Jay returned the cloth to its pouch. The camera was aimed at the door. Jay half expected something to come barreling out. He waited. Five seconds. Ten. Twenty. He spoke for the audience. "I don't know what the hell that was. We know the Amityville house has a supernatural history. Let's check it out." His hand reached out tentatively. The wind worked to wrench the door from his grip. Jay slid inside and muscled the door closed. Inside, the ocean water slapped and sloshed noisily, but he was sheltered from the elements outside.

Jay scanned the structure's interior. Seeing nothing of concern, he switched the camera to its infrared setting before switching his headlamp off. The small display on the side fed back everything in bright greens and soft grays. He pointed the camera along the planks of the U-shaped dock on the opposite side. Splayed across most of the pier on that side was a severely damaged net. Part of the net dangled off the edge of the dock and drifted in the turbulent water. The net was attached to a metal pole, which now lay on the pier, bent and snapped into two pieces.

"Hello?" He usually said this for effect. He said it now because his gut told him he was not alone. "Is anyone there?" Another pause. "Are you one of the DeFeo family members? If so, can you do something to make yourself known?" Nothing. "Are you an unfriendly spirit?" There was a thud under the dock where he stood. "Holy crap! Did you hear that? Something struck the dock where I'm standing."

Jay pointed the camera at the dock. In the dark confines of the boathouse, with only the tiny video display providing any visibility, Jay scuttled to the other side of the dock, careful not to fall into the water. He walked onto the mangled net. He kept his poise, focusing the camera near the place he believed the dock was struck. Something tugged on the net, causing Jay to lose his balance. He fell back, away from the water. Years of experience prevented him from losing a grip on the camera.

"Something just pulled on this net. Did you see that?" he said. When he attempted to stand up, he realized he had a small problem. The net was twisted around his right ankle. "I'm caught up in a loose net on the dock here, and I'm going to try and free myself from it." He placed the camera on the net next to him as he worked to untangle his shoes with his free hand, using the mini display to guide his fingers. Suddenly, there was another violent tug, only this time, Jay and the camera were pulled into the ocean. Jay thrashed around in the wild torrent, blind, with the water jouncing him in all directions. He had difficulty determining which way was up. He felt around his forehead for his headlamp, but it was gone. Something grabbed his legs. At first, he thought it was a shark. But it *gripped* his leg, with incredible strength.

Jay struggled to free himself, but whatever held him underwater was vastly more powerful. When it clawed his back, panic gripped him to the core. Jay desperately needed air. Imagine the press running with this story: Ghost Rustler drowns during lockdown at the famed Amityville house. It would only add to the mythos surrounding the house. He was losing the battle without putting up much of a fight.

Then he realized his head had resurfaced above water. Jay coughed out water before sucking in all the air his lungs could withstand. He doggie-paddled to a ladder in the corner of the dock, climbed out, and, while on his hands and knees, coughed out more water. Once he regained his breath, he noticed a burning pain span across his back, and he glared at the inky black water through chattering teeth.

What Jay did not realize was that the demon had been planning to keep him submerged until he drowned. But this would have been considered a direct killing, an act which would have violated the rules of the covenant. Instead, Lucifer, charged with monitoring each Test of Mettle, sent the demon a savage zap from Hell for the infraction. The demon released Jay, enabling the Ghost Rustler to reach the surface and climb to safety.

Jay staggered up the knoll, away from the boathouse and toward the driveway. The wind chewed through his wet clothes and nipped at his taut skin. He tripped over exposed tree roots next to the driveway. He picked himself up and lumbered forward. The muscles in his legs burned more and more with each step. Reaching the rear of the truck, he swung a limp arm at the side of the truck. He waited for what felt like an eternity before slapping the truck a second time. His arms felt heavy, too heavy to hit the door a third time. He stumbled to the rear of the truck and fell against the door. A face peeked out the rear window. Fritz's eyes went wide.

The door swung open, and before Fritz's feet hit the ground, he was on the radio calling in an SOS. Soon, Matt and Devry were sprinting toward the truck. Each held a camera. Both cameras were recording.

"Jay!" Matt cried out. "What the hell happened? You okay?"

"No, I'm not okay!" Jay screamed. "I was fucking attacked!"

Fritz pointed to Jay's back. "You guys might wanna get a shot of this."

Matt pointed the camera at Jay's back. His hold on the camera slackened at the sight of the gruesome wound.

"Damn, bro. You got some nasty claw marks down your back. Three long diagonal lines. Wow. Just... wow."

"It burns like a mother!"

Matt said, "Fritz, patch him up as best as you can with what we got."

Horrified, Fritz looked from Jay's back to Matt. "Dude! I think he's gonna need to see a real doctor. He's probably gonna need some stitches."

"No," Matt said sternly. "Spritz him with some of that antibiotic spray from the first aid kit and patch him up. We're not leaving. Then help him into some dry clothes. You got a spare set of clothes in here, Jay?"

"Yeah. Look in my gym bag. It has yesterday's clothes in it." They helped Jay pull off the soggy, shredded remains of his shirt.

Matt said, "Can't do much for wet shoes. You'll have to get around with socks only. Better to keep your feet dry. I see you wore your belt into the water. How's the two-way?"

"They're not waterproof." Jay unclipped the radio from his belt and flipped it off and on. "Dead." He tossed the ruined unit into the back of the truck.

From behind the group, Devry asked, "You get a glimpse of the ghost?"

Matt and Devry waited for Jay to answer. Instead, the silence was broken when Fritz sprayed Jay's back. He yelled out and pounded the metal door with his fists. "No," he muttered through gritted teeth. "No, I didn't see it."

"Where's the camera?" Fritz asked.

"In the drink. If you want it, feel free to go back there, dive in, and fetch it."

Everyone waited for Matt. His camera was recording the pain on Jay's face. This was the stuff viewers lapped up. By production standards, it was pure gold. He needed all the gold he could get if they were to see another contract. So far, this had all the makings for a ratings bonanza. Despite Jay's condition, Matt continued to take advantage of this fortuitous moment. Jay knew his brother would carry on. It was too important. When Jay refused to seek medical attention, Matt knew his brother was taking one for the team. This was the season finale, after all. They had a job to do and only one night to do it.

"Change of plans," Matt commanded. "No one mans the truck."

Fritz began to argue.

"I mean it," Matt scolded. Things were escalating. He couldn't believe his good fortune. The house was alive! They might record something truly supernatural for their show. As their leader, Matt took charge. "Everyone in the house. Now. Everyone carries a camera, electromagnetic frequency detector, voice recorders, whatever is charged and ready to use. Jay can snatch one of the static cams inside. Fritz, hand him one of the remaining two-ways, an EMF, and a voice recorder."

Fritz helped Jay with his shirt before gathering the equipment.

Jay grabbed his brother's arm. He spoke softly enough that only Matt could hear him. "Our gear won't last the night. You know that, right?"

"Yeah." Matt lightly slapped Jay on the chest with the back of his hand. "Time for an all-out blitz, bro."

They checked their equipment and headed toward the house. Matt led. He wanted this more than he'd ever wanted anything. Whatever was here in this house, it was his booty to plunder. When this was all over, he was going to be a superstar. They would make millions. The others bunched together behind Matt, panning their cameras in all directions, except for Jay, who took up the rear and walked backwards.

Matt's swagger evaporated when they reached the front door. The others froze in their tracks. Jay walked into Devry, who startled. Angrily, Devry shoved Jay in the back. Jay yelled out in pain before cursing out Devry.

Matt's camera focused on the entrance of the house.

"Dude, what the hell is that?" Matt turned to the others, but he was really directing the question to Jay. "What the fuck are we chasing?"

The others spanned out, gawking.

"Oh my God," Devry squeaked.

The door had been left wide open when they responded to the emergency call. They gawked at a newly created set of muddy, three-toed hoofprints. Whatever made these had traveled from the other side of the house, left deep impressions down the length of the now-empty dirt flowerbed, and walked straight into the house. It continued through the flour trap and up the stairs two at a time. The house was silent — not even the squealers had been triggered.

"What do we do?" Devry's voice was weak.

"Toughen up, Devry," Matt growled, keeping his voice low. "We still got a job to do. You're professionals. Time to earn your pay."

A spirit was, allegedly, vaporous, and Fritz was the maker of all things ethereal. He excelled at making things go bump in the night. This, on the other hand, was real. Judging by the length of the stride and size of each print, it was reasonable to assume the creature with the hooved feet had considerable mass.

Jay walked up to Matt. "I wonder if this is what attacked me in the boathouse. If it is, I don't think that's a ghost, bro."

"Ghost or not, we hunt down whatever it is. Debunking, last I checked, was in our job description. Look at the stairs, Jay, and tell me what you see. I spy footprints taking the stairs two at a time. It avoided setting off the squealer at the top of the stairs. How did it manage that?"

Jay considered the implication that this thing might be intelligent. The idea led him back to the boathouse in the water. Why did the thing stop attacking him in the water? It had him dead to rights. Why let him go? Was it the same creature that made the muddy hoofprints? Too many questions and not enough answers.

Before Jay had a chance to speak up, Matt demanded, "Everyone inside."

They all marched into the house in a tight bunch, walked past the staircase, and entered the foyer, where their pizza boxes and coolers were stored. The battery-powered lantern provided the room with a yellow glow, as if cautioning them of their decision. Jay, Devry, and Fritz retreated to the furthest corner in the room.

"Game plan. We got four levels to this house. There are four of us." Their future was at stake. To hell with their fear. Everyone had to take it up a few notches. If something was here, they would capture it on video or audio or both, then share the evidence with the world, and secure the future of *Ghost Rustlers*. It was time to up the ante. "We search the house two to a floor."

"No way," Devry said with a raised voice. "I'm not walking around this house armed with just this camera. Ain't gonna happen."

"You're such a chickenshit, man," Matt muttered.

"Me?" Devry argued. "What about them? You guys wanna split up with some fucking *it* prancing around this gateway to Hell?" The others remained silent.

"This isn't about them, Devry. It's about you," Matt said.

Devry fired back. "Whatever, Matt. No fucking way. Count me out. I'm not interested in your crazy-ass plan. Look at your brother's back. This thing is real. It ain't no ghost. I think we should just leave while we're still alive and in one piece. We got the hoofprints and Jay's back as proof. What more do we need?"

"What about the equipment in the house? Huh?"

"What about it?" Devry said. "We can get it tomorrow morning. We get more people, the cops maybe, I dunno. It'd be safer."

"You're not just a chickenshit, man, you are a coward. Plain and simple. You wanna take your ball and go home now? Fine, be my guest. Go. The door is that way. But you are *walking* back. All the way home. You jet now, then you are done. Game over. There is no turning back. So what's it gonna be, Dev?"

None of the others said anything. Matt had a point. They had been paid handsomely, doing what they did. Now they faced something new and un-expected. They had never encountered anything — real or ethereal — that made its presence known be-fore. Like it or not, Matt was the show's executive producer and had full rights to pull the plug on any-one not pulling his weight.

Devry dipped his head in shame and nodded. He cleared his throat. "Yeah, uh, I'm in, Matt. Sorry man, I'm, uh, just a little scared."

"We all are. But you have got to control your fear. Channel it. Get angry. Use it to do your job. Don't let it rob you. Use it against..."

A resounding boom shook the house, followed by a series of muddled thuds, thumps, and bangs. Growling and giggling and whooping and hollering came from the upper-level floors. Matt ran out to the lawn and pointed his camera up toward the sec-ond and third floors. The others followed suit. They witnessed an intense light show, mostly made up of orange and white light, flashing from the third-floor windows. Jay turned to Fritz, wishing it were one of his ingenious special effects, but, to Jay's chagrin, Fritz simply shrugged.

The banging carried on for a few minutes. Next came a low, hasty rumble that resembled a lead-footed runner giving chase. This was answered by the distinct sound of doors opening and slamming shut. The third-floor squealer was triggered. Matt ran back inside and pointed the camera up the stairs. The others followed. More rumbling came from above. The squealer on the second-floor landing activated. The cameras were recording, but they captured nothing physical or ethereal. It went quiet for a spell before they heard the echo of many unpleasant voices snarl *"GET OUT!"* The cameras recorded the entire supernatural event.

Then the activity ceased altogether in the same manner as the kitchen incident and the flies.

The alternating tones of the squealers fell silent after ten seconds. No one moved. No one breathed. Unnerving peace and quiet had returned. They were too stunned to move, fearing they might incite another dramatic outburst.

Everyone except Matt.

"Let's move. Fritz, Jay, you guys take the basement. You see something, you call us. Use the two-way, scream, do something to get our attention. I don't care how you do it. Dev and I are going upstairs."

"Ten-four," Jay said.

Devry swallowed. The room started to spin. He closed his eyes. His throat tightened, and his stomach twisted into unspeakably painful knots. He breathed in, held it, and almost coughed it out. He had to relax. The house was closing in on him, increasing his nausea.

"Dev," Matt called sternly. He was stepping

over the squealer's sensor. "Let's go."

* * * * *

Devry shouldered his camera and lifted a compact EVP voice recorder to his lips. He whispered, "Matt and Devry in the bedroom on the second floor where the little boy was seen."

Matt shook his head and snatched the recorder from Devry. He raised his voice.

"We heard you. We know you're here. Time to speak to us or show us who you are."

Silence. Devry pulled an electromagnetic frequency reader from his belt and aimed it in a wide arc.

"Nothing on EMF," Devry said.

Matt spoke aloud again. "Are you angry that we are in your home? Are you a little boy? What is your name? Why are you here?"

More silence.

"Anything, Dev?"

"Nope."

It was time to step it up. Matt said, "C'mon! We heard you a little while ago. That was pretty impressive for a little shit like yourself. You got game, kid. Why not give us a demonstration face-to-face? C'mon, you pansy! I'm waiting."

Still more silence. Seconds passed.

Devry shook his EMF meter. He put the camera on the floor and returned his attention to the EMF reader. He slapped it. "What's wrong with this thing?" he muttered.

Matt asked, "What's it doing?"

"Numbers are bouncing all over. One second it gives me a baseline 0.3. Then it spikes to over a hundred. Then back down to—"

Matt interrupted. "IR is dead."

"What?"

"My battery just had ninety minutes on it. I got nothing now. Devry, I need you to hang tight. I'm gonna run out to the truck real quick to grab another battery pack." Matt handed Devry the voice recorder. "Keep the camera rolling and the voice session going. See if you can get it talking."

Matt stepped out of the room, flipped on his flashlight, skipped over the topmost stair to avoid triggering the squealer, and headed down the stairs.

"Um, okay," Devry said, alone, listening to the stairs creak as Matt descended them.

Matt drifted around the flour trap.

"Hey guys," came a call from the radio. It was Jay. "We got a problem."

Matt walked toward the front door. It was wide open. *Hadn't they closed it when they reentered the house?* He was pretty sure they had. He pulled the two-way from his belt and responded as he studied the door and used the flashlight to check the flour trap and the immediate area. "Matt here. What's up, Jay?"

"Dude, Fritz and I are in the basement. The thermal is trashed."

"What do you mean 'trashed?' What's wrong

with it?"

"Matt, the camera is smashed. It's still attached to the tripod, but the tripod is..." Jay's voice trailed off.

"The tripod is *what*, Jay?" Matt demanded.

Fritz's voice answered, "It's jammed into the wall like a pushpin."

Matt was about to respond as he neared the back of the truck, but then the truck rocked close to its tipping point. Loud bangs, crashes, and growls came from within.

"Hey!" Matt yelled. "Who's in my truck?"

He ran to the back of the truck. The doors exploded outward, severed from their hinges. One of the doors struck Matt a glancing blow in the chest. It happened too fast to see or react. The demon followed the door, landed on the ground in a crouch, and, with its momentum carrying forward, sprang up and into Matt with its hardened mass. Matt sprawled backward through the air before his head bounced on the ground. The world disappeared briefly, and for a few minutes, a blank stare settled on Matt's face. Something loomed high over him, but his eyes refused to cooperate.

The demon wanted nothing more than to shred this frail, insignificant human, but the rules were being strictly enforced, as it had learned in the boathouse. The demon growled its displeasure, and it set off back to the house, intent on finishing the job. The humans being tested were not the only obstacle. Its master was watching, and that was motivation enough for the demon to return to Hell victorious, regardless of who — or what — stood in its way.

Matt rolled onto his abdomen and worked his shaky knees under him. He wobbled to the undamaged flashlight lying on the ground next to the truck. He pointed the flashlight into the back of the truck, and his shoulders slumped. Wires dangled from the roof and the side panel. Pieces of equipment lay scattered and unrecognizable. The sickly unmistakable odor of fried electronics was the cherry on the shit sundae. He pointed the flashlight at the smashed remains of the digital video recorders, a major cog to fame and fortune. All that remained were the handhelds and voice recorders. And if they, the Ghost Rustlers, had any hope for a future, it was time to grab the equipment, regardless of its condition, and leave now, hoping to edit whatever they had into a watchable show. Photographing their damaged equipment might help sell their frightful encounter on this historic night. His head hurt like hell, and he felt like complete dogshit, but Matt would heal. It was imperative to make damn sure he got every last bit of evidence out of that house.

* * * * *

Alone, Devry complied with Matt's wishes to continue the electronic voice phenomenon session. Devry sat cross-legged on the floor in the corner of the room, with his infrared camera pointing at the doorway. The EVP recorder and EMF reader sat to either side of him. The EMF reader continued to spike.

"I'm all alone. I am a peaceful person and wish you no harm. I just want to talk to you. Is that okay?"

Outside, the wind pummeled the back of the house. Like all old houses, this one creaked and settled.

"I really like your house," he lied, trying half-heartedly to be convincing. "You know, it's pretty famous. It's probably the most famous one in the whole world. Did you know that?"

No response. Devry cleared the knot growing in his throat. He sat forward and felt his shirt cling to his back. He swiped at the sweat on his forehead. Concern rolled in like the tide. *How long does it take to retrieve a flipping battery?* He wished Matt would hurry back. Devry started to pull his two-way out. If he made the call, he probably wouldn't hear the end of it. He did not want a repeat of Matt's wrath. Or to get lectured by the others. Or to find himself fired because he couldn't hold his shit together.

He set the equipment down, then he used the front of his shirt to wipe the sweat from his face. Was it him, or was the temperature in the room rising? He glanced down at the illuminated face of the EMF detector. It displayed three dashes. Maxed out. Not good. He plucked the two-way from his belt and placed his thumb on the push-to-talk button, when thumps and shuffling steps outside the room stole his attention. He slowly lowered the two-way to the floor, staring at the general direction of the doorway. He lifted the camera and watched for activity in the mini display.

"Is someone there? I'd like to speak to the little boy. Are there any other children here who would like to talk to me?"

The display glitched before going black.

"No, no, no," Devry hissed. He slapped the side of the camera, but it did nothing to change the fact that the camera was dead.

He heard faint buzzing.

Oh shit.

The buzzing grew steadily louder, and the temperature in the room plummeted. Devry's hands fumbled around to locate the flashlight clipped onto his belt.

"Hello?" Devry's throat nearly clamped shut.

The room sounded like an active beehive. He thumbed the power button and pointed it toward the doorway. He watched his warm breath huff out into thick clouds. Movement in the doorway caught his breath. A dense swarm of flies filled the threshold. In the center of the swarm was a shape devoid of flies. It was the shape of a child, and it stared directly at Devry with brooding black eyes.

"Oh my God," Devry whimpered. He tried to keep his shit together, but his courage was faltering fast. "Uh, hi there. I'm Devry. What is your name?"

The shape stepped into the room. The door slammed shut behind it. Devry grabbed his two-way and squeezed the push-to-talk button. It failed to squawk, but Devry took no notice that his two-way, like the camera, was dead.

He screamed into the dead radio. "Help! Help! Get up here! Oh my God, it's here!"

It glided toward Devry. Devry gagged at the odiferous emulsion of wilted flowers, death, and cooked flesh. The droning of flies, so intense now, more closely resembled a packed stadium of frenzied fans. Flies surrounding a shimmering arm rose. The stench intensified. Flies crawled over him, buzzing into his gaping mouth. He spat them out and flailed at the insects. The void extended its fingers toward Devry. At first, he did not know what to make of it. Then, the hand squeezed into a fist, as if to crush something in its grasp. The flashlight flickered once before it went dead, engulfing Devry in total darkness. He shuffled to his feet, dropping the flashlight. He dashed through air thick as soup and as cold as a glacier, kicking the camera and EMF reader hard enough that they each clattered into the wall. Devry ran straight into the door and bounced off. He fumbled in the dark until he located the doorknob. He pulled and tugged as hard as his adrenaline-fueled muscles could muster. It was useless. The door would not budge.

"Help!" He screamed as loud as he could. "Someone get me outta here!"

He pounded the door with his fists, screaming. The hair stood up on the back of Devry's neck, and he went still. The air thickened to the point that it was impossible to breathe, and his exposed skin felt the teeth of frostbite. He felt icy puffs tickle the back of his neck. The presence enveloped him like a scratchy blanket. Devry tried to scream, but he was breathing in ragged gasps. The rank odor filled his mouth with a vile cocktail of rancid licorice, crushed insects, and ammonia.

Devry retched. His mouth watered, which helped to spit out some of the cloying flies. The thought of them still flitting their wings and moving around in his mouth carried him over the edge. He bent over and threw up. When he finished, he stood up straight. The flies were gone, but the temperature painfully bottomed out. An elongated guttural word was uttered into his ear. *Leave.* The door clicked open. Devry bolted out of the room, colliding hard with Matt at the top of the stairs. Both sprawled across the second-floor landing.

From the top of the third-floor stairs came the ululating shriek of the squealer.

* * * * *

Unearthly whispers flooded in from all directions. Though mostly incomprehensible, there was little doubt of their agitation. A chilled, swirling wind came from nowhere, adding a supernatural element to the shrieking spirits.

"Jay, you recording this?" Fritz shouted over the wind and voices.

Die. Trespasser. Leave. Demon. Blood.

"Yeah!" Jay was bewildered. In all their years,

they had never encountered anything they could call supernatural. Tonight, the Amityville house was putting on a show. "Yeah, I am."

"My EMF is still maxed out," Fritz called out.

Jay asked, "You getting anything on thermal?"

"This is crazy," Fritz answered. "My thermal is still reading in the twenties down here. It feels every bit of it. I think our breath would be visible if it weren't for this damn wind."

Jay pleaded, "Who is down here with us? C'mon, be a sport and talk with us. You sound angry. Let's be civil. We just want to talk to you, okay?"

The wind and whispers stopped. Jay and Fritz shared bewildered expressions.

"Weird," Jay breathed.

Enmity, repulsion, and venom funneled into a single, palpable word.

LEAVE!

"Jay, I admit it. I have never been more scared in my life than I am now."

"Me too, Fritz."

"Jay?"

"Yeah?"

"I pissed myself."

The door to the basement burst open, and Matt and Devry ran down the stairs and sped around the corner, out of breath. Matt held a small utility flashlight. Its tiny beam reflected off two different jagged lines of blood trickling down the side of Matt's face.

Matt huffed, "Jay, Fritz, time to go."

"What happened to your head?" Jay asked.

"I was attacked outside. I came inside to grab the equipment, get you guys, and leave. I went up to the third floor. Along the way, I saw our static cameras, just like you described. There must have been a badass fight in one of the rooms. I only had my flashlight and couldn't make out whatever it was. I accidentally tripped the squealer. For a brief second, I thought I saw glowing eyes. Next thing I know, it sounded like a tribe of Indians whooping and hollering, and then this big fucking thing gets gang-tackled through a wall. The third floor looks like a goddamn war zone. Then the bedroom door slammed shut by itself. I ran as fast as I could to get Devry, but the door to the bedroom he was in was locked. Next thing I know, Dev mowed me over."

Devry nodded in agreement.

"Look, I've had enough," Matt said. "I think Dev was right. Let's just take what we got and get out. We can come back with a battalion tomorrow. Right now, let's dip."

The others assented.

They marched toward the stairway. Matt's flashlight blinked twice and died.

"Oh shit," Jay said as they fell into complete darkness.

Something moved with heavy footsteps along the main floor directly above them. They heard… Indians. It was followed by an angry, defiant growl. This was answered with another deafening boom that rattled the house. They backed away from the stairs.

"Montgomery. Oh my God," returned Devry's feeble, frightened voice. "It's back."

They regarded Devry in the dark, realizing too late what had spooked him all along.

He had had a demon encounter once before — a Test of Mettle he had neither won nor lost. As a result, he could be tested again, up to three times, based on the covenant between Lucifer and Jesus.

All eyes fell on the staircase after a sequence of a whinnying horse, a furious growl, and a flash of orange and white light that ended when a massive creature rolled backward down the stairs, slamming into the wall opposite the bottom of the stairs. The temperature fell even further, and they choked on an intense odor of decay and outrage. Electric-blue discharges gave them fragmented glimpses of the scene unfolding before them. The demon launched itself at the unseen opposing force, but never made it. A thunderous clap of bright orange lightning slammed into the belly of Hell's minion, propelling it into the four Ghost Rustlers, across the length of the basement and into the opposite wall. The impact sent the four men crashing across the floor. A gray form appeared in the darkness at the source of the lightning bolt. It took the form of an Indian chief with a full headdress, atop a decorated horse. The horse rose up on its hind legs. Its whinny came out as a horrible shriek. The Indian chief raised an ethereal hatchet into the air. The horse charged across the basement, passing by the demon that hung heavily in front of the severely damaged wall. The chief's hatchet plunged into the demon's chest. The demon slammed back into the wall before falling forward onto the floor.

Without a backward glance, Matt raced up the stairs, shouting to the crew. He ran through the open front door, pulled the keys from his pocket, and hopped into the truck. He jammed the key into the ignition, started it on a single turn, shifted into reverse, and slammed his foot on the accelerator. The truck jounced onto Ocean Avenue, leaving a trail of sparks in its wake. Large broken pieces of equipment slid out the back of the truck and skittered across the street. Jay and Fritz yelled as they ran out of the house. Brake lights gave the chasers their lone opportunity to leap into the back of the truck. Matt jerked the gear into drive before punching it. Jay and Fritz clutched at anything still bolted down. The truck sped down Ocean Avenue, away from the world's most famous haunted house. The sound of screeching tires carried up and down the street, then faded. A sense of peace and quiet seeped back into the neighborhood.

* * * * *

Devry remembered something rolling down the stairs. An Indian on a horse appeared out of nowhere. Devry covered his ears when the horse shrieked. There was a flash of light. Then something hit him hard, sending him sliding across the floor and into the far corner face-first. He was bleeding, but that was the least of his worries. He sensed a severe injury to his arm and shoulder. Using his good arm, he sat up to get his bearings. Devry could see absolutely nothing. Fear pumped through his veins. His bad arm and shoulder kept him from moving any more than he had to.

His voice croaked, "G-g-guys? Y-y-you th-th-there?"

A rough growl captured his attention from along the wall where he sat.

"M-M-Matt? Th-th-that y-you?"

A set of red-glowing eyes turned toward him. They were, at most, seven feet away. Devry watched, praying it could not see him. He held his breath and sat stone silent. The eyes remained trained on him. They didn't blink. They never wavered. Then, the eyes rose as the creature stood. It towered over Devry. He felt tears flow down his face.

The demon felt the pull from Hell, and not because Devry had laid eyes on it. Devry failed to face his demon mentally, physically, and spiritually. The demon growled — the same growl that had haunted Devry since Montgomery — before it charged the human, the human it had been sent to test.

Devry squeezed his eyes shut and let out a high-pitched scream of pure, unadulterated terror. There was a detonation of air caused by the demon's departure. The concussion forced Devry to strike the wall again.

Devry opened his eyes. The unnerving quiet

in the pitch-black basement broke something in him, and he filled the void of darkness with empty, silent screams, his damaged vocal cords incapable of producing any sound.

* * * * *

Dawn brought in the new day with a glorious sunrise. The cloudless sky melded with hues of gold, tangerine, and violet. The air was fresh, and the breeze was crisp. All indications were that the first day of November would begin in spectacular autumnal fashion.

A gold Lexus parked in front of 108 Ocean Avenue, and Wendy Titus stepped out of her car. She looked forlornly at the house before her. She searched up and down the street, but the Ghost Rustlers' truck was nowhere to be seen. It upset her that they hadn't notified her. She pulled a cell phone out of her pocket, scrolled through her address book to the entry for Matt Depone, and pressed the call key. She frowned when it went straight to voicemail.

"Hi, Matt. This is Wendy Titus of Amityville Realty. I am at the house now, but I don't see your truck. I don't know if you guys returned to your hotel or grabbed a bite to eat, but you agreed to meet here at dawn. Please return my call as soon as possible. Thanks."

She flipped the cell phone closed and dropped it in her purse. She nearly tripped on a smashed metal box. She surveyed the street and found it littered with an assortment of plastic and metal debris and frayed wires. She walked up the steps leading to the front door. She tapped her knuckles on the door, and it creaked open. *Odd*, she thought. *Why on earth would they leave the house unattended — with the door ajar, for that matter?*

She stepped inside.

"Hello? Matt? Guys? Anyone here?"

The floor was covered in a fine powder and footprints heading in different directions. She spotted remnants of indiscernible, muddied prints on the floor and the stairs. Wendy walked past the stairs and into the foyer. Empty pizza boxes, plastic water bottles, an unlit lantern, and assorted litter rested along one wall. She walked back toward the staircase and ascended the steps, then grabbed her chest in fright when the squealer shattered the silence at the top of the stairs.

For the next ten minutes, she went from room to room assessing the trail of damage. It worsened the further she went. She received another fright from the squealer at the top of the stairs leading to the third floor. The third floor was a scene from a warzone. Doors were ripped from their hinges. Huge gaping holes were found on the innermost walls, though the exterior walls, based on her survey, were untouched. The floors and ceilings had sustained spotty damage throughout the upper two levels.

She huffed past cameras that were thrust senselessly into the walls. What story would they concoct? Probably they'd come up with some nonsense about the house being haunted. It had been owned by a handful of people over the years, but none of them claimed to have seen ghosts or to have heard demonic voices. She'd sold hundreds of properties over the years, and not once had she ever encountered a ghost. People could believe what they wanted. As far as she was concerned, it was all a bunch of hokum. The damage laid out before her only rankled her ire even more. These guys had some serious balls to just up and leave after destroying half the house.

Nearly blind with rage, she decided to check out the basement before leaving. Her heels clunked and creaked as she descended the wood stairs. The opposing plaster wall had a spiderweb of cracks from floor to ceiling. Plaster littered the floor beneath it. Sunlight filtered into the basement's tiny windows.

She walked around the corner to the main area. She gasped, covering her mouth with her hand as her purse plopped to the floor. The wall on the opposite side of the basement looked like it had been targeted by a wrecking ball. Overlaying the round area of damage was an image burned into the wall of an American Indian chief on horseback with a hatchet in hand. And in the adjacent corner sat one of the Ghost Rustlers. If she recalled correctly, his name was Devry.

His eyes were wide open but unseeing. Dried blood smeared his battered face. One arm, bent at an odd angle, hung limply at his side. His knees were pressed into his chin, and his unbroken arm wrapped around his legs. Devry rocked steadily mouthing something, but no sound escaped his lips.

9 - THEODORE
GOES HUNTING

April 23, 1909: British East Africa

T he well-dressed man sat still on the train. He remained quiet, focused. Every so often, he pulled a notebook and a stubby pencil from a hidden pocket within his jacket to jot something down. When finished, he closed the notebook and tucked it away before resuming the same posture he'd been in since the start of the train ride in Mombasa, a port city along the Indian Ocean located on the east side of the African continent. His left leg rested across his right. Spectacles covered hard eyes deep in thought. The seat next to him was empty.

Sitting directly across from the well-dressed man was his twenty-one-year-old son, Kermit. The young man read a small book covered in worn, stained leather. The title etched into the leather was faded and illegible.

Next to Kermit was a man whose face looked as worn and leathery as Kermit's book. A trio of deep trenches snaked across his forehead. His eyes were sunken and ringed by darkened wrinkles. Those eyes were studying the well-dressed man.

"Why Africa?"

The well-dressed man maintained his deep concentration for a full minute before answering. "I plan to collect specimens for America's great museum, the Smithsonian."

The man guffawed. "What good is a museum but a place of death and rot and dust?"

This question seemed to snap the well-dressed man from his trance, and he directed a gaze of such intensity that it caused the man with the sunken eyes to shift in his seat, averting his attention to some other thing.

Finally, Roosevelt bristled. "What museums have you visited? Or, perhaps, were they mausoleums?" At this, Roosevelt dropped his folded leg to the floor with a mighty thump, garnering the man's attention once more. "The Smithsonian serves a greater purpose to mankind. They do not just display dull butterflies pinned to a board with faded identification labels. There are a great many scientists, professors, and those like me who have a curious passion for our living world. There are a great many men and women who dare to know more. Life begets knowledge. I am here to collect specimens for research. Knowledge is a treasure. Our world is bustling with life. How can you truly live it without knowing of its treasures? And treasures will return with me, yes indeed. I will not let down those who have paved the way in the name of science. So, you see, I would not be on this expedition if it were not for those fine people at the Smithsonian."

"And it had nothing to do with your successor, Taft?"

"Hardly. I admit I had a certain fondness for dear William. Until, that is, I learned what a puzzle-wit he truly was."

"Hmm."

Theodore leaned forward, his face reddening, his eyes menacing. They fixated on the leathery man.

"Let us be clear about one thing. I am no longer in politics. I am on the hunt, Shamus, to collect specimens for the Smithsonian. They paid a great deal of money to finance this trip. I believe we are indebted to them. One debt, I hasten to say, that will be repaid in full. Scribner's provided me enough equity to finance my share of this safari. In return, I will repay them with a detailed account of this trip," he said, and he tapped the book hidden within the breast of his jacket. The twenty-sixth former president of the United States inched closer. "Does that satisfy your curiosity, Shamus?"

The leathery man shrank back into his seat and nodded, wanting no further interaction, while Theodore slid back into his seat, settling himself until he was comfortable once more. Once he seemed satisfied, he returned his leg to its crossed position atop his other leg, pulled out his notepad, penciled a few lines, paused, eyed Shamus with a long, hard stare, jotted something else, and returned the pad to his jacket.

Like many who found themselves face-to-face with the former president, Shamus did not realize Theodore was blind in his left eye. It had been injured during a boxing bout last year, but that bit of information was kept private. There were many people with two functioning eyes who did not have half the boundless energy Theodore exuded, so there was no reason to theorize such a ludicrous notion. Engrossed in his book, Kermit could not help but crack a wry smile, knowing Shamus had just been stared down by a half-blind man.

With hundreds of miles behind them, they reached camp with little more conversation. The campsite had been assembled ahead of their arrival. For that, the team was grateful, for they entered their tents and promptly fell asleep.

Over the course of the next few days, the camp was actively organizing their activities, breaking off into smaller teams to gather specimens.

One such morning, shortly after the break of dawn, Theodore awoke refreshed and perky. In the adjacent cot in the cozy tent, Kermit was snoring. Theodore opened the flap of the tent and stepped outside. The sky swam with rich ocean blue mingled with twists of orange. A single condor circled overhead. After breathing in the fresh morning air, Theodore stretched to the usual pops and snaps in his aged joints. Shamus sat upon a crate shaving his face with a straight razor in one hand while holding a simple round mirror in the other. Seeing the bleeding nicks, Theodore was surprised half the carnivorous beasts populating the plains around them were not already feasting on his face. Theodore opened his mouth to speak, thought better of it, peered up at the circling bird once more, and decided to head for the nearest carafe of coffee.

One of the porters poured hot coffee into a ceramic cup and handed it to the former president. Theodore watched Shamus from across the way as he sipped his coffee. Shamus jerked the razor away once more and inspected the newest nick on his face. Theodore sipped his coffee, contented to watch Shamus, who reached for a bowl of water on the ground and dipped his face in it. Theodore stood and walked up to Shamus. He lowered himself to one knee. With his eyes squeezed shut, Shamus used a small towel draped over his shoulder to pat his face dry, careful not to reopen the many cuts. When he reached for the mirror to inspect his face, he was startled by Theodore's reflection.

"What is it?" Shamus huffed in irritation.

"You are an attractive man," Theodore said.

The scowl on Shamus's face was replaced with a wide smile. "Why, thank you, sir." His chest puffed out with the compliment. Theodore carefully rose so as not to spill his cup of coffee. He placed a hand gently on Shamus's shoulder as he bent toward the man's ear.

He said, "That is, I am sure the animals will find you an attractive appetizer." Shamus's smile evaporated. "First, the big cats will have their fill of you. Then, the vultures will pick your bones clean. When they're done, the swarms of bloodsucking insects will finish whatever's left after laying eggs in your carcass." With a powerful hand, he grabbed Shamus's head and pulled it back so the man could see the large bird circling overhead.

Theodore headed toward another tent where four men huddled around a campfire. They held plates piled with freshly cooked eggs, links of sausage, and cups brimming with hot coffee. Guides and porters prepared breakfast for the men.

"Teddy! Top of the morning to you."

One of the four men raised his cup in salutation.

"McKittrick," Theodore responded flatly. "Gentlemen." He nodded to the others.

After greeting one another, they each shared their backgrounds, which mostly consisted of hunting and their most significant kills.

"Speaking of kills." Theodore turned to McKittrick.

"Done. Our specimens are safely packed away, mate. As you know, we had four tons of salt to preserve big game for the return trip. We have a fair amount left."

Theodore nodded. He pulled his notepad out and scribbled a few notes before returning it to his pocket.

"Tell me, Teddy," McKittrick said, "what have you and your son bagged?"

Theodore loathed being called Teddy. Since early childhood, family and close friends had called him Teedie. To everyone else, his name was Theodore, and that was what he preferred. Theodore had grown accustomed to such banter and rarely found any reason to draw any attention to the matter.

"A few antelope, a zebra, a pair of warthogs, and a water buffalo."

The men nodded their assent.

"Not bad, Teddy," McKittrick said. "But were any of them a threat?"

"A threat?" Theodore repeated.

"Aye, a threat." McKittrick sneered, showing two rows of yellow, crooked teeth. "Did the big scary antelope come a-chargin'?"

The men snickered.

"Antelope can leap when they run, making them far more difficult to bring down than some lumbering beast bearing down on you with his head lined up with an elephant gun. Though I admit, an element of the hunt — that thrill of man versus beast — is lost."

The men nodded at the truth in his words. McKittrick's face began to color.

"Also," Theodore added, "while I was collecting smaller specimens, insects and arachnids, you understand, I came across an entire nest of rare seven-legged African plain beetles. Did you know their eggs have the same color and flavor as coffee, except that they are said to lean toward the bitter side? I boxed the whole nest, but it seems it was confused with our rations." Theodore took a sip of his coffee and swished it around thoughtfully, before leaning forward to spit it out. He turned to a man next to him and asked, "It does seem more bitter than usual, doesn't it?"

The man took a reluctant sip. He nearly choked on the liquid when he found himself stuck between swallowing and spitting. Caught in the middle, he coughed out the coffee. Some of the men tipped over their cups, pushing their meals aside and mumbling on the way back to their tents. McKittrick guffawed in disbelief. He picked up his cup and took a hearty swig, swallowing for all to see, then smacked his lips. He was about to place his cup on a crate but peered into it first. The color of his face drained away at the sight of an unmoving insect floating inside. McKittrick swiped the plate of breakfast from his lap, dropping the coffee cup to the hard dirt as he staggered a few steps on wobbly heels. He groaned as if he had taken a shot to the gut. The remaining men snickered. McKittrick spun to condemn Theodore, his forefinger pointed straight up in the air in a prepared measure to denigrate the former president. The man went perfectly still, then fell to his knees and lost his breakfast. Applause and laughter permeated the campsite.

The men patted Theodore on his back as he headed toward McKittrick, who was now on his knees, drawing deep breaths. McKittrick swiped at his face with his sleeve but missed most of the mess surrounding his mouth.

Theodore leaned over and spoke in a tone meant only for McKittrick. "Beetles are insects. Insects have six legs, not seven."

McKittrick shot him a deathly look, but it carried hardly any of its intended ferocity. The man had dried grass, runny eggs, and a long strand of snot stretching from his nose to his mouth to the barely digested breakfast splattered along the ground. Theodore patted the defeated man on the back.

Theodore entered the circle of tents surrounding their campfire, which was barely smoldering. He spotted Shamus studying his reflection in the same mirror he'd held earlier. His thumb held open his nose while the other held a pair of scissors. Theodore dropped a plate of food atop the mirror just as he snipped.

"What is the meaning of this?"

"Breakfast," Theodore responded matter-of-factly. "Enjoy."

Dressed and cleaned, Kermit sat on the crate his father had used earlier, enjoying a fresh cup of hot coffee. An untouched plate of food rested next to him.

"Anything new?" Kermit asked.

Theodore rolled a log from a woodpile next to their tent and sat upon it.

"Seven-legged East African beetles."

Kermit gazed questioningly at Theodore before replying, "Father, there is no such thing. Beetles are insects. Insects have six legs."

"Indeed."

Hours later, a line of thirty men — hunters, porters, guides, and photographers — crossed an area of the plain dominated by wildlife. They set up a temporary base camp and held a short meeting to discuss their day's activities. They split up into small teams before heading out to hunt. A native guide led Theodore and Shamus. On their team was a seasoned hunter by the name of Captain Arthur Slatter. Arthur was an excellent hunter, despite having only one hand. The lack of limb did nothing to impede the man. He was as agile as any of the seasoned hunters in the camp.

The surrounding grass ranged in height from ankle to waist. Short, scant trees dotted the landscape. Their usefulness was limited to small birds that used them for nesting and large birds to rest weary wings. They provided little shade, and cobras were known for taking residence in the nests, which were often three to four feet in diameter. Advice to steer clear of the trees was well received.

Theodore's team stopped behind a ridged mound adjacent to a clearing. About two hundred feet away in the open was an adult white rhinoceros. The creature flicked its tail and ears in a fruitless attempt to repel irritating insects. The stubborn rhino stood perfectly still. The curved ivory tusk on its massive head measured at least two feet in length. Its impressive armored plating was battleship-gray and remarkably ironclad, having only a few blemishes on display. It was an alpha male that did not lose in battle, nor did it encounter many willing challengers. Perhaps most competitors saw what Theodore, Arthur, Shamus, and the guide witnessed. This behemoth was a veritable two-thousand-pound fortress.

Theodore whispered instructions to the guide. The guide nodded. Shamus released his camera and tripod against the mound with a clatter before plopping down and fanning himself. Theodore's reprimanding stare shrank the man into the grassy knoll. Arthur kicked Shamus in the pants, following it with a stern "Shh!"

After peering over the mound once more, both Arthur and Theodore stepped with a hunter's grace in the direction of the beast's rump. They faced a light breeze, which was good news, because it carried their scent away from their intended prey. With their weapons poised and ready to fire, they changed directions as they closed in, positioning them along the animal's flank. They were a mere one hundred feet from this dangerous yet magnificent animal. It would serve as one dandy specimen if they were successful.

The animal shifted. Theodore and Arthur stood stock-still, their rifles pointed. The rhinoceros snorted and plopped onto the soft grass. Theodore and Arthur shared a knowing look, one that communicated that the creature, known for its poor eyesight, was clearly unaware of their presence. Theodore sidled along the animal's flank while Arthur positioned himself behind it. The rhinoceros shook its head, flicking its ears to deter the abundance of pesky insects. In doing so, the beast spotted Theodore and rose with the speed and agility of a polo pony. Its head lowered. The battle had begun.

Theodore emptied the right barrel of the double-barreled Holland rifle. It struck the animal in the side, piercing both lungs. The animal wheeled around and charged full-on. Blood sprayed from its angry nostrils as it rapidly closed the gap between them.

The hunters never wavered as one ton of ferocity came hard and fast. This was an animal not accustomed to losing. It moved despite a pair of collapsing lungs, protecting its territory from an unwanted rival. The point of its horn was now aimed to kill. Two more shots were fired. At the same time, Theodore emptied his left barrel. The final shots proved fatal. Theodore struck the rhinoceros between the neck and shoulder, piercing its heart. Arthur severed vertebrae in the rhino's neck. The bulk of the animal's weight shifted forward. Its massive head plowed deep into the earth before coming to a rest.

Shamus wiped his sweaty brow with a handkerchief. He glanced over the mound to see the huntsmen shaking hands; the lifeless monster lay behind them. The freshly tilled earth around its head gave the creature the appearance of having a beard.

"Shamus!" yelled Theodore. "Come at once and take our photograph. We have captured our most formidable opponent yet!"

The sun dipped behind the trees and distant mountain ridges. Fiery colors painted the sky. It was a good day: everyone returned safely to the main camp. Smoke rose from roaring fires, and hovering above those flames was sizzling meat on iron roasting spits. Arthur and Theodore's trophy specimen was cause for a celebration that was soon underway with the pops of champagne corks. The outdoor party continued well after brilliant stars and a glorious half-moon filled the sky, providing ample natural light. Shadows grew sharper and stretched deeper into the lightless pockets across the plains. The effect painted a cool, bluish hue across the surrounding grassland. It resembled a great lake. The subtle breeze oscillated waves into the fluid grass.

The celebration dwindled, conceding to the sounds of nocturnal nature.

Theodore, Kermit, Shamus, and Arthur sat in front of their campfire.

"That was fine sport today, eh, Teedie?" Arthur slurred his words, but displayed no other signs of drunkenness. His movements remained crisp, his eyes were sharp, and his rifle stayed within an arm's length. If a predator made its way into camp, odds were that Arthur would fire the first shot.

"I shall remember it for all my days," Theodore responded with a similar inebriated slur. He turned his attention to Kermit. "My boy here bagged himself a trio of hyenas. He found their tracks a quarter-mile away, circling our camp."

Arthur slapped Kermit on the back. "Good

show, Kermit. Good show indeed."

"And Shamus here was the best shot of all. For we salt animals and spew imbibed tale, but this man brings the hunt home. He makes it real now and for all eternity."

"A toast, then!" Arthur raised a bottle. "To Shamus, master hunter!"

The rest echoed, "To Shamus!"

Shamus blushed. He tried to rise from his crate. He tipped forward toward the fire, thrust his shoulders back to regain his balance, and overcompensated. He stepped back into his crate, lost his balance, and landed on the ground with a dull thud. Only the soles of his boots were visible above the crate.

The men slapped their legs, laughing themselves senseless. Shamus's foot twitched once, then did not move again.

"Well, it seems Mother Nature is not without a sense of irony, for she has poked at my bursting loins. I must relieve myself," Theodore said. "Please excuse me."

He slung his rifle over his shoulder and snatched a brown wool blanket from his crate. He walked over to Shamus.

"Out cold," he said, and he covered the man with the blanket.

An area at the corner of the camp was designated as a toilet. Theodore unslung his rifle and entered one of the makeshift stalls, pinning the cloth door for privacy. He rested his rifle against a wall and stared up at the heavens.

After a moment, he said, "Surely, God exists. To have provided us with such a bounty of nature. There is nothing quite as magnificent. Who else but a supreme being could have created such splendor? Even the heavens above are indescribably beautiful. I hope never to witness the wrath of God. But if I ever should meet His foes, I will protect His land until my dying breath. And I promise the last thing they will see is the end of my rifle."

A fit of wild laughter interrupted Theodore. He heard pattering through the grass not too distant from where he squatted. Something ran by and bumped the latrine. Theodore scrambled to his feet, yanking up his trousers with one hand and reaching for his rifle with the other. A second whooping cackle joined the first.

Then there was silence.

Hyenas? Couldn't be. They're predators, sure, but they're known for being opportunists. Scavengers. They prey only on wounded or small animals, and they do so in packs. Hyenas leave the dirty work of hunting big game to the lions. It's unusual for them to enter a camp, or even approach it. No, they would skirt the perimeter at a safe distance. If there's any animal bold enough to approach and enter a camp, it's the lion. The pair of creatures stirring about do not sound like lions. There's something curious about the laughter; it almost seems human.

Theodore unpinned the cloth and stepped out of the latrine just as Kermit and Shamus turned a corner, with half the camp behind them in varied states of dress and sobriety. Shamus wobbled unsteadily, needing to steady himself by grasping Kermit's shoulder.

"Hyenas?" Kermit asked.

"I thought that very thing, but I'm not so certain," Theodore said.

McKittrick pushed through the group of people.

"What the hell was that? Didn't sound like any hyena I ever heard."

"Hyenas," Theodore corrected.

"What?" McKittrick said.

"There were at least two of them. I heard two distinct sets of laughter."

"Two?" McKittrick said unconvinced. "Makes no damn sense. Hyenas hunt in packs, not in pairs. The whole family stays close."

"Kermit bagged three of them today some distance outside of camp."

McKittrick added, "Maybe they're fractured."

"Not likely." Arthur approached from behind Theodore, carrying a torch. His rifle was slung over his shoulder. "I just spotted a set of fresh tracks. It did not belong to a hyena."

"If it is not a hyena, then what the hell was it?" McKittrick asked.

"I…" Arthur hesitated. "I don't know. It's unlike anything I've ever seen."

Maniacal laughter came from somewhere in the camp. Another fit of laughter joined it nearby.

Some of the men who were not hunters and carried no weapons grew unsettled, keeping within safe proximity to those who were armed.

"It's in camp!" McKittrick yelled. "Follow me!"

Dozens of men chased after McKittrick.

"McKittrick!" yelled Arthur, but he was gone. "Damn fool. This is how people get killed. Just a-whoopin' and a-hollerin' with guns a-blazin'."

"Let's be smart about this and remain calm," Theodore said. "Arthur, I need you to track these things. Perhaps their tracks will lead to a den. If they are fractured, then McKittrick and his posse will bag them."

"Okay," Arthur said with obvious sarcasm. "Hunting in the dark. Great idea."

"Wait here," Theodore said. He disappeared into the city of tents and returned a minute later with a torch in hand. "Here," he said, handing the torch to Shamus.

"What am I supposed to do with this?" Shamus protested.

Theodore said, "Carry it. And if need be, make shadow figures using the firelight to scare off anything that isn't human."

Shamus looked upon the man in disbelief. Arthur, already ten paces outside the camp, carrying a torch of his own, called to Shamus. Shamus sighed heavily and chased after Arthur. Kermit and Theodore readied their rifles as they fell behind.

Ten minutes later, Arthur stopped suddenly and squatted low to inspect the ground. He studied the soil, moving the torch to gain the best possible view. Shamus glanced nervously at the ground Arthur studied. A hand grabbed Shamus's shoulder, and he yelped.

"Easy does it, Shamus," Kermit said. "They fear you more than you fear them. You need to calm yourself. Predators can sense fear."

Rivulets of sweat ran down his forehead and cheeks. Shamus swallowed hard and nodded. Arthur handed his torch to Kermit as he circled the area of concern. Arthur squatted once more. Theodore watched Arthur paw at the ground, his lone hand flicking pebbles. The man's mind seemed to be a million miles away.

"What is it?" Theodore finally asked.

Arthur looked up to Theodore as if he had just arrived.

"Arthur?" There was grave concern in Theodore's voice. "What is it?"

Arthur pulled at a blade of grass until it snapped in half. He rubbed the grass between his fingers before discarding it. His eyes scanned the area, then turned in the direction of the camp. He stood, having reached a conclusion.

"I was right. This is no hyena."

"Fine. What are we hunting?"

"We are not the hunters."

"That's preposterous. We are armed men. If we are not the hunters, then what are we?" Kermit asked.

Theodore strolled up to Arthur and planted a

firm hand on the man's shoulder. "Arthur, you need to tell us what you know."

Arthur sighed in resignation. "The tracks end here."

"So?" Kermit said.

"Do you not understand, young Kermit," Arthur said, his timbre bereft of the effects of the earlier celebration. Theodore knew this was a man not accustomed to being rattled in the wilderness. He, like Theodore, stood rooted to the ground while a two-thousand-pound rhinoceros charged at them. Neither man flinched. As hunters, fear was not in their blood. Though Arthur may not have been afraid, his uneasiness had amplified the disquiet Theodore and Kermit both shared. "We followed the tracks to their origin. This is where they begin. There is nothing else around here. No den. No flattened grass. Look around. It's undisturbed." The stub of his arm arced across the starlit vastness. "How does an animal begin from nothing?" They stared at Arthur, said nothing. "It cannot. Further, not one but two sets of tracks *begin* here. Standing. Side by side. Then they run toward camp. Bipeds. Not quadrupeds. They are not hyenas. They are not lions. They don't have typical footprints for this region. I have hunted for decades. I have hunted all over the world. I have never seen anything like this."

"Could it be some sort of bird that just landed here?" Kermit asked.

"First, there are two of them, so that would be *birds*. But these are not birds. When a bird lands, its weight is distributed through its feet as it grips for purchase. The prints would be deep and intrusive, with particular attention to its talons. Most bird feet are proportionally small for their bodies. That would suggest these be... I don't know. Maybe ten feet tall. But these prints do not suggest a landing. Here." He pointed at the area he'd circled. "They started here, standing. And these creatures were close together. They stood next to one another, facing in the direction of our camp. If they were birds, why not just fly to camp? But these so-called birds ran. Why run?"

"What about emus, rheas, or ostriches?" Kermit asked.

Arthur shook his head. "The crux of the problem is the fact that their tracks begin here. The only possible way for that to happen is that these creatures must be able to fly. I am unaware of any birds on this planet as big as this duo that can run and fly. So, no, I do not believe these to be birds, Kermit."

"What do you think they are?" Theodore asked.

"I don't know. But these creatures are not of our world, since they appeared out of thin air and ran toward our camp, laughing, supremely confident in what they are doing. I fear, Theodore, we are not the hunters. They are hunting us."

There was a long moment of silence as they absorbed the information. It was sound, logical, and backed up by reasonable fact.

"No, my friend, I disagree. If what you say is

true, then these creatures are unfamiliar with the surrounding terrain. In that, we have the tactical advantage. We take the fight to them. Let us be the hunters this night."

As they approached, a gunshot roared from somewhere in the camp. The four of them instinctively ducked. Three more shots fired in rapid succession were followed by screams and curses.

"We must alert them of our approach lest we be shot," Theodore said.

Each of them entered camp, yelling. After turning a corner, they found McKittrick hunched over another man, one of the cooks. The cook was flat on his stomach, slapping the ground in pain. Blood leaked from a trio of small holes in the back of his shorts.

"What is the meaning of this?" Theodore demanded.

The cook turned to see Theodore standing nearby. "Damn bloke shot me! I can't believe the damn fool shot me in my arse!"

Wisps of gray smoke swirled from the muzzle of McKittrick's shotgun. He stepped back to allow a pair of medics to aid the injured cook. They lifted the man by his arms and legs and carried him to the medical tent.

"They moved like lightning," McKittrick revealed. "I've never seen anything so bloody quick."

Arthur stepped forward, his rifle slung over his shoulder. "You saw them?"

"Yes. No. Well," McKittrick said with uncertainty. "No, not really."

"Then how do you know it was *not* a possum?" Arthur practically shouted.

"It stood, I guess. Well, what I mean is that it ran. Like people."

Theodore said, "We saw tracks outside the camp, bipedal by nature. Arthur, go with McKittrick to the place where he spotted them and examine the tracks." The two of them departed and returned a minute later. Arthur nodded in assent.

"McKittrick," Theodore said, "you shot a man. You are, therefore, liable for his life. You will stay here and guard the medical tent."

"What?" McKittrick said, clearly insulted. "You mean to leave me here? I want to bag this thing for what it did."

"I think not. We don't need anyone else shot tonight." McKittrick's face grew apple-red. Theodore stepped past McKittrick and into the gathering. "We have two unclassified animals out there waiting to be discovered. I want everyone huddled together while the four of us — Arthur, Kermit, Shamus, and I — hunt them down. I want a pair of armed guards stationed at each corner of the camp and each vulnerable point in between. You are not to fire unless they enter the camp. Do you understand? We don't need someone else filling a cot next to the cook." His eyes locked with McKittrick's. They were like two dominant male rams locking horns following a dizzying collision to gain breeding rights on a rocky crag. In this fight, Theodore stood his ground while

McKittrick took a vulnerable step backward. "Or worse."

McKittrick grumbled, "Shamus is no hunter."

"Shamus never shot a man, either," Kermit said. McKittrick spun around to see Kermit standing directly behind him.

Theodore and Arthur each carried an ammunition satchel. Kermit nudged McKittrick as he stepped forward.

Kermit and Shamus were relegated to torch duty. Kermit slung his rifle over his shoulder. A rifle was offered to Shamus, who stared at it with the same disgust he felt after witnessing the gutting of an animal. The stink of blood and entrails were enough to make him swear off meat for the rest of his life. Shamus held his hand out in refusal. He shot with a camera, not a gun.

Shamus said, "I've never fired a weapon in my life. I don't even know how to use them."

McKittrick snorted. Theodore ignored him.

"Fair enough," Theodore said and slapped a sheathed dagger into his outstretched hand. Its hilt sparkled in the moonlight. Shamus stared at it. "Try not to cut yourself shaving."

"B-b-but I'm no hunter," Shamus stuttered.

Theodore was already heading out. "You are tonight," he called out.

The four of them left the gathering. McKittrick shot one final murderous glare at the four of them. Another hunter issued instructions to the remaining group, directing men to secure the camp in pairs. McKittrick slipped into a nearby tent and through the flaps on the backside. He headed for his tent. A moment later, McKittrick dashed out of the camp, armed and unnoticed. And not a moment too soon, for a pair of huntsmen arrived to guard the area where he had slipped out.

* * * * *

Mad bursts of laughter came from some distance to their left. A second maniacal fit of laughter emerged from their right.

Theodore's hand was up and signaling. Shamus stopped when everyone else stopped. He was unaccustomed to their hand signals, deft and decided movements, or how to use a weapon to kill or defend. He had hoped they would take pity on him and shoo him back to camp. Theodore's hand flicked about, issuing instructions. He wanted to split up. He and Shamus would go left, Arthur and Kermit right. Not a single word was spoken. Shamus sighed loudly. Kermit and Arthur nodded. They headed off to the right, with Arthur leading and steadily pointing his rifle with one hand. Kermit held a torch in one hand, and, Shamus noticed, a long blade wielded in the other. Shamus squeezed the hilt of his sheathed dagger until his knuckles were as white as the moon. Shamus, wiping the sweat from his timid brow, turned to find Theodore already on the move. He hurried after him, bearing the crackling torch. He could hear another reprim-

and from Theodore echoing in his mind. *Running with a torch is a foolish endeavor, for not only can you see nothing before you, but when you fall, you will most certainly fall atop the torch and set flame to yourself and everything else around you.* Inevitability has a way of making fate seem a prophet. His left foot struck something hard in the grass, and he tripped. At that moment, everything slowed. He glided through the air with all of the grace of a wingless falcon. His body torqued around until he was able to gaze upon the stars above. Something metallic glistened as it shot across the starry backdrop. He lost the torch at some point. The grass did little to soften the blow to the back of his head. Something long and round bit at his lower back.

"Shamus!" came that familiar, reprimanding tone.

Shamus shrieked when Theodore snatched his arm and pulled him over like a rag doll. The former president began slapping his backside with heavy blows.

"Shamus!" roared Theodore. "Roll, man, roll! You're on fire!"

Shamus did as he was instructed until all that remained were the charred edges of his trousers and shirt. His back and arse were clearly visible. A belt kept his trousers around his waist.

"Are you all right?" Holding the lit torch, Theodore gripped the man's shoulder to inspect his back. He firmly swung Shamus around when the man failed to reply.

Chin quivering, Shamus stared back, wild-eyed, at Theodore.

Theodore held out the torch. Shamus glanced at it before snatching it from Theodore.

Theodore turned and began walking away. "Never run with a torch," he reprimanded.

Shamus followed glumly after Theodore, feeling defeat ooze from every pore. He held the torch out to one side, away from his body. Mixing with the surge of apathy coursing through his blood — misery, lack of confidence, terror — he could now add one more to the list: vulnerability.

* * * * *

Arthur walked at a brisk pace but suddenly knelt, going completely still. He caught a flash of a pair of golden orbs peering back at him. The grass rustled, and the glowing eyes disappeared into the tall grass bordering a nearby woodland. Kermit held the torch high and away from his body. Like his fellow hunter, he was uncertain about what he saw. By the time either of them realized what they'd observed, it was gone.

* * * * *

The demon pressed on through the trees as the hunters approached. The humans moved fast and with astonishing precision, catching the demon off guard. This was not the way this hunt was supposed to go. Instead of hunting the humans, the demon found itself the unlikely prey. It observed the men as they approached the unfamiliar trees. It sidled behind a thick trunk to peer at them. In the process of doing so, it stepped on a dead branch, snapping it in two. They both looked in the direction of the demon. It moved out of their line of sight in time, barely escaping being sucked back to Hell.

The demon ran away. From humans. It had not envisioned this Test of Mettle going awry. It stopped again. It could not keep running away. It had a job to do. The demon snarled as the persistent humans continued to give chase. It scanned the woodland in all directions, trying to find some way to shift the advantage. Slowly, its grotesque head lifted upward, and a hateful smile displayed pointy teeth.

* * * * *

The ground began to tremble. Arthur turned to Kermit, confusion molded into the contours of his face. Kermit could only shrug. The forest burst with life. Birds screeched and flapped noisily into the air. Animals growled and hissed. Eclipsing it all came that unsettling maniacal laughter.

Then things turned south.

Trees shook and snapped. Animals burst out of the small forest in all directions. A herd of zebras stampeded past Arthur and Kermit, who could do nothing but hold their ground. One of the animals came straight at them until it tried to leap out of the way at the last moment, clipping Kermit in the shoulder. Kermit fell on his back, wincing in pain. Coughing, Arthur slung his rifle and waved at the dust kicked up by the frightened animals that filled the air around them.

"Kermit? You okay?" he asked.

Kermit slowly stood up. "What the hell was that about?"

That same uncertain look dug deeper into Arthur's features as he turned to face the trees, still waving at the dust permeating the air. Something beyond the wave of his hand caught his attention. Arthur unshouldered his rifle and pointed it into the trees just as something dark and massive flew at them. The trees lit up from the muzzle flash. Whatever had come at them struck the ground fifteen feet shy of where they stood. They waited it out, but it remained motionless. Kermit carefully stepped toward it, holding the torch overhead. Arthur's finger tensed on the trigger, anticipating any sign of life.

It did not move.

Kermit unsheathed his blade, walked past Arthur, and stabbed it with a short, quick stroke.

No movement.

A sickly odor replaced the dusty air. A black leopard reflected in the torchlight. Its belly had been ripped open, and its entrails littered the surrounding ground. Arthur's single shot and Kermit's knife were not what had ripped open this animal's belly. Whatever they were chasing, whatever appeared from nowhere next to the camp, whatever owned the glistening golden eyes, whatever nearly trampled them, it was guilty of slaughtering this magnificent creature.

Flies honed in on the carcass. Soon, this place would be crawling with insects and other nocturnal predators.

Given their encounter so far, somewhere in the back of their minds they knew this was not the work of man. Nor was it an animal of this world. It did not fit in with any of their academic research or field experience. It was an answer to an unknown question, and Arthur and Kermit meant to hunt it down and bag it.

Kermit jammed the base of the torch into the slain animal. That would repel the flies and other scavengers for the time being.

In the torchlight, the hunter glared vehemently at the trees, his words uttered with murderous intent. "Let's hunt, young Kermit."

Kermit wiped his blade and sheathed it. He brushed off the pain in his shoulder and unslung his rifle. "Let's," he agreed.

And with that, the two stepped into the forest.

The forest, for the most part, was easy to navigate because the ground remained relatively flat, and it sported little shrubbery and foliage along its base thanks to the relatively dry conditions. The trees grew tall here. Most were as thick as a man's thigh and carried a dense amount of foliage atop their canopies. A soupy fog swirled over the ground.

Light from the moon and stars peeked through the trees, giving the fog a haunting glow.

The two men stepped deeper into the silence. Each man knew they were being watched. The silence within the forest made this fact loud and clear. There were no night sounds. No chirps. No shrills. No clicks. Just the unsettling quiet of an unwelcome intruder. Normally, they would chastise themselves for breaking the silence by snapping a twig or crunching the ground, but that was not the case here. They were as much the hunted as the hunters. Because they felt the creature's eyes on them, there was no need to maintain discretion. They pressed on, fifteen feet apart.

A resounding crack of wood and the rustling of leaves halted both hunters. It was followed by a series of cracking and popping sounds and grunts and growls. They heard leaves being thrashed about as if a windstorm swept the trees. They looked up, but the treetops above them were barely stirred by the mild breeze.

A tree, snapped in half, arced overhead, barreling through the canopy above before it came crashing down. It pierced the forest floor close to where Arthur had stood seconds ago. Another tree swept the treetops and slammed mightily into the top of an older tree above Kermit, snapping it at the point of impact, sending both spiraling to the earth. Kermit hastily retreated several steps, narrowly avoiding being crushed. A few more trees were tossed in their general direction before it grew quiet once more. The hunters checked on each other before pressing on, to the chagrin of the demon. They passed by several tree trunks that were twisted and spiked. They saw them but said nothing.

Kermit spotted a fast-moving shadow darting through the trees. He raised his rifle and fired. The shot struck a tree, and the demon answered with a wild fit of laughter. Arthur pointed his rifle in the general direction Kermit had fired, scanning the trees for movement. A fist-sized stone struck Kermit's rifle, knocking the weapon from his hands. The man yelped in surprise. He shook his hands in pain as he bent to retrieve the rifle from the ground. He inspected it. The barrel had suffered damage where the stone struck it. Kermit cursed and tossed down the weapon. From their right side came another chorus of crazy laughter. The demon circled them at a dizzying rate.

"What the hell does something like this?" Kermit said over the demon's laughter.

"What the hell, indeed, young Kermit," Arthur replied solemnly.

Kermit pulled a Colt M1900 handgun from a holster on his belt.

"Let's kill this thing once and for all," Kermit demanded.

"Good show," Arthur said with a wry smile.

They chased after the demon with renewed determination. It was not long before they spotted a shadow moving from left to right with incredible speed. This was an apex predator, Arthur figured.

Something new for the ages. And something they were going to bag, or die trying.

Arthur pointed his rifle at the shadow and fired. A tree splintered near the shadow, and the creature released a guttural cry. Arthur lowered his barrel, opened the chamber, and reloaded. Kermit covered him, but the creature was gone.

"Where did it run off to?" Kermit asked.

Arthur stared into the gloom as the demon barreled into him from the side. The collision sent him sprawling into Kermit, who stumbled into a tree, striking his head and falling to the ground. Arthur rolled on the ground, groaning in pain. He located his rifle some distance away. He searched in all directions. Finding no movement, he rose to his feet.

"Kermit?" he called, fetching his rifle from the forest floor.

Kermit responded, "Yeah, I'll live. Head's bleeding, though."

A rustle of leaves compelled them to look upward. Wild laughter filled the treetops. Arthur focused the eye he'd used hundreds of times before to center his quarry, aligning the dark shape with the sight at the end of his barrel. The demon, palming a large stone, cocked its arm, prepared to launch it at the hunter with the rifle. A pair of golden orbs locked eyes with Arthur as the hunter's finger tensed on the trigger. There was an explosion in the trees. Thousands of leaves and fractured twigs rained down through a massive cloud of smoke. Among the litter showering down was a stone.

They were unable to see through the misty cloud covering the treetops. Kermit and Arthur homed in on the tree to which the creature clung.

As the vaporous mist rapidly dissipated from above, they combed the ground surrounding the trees but found nothing. They peered upward but again found nothing. It was as if the creature had been blown to bits. Only... where were the bits?

With the Colt lowered, Kermit spun in a complete circle, surveying the woodland one last time. Frustrated, he yelled, "Where is it?"

"Where indeed," murmured Arthur, who slowly lowered his rifle.

"Arthur, you shot it! Where is the body?"

"Kermit," Arthur spoke in a flat tone. He held out his rifle. "I never got a shot off. It's fully loaded." Perplexed, Kermit eyed the rifle, then Arthur. Arthur returned a gesture indicating he was equally baffled. "Just as it appeared out of nowhere, the foul creature disappeared back to nowhere."

* * * * *

Where was Theodore? Shamus walked as fast as his legs could muster. The ground was rough and uneven in spots. He thought he heard something to one side, but, to him, the wild was vocal. Another sound caught his attention. Something was off about it. Then the realization slapped him like a cold shower, and he shivered. It was the *only* sound he had heard. He picked up the pace, peering around nervously. Then the ground collapsed into an old burrowing hole. His ankle buckled, and he face-planted in the ground. Shamus cried out. A thin line of fresh blood flowed from an ugly gash across his left cheek. Dirt, grass, and small pebbles adhered to the perspiration coating his face and hands. A dull ache radiated around his ankle. He needed to keep moving, or it might swell, rendering him an easy target. Shamus was on the move, jogging with a slight limp. He cried out at the approach of rapid footsteps at his back. The demon rammed into his back, sending the slender man sprawling through the air with his arms and legs flailing. The ground knocked the wind out of him. He knew beyond a doubt that he was no match for whatever hunted him. It was futile to run away.

* * * * *

   Trees outlined a clearing along the rolling terrain. Theodore worked his way through the trees before he settled into position. He was far enough away that he might have had a clean shot, but Shamus had continued to run away from Theodore. The man was not only fast on his feet, but was also scared, and quickly outpaced Theodore. The man blindly sprinted over the coarse terrain, tripping several times, giving Theodore an opportunity to catch up. The creature had done a remarkable job of splitting them up and was now hunting the weaker and unarmed one of the two. More than once, Theodore had to breach the safety of the trees to track Shamus down by studying the grass or searching the open dirt for footprints. Theodore tracked Shamus with little difficulty.

The illusory effect the moon and the gentle breeze had on the field gave Theodore the impression that Shamus was running atop electric blue water. There was no splash when Shamus took a tumble. While Theodore did not witness the fall, he heard the man cry out. Theodore was now running full speed alongside the wall of trees to gain a better vantage point. Theodore had no intention of firing his rifle at this distance for fear of striking Shamus. Shamus was on the move again. Then, a shadow shot out of the adjacent tree line. It moved impossibly fast. Theodore could barely make it out as it hugged the ground, hidden by the tall grass.

Theodore changed direction, heading onto the plains toward Shamus. The creature created a dark line in the sea of blue. It slammed into Shamus and raced back into the trees.

Theodore called out when Shamus disappeared from view. The demon answered with mocking laughter. Ignoring it, he continued on a direct path toward the area he'd last seen Shamus. He came upon an oval area barren of grass and knelt. Footprints. Two sets. One set belonged to Shamus and ended abruptly. The other set was identical to the ones near the camp. It belonged to the shadow creature. Theodore observed the area around him before marching in the direction of the mysterious three-toed footprints. The thought that disturbed him was that it had a hunter's intellect. After somehow forcing Shamus and him to separate, this creature wisely had them moving away from the safety of the camp.

After several minutes of tracking, Theodore found an area of land bereft of trees. The grass stood tall enough to conceal the likes of a king cobra. The breeze had died down, and the temperature felt like it had dropped ten degrees. Theodore watched as, many miles away, heat lightning flashed through an advancing cloud wall. Several seconds passed before he heard, and felt, the familiar rumble of thunder. He followed small clumps of clouds overhead to gauge wind direction and speed. The distant storm was not going to threaten the camp, and the stars and moon shined a welcome amount of visible light for tracking. The creature created a natural trail in the grass, its hoofprints left as its signature. He smiled inwardly at this fortuitous development and was now chasing at a near-sprint.

After some distance, Theodore reached a small hillock and ascended it with ease. At the top, he froze. It resembled a mini mesa. Along the grassy top were fresh rifts in the grass, crossing in multiple directions. Wild laughter came from somewhere in the grassland. Was the creature toying with him? For the first time, Theodore contemplated returning to camp. Having not seen Shamus and receiving no response when he called, Theodore was left to assume the creature had captured Shamus. For all he knew, the creature could be feasting on the skinny man right now. If Shamus was dead, Theodore could not possibly leave him behind. He liked the man, even if he was infuriating and dense. Of course, Shamus could be alive. He could be injured and in need of medical attention. Theodore kept the muzzle of the rifle pointed as he crossed the grassy flattop before reaching the far side of the hillock and descending along another animal trail.

A low, feral growl caught Theodore's immediate attention. He swiveled to his right with his rifle poised. The grass was waist-high here. Two sets of golden eyes shone just above grass level, maybe forty yards away. He knew the growl instinctively. Lions. One of the cat's manes reflected in the moonlight, so at least one of them was a male. Four hundred to six hundred pounds of feline prowess on full alert for an easy meal.

Something else moved. A shadow, perhaps, lurking low and slow. The hungry eyes that feasted upon Theodore's form now turned their attention toward the shadow. But the cats were too late. The shadow accelerated and lunged at the lions.

The damned shadow is attacking them?

One of the lions leaped at the shadow. There was a horrible midair collision. The other lion, flanking the shadow, jumped onto its back. The shadow let out an unearthly howl, and it dropped to the ground.

Theodore dared to move closer and was now thirty yards away. He wanted to improve his vantage point, but he was uncomfortably close as it was. Manes flashed about, and the big cats roared. The shadow let out a final deafening growl.

Silence ensued.

Theodore walked backward about ten yards to avoid attracting any attention. He watched as one of the cats rose into the air. There was a loud grunt, and the massive feline was tossed like a rag doll. For the briefest moment, Theodore watched the silhouette of the lion against the moonlight, limp and unmoving, until it disappeared into the darkness.

The other indignant lion rejoined the melee. The shadow ran away with blinding speed, and the lion gave chase. Theodore lost them to the darkness. The lion issued an ear-shattering roar. The shadow responded with a delirious cackle. There was a mighty blow, as if the battle had begun anew with the two beasts clashing with one another.

It ended in the same abbreviated fashion as before.

Theodore waited. Ten seconds. Thirty seconds. Two minutes. He swallowed hard and moved backward again. The realization of what he had witnessed was too much to bear. Two full-grown male lions attacked *something*. One lion, presumably, was killed. If the shadow creature defeated two full-grown lions, then what odds did Theodore have of surviving a one-on-one confrontation? His survival instincts screamed for him to abort and flee hard and fast. Instead, he worked to steady his breathing. His keen senses were on high alert.

There was a heavy grunt, and something flew at him. He threw his arm up and ducked just as the thing passed over his head. The object landed on the ground with a sloppy, wet smack. Theodore sprinted toward it with his rifle aimed dead center. It was the second lion. The sight and smell were ghastly. Theodore choked, not out of fear, but revulsion. Its belly was splayed open, and a tangle of guts lay strewn across the surrounding grass. The cat's limp tongue hung from the side of its mouth. Its eyes were open, but there was no life behind its blank stare. Theodore saw several brutal gashes along its body. Three parallel lines made up each nasty wound.

Three toes, Theodore thought, and, perhaps, three clawed fingers.

Theodore sidled past the dead animal, keeping the rifle trained on the lion. He hurried toward the hillock. The grass rustled behind him, and with it came the maniacal laughter. He felt a heavy blow on the small of his back, propelling him forward. The rifle spiraled in the air until the darkness swallowed it. Theodore groaned as he pushed himself from the grass. More rustling. More laughter. While on the ground, the creature struck him in the side. He felt his ribs crack. Finding it difficult to breathe, he opened his eyes to millions of twinkling stars.

There is a time in a man's life when he knows Death is near, standing nearby, scythe in hand, waiting with eternal patience until the final breath. Theodore ignored the pain and sucked in a deep breath, then let it out with spittle flying and a high-pitched whine. He turned onto all fours and crawled up the length of the trail toward the hillock. Drool slithered out of his mouth. Hand. Knee. Hand. Knee. Onward he went, until his fingers struck something long, metal, and familiar.

He picked it up and rolled onto his back. The inclination of the hill enabled him to overlook the open field. He fired blindly down the trail. It was a panic shot. He cursed himself while he worked to reload the weapon. His fingers trembled as he opened the satchel at his side to retrieve a round of ammunition. The pain from his movements stabbed his ribs. He gasped for air while attempting to chamber the round.

He glimpsed a shadow in the middle of the field. It was watching. Theodore returned his attention to the rifle. He tried to thumb in the round. It caught the side of the chamber and fell away from his shaky fingers. The shadow raced through the field. He jammed his fist into the bag and grabbed a handful of ammo. All but one slipped through his fingers. He worked the round into the chamber and cocked the bolt. He aimed the rifle toward the field, but the shadow was gone.

His gaze shifted to where the second dead lion lay. He followed the scattering of lines in the grass until he spotted the shadow. It was eighty yards away and still as a scarecrow. He thought he glimpsed a pair of glowing eyes.

Then it came straight at him.

It was fast. It moved like living energy. He

remembered a story that was told to him when he was young and spry. He heard about how energy was maybe a living thing — the same energy some people foolishly thought gave lightning its power. After all, how can lightning just appear out of thin air and strike down a tree? Sometimes it missed and hit the ground instead. Or a building. Or a person. Occasionally it would misfire like a gun, and all you would see was the misfire spread across the sky. He remembered a dull wit of a boy named Tommy. Tommy said lightning creatures would consume unspeakable power they stole from Mother Earth herself. Before she could recapture her stolen power, they jumped off the clouds and fell from the sky. The lightning creatures fell so fast that the wake they created in the air was what people called thunder. Funny, Theodore thought, that his final fleeting thought would be about Tommy and his lightning stories. Maybe, Theodore wondered, this was one of them. Maybe this was one of those lightning creatures.

His mind wandered. Maybe a second passed. Maybe an hour. He did not resist. Perhaps the shadow took his life.

Theodore Roosevelt, former president of the United States of America, father, husband, friend, outdoorsman, hunter, author. He was a great many things; there were not nearly enough labels to describe who he was in life. Many of his accomplishments had been inspired by his love of the open country. He had launched one of the greatest international projects in history: the Panama Canal. He took particular pride in many others. He extended federal protection to land and wildlife. He established the United States Forest Service. He created five national parks and eighteen new national monuments. He was also responsible for establishing the first fifty-one bird reserves, four game preserves, and one hundred and fifty national forests. Of the latter, one of them, Shoshone National Forest, was the country's first of its kind. He believed he had performed a tremendous service to his nation.

Then a memory came to him. He recalled a time when he and his brother peered outside a second-story window of their family's mansion as Abraham Lincoln's funeral procession slowly passed. It was a sad time in his nation's history. America grieved. Thousands gathered to pay their final respects to one of the greatest presidents the United States had known.

Abe Lincoln, he thought, was great. As great a president as there ever was. "Greatness," he huffed, as he considered what to think of himself. Here he was, practically cowering in the face of adversity. His opponent was mighty, no question about it. Theodore calculated his chances of victory to be between laughable and none. He opened his eyes and adjusted his sitting position, but a pain in his side blazed upward and inward, stealing his breath. He felt broken. Resignation had never crossed his mind until now, but still, there was a little fire left in the old boy. If he were to die, he would die on his terms:

fighting. Shaky hands worked to hold the rifle steady. He puffed ragged, painful breaths. The muzzle of the rifle lifted off the ground several inches, but his side flared with a flash of searing pain. He cried out and tucked his elbow to his side. The rifle slipped from his grasp and fell away. Gasping, he knew beyond certainty that he had lost. He surrendered himself to the superior hunter. The creature cackled as it drew near.

Theodore covered his ears and closed his eyes, cursing aloud. After a moment, he opened his eyes again in time to witness a massive cloud envelop him. The world glowed white in all directions. He turned back to see two silhouettes. The wind had picked up again, allowing the lazy cloud to drift past the two figures standing atop the hillock.

McKittrick stood stout and resolute. Next to him was a bloodied mess of a man. It was Shamus. He was alive but struggled to remain upright. McKittrick held his shotgun by the stock with the muzzle resting against his shoulder. With a deft twist of his wrist, he flicked a dagger, impaling it into the ground next to Theodore's leg. Theodore recognized the blade. It was the one he'd lent to Shamus.

"Mr. President," McKittrick announced, "never send a servant to do a hunter's job, or the food might eat him."

10 - RESTAURANT NOIR

June 29, 2007: New York City, New York, United States

Eleven thirty on a Friday night, and the restaurant showed no signs of slowing. Most restaurants and bars stayed open until the wee hours of the morning in the city that never sleeps. And why not? This establishment had opened a mere two months ago and had already become the rage. The owner and executive chef, James Barlow, was scheduled to make television appearances ranging from the Today Show to a spot on the Food Network. The Travel Channel had called last week expressing interest in documenting a hot dining spot for one of their new shows.

"Restaurant Noir is heaven to the senses, for it is what the gods put into food and wine that makes it truly divine." – Saveur magazine

"Impeccable, delightful, and astonishing feast that lingers tantalizingly long after savoring its five-star goodness." – The New York Times

"The wine was crisper, the berries plump and sweet as if freshly picked, and then there was this hint

of chocolate and coffee that covered my tongue like silk. I couldn't get over how fragrant it was. Not overpowering but enough to make me nostalgic for days of homemade strawberry rhubarb pie and hot cocoa. I lost myself to culinary bliss." – Food and Wine magazine

"I've never seen so much while viewing so little." – FineDining.com

Restaurant Noir became Chef Barlow's fifth restaurant. There was no denying his skill in the kitchen. Talking business and managing his establishments made him an unmitigated genius. As his reputation flourished, so grew his financial backing. At the announcement of the new project, financiers fought for an opportunity to back the new restaurant, until they learned of the intended theme. Unbothered by the blitz of rescindments, James funneled in his own money. Those who had withdrawn their monetary backing were kicking themselves in the pants for second-guessing. Restaurant Noir became an overnight sensation because it melded impeccable food flavors with its themed atmosphere, a thorough dining experience if there ever was one.

The restaurant served highly rated culinary meals in complete darkness.

James got the inspiration from performing a competitive taste test with Cheryl Paxton, a friend who was legally blind but also once a highly touted sous chef. A blindfolded James lost the competition and was left dumbfounded. Cheryl then went on to train James in the art of tasting his food, truly savoring it. Cheryl explained that before her accident, she had taken her sense of taste for granted. As concocters of delectable dishes, she explained, it was their duty to plate the best possible flavors. When an artsy dish is placed before you, she said, you ogle its presentation, and no rational person dives in with a knife and fork. She equated it to a museum patron eating a painting. But food was not just about looks. Though the presentation is important, food can best be enjoyed through the sense of taste, not the sense of sight.

For the next few weeks, she blindfolded James and had him try a series of dishes served from his kitchen, dishes that rated high in the opinion of the public and critics alike. He learned his dishes were imperfect. All of them, he determined, tended to lack a little something. Under Cheryl's tutelage, he improved upon those dishes. When they were perfected, James trained his staff.

Lying next to Cheryl early one morning, his mind worked on a problem. He had retrained his sense of taste. The kitchen staff in his restaurants was similarly trained. Overnight, the output from his kitchen improved dramatically. The clientele continued to flow in and out of his restaurants; their numbers never dwindled. The write-ups from his critics continued to describe the excellence of the food and service. Those critiques used creative spins and flashy adjectives to make the reviews pop. Never did they describe the effort he and his staff put into enhancing the overall flavor. No one interviewed him or his team about their techniques. He had hoped his success was not the result of wealthy, overindulgent snobs who came simply to stuff their faces and drink their senses dull. His prices ranged from moderate to upscale. The numbers suggested business was better than ever. He was left to question the knowledge of his patrons — if they were getting the most out of the culinary experience. James wanted to do for them what Cheryl had done for him.

Cheryl laughed when he shared this with her. He gazed at her with a puzzled expression.

"Look," she said, placing a finger over his lips, "with your other senses."

His retort carried a little bite. "I don't understand. What does that even mean?"

She walked her fingers up his face and gently brushed his eyebrows. "Close your eyes. What do you see?"

"Nothing. Not a damn thing."

"What do you smell? What do you feel? What do you taste?"

James sighed in exasperation. "Nothing. What is the point?"

"You are a customer in my bed."

"Huh?" James was taken aback. Cheryl had a way of making his mind spin like tires on New York ice in January, leaving him going nowhere fast.

"Think, you big dummy." Her hands caressed the sides of his face. "The answer is right in front of you."

His mind waded through a sea of thoughts,

working to come up with a solution. Then the answer revealed itself. The darkness. The blind-folds. The training. It was there all along. A smile stretched across his face.

"Yes," she said, "you see now."

"No," he exclaimed, "I don't see. That's the answer. Son of a gun! That is the million-dollar answer. I can train my customers by removing the light. Sweetheart, you are a genius!"

An hour later, he and Cheryl sat at a small table in a crowded café discussing the plans for what would become his crowning achievement. He jotted notes on paper napkins. At the top of one, he wrote Restaurant Noir and underlined it twice.

That name now stretched across the façade of his restaurant. The letters were black. At night, the opaque letters were backlit, displaying the desired thematic effect. Dining at the Noir became a rage with New Yorkers. Clients flew into New York from all over — curious Europeans and Asians were among the restaurant's clientele. All eager to dine in the dark. Reservations were required, and calls came from all over the world. James observed his restaurant with renewed confidence and with a blind set of eyes. And why not? He had elevated himself to the next level, something his peers could not, or would not, conceive. He was a master. The evidence was right there in front of him. His restaurant was booked solid for the next six months. There was something unique to the experience, and it was apparent James did something special. After learning about the menu from the waitstaff before the lights went out, the patrons seized the opportunity to openly discuss each course with other diners, whom they could not see. Customers had fun. More importantly, they learned to use their heightened sense of taste.

The critics were next. It would not be long before the first reviews made the newspapers, magazines, and the Internet. Even with his history of success, it still gave James butterflies waiting for that first review. Restaurant critics would show up as ordinary patrons. The next day they would post their experience, good or bad. Like them or hate them, critics wielded a different sort of blade. Critics could be particularly kind or especially vicious. A review from an experienced or renowned critic could be the difference between everlasting success and failure. The relationship between critics and restaurateurs was a peculiar one.

James stood at the end of a stainless-steel table. The kitchen bristled with activity. He had hired a trio of top-notch sous chefs. He trained each of them to cook in a new way. Each chef tasted his or her dishes while wearing blindfolds, then tweaked the ingredients.

With one of the three sous chefs off for the night, the other two now worked feverishly over pans that occupied every available burner. James inwardly celebrated the fact that he'd managed to steal a prized pastry chef away from a rival restaurateur. The pastry chef focused on the preparation of the aptly named Chocolate Experience. It was four layers of chocolate decadence with incredibly smooth cream fillings flavored with amaretto, combined with a cherry reduction using the sweetest fruit grown in Washington state. The chef set aside a bowl of chocolate ganache, the cake's pièce de résistance.

* * * * *

Restaurant Noir was centered along a block of buildings varying in width and height. Behind the restaurant was an alley with streetlights that painted it a jaundiced shade of yellow. Each business had a rear entrance and parking for employees. A cloud of moths flitted wildly in the warm summer night under each light. Even though there was nary a breeze, Styrofoam containers, small boxes, plastic water bottles, newspapers, and other assorted garbage were suddenly swept up and tossed haphazardly around in an unnatural gust of wind that seemed to come from nowhere and everywhere at the same time.

As quickly as it began, the wind died. A rolling mist covered the pitted, stained asphalt. Little reptilian three-toed feet scampered across its surface past several parked cars. Near one of the lighted doorways was a shiny blue BMW. The demon felt an odd connection with the sports car. It raised itself on its clawed toes to get a better look at the inside of the Beemer through its back window. The top of its ridged head was barely visible over the trunk. It stalked over to the driver's side, careful to remain in the shadows.

Next to the BMW was a vehicle that had seen better days. It was far older, far less sporty, and appeared to be a magnet for scratches, dents, and rust. The demon moved to the front tire of the BMW and peered over the hood, slit eyes darting left and right. Seeing no activity in the alley, it twisted off the air cap of the tire and inserted a clawed fingertip into the valve stem until there was a steady hiss.

This was not a demon of power. It was not one of Lucifer's overlords, generals, or lieutenants. It was not one of the promising mid-tier demons, who were irritatingly bent on proving their might. Lucifer favored the chaos demons above all. They were among the lowest class of minions in the underworld, and, like their stature, their duration for the Test of Mettle was always short. While the chaos demons posed minimal threat due to their abbreviated visits, they often wreaked an unbelievable amount of terror and turmoil. How something so insignificant could pack such a sizable wallop in the span of a whisper's breath! Chaos demons tended to receive a considerable amount of admiration from Lucifer. They lapped it up like puppies before being cast back to the grungier parts of Hell they inhabited.

* * * * *

James felt his chest swell with pride, watching these exceptional professionals at work. He dreamed of being named among the greatest to have graced the culinary world — from Auguste Escoffier, Fernand Point, Paul Bocuse, Alain Ducasse, and Julia Child to modern celebrity chefs like Gordon Ramsey, Wolfgang Puck, Masaharu Morimoto, Anthony Bourdain, and Emeril Lagassé — and Restaurant Noir brought him one step closer to making that a reality. He checked his watch. He and Cheryl were flying to Miami in the morning for a much-needed vacation. He not only planned on enjoying the fruits of his labors around South Beach, but he also planned to propose to Cheryl. James reached into an inner pocket for the millionth time to touch the little felt box. With car keys in hand, he looked around once more before announcing his departure. They all wished him well before returning their attention to their work.

* * * * *

The alley entrance was wide open, venting the stifling heat from the kitchen. The demon walked past the open screen door. It sensed the connection immediately and watched the man — the one the demon had been sent to test — turn away from a steel table, take a few pensive steps toward the rear door, and spin around to address the kitchen. The demon dashed into a walk-in refrigerator, leaving the door ajar to spy on the well-dressed man. There was laughter throughout the kitchen, and a moment later, the man, James, walked out the back door. The demon watched James release the catch, and the screen door slapped shut. The bustle around the kitchen resumed.

The demon eased its way out of the refrigerator, pausing in an adjacent nook. There was a small punch clock on the wall. Alongside it was a bin filled with time cards. There was a first aid kit and fire extinguisher affixed to the wall next to a desk. A series of storage racks surrounded the remaining space, each packed with boxes neatly labeled.

One open box caught the demon's attention. Stacked in a tall column were paper chef hats with the restaurant's logo. The demon pulled one from the stack and placed the paper hat atop its scaly, rippled head. After several failed attempts to keep the paper hat in place, the demon reached for a stapler on the desk and stapled the hat to its head. Happy with the result, the demon resumed its work. It peered through a wire rack to view the entire kitchen. Along the opposite and right-side walls were the stoves and ovens and sinks and dishwashers. The chefs and dish handlers had their backs turned and were focused on their tasks. On the left side, closest to the demon, was a steel table that made up the pastry chef's station. The pastry chef finished pouring some of the contents of a large glass mixing bowl over a tall, round cake. The bowl was filled with chocolate ganache. The demon sneered, licking its purple-green lips as the chef placed the glass bowl on the table before attending to the cake; ganache glistened as it traveled in rivulets down the sides. The chef worked the ganache using a long pastry spatula to coat the cake evenly. A paper hat bobbed down the aisle, stopping behind the busy pastry chef. The demon reached a clawed hand up and into the bowl of ganache. The liquid chocolate coated the demon's hand, drizzling onto the floor before it scampered down the aisle. It licked the back of its hand as it pushed through a pair of swinging doors.

It found itself in a hallway painted black and lined with dim track lighting. Unassuming twin ceiling lights gently illuminated a set of doorways on the right side of the hallway. It was pitch black at the end of the hall, which was draped closed by a thick black curtain. The demon passed the first door and froze at the sound of giggling, its slimy tongue seemingly glued to the back of its hand. It watched as a pale arm flailed blindly through the drapes. The demon leaned into the second door, straining to push it open. The bulky door resisted, but it gradually opened. The demon slipped into an elegant bathroom colored with serene hues of peach and cream. On the right side was a double vanity showcasing a pair of fancy chrome gooseneck faucets centered between widespread shiny hot and cold handles. At the end of the vanity was a silver tray topped with several bottles of lotions. Next to the tray was an orange box of tissues. Mounted over each well-lit sink was an ornate oval mirror. Small potted trees dotted the corners of the bathroom. A trio of private stalls graced the left side of the bathroom. The demon retreated into the center stall, latching the door just as the bathroom door opened. The demon hopped up onto the toilet seat as two women entered. One was fresh and perky. The other had lost her perkiness a decade ago. Both wore little black dresses that leveled off at mid-thigh. The sultriness of their designer dresses was surpassed by the finest enhancements money could buy, which bulged out gaudily. They spoke softly, as if in a library, while they checked their makeup, giggling fiercely between touch-ups. With their faces in order, the older lady entered the left stall. The younger one entered the unoccupied stall on the right. The restroom went quiet for a full minute.

The older lady broke the silence, her accent thick with the city.

"This place is beautiful. I mean, if the rest of it looks anything like this bathroom."

"Oh, I know," replied the younger lady.

"Even the stalls are decorated all fancy."

"Yeah, it's like, wow. You know?"

"Would you look at that? Even the toilet paper is fancy."

A claw oozing liquid chocolate reached under the left stall wall.

A gruff voice asked, "Can I have some?"

The older lady screamed. The demon exited the stall with a coarse giggle, thick with decades of brimstone. It scampered across the floor, ducking behind the bathroom door as it swung open. A male waiter, having heard the scream, rushed in. He wore a paper hat and night-vision goggles, which were pressed against his forehead. The demon sidled out of the bathroom as the door swung shut. It headed toward the black curtain at the end of the dimly lit hall, peeking through the curtain before ambling into utter darkness, its white paper hat bobbing up and down unseen in the dining room.

The demon muted its glowing red eyes to matte black to maintain its concealment in the darkened room. The modified vision limited the demon to shades of silver and gray, which it found perfectly acceptable. The demon took in the quaint, boxy dining room, purposely designed to enhance the dine-in-the-dark experience of its patrons by allowing them to speak openly and be heard by others. It was to engage an entire dining area, a space that held fifteen tables, each seating two to six persons, spaced equidistantly apart to offer a scant amount of privacy. The demon ducked under the linen tablecloth of the only empty table. The patrons reserving the table were not present. The waiter from the bathroom rushed past, the night-vision goggles showing him the way. He had no trouble maneuvering through the dining area. Moments later, the headwaiter, also wearing special goggles, stormed past, with the waiter in tow. Both slipped through the black curtains, heading for the women's bathroom.

From under the table, the demon wiped chocolate from its three-fingered claws onto the linen cloth. There were forty-five blind sheep in the dining room. A hideous toothy sneer crept across the reptilian face. It turned its attention to an adjacent table, where a man and woman in their thirties sat. The woman wore a dress that was as elegant as it was provocative. The demon reached up and plucked a spear of olives from the man's martini. They were engaged in a conversation about Wall Street. The low chatter and clatter of glasses and plates filled the room with a constant source of white noise. The demon ate two of the three olives, then it took careful aim with the third olive and tossed it. The woman's eyes shot wide open when the olive landed in her cleavage. The unseeing woman clutched at her breasts, feeling the wet sensation of the fruit roll down her dress. She wiggled around as the olive worked its way down. The oblivious man continued to gab about high rollers in his office, who shared success using some technique he'd developed. She ignored him, squirming in vain until the olive rolled past her waist. She thrust her hips until it made its way to the floor, then patted down her dress, looking mortified. Thoroughly entertained, the demon moved on to the next table.

There were two men seated at the next table. The one in his late twenties fidgeted with an air of impatience. He pushed a button at the side of his watch, and the watch face briefly illuminated. Using the temporary luminescence, he jammed two fingers into his water glass, plucked out an ice cube, and popped it into his mouth. The other man, in his early forties, sat with folded hands, listening to his companion crunch at the ice. He pulled more ice from the glass, repeating the process of illuminating his watch. The demon slipped under their table undetected. Moments later, the headwaiter and the waiter who'd trailed after him now assisted the two women from the bathroom to their table. The rectangular table seated six persons, but, for this ninety-minute dinner, its side chairs had been removed, and it comfortably sat four. When the younger of the two men asked what the problem was, the headwaiter offered a generalized explanation that one of the ladies had a small situation. The other waiter checked to see if the older woman was okay.

"Yes, yes, yes," she huffed resentfully. "I'm fine, for the hundredth time."

"Yes, ma'am," he said nervously.

The headwaiter whispered in his ear. The waiter politely responded before leaving the group to tend to his tables. A man in his fifties sat across the table from the older lady. He was already leaning forward, inquiring, "Lorraine, what happened? What's going on?"

The younger man stopped fidgeting so he could position himself to eavesdrop about the uproar.

The headwaiter leaned toward the older gentleman. His calm voice reassuring, he said, "Nothing to be concerned with, I assure you. Just a small mishap in the ladies' room. Please, let me buy you and your friends a drink."

The older lady huffed once more in indignation. The older man knew when to button it. He ordered another cocktail. The others placed their drink orders. The headwaiter thanked them for their understanding.

After the headwaiter left, the older woman droned on about her disturbing experience in the bathroom, how shocking it was that management would allow some practical joker through the doors of a place hell-bent on its image. Despite four pairs of legs under the roomy table, the demon sidled past to peek over the edge of the table. The younger woman rolled her eyes. The older man feigned his understanding and concern as he swirled the ice in his now-empty cocktail glass. His left hand moved near the corner of the table. It continued to slide along the edge of the table, inches from an observant pair of eyes, where it stopped. A small, well-manicured hand approached from the opposite side to meet the man's hand. The demon raised a reptilian brow with sinister understanding when the hands coupled. It ducked under the table when the headwaiter returned with a tray of drinks. The older woman gave another dramatic huff when the headwaiter placed her drink on the table.

"Please enjoy, compliments of the house," the headwaiter announced before leaving the dining area.

A clawed hand stroked the younger woman's knee. Her skin was buttery soft. Not only did she offer no resistance, but she also shifted her hips forward toward the older man, brushing one leg against the demon. Feeling the spontaneity of a welcome, and wanted, presence, she spread her legs apart. The clawed hand moved gently once more up and down her thigh. She continued to offer no resistance, so the demon obliged. It stroked her delicate skin, daring to move further up her thigh.

The younger woman sighed, closing her eyes as the reptilian hand made its way to the front of her lacy underwear. Her breaths shortened as the demon worked its fingers in rhythm to her gyrating hip. She slunk even further down the chair, her breathing becoming more energetic. Her manicured hand gripped the side of the table. Her head fell back, and her body gyrated with animalistic need. Her mouth formed a small O as her hand gripped the edge of the table. The magical moment arrived, and she gave herself to ecstasy while stifling the compulsion to scream. The hand that gripped the table balled into a fist before her fingers straightened suddenly. Her skin crawled with wave after wave of pleasure. The heat from doing such a naughty thing in public, let alone a restaurant, melted her slackening body into her chair. The demon continued to stroke the wet patch of her panties. The moment was more than she could bear, and she allowed her hands to casually roam over the front of her skimpy dress until they reached her yearning breasts. She groped herself, allowing one of her nipples to pop out. Lost in a realm of sexual bliss, she tugged the front of her dress, freeing her breasts. It sent a raging surge of electricity down her legs, prompting her heeled feet to kick out, striking the demon along the top of its scaly head, ripping the stapled paper hat from its head. Her hand gripped the table again as another powerful orgasm overtook her.

The older man found her hand convulsing on the table, and he placed his hand over the top of hers. Something was wrong. In a raspy and barely audible voice, she called out her fiancé's name. "Kevin?" The older lady, who sat to her left side, stopped mid-rant.

"Yes," the younger man, seated across from the older woman, answered with a disinterested response. All three were accounted for above the table. Horrified, she yanked her hand back and slapped her legs together. The demon hopped back, realizing too late that it had overstayed its welcome. She kicked her legs hard, catching the demon square in its scaly face. Dazed, it rushed out from under the table to the other side of the dining room and ducked, unnoticed, under another occupied table.

After pulling up her dress, the young woman yanked up the tablecloth of her table, holding the illuminated display of a cell phone, drawing the dismay of nearby diners. She saw three pairs of legs under the table. Lying on the floor nearby was a paper chef hat. The same one she saw on the waiter in the bathroom. She swallowed down her revulsion, but the bile crept up again. The second swallow was harder to hold down. Her face flushed with a cold layer of sweat. Her eyes were trained on the paper chef hat until the display of the cell phone dimmed.

As the demon rubbed its head, it stood next to two pairs of plump male legs seated at the small table. With its time nearing an end, the demon began to feel sluggish. It listened to them talk about a professional interleague baseball game between the Yankees and the Mets. They rambled on about pitching, batting, fielding, and how the umpires blew a call, costing the Yankees the game. These two bored the demon. With little time remaining, the demon opened its mouth and bit one of the men in the leg. The man yelped midsentence and thrust his weight backward. He followed it with a high-pitched scream as he and his chair toppled back. He landed with a heavy thump on the carpeted floor.

Some patrons were grumbling their displeasure at the young lady with the cell phone. She snapped back with a few crude expletives. The headwaiter arrived at the table to sternly issue a final warning to the disruptive young lady and her acquaintances. Just as the headwaiter was about to speak, a man on the side of the dining room screamed and toppled backward. Unable to see, patrons from adjacent tables called out to see if the patron was okay. Angry, the fallen man shouted that he had been bitten. Some worried patrons were speaking in hushed tones, which included the word *rat* among adjoining tables.

From yet another table, a man flipped on his cell phone and threw a linen napkin into the chest of one of the waiters. He and his olive-plucking lady friend walked toward the entrance and disappeared through another set of black curtains. The young lady, using her cell phone for light, walked up to the waiter who had assisted her in the bathroom, called him a bastard, and slapped him across his face. His paper hat fell to the floor. Mouth agape, the stunned waiter rubbed at his face. Using the light from her cell phone, she stormed toward the exit with her friends. The older lady in the group was complaining again.

The demon had made its way under an available small table and watched the commotion unfold. The heavyset man who fell back had pulled a lighter from his pocket and was on his knees, flicking it until it sparked a flame. Nearby patrons gasped in surprise at the unanticipated light and sight of the big man on his knees inches from their table. Oblivious to their annoyance, he swung the lighter under their table and side to side, searching.

"Something freaking bit me," he cried out.

A nearby table of six whispered to one another, stood, and made their way to the exit. Patrons from three other tables followed in their wake. The apologetic waitstaff urged them to return to their tables, offering free drinks and discounted meals, but to no avail.

The fat man clumsily got to his feet with the lighter held out as his friend pulled up their tablecloth. They found nothing, and decided to check under another table. The tug from Hell pulled hard at the demon. The friend walked around and pulled up the tablecloth while his fat friend thrust his lighter under the table. The friend had his back toward the table where the demon hid. The demon lunged forward and bit the man in his plump calf. The man screamed and let go of the tablecloth. Its time expired, the demon returned to its domain, leaving with a small *pop* as if a single small firecracker had ignited. Startled, the fat man with the lighter poked his head up like a chubby prairie dog to see why his friend was yelling and to find the source of the firecracker.

"What happened?" the fat man cried out.

"The rat! It bit me in the freaking leg!" his friend yelled, dancing around in circles.

A miniature cloud rolled across the carpeted floor where the demon had last stood.

The fat man watched his friend dance around. Failing to keep his attention on the lighter in his hand, he had not realized he was now holding it directly under the linen tablecloth, which was being held aloft by his other hand. A dark circle grew in circumference until the cloth caught fire. The fat man yelped, letting go of the burning tablecloth. He scooted back, afraid, as the flames trickled up to the tabletop. His friend grabbed him, shouting that they needed to get out of there.

The two big men lumbered past the headwaiter, who held a $200 bottle of fine red wine. He walked up to the fire and doused it with the expensive wine. The tablecloth was ruined, and the table probably sustained some damage. The headwaiter stood there in shock, holding the empty wine bottle, wondering how things had gone downhill so quickly.

Shouts from the front of the restaurant pierced the now-quiet dining establishment. Someone threatened that the restaurant would hear from their attorney. From far away came the faint cry of a police siren. When the dining room lights flicked on, he realized he had lost his night-vision goggles, which probably occurred during the fracas.

James Barlow walked into the empty dining room with a tire iron in one hand and his suit coat draped over his other arm. The pastry chef and the waiter who had been slapped stood at his side. All three of them stared slack-jawed at the smoky mess in the dining room. The headwaiter's eyes were drawn and emotionless. He hobbled to one of the tables with the wine bottle and plopped himself into a chair. He checked the label, put it to his lips, and lifted it high, wishing for a few drops. Alas, it was empty.

* * * * *

The wreckage of James Barlow's elegant restaurant went beyond the damage in the dining room. Rumors spread about the waitstaff taking liberties in the dark, which led to more scandalous stories. Then there was the incident involving a rat and two male patrons who had been bitten. More rumors — mostly tasteless jokes — surfaced over the radio. "The appetizer that got away" was one of the popular wisecracks.

The restaurant fell further into disrepute when a class-action lawsuit quickly surfaced, filed for damages due to a claim that the waitstaff had taken sexual liberties when patrons, veiled by complete darkness, were at their most vulnerable.

Even though the restaurant passed a series of health inspections, there were two men who claimed to have been bitten by a giant sewer rat that fateful night. They were each treated for an animal attack, though it could not be concluded what animal caused the bite marks. With medical evidence supporting them, they filed a separate lawsuit citing physical and mental anguish.

Business regressed. Not once was the upscale restaurant able to seat even a dozen patrons. Often the dining room was devoid of customers. As the restaurant was unable to find new clientele or reassemble the broken shards of trust from the surrounding community, the Noir dream ended when the doors were locked for the final time less than six months later.

Though James had survived his Test of Mettle, he never faced his demon. The draw granted Lucifer up to two more opportunities to test the human, should he desire.

The Test of Mettle was a marathon, not a sprint. Sometimes, breaking down barriers, like faith, love, trust, and confidence, was vastly more important than claiming a soul, mainly when it impacted several humans at once. To perform such a

delicate task, who better to employ than chaos demons. It further underscored Lucifer's fondness for
his lower-class minions.

11 - RUN FOR YOUR LIFE

March 26, 2010: Okeechobee, Florida, United States

A t 11:34 on a humid Friday night, a demon materialized amid six alligators lying along a bank of Lake Okeechobee. A fourteen-foot male was in the midst of the five females with whom he'd chosen to mate. The territorial creature took exception to the demon's appearance, and instinct beckoned the reptile to react with aggression. The alligator's golden eyes were as menacing as the reverberating growl rippling from its belly. It darted toward the demon, cutting the distance between them in half before halting and hissing a final intimidatory warning to the intruder.

The demon dropped to all fours. Its joints popped and snapped as it transformed into a quadruped. When it turned to face the alligator, it responded with its own menacing growl, one hatched from countless decades of torture and brimstone. The ferity and stature of the demon were exceeded only by the supernatural deviltry it possessed, causing the alligator to do something that did not come naturally to it as an apex species. It hesitated — a fatal mistake. The demon lunged. The five female alligators along the bank retreated to the safety of the water. Demon and alligator rolled along the bank. The demon timed the roll, tucked in its legs, planted its three-toed feet against the alligator's abdomen, and, when the demon's back met the ground, it kicked out, launching its eighteen-hundred-pound adversary sideways through the air. The reptile slammed its back against a palm tree. The collision yanked the roots from the sandy soil, and the tree toppled over with a pronounced thump.

This alligator had owned these waters until tonight, and decided it best to concede its territory to the newcomer. The reptile limped toward the lake, but the demon stopped at the water's edge, blocking the gator from escaping. When the alligator took a step back, the demon charged.

The alligator swiveled its head to bite its aggressor, attacking with speed and precision honed through millions of years of evolution. The demon was otherworldly fast and avoided the lethal bite with no trouble. The motion of the attack placed the gator at a disadvantage. The demon hopped over the gator's back and wrapped its massive arms around the alligator's powerful neck. The alligator rolled — exactly what the demon wanted. The demon halted its progress halfway into its roll and landed heavily atop the gator's soft belly. The alligator was helpless on its back as the demon straddled its prey with its powerful legs. The alligator thrashed, its massive tail whipping about, fatigue setting in. The demon snatched the gator's closed maw, then paused for an instant, expecting a warning from Hell for what it was about to do. It yearned to kill and destroy, but it was bound by the limits of a contract made long ago. As it hovered over the helpless alligator, the demon received no alarm, felt no otherworldly dissuasion. The pact between Heaven and Hell clearly stated that no outright death shall befall man. It declined to mention the millions of other creatures roaming the planet. Demon muscles rippled as one hand pushed and one hand pulled. Two thousand pounds per square inch strained to keep the gator's jaws clamped shut. Despite its extraordinary jaw strength, the mouth opened very slowly, the top and bottom jaws growing wider and wider apart until resistance from muscles, tendons, and bone could open it no further. The demon, however, was not finished, and with one massive heave, it was greeted with a resounding crack. The injured alligator writhed, letting out an unnatural squeal. The gator tried unsuccessfully to unsaddle the demon, but all it did was make the minion more determined. The demon strained harder, until there was one final crack. The lower jaw gave way. The demon torqued its massive arms and rent the entire bottom jaw, along with a portion of the alligator's throat.

The demon hopped off the back of the gator, watching blood spurt from the fatal wound. The demon lobbed the bloody jaw into the lake amid five wary sets of golden eyes.

The demon had exhausted a great deal of energy but felt so alive, so full of vigor. If the creatures of this world could be overtaken this easily, then it looked forward to exerting a swath of ruination in about six hundred years.

If it could escape the constraints of its hellish leash, it could commence an apocalyptic event starting now. As if on cue, the invisible leash tugged all the way from Hell to regain obedience. It would not do well to anger Lucifer, and the demon acquiesced to its role of subservience, collapsing to its knees.

* * * * *

A popular cross-state race called the Sunset-2-Sunrise Relay was well underway. Fifteen teams with ten to twelve runners each began a nightlong sojourn commencing in Fort Myers,. Their goal was to reach Jensen Beach. From the western shore of Florida to the eastern shore. Begin running at sunset. Run all night. Finish around sunrise, nearly twelve hours later.

The distance is about 180 miles, and the race has thirty-six legs. Each of the twelve members covers an average of five miles per leg and runs three times throughout the race. After completing a leg, the runner passes a bracelet to the next runner and gets a rest before it is their turn to run again. For safety, all runners are required to wear reflectors on their clothes. Each runner wears a headlamp for additional protection and visibility.

If running 180 miles is not daunting enough, runners must be shadowed by a bicycle ridden by one of their twelve team members. Cyclists, like runners, switch at the end of a leg to rest.

At a quarter to midnight in the middle of a clear, starry sky was a luminous three-quarter moon. A whispering breeze and a seventy-one-degree temperature yielded perfect running conditions. A racer and a biker made their way on a packed-dirt trail along Lake Okeechobee. Evergreens lined both sides of the broad path to the upcoming dike. The patter of feet and the crunch of bicycle tires served as white noise for the participants, who were busy concentrating on the physical course. Loose stones — some large enough to turn an ankle — littered the trail. Ruts created by truck tires added another layer of peril to the rough road. Through traffic consisted of the Army Corps of Engineers, who monitored levees, dikes, and rain erosion around the lake.

Sweat stained the athletic apparel worn by both athletes. Pauline ran alongside the rut on the right side of the dirt road, keeping with the lawful flow of traffic. Safety was relentlessly preached in the race's literature, at the race meetings, and on its website. No one wanted to be hurt, or hurt a team member, due to senselessness. Even though it was technically a race, finishing, rather than placement, was of the utmost importance. Greg cycled on the opposite side of the rut. They were three miles into a six-mile leg. Pauline had a good rhythm going. Greg requested riding this shift because he needed to keep his knee from stiffening — an old sports injury that occasionally flared up — and wished to warm up before running his upcoming leg.

Greg was a regular guy, with average height and above-average weight. He loved exploring new places on his bike and could knock out twenty or thirty miles. There was something special to him about pizza, beer, and friends.

Something even more special was a goddess named Pauline. Her daytime training regimen in the Florida sunshine allowed her to maintain a natural golden tan year-round. Pauline was an outdoor girl with a hearty appetite for running, outdoor yoga, swimming, and sunbathing. She was the only woman he knew who carried a six-pack that didn't have a beer brand affixed to it. A blonde braid swayed in time with her perfect stride. She had lively blue eyes that sparkled with unrelenting energy. The girl always seemed stuck on *Go*, and her tenacity — along with a deep-rooted commitment to a positive, healthy lifestyle — was entertaining to Greg.

Greg explored and cycled in spurts. When the feeling struck, day or night, he hopped on his bike and rode as far as the urge took him. It could be five miles, it could be thirty. He didn't mind exercising, but there had to be a balance to life. He had a philosophy: Sometimes, you gotta shift into neutral.

Pauline, on the other hand, kicked it into overdrive at the start of her day and left it there. She had completed a handful of triathlons, finished dozens of marathons and mini Ironman events, participated in a few relay races — her favorite was the Sunset-2-Sunrise Relay — and got grimy over countless mud runs. She threw herself into a million other activities and loved doing all of them.

Pauline was the team's organizer and had captained the squad for the past three years. Everyone, Greg included, looked forward to the event. Pauline had a large circle of friends. Her magnetic personality allowed her to do a great many things with people she knew and liked. So it came as no surprise when she announced that unless you were hospitalized or pregnant, stick with it or someone will replace you. It happened once to some jock jerk named Jeff Boone, Greg remembered. Or "the Great Jeff," as he'd self-proclaimed. The guy was built like a brick shithouse and had a hard-on for Pauline. They dated briefly, but not even the Great Jeff kept up with her. Or, from the rumors, could keep *it* up *for* her. He skipped a race following their breakup and made a scene when he tried to get back into the circle — and Pauline's pants — the following year. Greg heard about the guy from the others because he was the one who'd replaced the Great Jeff.

Greg and Pauline began dating, which pissed off Jeff to no end. As a result, Greg became his mortal adversary. Greg proved to be the better man, surrendering with his hands in the air when Jeff tried to pick a fight during a friendly get-together. Greg woke up on Pauline's couch with a black eye and a concussion. From then on, everyone dismissed the

Great Jeff. They had all but forgotten him until recently, when Jeff's social media page showed him hugging his fiancée in another region of the country. The Great Jeff had moved on, and Greg couldn't be happier for the guy.

Dating Pauline was a dream — when they dated, that is. It was on-again, off-again. He could never tie her down for any length of time. But there was a spark between them, and they enjoyed a flirtatious relationship even when they weren't dating. When apart, they remained close, but Pauline loved her freedom more. She was a wild mustang. Being single and living life, experiencing new adventures — all of these were at the core of what made Pauline truly happy. If someone was there to keep her company — and could keep up with her — all the better.

While they were dating, Greg shared with her his philosophy: Sometimes, you gotta shift into neutral. She laughed before realizing he was serious. He remembered the humiliation of that moment. She countered with a question: If someone handed Greg the keys to a brand-new Ferrari with an endless stretch of isolated highway in front of him, would he shift to neutral? He shrugged. No, she added. Sure, you have to stop for gas along the way, but when faced with an open road, you drop the top and put the pedal to the metal.

Greg was thirty-five and never married. He'd been engaged once. Three years into the relationship, he came home from work and found her and her things gone. No call. No note. No reason or closure. They rarely argued, and she never displayed signs of being unhappy. They both had great jobs and enjoyed doing things together. The oddest part of this was the timing: They had just returned from Mardi Gras. Two days later, she left him. Greg called her parents. They hung up on him. He was baffled.

Greg had dated others in the past seven years, but no one stacked up to Pauline. Pauline dated others, too. She liked Greg. Maybe even loved him, because she always came back to him. No one had ever received that sort of attention from Pauline.

Here they were together on a lonely road along Lake Okeechobee, side by side, participating in an activity she craved. Pauline pointed it out a half mile ago, telling him the view along the lake and the moon and shining stars and running and being with him — all of it — was her idea of paradise. Greg responded by nearly crashing the bike.

At last, he understood. It was perfect in every way. Earth, sky, air, water — it was all present and accounted for. They were sweating together, playing a cat-and-mouse game. Wrangling the wild mustang. It was strangely arousing, in a Pauline-coquettish sort of way. And he enjoyed it. Another realization struck him at that moment: He wasn't stuck in neutral. This was the Ferrari, and they were driving it down that straightaway together. He could not believe his naiveté. He'd had the answers all along.

Greg looked over at Pauline and sucked in a breath at the sight of her. She was the most beautiful woman he had ever laid eyes on. He watched her lithe form gliding over the dirt road; the reflective tape on her clothes caught the moon just right and cast an angelic glow all around her.

"What?" Pauline said with a coy smile, looking right at him.

"Huh?"

Greg had been caught ogling and jerked the handlebars. The bike struck a large stone embedded in the dirt. The front tire popped, and the bike steered into the rut, sending Greg sideways onto his butt.

"Oh, come on. Not now," Greg groaned. He took a few deep breaths before standing up and batting the caked dirt off his sweaty bare legs and shorts. He smacked the dirt from his palms while he checked the damaged tire. It was a road bike, skinny frame and tires, built for pavement and speed. Greg owned a road bike and a trail bike. They were very different bicycles, indeed. Road bikes were not equipped to handle rough roads like this one. His trail bike had a carbon fiber frame and dual suspension. It would have treated the rocks and potholes with indifference, apathetic toward whatever the road threw at him. This bicycle belonged to another member of the team. At least they had a cargo box fitted to a rack over the back tire.

"Are you okay?" she said, giggling. Seeing his dismay, she said, "I'm sorry," but the giggles came gushing out. There was something cute about Greg when he became flustered. "Oh gosh, I'm so sorry. I can't help it." The floodgates opened, and she howled with laughter. Greg could not help but smile. And maybe he would have found hilarity in the moment if he didn't feel like he'd blown out his manhood. His stomach felt crammed with icy butterflies.

"I'm fine. And don't be sorry. I'm sure that would've had at least a million hits on YouTube."

"Oh no," she said, realizing they were down a bike. "What are we going to do?"

Greg unsnapped the chin straps of his helmet and dropped it to the ground. Pauline smiled. She put a hand on his shoulder. It felt warm and comforting.

"Are you okay? Really?"

"Yeah, I'm good." He pulled his cell phone from the cargo box. "I'll call Benji. He or Christina should be with the RV. I'll let them know what happened. You keep going, though. It'll take me a few minutes to repair the tire. It's no big deal."

"Darn it. I was really looking forward to running this stretch with you," Pauline said. She gave his shoulder a tender squeeze. Then, she was off. He watched her shrink into the distance until her reflective tape was no longer visible.

"Me, too," Greg finally muttered, and he kicked the bike extra hard for good measure.

Greg picked up his helmet and aimed the headlamp into the cargo box. He probably should have inspected it before the start of the race. When Pauline's turn came up, she was stretched out and ready to run. In his excitement, Greg forgot that his bike was mounted on the RV. He had no choice but to use this bike, dutifully taking it from Christina at the end of her leg.

He rummaged through the cargo box. Its contents included patches, glue, cable lock, small medical kit, and a toolkit. *Great*, he thought, *no tire pump*. Anyway, it was too dark to patch a tire, and he certainly was not about to go anywhere near the water to dip the inner tube to locate the puncture. Alligators and moccasins inhabited the ponds, canals, swamps; and lakes. Greg flipped open the cell phone and pushed a few buttons before putting it to his ear.

A bubbly female voice answered. "Hey, Greg! What's up?"

"Got a blowout, Christina. I'm sitting here near the first dike."

"Ouch," she responded. "Where's Pauline?"

"She went on without me. Meantime, I plan on walking toward the next checkpoint, unless you could meet me along the way. Since the bike's dead and Pauline is alone, can you ask Benji if he's willing to grab my bike and meet up with Pauline?"

"Sure, hold on." Greg waited while he heard muffled voices. Benji was catching a few winks before his next leg. "I'll fill him in, Greg. He's a little out of it at the moment."

"I'm awake! I'm awake!" came a booming voice in the background. It was followed by an audible *thunk* and a string of profanity.

Christina broke out into a long, wheezing fit of laughter. Greg cracked a smile, imagining what was going on in the RV. Christina and Benji were a couple of nut jobs that brought the party bus. Everyone liked them, and why not? They were a humble couple who could make anyone laugh, even if it happened at their own expense. Even now, Greg found himself unable to resist a chuckle. Christina could barely speak. "Oh my God! That's too much. Benji just wiped out." This was followed by more raucous laughter and squeals of delight from the other teammates who'd witnessed the mishap. Benji let fly a few more colorful words. Christina snorted. "Thought he was going in the bathroom, and instead he walked face-first into the side door as he pulled his shirt on. Oh, God, wish you could've seen it. One for the books, I swear."

"That was awesome!" he heard someone shout in the background.

Christina coughed before she was able to speak again. "We're on our way. Keep to the road. We'll drop Benji off with Pauline on the way, if he doesn't cripple himself before we get there. Then we'll come get you."

"Okay. Thanks."

Greg folded the phone and dropped it into the cargo box. He lifted the hobbled bike out from the rut and tried to push it forward. The flat tire slogged over the dirt. Unwilling to risk another misadventure, he eased the bike back down on its side.

From his right came an aberrant laugh that had the embodiment of someone who swallowed a cup of nails and smoked four packs of cigarettes a day. It raised the hair on his arms and sent a shiver down his spine. Greg considered walking away, leaving the bike. It was the middle of the night on an isolated road. It should be safe, and his team could reclaim the bicycle using the RV. Greg waited, listening intently, while he considered his next move. There were none of the usual trills, chirps, twitters, or buzzing sounds. After strapping on the helmet, Greg used the headlamp to scan the evergreens. Then he pushed the bike toward the left side of the road. Never did his eyes veer away from the trees along the right side.

Another fit of ghoulish laughter permeated the night. Greg stopped cold when he caught movement in his peripheral vision. It was something big. Really big, and really fast.

"Hello? Who's there?"

No answer. Even the subtle breeze subsided. It was as if every living thing held its collective breath.

Greg announced with a modicum of humor, "I don't wanna have to use force. I've got a sharp set of tools and a medical box. If I cut you, I swear I'll pour alcohol on it to make it burn."

He heard nothing, not a sound.

"Shoot," Greg muttered. "Hey, if this is some kind of initiation or a practical joke, then you got me. Okay? I'm scared. You win, okay? So why don'tcha come out?"

A dim circle of light bobbed from tree to tree while he waited — hoped — for a human reply. Greg barely saw it in time to react — a volleyball-sized rock slammed the rear frame. The bike whipped back, striking Greg in the shins with enough force to kick his legs out. Greg landed atop the bike. The seat jabbed him in his ribs, knocking the wind from his lungs.

Greg grimaced. His shins screamed, and his ribs barked, but thankfully nothing seemed broken. A snapping sound from the trees stole his attention, not far from where he stood. A shadow? In the trees? After blinking several times to work the tears from his eyes, he saw nothing there.

Greg checked the condition of the bike. To his chagrin, the right pedal was missing. The frame bent inward and was now visibly cracked where the stone struck. He considered what would have happened if that stone had hit him instead of the bike.

In addition to the extensive damage to the bicycle, the cargo box now lay in pieces, its contents ejected toward the right side of the road, close to where the stone had come from. Greg searched for one item: his cell phone. Three feet from the furthest scrap of the shattered cargo box, mere inches from where the grass mixed with sandy dirt, was his cell phone. The impact had somehow flipped it open, causing the LCD panel to illuminate.

Greg took a painful step toward the cell phone. Rivulets of fear and sweat trickled down his dirty face. He swore at his dodgy knee when it cracked on the second step. He took another tentative step forward when the nearest evergreen began to shake, violently swaying side to side until the tree uprooted. It rose gracefully like an angel before the tip lowered like a spear. Greg started walking backward, stepping on the shattered plastic pieces of the cargo box. The tree moved back like a bolt set on a crossbow. Then it shot forward, striking the cell phone, skidding across the dirt road and into his bruised shins, felling him onto the tree. Greg did not have time to work through the pain in his legs. Another tree was freed from the ground and pointed at him once more. He rolled off the tree and hobbled down the road in the opposite direction of the race. Greg slid to a stop when the second tree soared overhead and landed sideways across the dirt road twenty feet ahead. The thing was on the move, brushing every evergreen along the way, closing the distance between them.

Greg sprinted back toward the broken bike and the first fallen tree. He heard another tree being uprooted. Greg suddenly cut right. The third tree struck the road where he had turned, skipping like a flat stone across water. The beam from the headlamp bobbed up and down as he ran, stumbled, regained his balance, and ran harder.

Something was chasing Greg, and it was gaining. And with it came a coarse, wild laugh.

Then the thing spoke a single word in a gravelly voice: "Pauline."

Greg looked over his shoulder. He'd had barely enough time to catch a glimpse of a shadow and glowing eyes before his foot struck something substantial. Greg belly-flopped in the damp grass along the shore just as the shadow dove at him. The thing sailed past him and into the lake. Greg groaned. He eased himself up and watched the spectacle in the lake. The creature that chased him growled and splashed about furiously as five sets of golden eyes closed in. Greg hastened back from the water until his heels knocked against something hard. He continued to watch the thrashing as the alligators attacked. The creature was being torn apart, depleting its hellish reserves to nothing. Summoned back to Hell, it gave one last otherworldly howl before the lake exploded at the opening and closing of the portal.

The concussion of the blast sent Greg sprawling back over the log he had just tripped on. A massive plume of water rose from the lake and rained down upon him. A geyser of hellish fog followed the plume of water. The thick cloud rolled back down to the lake, and a thin layer of mist spread out over the murky water.

Greg watched the spectacle, wondering what had attacked him. It appeared the alligators in the lake had finished it off.

After swiping the sand and dirt from his shorts, Greg followed the beam of the headlamp with his eyes. The light illuminated the side of not the log he assumed he'd tripped over, but a sizeable reptilian body. The light tracked up each foot of the alligator until he realized why it would not attack him. The ground surrounding the disfigured head was saturated with blood. This was a fresh kill; blood was still oozing from its mortal wound. Upon closer inspection, Greg realized the lower jaw and a good chunk of its neck were missing.

Greg surmised he'd narrowly escaped whatever killed the massive alligator. Where this beast lost, Greg won, because the gator had saved his life by tripping him, and the alligators patrolling the waters had done the rest. The water was, after all, their domain. He looked back to the lake once more as the curious fog slithered over its surface.

From the dirt road, the RV's horn blared. Greg limped toward it, trying to piece together the last ten minutes. Eight-foot shadows lurking in the dark. Evergreen trees uprooted and tossed like footballs. Heavy stones thrown with accuracy and force. A mauled alligator he mistook for a freaking log. Then there was that awful laughter. It sent another shiver down his spine. He would never, *ever* forget that. One fact would elude him for the remainder of his days: From now on, he would be untouchable by Lucifer and his minions. Greg had won his Test of Mettle.

Greg limped out of the darkness and into the face of the RV's high beams. He was caked in mud, sand, and dried blood from head to toe. His barely recognizable form staggered forward until he stood directly between the bright headlights. Eight team members stared back through the windshield, concern etched in their faces.

12 - WILD, WILD GUEST

July 15, 1863: Cheyenne, Dakota Territory, North America

A curly wolf of a man with a face of leather and whiskers and a body shaped by gristle and grit. Slade was his name, and he towered over the much smaller man, who was on the ground working to gain traction in the soft dirt with his elbows in an attempt to escape the broad figure towering dangerously over him. He twisted onto his stomach, preparing to stand and run, but Slade kicked him solidly in the ribs with the toe of his boots. There was an audible snap. The smaller man curled into the fetal position and began sobbing.

Quiet, yet equally dangerous, were seven other men. All were hardened, all shared the same guarded, loathing eyes, but they displayed nothing like the reeking hatred emanating from Slade. None of the seven men had their weapons drawn, but their ready fingers were itching plenty. Slade held his pistol like a hornet set to sting.

The man stared at the end of the weapon. "I didn't tell nobody! I swear to almighty God!"

"Michael and Ty saw you. They followed after you. Saw you speaking to Turner's boys," Slade spat.

The little man sputtered a senseless string of nonsense. Slade shook his head in disgust and took two resolute steps back.

"That's right. You been spotted. You ain't nothin' but a yellow-bellied, flannel-mouthed liar." A calloused thumb drew back the hammer. "And I'm meanin' to fix that."

The small man cried for mercy, raising a dirty hand to shield himself. The weapon roared, and the shrieks came to a sudden finality. Smoke billowed from the end of the pistol. The towering figure holstered the smoking weapon and let fly a stream of brown tobacco juice onto the dead man's forehead. Tobacco juice oozed over the frozen moment of terror in the man's eyes. Slade brushed away the backsplash of spittle clinging to his whiskers with a swift swipe of an arm.

"Serves 'im right, Slade. Damned fool had it comin' to 'im," one of the men said. It was Ty. Slade spit, aiming for a grasshopper on a nearby rock, and struck it squarely. The insect, caught in the slimy spittle, oozed down the side of the rock. A sleeve stained brown from elbow to wrist again swiped at the dark brown spit caught in Slade's whiskers. Then, with the grace of a snake, he slithered onto his horse.

Nick called out, "What should we do with the

body, Slade?"

The same question was on the minds of the others.

Slade aimed those deathly black eyes back at the body before turning his attention to the young man he knew so well, but his voice lost none of its seriousness. "Son, you leave 'im for the coyotes, y'hear?"

He spurred the horse's flank and whipped the reins, sending the horse into a full gallop south before merging onto the main trail, toward the dying sun, and into Cheyenne. The rest of the men saddled up without another thought, leaving Nick, who stared down at the destroyed corpse for another moment longer before tethering the extra pony to his own.

They returned to the ranch to strip down their newly begotten horse of its former owner's goods and put it to pasture with their others. Once that chore was done and the evidence safely hidden away, they saddled up once more and rode into town. Some loose ends needed to be tied up.

The wooden structure mimicked every other building in town. That is where the similarities ended. Dusty's Saloon had swinging doors at the entrance and almost always had horses tied up outside. The men tied their own and went inside. The tavern reeked of a mix of tobacco smoke, body odor, and dried blood. The floorboards creaked with wear. Slade emptied the chaw from his mouth at a spittoon next to the bar. He fished around his cheeks for stray pieces of tobacco and spat the remaining bits somewhere near the vessel. Tobacco juice had darkened the floor over time.

The men bellied up to the bar after removing the tobacco from their mouths.

The bartender nodded at Slade while wiping a glass.

"Usual, Dusty."

The barkeep gathered a bottle from a hidden shelf and placed it and a clean glass in front of Slade, who lit a cigar. After placing a stack of coins on the bar, Slade carried the bottle and the glass to a quiet table in a dark corner. The position was perfect for scouting. It gave Slade an unobstructed view of the bar.

The bartender pulled a bottle from one of many lining the shelves, uncorked it with his teeth, and filled seven glasses with whiskey. Slade preferred the private stock. It was smoother, more flavorful, and pricier than the firewater shared among his men and the regulars who frequented the establishment.

Dusk settled in, and activity at the saloon picked up. Soon Cheyenne's finest whores began to doll up the place. The smell of soap and perfume made the stale air more tolerable. They wore corsets, which helped to display their bountiful cleavage. Kerosene lamps furnished the saloon with enough light for patrons and card players.

It didn't take long for alcohol and testosterone to create a volatile situation. A pair of men argued bitterly over which prostitute displayed a prettier set of teeth. The girls scurried away from the inevitable. After a few more vile retorts, one of the men lunged. Punches were thrown, and the men crashed to the floor, wrestling amid the foul mix of fluids and grime.

A stout, gray-haired man rushed into the saloon, two young, beefy men on his heels. Each wore a shiny star over his left breast. The surrounding patrons scurried out of their way. Slade watched as they overpowered the pair of drunkards and dragged them outside, where they would be smacked around a bit. The purpose of these extracurriculars was to induce the drunkards to vomit. After the drink was purged from their systems, they were more obliging with the jailing effort. It also made cleanup of the jail cells palatable. Even with puke pails in each cell, roostered cowboys always seemed to throw up everywhere else. Getting it out of their guts ahead of time made the jail a more bearable environment.

Tomorrow those two brawlers would be hobbled with hangovers in the hoosegow until high noon, at which time they would either pay their fines or find the calaboose their home for three whole days. The cost of the fine was a tidy sum. One could knock boots with a whore and still have enough left over to sup and drink himself into a sated stupor. The sheriff did not take too kindly to those who could not afford their fines. It was public knowledge that three days in his hoosegow was no picnic. Some men were lucky to walk away with black eyes, bloodied noses, and their teeth intact.

Slade pulled another cigar from inside his coat and lit it with the dim fire of a nearby lantern. A flame spurted out the end, momentarily casting the creases in his hardened features. There was a time, long ago, when he enjoyed what each day brought. He'd smiled his last smile sometime back then. In the present, Slade preferred the camouflage of darkness, and he settled back into his chair. His eyes reflected twin white dots in the lantern light, and they flashed like those of a coiled snake searching and studying the patrons, patiently waiting for an opportunity to feed, for that perfect moment to strike.

The sheriff reentered the saloon with the grace of a cat. His eyes roamed the darkened areas until they settled on Slade. Slade briefly pressed against the back of the chair.

The sheriff made his way to Slade before removing his hat and placing it on the table. He eased himself into the creaky chair opposite Slade. "Slade," he said.

Slade refused to call the man by his title. They'd grown up together in Cheyenne, attending the same school, going to the same church on Sunday, playing in the same patch of dirt. As they got older, their relationship grew increasingly strained as their philosophies differed widely. The two men inevitably quarreled. Slade had fought many men in his life. There was only one who'd bested him. "Turner."

A waiter seemed to magically appear, and he asked the sheriff what he'd like. The sheriff waved his hand, eyes locked on Slade. The waiter disappeared back into the bustle.

The chair creaked when the sheriff shifted his weight forward, resting his thick forearms on the table. Slade puffed on his cigar, the end burning hot, before plucking the cigar from his mouth and letting the smoke curl from his mouth in slow twisting plumes. The sheriff watched. Slade knew the man and chose to wait him out, let him be the first to speak. He took another long, lazy drag from his cigar. Too many men crumpled under the sheriff's glare, and, before even realizing they were doing it, found themselves confessing to every sin they ever committed. Slade was not so easily swayed. He eased back into his chair and bored those twin white dots into the sheriff.

The staring contest continued for several moments before the sheriff broke the icy silence. "I heard an interesting rumor," he said, settling back into the creaking chair and giving Slade a look demanding an answer.

Slade said nothing. This was another tactic the sheriff used. Most men quivered in fear and babbled away.

Seeing no reaction, the sheriff chuckled. He'd figured it would be pointless to go this route, but it had been worth a shot. It was time to get straight to the point. "Word is you and your boys took down a wagon."

Slade appeared relaxed on the surface, but inside his muscles tensed, ready to strike. Slade pulled the cigar from his mouth and studied it. He responded flatly, "That right?"

"Killed four men. Two of them law." The sheriff watched Slade for any kind of tic, reflex, or giveaway. Slade grunted as if it were news to him, but he knew all too well that the actual body count was a dozen men. Two drivers and ten marshals.

The sheriff continued to stare. Slade acted offended and drew in toward the table. "I'm a simple rancher. My men see to their work. We got better things to do than fuss with some witless acts of lawlessness. And you should know I don't take to no funny business."

"That right?" the sheriff asked. His lips curled into a half smile. A hand stroked the top of his hat before plucking it from the tabletop. "Well, I guess that settles that."

Slade responded, "Guess so."

The chair scraped the floor as the sheriff stood. The man returned the hat to his head. After he slid the chair under the table and was about to turn and leave, he stopped. A finger pointed up as if a thought had just occurred to him.

"Funny, though. There were a lot of footprints and hoofprints — I'd say up to ten people — some distance away from the robbery, as if it was an ambush. Hard to think twelve men could be so easily slaughtered. It would have taken some solid planning, probably by someone intelligent." The sheriff stared straight into Slade's unblinking eyes. "Know what I mean?"

Slade's voice remained low and level. "Thought you said there were only four men."

"So I did." The sheriff rapped the table twice with his knuckles. "I'll see you around." The sheriff walked out of the saloon with the same catlike movements.

Slade eased back into his chair once more. The tenseness in his muscles drifted away with each puff of his cigar. As he relaxed, his mind toiled away, contemplating. Things were getting mighty dangerous now that Turner was sniffing around. He knew that McGrady or McGirty, or whatever the hell his name was, was a dirty, rotten polecat, and now word had made its way to the one person he'd wanted to avoid. Turner was not going to go away. The sheriff and his boys would be sniffing after them every chance they got. Probably not tonight, given the recent acquisitions at the hoosegow. But he knew Turner. He was as deadly as he was dangerous, but most of all, the son of a bitch was just plain unpredictable.

An hour had passed when Earl and his two larger-than-life sons shoved open the tavern doors. The father was lanky, and age had put a crook in his back. He strolled up to the bar while his sons threatened two men to leave their table. The angry cowboys kept their wits about them and wisely left the saloon.

Slade's men, no doubt, were upstairs getting their rocks off with the ladies of the establishment.

There was a job to do, and he wanted them to keep out of sight. He turned the key on the oil lamp until there was barely a visible flame. The darkness around his table provided ample concealment in the busy saloon. He melted into his chair and tilted the brim of his hat forward to conceal his face.

Earl's sons were in their twenties. Both were hatless, witless, and strong as oxen. They were heaped in muscle and thick as mules. While they waited for Earl, one picked his yellow teeth with a dirty thumbnail while the other one drilled into his nose and licked his finger clean before grooming the other nostril. Earl returned with a small stack of four glasses. The waiter followed in his wake and set a half-empty bottle of whiskey on the table. Earl passed around glasses, putting the fourth on the side of the table nearest the swinging doors. One of the boys hulked over to another table and took the empty chair without a word. One of the men launched out of his seat, but the others grabbed his arms and shoulders to hold him back. The boy walked away with the chair, holding it by a single leg above the crowd. He placed the chair down roughly just as one of Turner's boys entered the saloon. Earl beckoned him over, and the man sat in the empty chair. Slade watched as Earl slapped the shoulder of his nose-picking son, scolding him about his manners. The boy held the nose-picking hand out for a shake. Turner's son eyed it cautiously and gave the boy a polite nod instead. Earl poured whiskey into the man's glass. Turner's son raised the glass and nodded to Earl. With a greasy flick of the wrist, he gulped the liquor and slapped the glass upside down on the tabletop. His facial expression was no different than if he'd downed a glass of water. Earl's two boys' faces lit up red, as if they'd just eaten coal straight out of a campfire. Earl's face twitched as he drank his own, but he maintained eye contact with Turner's son, then he, too, slapped his glass upside down.

Slade noted this demonstration.

Earl and Turner's son spoke while the two boys sat there looking as stupid as ever. Before long, the two men shook hands, and Turner's son departed. Earl slapped his two hulking youngsters on the shoulders, and the three men left the saloon. Slade sat quietly for a few minutes before he stood up and headed out.

As far as anyone else was concerned, Slade was nothing more than a rancher with a group of dedicated workhands that looked after livestock. Most figured him to be an honest-to-goodness civilian.

That was partly true.

He'd worked for years at keeping, maintaining, and selling his livestock. He still kept a decent number of them corralled at the ranch, mostly for appearances. Nowadays, his business ran down a different avenue, a venture that was risky and extraordinarily profitable. It had shaped him into an apex predator, one who would go to any length to succeed.

Turner, Earl, and their sons would need to be dealt with. Until today, things had been quiet. But Turner clearly knew something, and his old pal Slade had made his list. Slade thought the operation had been flawless, but someone must have squealed.

As far as he could tell, McGrady was in cahoots with Earl and his boys. He figured them boys planned to steal what Slade and his boys rightfully took. Once Slade and his men were incarcerated or put down, they could profit greatly, and with minimal effort, since they would merely be *confiscating* stolen evidence. Turner and his boys may have taken an oath to uphold the law, but it didn't stop them from using their position of power to tarnish the stars they wore.

It might have worked, if not for Slade's untrusting nature. Ty and Michael had kept a tail on that McGrady fellow. He was the one with all the connections, and he was the only one who could sell the goods. Now, Slade figured he could learn about those connections as he developed a backup plan.

Michael and Ty had found treachery afoot when they eavesdropped on a meeting between McGrady and one of Turner's boys. He tried to convince the boy that Slade and his men had a big hand in the death of all those marshals. But Turner's son was unconvinced. How could a simple rancher with less than a dozen cowhands cut down armed and battle-ready men? McGrady shrugged; he had assumed Turner's boy a dolt. Then Turner's boy asked him point-blank why he thought it was Slade. Why would a rancher assail a munitions run? McGrady offered no answer, and the boy suspected McGrady was less than forthright. He could beat it out of him, but, instead, he would share what he learned from McGrady with his father.

That was why Turner had questioned Slade at the saloon instead of arresting him. Turner was searching for anything to take him down, but Slade had given the sheriff nothing. This meant that the next person Turner was likely to go after was McGrady. And Slade could not let that happen. McGrady knew everything. Turner and his boys would pound the truth out of him in short order.

It was unfortunate that Slade could not listen in on the actual conversation between Earl and McGrady at the saloon. It would have been convenient to know what beans were being spilled. Slade figured it had to be another layer of treachery. McGrady failed to convince Turner's son, so they needed to come up with another plan. If they could not convince Turner that Slade and his boys were behind the heist, then maybe they wanted to remove them from the equation altogether and set it up like some infighting gone wrong. Whatever their plan, it was imperative for Slade to take quick and decisive action.

Slade watched Earl and his two boys riding east out of town, as expected. He knew where they were going. He focused his attention on Turner's son, who was harassing a pair of drunks sitting against the side of the general store. He hauled off and kicked one square in the hip, which got the man to roll onto his side and stumble onto his feet. He threatened to jail the two men if they were not able to walk home. The two drunkards stumbled down the dark street, with Turner's son in tow. Slade followed, unsheathing a blade hidden inside of his right boot as he did so.

The drunkards turned a corner, exiting the shadowy path between buildings. Before Turner's son reached the corner, Slade reached up from behind and slid the blade across the man's throat. The boy dropped to his knees, clutching his neck and sputtering wet, gurgling noises. Arterial blood spurted from between his fingers. Slade relaxed his breathing while he watched the dying boy's arms sag. The boy crumbled forward face-first. Slade wiped the blade on the back of the boy's shirt. After detecting no witnesses and hearing nothing warranting additional action, he peeked around the corner. The two drunken men staggered into a small house down the street. Slade smirked with a small amount of satisfaction before slipping back into the shadows.

* * * * *

Ty, Michael, Billy, Julius, Walt, Filmore, Slade's son, Nick, and two women stood outside on a second-floor balcony.

"Anna, I thought... I dunno, maybe I can see you tonight," Billy said. Nick scowled at him, so Billy amended, "But it will have to be late. I'll wait up for you."

"I'm sure you'll be up for me," Anna giggled. The other prostitutes sitting close by also giggled. Billy blushed and looked down at the wood planks to kick at an invisible rock. Anna lifted his chin gently and said, "Don't you go and get unsettled in your britches. I'll make a special trip to see you. Who knows? Maybe Elizabeth will tag along to get some fresh air later." This comment was greeted with a rousing chorus of giggles and catcalls, which deepened Billy's crimson color.

"All right!" Billy shouted. Realizing it sounded harsher than he'd intended, he added a calm, "That would be just fine, Anna, should your friend want to come by to enjoy the fresh air."

Nick, standing next to Billy, gave him a sharp what-are-you-doing elbow in the ribs.

"Well, we best be gettin' back inside before your brother breaks anything we might not want broken." She winked at Nick before turning her attention to Billy once more by giving him a slow, gentle kiss on the cheek. She waved before heading back down the balcony with her companion, both giggling as they stepped inside the saloon.

"Dang, Nick, what was that for?" Billy asked, rubbing at his side.

"I don't know how you do it," Nick said, "but get focused. We got a hard ride ahead of us."

Billy answered with an impish grin.

"What?" Nick said. It took a moment before he

finally understood the reason they were all staring intently at him, snickering. "Jesus Christ almighty, you idjits need to grow up."

They let out a chorus of laughter.

"Well put, Nick," Michael said, and the others laughed again.

Nick punched Billy in the shoulder, grinning widely.

"And what's with you? I never seen a man go into a whorehouse and leave with a whore. Never seen it," Nick said. They all stepped forward to praise Billy with a few slaps on his head and shoulders. Billy could not help his ability to charm. It came naturally to him.

"Let alone two whores." Michael slapped Billy twice on the back.

The men quieted to keep watch from the balcony's shadows. It wasn't long before Earl and his boys lumbered out, saddled up, and galloped east. Turner's son came out as they climbed their horses. The man kicked a pair of passed-out drunks lying against the saloon wall, shouting obscenities as he reared back to give them another taste of his steel toe. The drunks stumbled to their feet and staggered away while Turner's son chased after them. They never saw Slade exit the saloon and meld with the darkness.

Nick climbed down, and the others followed, keeping to the shadows as much as possible. They waited in a tight circle along the side of the building, focusing their attention on the activity involving Earl and his two massive boys. Nick was about to address the group when he realized someone was standing next to him, leaning almost cheek to cheek with him.

"Jesus hollerin' Christ, Pa! You damned near spooked me to my grave."

None of them had picked up on Slade's movements.

"Slackers," he said. "I tol' each one of you to keep guard. One day it's gonna be your ruination, y'hear?" They murmured in reply. "All right, let's get down to it. That McGirty fella…"

"McGrady," came the corrections.

"Yeah, right," he said. "He went and squealed to Turner, as y'all know. Told 'im about our little operation out west with the munitions run. Probably took every last drop to keep Turner from hauling his ass to the calaboose. Turner let 'im go, but I bet he asked around. Probably learned McGirty was one of Earl's partners. Then it gets real interestin'. See, Earl and his boys meet right inside here with Turner's boy. Earl's a-tellin' him a good deal to make us look like we done did all the killin'. He comes out meaner than a kicked snake and does some kickin' of his own. I know he's itchin' to tell his daddy what he learned. All of a sudden we's lookin' mighty appetizing. But I shut him down 'fore he had a chance to blab. As far as I'm concerned, we're in the clear. He was last seen with Earl and his boys. McGirty up and disappears. Looks real suspicious. But then Earl and his boys disappear. Looks a whole lot more suspicious. Seems to me that would get the sheriff all riled up. Suddenly we ain't even an afterthought. If I know Turner, I'm thinkin' he might be chasin' after Earl."

They processed the information, then Nick spoke up.

"Pa, that sounds real good and all, but what if Turner gets to thinkin' maybe we was workin' with McGrady and Earl? We ambushed them marshals real good. Your plan was pure genius, but someone like Turner's bound to figure Earl and his kin wouldn't be wise enough to know you can pluck the feathers off a bald eagle."

Slade scratched his scruffy chin as he considered what Nick said.

"Son," he said, "I fear you may be right. That means we gotta take down Earl and his kin. We can't have them anywhere near us. And I know they're aimin' to get our claim and hightail it out east to meet with them Confederate fellers. But they's too stupid to run in the night. Plus they probably need horses and carts. So they's planning to wait 'til morning to make a purchase for ponies and carts."

"Unless they're aimin' to steal 'em," Michael added.

Nick nodded, then responded, "Hell of a risk, but I wouldn't put it past them if they find themselves desperate enough."

Slade scratched his chin, nodding. "We take them down now," he said with a cold note of finality.

* * * * *

They arrived in open country, leaving behind the staleness of booze, the taint of whores, and the clamor of civilization. Stars painted the broad sky, each one more brilliant than the next, twinkling like little crystals rotating under sunlight. As bright as they were, the full moon was the star of the stage. It hovered directly overhead with a gentle wisp of gliding clouds, amping the countryside with a glorious bluish-white glow.

The prints in the dirt trail were easy enough to track, and even easier at the small, inconspicuous path adjacent to a massive boulder displaced by retreating glaciers thousands of years ago. They followed the prints up the narrow path. The surrounding terrain grew increasingly rocky and uneven, and the tracks became much more difficult to follow. Slade tugged at the reins to stop his horse and dismounted. The others did the same and drew their weapons. Slade didn't need to scan the ground for tracks. He knew where they were holed up.

The landscape was pimpled with grassy domed hills like the one where they now stood. They crouched behind a tentacle of rock barely five feet tall at the southeast corner that grew increasingly shorter as it snaked away from the hill. There they waited, watching the cave entrance along the southwest side. Twin oil lanterns, shiny and new, hung at each side of the cave on rusted nails pounded into wooden beams illuminated the entrance.

It wasn't long before one of Earl's sons — Slade recognized him as the one that had nearly started a brawl when he took the patron's chair at Dusty's — wandered out from the cave carrying a lantern.

Slade motioned to Filmore, a bastard son whose father was white and mother was Native American. Slade knew neither father nor mother. He'd come across Filmore in Cheyenne fifteen winters ago, barely clothed and clinging to life, begging for food and coin. Slade had walked up to him and handed the boy his coat. Filmore looked up at him, frightened and unsure. But he put the coat on, and Slade paid to put soup and bread in his starving belly. Filmore had remained loyal to Slade ever since.

Filmore leaned his rifle against the rock wall, rolled over the top of the wall, and deftly freed a blade from his pants. In one soundless, silky movement, he crouched low on his feet, moving with deadly swiftness toward Earl's son, who was kicking pine cones as hard as he could while laughing and announcing dumbly how bad he had hurt them.

The breeze remained light and steady. It swirled in the clearing outside the cave, and as Filmore drew closer, he wrinkled his nose. Human waste. The lumbering boy seemed oblivious to it and continued his pine cone-kicking game until he reached a shithole dug up next to one of the many glacial boulders dotting the landscape. He untied his pants and let them drop to the ground before kicking them off. With his back pressed against the boulder, he bent his knees until he hovered over the hole. The boy never saw the blade, nor did he even seem to register the pain it inflicted. He turned to see Filmore standing in a defensive posture, fresh blood running down the perfectly sharp blade. There was no threat of aggression in the boy's cherubic face. Filmore thought of the number of men — and women — who had fallen for this skullduggery before the beast unleashed. The knife remained poised and ready. The boy's mouth opened, but not even a whisper escaped. The boy dropped to his knees, raising a hand to feel his throat. It came away with the same blood dripping off of Filmore's knife. The boy's passive face gave way to sorrow. He slid down the wall, dead.

Witnessing the boy's ability to tune out pain, Filmore jabbed him under his kneecap. Blood leaked from the wound, but the boy never twitched. Filmore wiped the blood using the boy's pants before hightailing it back to Slade and his brothers at the stone wall. There they watched and waited. They could make out the silhouette of the slain boy leaning against the rock. Someone that large wouldn't be overlooked when the devil came calling. Slade considered the idea of what it would be like immediately after death. Would something from Hell be standing next to his corpse. waiting to claim his soul? Way out in the distance, he thought he spotted a pair of glowing golden eyes, but a shout from the cave distracted him.

"Stevie, where the hell you run off to, ya big

dumb oaf? I's ain't for chasin' after you ever' time you gotta squat." The other brother lumbered out of the cave hoisting a lantern at arm's length and heading straight for the rock. Before he could react, Slade realized Filmore was right on the heels of Earl's other boy. It brought a semblance of satisfaction to Slade's craggy face.

The boy stomped around the boulder, calling his brother once more. He stopped dead in his tracks when he saw the lethal gash across his brother's throat and a shirt soaked with fresh blood.

"Stevie?" The word was as grim as it was weak. He took another step forward when a hand wrapped around his forehead and pulled back. A trace of cold steel slid across his throat. The intended cry became nothing more than a mere rasp. Blood from the fatal wound spattered the ground. The lantern clanked to the earth as a pair of thick fingers clawed at his throat. It was not long before his dead brother had company.

Filmore cleaned his blade on the boy's shirt as Slade and the others joined him. Slade inspected each body, nodding his assent to the others. He stood up and walked toward the cave, the others in tow. The pair of glowing golden eyes followed.

Slade followed a long passage that steadily descended into the earth. A glowing lantern hung from a nail every third or fourth beam. The passageway opened into a natural underground hideout. The area was spacious enough to house a dozen men and their horses comfortably. On the opposite side of the cavern was an unlit passageway. Smooth stones circled a small pit in the center of the room. The wood used to warm the damp cavern had burned down to orange embers.

Sitting atop a smooth oval stone was the target of Slade's wrath. Slade drew his revolver and pointed it at the man. Earl tossed a fresh log in the pit. He used a stick to poke around the crackling coals. Tendrils of flame licked the sides of the wood. The serenity of the cave was broken when Slade cocked back the hammer. The man dropped his stick and reached for his rifle. Instead, his hand clutched empty air. He twisted around and found Nick holding his rifle. Filmore stood next to Nick, flaunting his gleaming blade menacingly. Earl rose to his feet and found himself surrounded by Slade and his boys.

"Slade!" Earl cried. "What's the meanin' of this? Have you lost your damned mind?"

"Michael, take Billy, Julius, and Walt with you and search the cavern. Stay in pairs if you need to split up." The four men hurried toward the back of the cavern and disappeared into the passageway. "Ty, stay here and cover me." Ty lowered the barrel of his rifle at Earl.

"Slade, this ain't right!" Earl shouted. "You ain't got no right treatin' me like this. We're partners, for Christ's sake."

"No, Earl, we ain't partners." Slade sat on a stone across from Earl. Using his revolver, he beckoned Earl to sit. Earl locked eyes with Slade, fury boiling in his pupils as he slowly sat back down.

"Okay, Slade. I'm sitting. Do you mind telling me what this is all about?"

"Well, Earl, for starters, you went and hired that McGirty fellow."

The name did not immediately register with Earl. There was an unmistakable fire in Slade's eyes, and Earl figured Slade knew more than he let on. "Are you meanin' McCleary?"

"Whatever!" Slade snarled.

"What of him, Slade? He's harmless. Where is he?"

Slade's men sniggered. Earl was beginning to sense a feeling of hopelessness but chose to play dumb. What would it matter now? Slade leaned forward, his eyes twinkling in the firelight, like a big cat toying with a mouse before its interest dissipated.

"Seems someone sent the law my way. They got wind some ways that I went and robbed that stagecoach, Earl. Six marshals came to my ranch asking me all about it. It made no damn bit of difference what I tol' 'em, 'cause they's just come to arrest me. One of them wanted to carry out the hanging right there on my property. Earl, the man put a rope around my neck, which made me very uneasy, ya see."

He waited to gauge Earl's reaction, but Earl was bereft of emotion.

Slade used the barrel to push up the brim of his hat. He leaned back and tapped the revolver against his cheek when he asked, "It got me to thinkin', Earl. What were they doin' at my doorstep, hmm?"

Earl swallowed hard when the end of the revolver aimed between his eyes. He wrestled with a few ideas. Should he lunge at Slade? Should he bolt from the cave? Should he continue to play dumb? The revolver was ready to smoke him if he moved. Earl played it cool.

"What are you talking about, Slade? I sure as hell didn't send them."

Slade smiled. "Of course you didn't." Slade broke into a laugh, and the others joined in. "Well that does it now, doesn't it? Shoot, I got to tell you I'm mighty glad we got that cleared up. For a minute there, I was worried you double-crossed me and my boys. But you's totally innocent, right?" Slade stood up in mock satisfaction. He slid the revolver into its holster before extending the same hand out to Earl. "Shake?"

Earl squirmed. He rose slowly, extending his hand with apparent reluctance. Slade reached for the man's hand and shook it firmly, eyes meeting Earl's. Then he turned his back and stepped away from the man.

Earl wondered for a split second if it was truly over. He let out a long, heavy sigh. Slade stopped ten feet away. His back still facing Earl, he added, "Now that I think about it, there was the matter of the balls."

Earl had no earthly idea what Slade was talking about. His brows bunched up. "Balls? What balls?"

"Oh, shoot. I guess you hadn't heard, although I imagined every person within a hunnerd miles would've heard. You see, Earl, this one marshal, well, he got mighty brave and all. We did things to him that would make most men cry like little sissy girls. But he was tough, I gotta give him his due. He had grit and stayed tough right up until we yanked that man's pants off and sliced off one of his balls. We even held it out for him to see. Guess a man does think with his balls, 'cause his memory got real good and clear." The men chuckled at the memory. Slade turned with catlike grace, and the hair along Earl's nape stood straight up. "Know what he tol' me, Earl?" Earl began to shake involuntarily. "Come on, Earl. You know, don'tcha?" Earl tried to swallow, but his mouth was as dry as a dusty riverbed. He looked away from Slade. Slade closed the distance in a blink of an eye, unholstered his revolver, and shoved it under Earl's chin. Slade was cheek to cheek with Earl. Earl froze. He could feel Slade's deceptively calm breath on his earlobe. Slade's voice dropped so low that he could barely make out the word "McCleary."

Earl's eyes went wide. Slade took a few steps back.

"Seems that yellowbelly fellow of yours got awful tight-lipped when I asked him about your little hidey-hole out here. I handed him the marshal's balls, then asked him for directions. He led us to this very cave."

As if on cue, Nick reentered the cavern. He said, "Found it, Slade. Them crates back there."

Earl's eyes widened. Slade tilted his head at Earl in a rueful manner. "Care to change that bullshit story of yours?"

Earl said nothing. It was over.

"No?" Slade gave Earl a chance to reconsider. "Hmm, what a pity."

Slade flicked the barrel of his pistol. "Walk. Nice and slow like. I'd hate to shoot you in the back."

Earl eased himself up with his hands half raised and walked toward the area Nick had just scoured. Slade stopped, whispered something to Nick. Nick nodded and answered, "Sure thing, Pa." He ran toward the entrance, tapped Ty on the shoulder, and the two men scampered off.

Slade turned to the rest of the men. "Filmore. Come with me. The rest of you, be ready."

The extension was wide and tall enough for them to walk side by side without bumping each other. The path continued to curve and descend with a subtle grade. They reached a dimly lit chamber. Inside were six crates. Slade gave Earl a firm shove in the back to keep him moving forward.

"See the crate with that metal bar against it? I want you to open that there crate," Slade demanded.

Earl's hands remained raised, but he looked at Slade with a quizzical look upon his face. Slade's demeanor remained neutral. Filmore moved next to Slade, arms crossed. Both waited. Why did Slade want him to open this crate? Or any of them for that matter? He slowly stepped toward the crate. He noticed a reddish-brown X painted on some of the corners. Earl had an inkling of what was used to paint the symbol. He lifted the bar and forcefully wedged its thin edge into a seam and wriggled it in deeper. Once it was deep enough, he pushed and pulled until the lid yawned open. A sweet and sour odor filled the cave; it made Earl gag. He placed a hand over his mouth.

His reaction was not only a result of the smell but also the contents of the crate.

In it was the body of McGirty and two others Earl had hired.

"Get in," Slade said.

Earl did not move. The stench burned his nostrils and hung thick in the still air. He stared helplessly at the three dead men stuffed in the crate.

"Where are my boys?" his voice cracked.

Slade's voice dripped with venom. "Dead."

Earl lowered his hands. It was over. He'd made a grave mistake crossing Slade. It was a risky venture, he knew, and could have made him a wealthy man. He and his team had been made a promise by the United States government of a substantial amount of money for completing jobs like this. The North wished to crush the South in a decided fashion.

"Get in."

Earl said no just as Slade fired his revolver. Earl dropped to the ground, his eyes open and lifeless. Slade and Filmore tossed his body into the crate like a sack of potatoes. Slade retrieved an oak barrel from the back of the cavern and tipped it over. A rush of black powder poured out against the crates. Filmore joined in, and they rolled the barrel to the main chamber, tipping it along its open end. Once they arrived in the main chamber, Filmore stood the barrel up and walked it away from the thick line of black powder.

Slade said, "Everyone out." He turned to Filmore. "You, too, son. I don't know what happened to Nick or Ty, but if you see them, tell them to stay clear. Ya hear?"

Filmore nodded, and the men followed him out of the cave. Slade waited to give them a chance to get to a safe place. Then he lifted one of the lanterns from the wall and slammed it into the ground next to the trail of black powder. The kerosene erupted into flame. The mound of black powder sparked to life with a *whoompff*, and a ball of sizzling white-hot sparks and flame followed the long line of black powder deep into the cave.

Slade snatched a lantern from the wall and ran full tilt out of the mouth of the cave, expecting the men to be grouped together a safe distance away. What he encountered made him stop dead in his tracks and forget about the cave, the black powder, Earl, and the deception against him and his boys. The trees. The rocky terrain. The horses. Cheyenne. They all disappeared.

On the ground at his feet was the crumpled form of Julius. A rock the size of the man's head lay on the ground, covered in gore.

"Look out!" someone shouted.

His feline-quick reaction saved his life, as it had done so many times. Slade dropped to the ground, still clutching the lantern, just as another large stone zipped by his ear, leaving a small tear in his shirt. The stone struck something behind him. Slade bounced back up and turned in the direction from which the boulder had been cast. An unearthly cackle came from somewhere over there.

"Filmore! No!" Billy cried. Slade spun around in time to see Billy clutch the headless corpse of Filmore. The boulder that grazed Slade had decapitated Filmore, who was standing behind him.

Someone else — it sounded like Ty — yelled in the distance. It was answered with an unearthly howl. In all his years, Slade had never heard such a noise. He was a hunter. There were times in his life when he'd practically lived in the wilderness, but this confounded him.

The earth jerked violently from the concussion of the blast in the cave, causing them to fall onto their asses. Smoke poured from the mouth of the cave. They rose to their feet, shaken by the sudden blast. But the momentary calm was chased away by hoarse, mocking laughter.

Slade checked to see who was left. Billy dusted himself off. Nearby he saw Michael and Walt. Filmore and Julius lay dead. That meant two of his boys were missing.

"Ty! Nick!" he shouted. "Where the hell are

you?" Slade shouted out their names again but was met with silence.

Slade circled back to the two boys lying on the ground. He shrieked, pulling his revolver from its holster. Tears rushed down his cheeks. Someone was going to pay. The lantern he'd snatched from the cave lay on its side nearby. When he picked it up, something on the ground caught his attention. Slade knelt to examine it, resting his pistol against his knee. He moved the lantern around an odd footprint. It was fresh, pressed deep into the top layer of loose dirt, more profound than the two sets of footprints near it, presumably belonging to Nick and Ty.

"What the hell?" Slade's voice trailed off. He lightly brushed the dirt around the three-toed print. Slade's head followed the direction the three sets of footprints traveled, scanning the darkness but seeing nothing.

Bewildered, Michael asked, "What kinda animal leaves a print like that, Slade?"

"That ain't no bear, is it?" Walt asked. "I ain't ever seen no three-toed bears."

"That ain't no bear, ya half-wit," snapped Michael. "That's gotta be some kinda cat."

"Cat?" Billy shot back angrily. The tears that streaked down his face had mixed with dirt, giving his skin a fierce, painted look. "Tell me what cat has three toes."

"I dunno," Michael said, not appreciating Billy's tone. "I dunno. A three-toed mountain cat?"

"Quiet," Slade ordered.

"What?" Billy ignored Slade. "Ain't no such thing, ya ignorant galoot."

"Oh, so now you's an expert in cats, are ya?"

"Quiet," Slade repeated.

"It don't take no expert to know cats ain't got three toes!"

"If I were to cut two o' yours off right now, I'd bet you'd be skipping threes in the dirt just like that damned cat."

"I'd like to see you try."

A scream pierced the night air, and they all fell silent. It was not a cat or a bear or whatever creature had howled earlier. This scream was human.

"Sounded like…" Slade said.

"Nick," Walt whispered.

"The sheriff," Michael said. They all turned to regard him. "Has to be."

Slade rolled his eyes and continued to listen.

Michael thumped his chest as if he'd just won a medal. Billy and Walt eyed Michael the way someone might look at a two-headed goat.

"You's kiddin', right? The sheriff?" Billy said with a trace of exasperation. But Michael waved Billy off. It only infuriated Billy more. "Why would the sheriff be out there? He arrestin' the trees, rocks, or your damn three-toed cat? How in the high heavens is the sheriff goin' to say to himself, 'Gosh, I ought to head out miles and miles into the middle of nowhere 'cause I jus' knows I got someone there I needs to arrest for a reason I don't quite know yet.'"

"He's smart," Michael argued.

"The sheriff. Out here. In the middle of no-where. In the dark of night. All. By. His. Lonesome," Billy said, with eyes narrowed. "That is about the dumbest thing I ever heard in my life. Why would anyone, including the sheriff, go out into the middle of nowhere, in the middle of the night, with no help?"

Michael hadn't considered this, but his answer came out more like a question. "He's brave?"

"You's an idiot!" Billy shouted.

Michael had enough and squared up to Billy. "How 'bout I knock some teeth from them flappin' gums of yours?"

Billy shoved Michael.

"Dammit! I said quiet!" Slade admonished.

Before the men had a chance to tear into each other, something massive flew past the trio... and it took Walt with it. Protruding from Walt's mid-section was five feet of dead tree, about as thick as a man's fist. Another five feet stuck out his back. Slade fell to his knees, his face inches from the boy's face. Walt tried to speak, but blood spurted from his mouth. His eyes stopped seeing, and his body went limp. Slade gently closed the boy's eyes. Tears dripped into the dirt.

Slade rose to his feet, his eyes fixed on the log. It had to weigh at least a hundred pounds. Maybe two hundred pounds. Who could throw such a heavy, unwieldy object with such deadly force? It was impossible. Incomprehensible. Beyond belief. Walt had been nearly cleaved in half by the log.

A revelation hit Slade as cold as a slap in the face. No man — not even Earl's boys — could have lifted this and thrown it with such deadly accuracy. Slade pointed his revolver into the distance and cocked back the hammer. He spun in a circle with the gun pointed, inducing Michael and Billy to duck.

Michael gasped. "What the hell did this, Slade? Ain't no man could've done this. No cat or bear, neither."

Lowering his weapon, Slade stepped up and backhanded Michael across the face. Michael cowered at the twin points of fury directed at him. "Damn it, boy, I said stay quiet! Don't go and make me repeat myself again, y'hear?" Slade said through clenched teeth. Those same fiery eyes turned to Billy. "That goes double for you, boy."

Those enraged eyes returned to Michael, who felt blood leak from his nose but did not dare wipe it. Almost inaudibly, but losing none of the rage, Slade said, "Get up. Get your weapons."

Billy held out a hand. Michael took it and pulled him up. Both men walked to the spot where they'd dropped their weapons. As they bent down to pick them up, they heard the ground crunch from behind. There was no time to react — something bowled all of them over. They shot to their feet, but it was gone. In its wake was that sinister hoarse laughter.

They shot back up to their feet. Slade plucked his revolver and pointed it into the distance. His head swiveled back and forth, simultaneously checking the ground and watching for the thing. He stopped when he saw three-toed hoofprints. The boys looked at each other in disbelief.

"Well, look at these two scaredy-cats," Nick teased.

Nick casually walked toward the three of them. Ty followed two steps behind him.

Billy screamed, "What the hell is wrong with you!"

Nick and Ty stopped short when they spotted Walt.

Nick cried, "What happened?" He glanced up at Slade. "Slade?" was all Nick could muster.

Slade shot a furious stare at Nick and Ty. "Where you fellas been?"

Nick answered, "We came looking for the bodies, like you told us to. When we got out here, we saw something pulling one of Earl's boys into them trees over there," he said, pointing. "We chased after it, figuring it was animal. We shot at it, but it moved like a deer with a blood tick on its rear. We gave chase and shot it."

"We heard you scream," Slade said.

"Well, yeah, look at me." Nick was bloodied and bruised, and his clothes were tattered. "That heavy sack of shit got tossed like a damn doll. Slammed right into me. That big boy hurt like hell. After I catched my breath, I yelled."

"Did you see who done it?"

"Um," Nick said shamefully, "no, not really. It was dark in the trees. Took us a while to get our bearings just to find our way back. Damn near got lost."

"So you didn't see what took the body? And you didn't see what threw the body? And you didn't see what you was chasin'?"

"No, Pa," Nick said, "we didn't. Sorry."

Ty's voice cracked. "Where's Filmore and Julius?"

Slade shook his head. "By the cave. Go see for yourself."

Slade handed Ty the lantern. Ty and Nick walked toward the mouth of the cave.

"Oh Lord. Julius!" Nick gasped.

Ty stood next to the headless body. "Oh gosh. This is…" He retched.

Slade, Billy, and Michael gave them their space. It was unreal. This could not be happening. Billy wiped his eyes. He turned so no one could see him tear up.

"Slade," Billy said, his voice low. "Where's Walt?"

"Over yonder," Slade pointed. He froze.

Walt's body and the log that had impaled him were gone. All that remained was the blood-soaked ground. Slade snatched the lantern from Ty. He searched the ground, then crouched low and pawed around a small patch of earth.

"What'd ya find?" Nick asked.

The men craned over an area Slade studied with his lantern. It was the same weird three-toed print.

"What is that?" Ty asked. "Some kind of bear?"

Michael, Billy, and Slade all stared incredulously at Ty. They were in no mood to do this again.

Michael answered, "Ain't no bear. Ain't no cat. Ain't no man."

"Hey, Pa," Nick said. "I ain't seen nothing like that. What do you think it is?"

Slade stared down at the tracks a moment longer before answering. "Probably the same thing that threw Earl's boy at you. The same thing that killed Filmore, Julius, and Walt."

"Which is?" Nick pressed.

"Anyone know what happened to Earl's other son?" Billy asked.

Slade didn't answer either of them. He rubbed his chin ruefully, using the back of the hand holding his revolver. They were being picked off, one by one. He considered the terrain around them. The cavern was far too hazardous for refuge. Smoke continued to drift lazily from the lip of the cave. They could build fires and wait it out until sunrise to be able to see. But three of his boys had been killed by impossibly heavy objects that were thrown as if they were mere matchsticks. So who — or what — had thrown them? Slade's mind was stuck on the word *what*. He murmured Michael's words: "It ain't no bear. It ain't no cat. And it ain't no human." Michael was right. So what the hell was it? Turner might be a welcome sight right about now. Sure, it might be weird, but he had to admit he liked the idea of having a few more capable men around. If they survived, Slade and his boys would have to return to inter the dead. He needed time to get his mind wrapped around every-thing. The questions outnumbered the answers. He'd lost three of his own. There would be a time to grieve. But now they needed to focus on survival.

"Back to the ranch," Slade said. He twisted a key on the lantern to lower the flame, then blew it out. He placed the lantern on the ground and started walking toward the trail.

Nick watched in disbelief. "Shouldn't we get some lanterns? We need light."

"Leave 'em."

"But, Pa." Slade kept walking. Nick jogged to catch up. Michael and Billy followed. "Pa?"

Slade stopped and turned to Nick.

"Yeah, I heard ya, all right. I says leave 'em, Nick. Ain't no reason to bring 'em and be all lit up for the world to see. We can't be seen around these parts by nobody. Not now. Not ever. We got to stay invisible."

"What about Julius, Walt, and Filmore?"

"Son." Slade stopped and placed a powerful hand on Nick's shoulder. Nick thought he felt his father's hand tremble. "Enough already. We'll come back to give them a proper burial. I give my word. But if we stay now, we all die." Slade patted Nick's shoulder, gave it a squeeze, then marched down the trail again.

Nick saw something remarkably close to fear behind his father's eyes. He had never witnessed this in Slade before, and it chilled him to the very core. Slade was determined to leave and do so in a big hurry. The others had to trot to keep up with Slade's long strides.

Billions of twinkling stars and a glorious moon painted the night sky.

And then there were flies. There seemed to be one buzzing for every star in the sky. Slade, who seemed oblivious to the pests, maintained a brisk pace. When they reached the clearing, Slade stopped as if someone had nailed his boots to the ground. The others gathered on either side of him, horrified.

"What the hell?" Slade said, mortified.

Every horse, save for one out in the open field, was decapitated, and their bellies were slit wide open. Organs littered the ground, and the strong mineral scent of blood and the putridness of perforated intestines perfumed the air. The insects swarmed in delight.

Michael whined, "What the hell done this to 'em, Slade?"

The pitch in Michael's voice, at times, was as uncomfortable as having an icicle rammed up your ass on the coldest day of winter. Slade shifted an icy gaze to Michael. Then he was off again, strolling right by the dead horses as if they didn't exist. The others hesitated, wondering what to do next.

"Let's go, dammit!" Slade growled. "Everyone, move!"

"What about the horses?" Michael whined as they chased after Slade.

"We walk. Stay together. Remain vigilant," Slade thundered. "And, Michael, shut your piehole."

They returned to the main trail a few minutes later and turned right, walking west toward Cheyenne and their ranch. A horse trotted across the field, keeping pace with them, angling closer to the trail as they hot-footed it. Slade watched for a moment to be sure it was not a threat. He counted the dead horses; this one must belong to someone else, or was wild. Seeing the unorthodox movement of the horse made Slade chary. He slowed his pace. Maybe it was injured. Whatever the case, he saw no reason to rein it in. He needed to be able to hide at a moment's notice, and he had no need or patience for a broken animal. It would surely slow them down and add unnecessary risk to their current situation.

The horse stopped to feed. Then it trotted past them in that odd gait across the field, and stopped to feed once more. All the while, it moved closer to the trail. The men found themselves watching the animal. It was close enough to the trail that, even under the moonlight, they could see the horse lowering its head... and they could see that it was not feeding on grass.

Slade picked up the pace, and the men followed suit. Slade began to pull his revolver out. He considered firing a round in the air to shoo away the pesky animal. The animal was stealing the attention of his men when they should be concentrating on whatever killed Julius, Filmore, and Walt, and keeping an eye on the trail for travelers and highwaymen. Firing his revolver would surely attract the type of attention he wanted to avoid. He snorted and holstered the weapon.

The behavior was odd for a horse, but Slade was beginning to have second thoughts about putting it down. The right thing to do would be to put the animal out of its misery, especially if it was injured and could not care for itself. He asked one of his boys for something that would do the job. One of the men handed him a loaded shotgun. What choice did he have? This was a broken, suffering animal, not anything that represented an immediate threat. He had a particular fondness for horses, given all the work they did. He walked in a straight line toward the animal's right flank, intending to fire a shot into its heart. If he got close enough, it would require only a single shot. Two at most.

After Slade covered half the distance, the horse raised its head. Slade pointed the weapon in case the animal charged, but lowered it once he got a glimpse — a real glimpse — at the creature before him. The eyes glowed gold, and the horse let out an unnatural whinny, oddly similar to the mocking laughter they'd heard back at the cave.

The creature looked directly at Slade; Slade looked directly at it. Nothing happened. The demon was not banished back to Hell, because it was not in its demonic form. It strained mightily — painfully — as its power depleted with greater rapidity. It reared up on its hind legs in agony. Then, as if it had been branded on its rump, it squealed. Slade took several steps back, raising the barrel of the rifle. He never got a shot off. The creature ran away with a speed as unnatural as its whinny. Slade stood as slack-jawed as his boys, unnerved by what they'd just witnessed. The horse ran on its two hind legs — its legs moved like an ostrich's — and with the speed of a cheetah. Maybe faster. Slade had heard tales about such animals, but he'd never seen one up close and personal.

Slade rushed back to the trail, shoving the shotgun at one of his boys, and marched on in silence, his head on a swivel.

Michael cried out, "How the hell can that thing run like that? Horses can't run on two legs."

"You can't kill what's already dead!" Billy added.

Slade wanted to shut them up, but they were right. And they were afraid. Hell, he was afraid.

"What do you mean, Billy?" Nick asked.

"I'll tell you what he means," Michael interrupted. "That there was a ghost."

Billy often questioned Michael's quirky logic, but this time he wondered if his brother was right. It had spooked him to his very core.

Michael's whine carried a deeper, grimmer timbre. "Yeah. When I was young, my mama tol' me that ghosts that float are saying their goodbyes for the last time. And those that don't float are evil spirits, sent to terrorize people who done bad things."

Ty, who was unusually silent, chimed in. "You sayin' that was an evil spirit?"

"Think about it," Michael answered. "We done some bad things. We killed people. A lot of people. Men who won't see their wives or their sons and daughters no more. We stole and we killed. Something took notice. We are being judged."

"That's a bunch of bull!" Nick cried, not able to take any more.

"Oh really? Then tell me — tell us all — what you just saw out there. Tell me I'm wrong," Michael said shortly.

"Well, hell, I dunno," Nick said, "but..." The others stared back at Nick, which gave him pause. "I just dunno," he said, his voice trailing off.

No one argued with Michael. Not even Slade. The surrounding fields and tree lines were deathly silent. Their footsteps and heavy breathing made the only sounds as they trooped past another open field, followed by a rocky outcrop and a grouping of pines.

After several minutes, Slade broke the silence.

"You may be right, Michael," Slade said. "Judgment Day has arrived, and we all have our crosses to bear."

The remainder of the long, arduous route along the rutted, rocky trail was accomplished in silence — without flying trees, thrown boulders, or ghost ostrich-horses. Their legs were tired from the relentless pace set by Slade, but no one complained, not even Michael.

They turned north along a narrow side trail a little more than a mile east of Cheyenne. They hadn't made it a hundred feet when Slade threw his hand up in a motion to halt them. He squatted and studied the ground. He took a few crouched steps, then turned his attention to the trees on the east side of the narrow trail. The men leaned in, curious to see what had captured Slade's attention. In the packed dirt were three-toed footprints, easy to locate thanks to the bright moon overhead. The gait of the prints suggested it had walked calmly toward them before running off into the trees. How did it know they would take this trail? The ghost theory was sounding more plausible. Slade followed the path of the three-toed prints to the eastern side of the trail into the trees. He assumed the thing was nearby. Close enough to be watching them right now.

Another thought struck Slade, one that sent an icy chill down his spine. He was piecing it all together: the oddity of the footprints; the accuracy and force of the boulders that killed Walt and Filmore; the tree that crushed Julius to death and was taken away with them standing near; and the ghost horse-ostrich with the glowing gold eyes. First, he knew they were being hunted. That was obvious. He figured they were at a significant disadvantage, because this thing could see in the dark. Second was the thought that gave him the shivers — the creature that hunted them was the horse-ostrich. He did not believe that was its true identity. How could a horse throw a boulder or a tree? How could an ostrich do those things? And how could anything run faster than the wind? He was darn confident none of that was possible. Nothing on earth could do that. He believed, instead, they were dealing with something not of this earth. Ghost or otherwise.

A twig snapped from somewhere up the trail. Five heads jerked up at once with weapons drawn and pointed. Patiently, they waited. The moonlit trail appeared to be clear. An uncomfortable minute passed. Then two. Still, they waited. Somewhere in the grouping of trees on the western side of the trail, the creature screeched. Trees shook. Then they heard the unmistakable snapping and felling of trees. They had no time to react. Several animals — raccoons, possums, squirrels, deer, and a brown bear with two cubs — scuttled around, between, and past them. None of the wild animals gave the five humans a second glance. They only sought the safe refuge of the trees on the eastern side of the trail and beyond, safely away from the unearthly creature. A twelve-point buck and a group of does emerged from the western tree line, leaped passed them, and disappeared into the trees on the east side of the trail. Eagles, owls, and other avian animals took to the air, all flying in an easterly direction, squawking their displeasure at being forcibly dispersed.

The emigration of animals left the forest unnaturally silent. Even the wind seemed to hide.

Still, they waited.

Five minutes passed.

Ten.

Slade was about to order them to continue when movement caught his attention from above.

"Look out!" he yelled. Slade stumbled and fell on his backside.

Michael and Nick sprinted up the trail when a full-sized, uprooted tree landed along its length where they'd stood seconds before. Ty and Billy helped Slade up.

Slade dusted himself off, trying to comprehend what earthly creature could have pulled that off. The word *otherworldly* repeated in his mind.

"What the hell can do that? What can throw a tree like that?" Michael whined.

Slade had no desire to stick around any longer. "Run," he growled through clenched teeth. Michael, Billy, and Slade raced around the tree. Slade yelled, "Get to the ranch!" The ranch was a quarter mile down the winding trail. Its entry was constructed of thick wood posts and a carved wooden arch with a buffalo skull centered overhead. Wood fencing surrounded the property to corral the livestock.

Down the trail, the demon stood next to the tree. It watched and laughed its terrifying, maniacal laughter.

They ran fleet-footed under the archway and up an arcing dirt trail. A series of structures stood on the left: a horse stable, barracks for the boys, a pair of outhouses, and a simple ranch house. About twenty paces from the house, next to a glacial boulder, stood an extra-wide tool shed with double doors. Beyond that was a massive barn, three times the height of the house. Beyond the barn was an open field with a few dozen cattle. They ran past the stable, past the house, past the boulder. They fled into the shed. The doors slammed closed, and they barred it with a beam of wood. Someone fired up a lantern, and all five men sagged heavily against the walls, working to catch their breath.

Legs tired and achy, Slade stumbled toward the back of the shed. He was breathing too hard to speak. He slapped Ty along the way, beckoning him to follow. Finding another well-used lantern atop a small workbench, Slade lit it and handed it to Ty before reaching for a hidden lever slotted between the workbench and the wall. There was a click, and the workbench swung open on well-oiled hinges. The warm yellow glow from the pair of lanterns revealed a stairway leading underground. The way down was wide enough for two men shoulder to shoulder. They reached the bottom of the stairs and lit another lantern, which hung on an iron nail secured in one of the many thick wood supports seen down the long tunnel. Like the barn, the tunnel was well constructed. Slade had seen to it years ago. Braces and support beams kept the hard, rocky ground surrounding it from caving in.

They lit the lanterns hanging along the length of the tunnel until they reached an alcove, where they lit a trio of lanterns. On the opposite end of the spacious area were tunnels used for additional storage.

In the alcove were dozens of barrels, crates, and an assortment of goods, all protectively covered. In all, there were forty-four barrels. Each barrel had two words branded into its side, BLACK POWDER. The word MUNITIONS was branded into the crates.

Slade examined the packed alcove and the storage tunnels before walking the remaining length of the shaft with the lantern he'd carried from the shed. After a quick inspection of his inventory, he scouted the passages to ensure no unwanted visitors were down here, finishing at the end of the tunnel opposite the shed. Slade hung his lantern on a nail and worked a crank. Hay slid down the ramp as it lowered.

Slade had built the underground passages with two openings, something he felt strongly about, given the tragic mining stories that regularly circulated in Cheyenne. If it caved in at one end, there was another way out. In case he or one of his boys were stuck in the alcove or the storage tunnels after a cave-in and had no way out, he'd stowed pick-axes, lanterns, rope, and other digging necessities to give them a fighting chance. And if law ever found a way in at one end, then he and his boys had a chance to retreat out the other.

After the ramp touched down upon the twin floor beams, Slade walked up. The secret ramp led to a pen located in the rear corner of the barn. Slade swung the pen door open and walked around the barn, lighting lanterns that hung on support beams. The barn doors were secured from the inside. As Slade returned to the ramp, he heard more of that hair-raising laughter outside and quickened his pace.

While neither Slade nor his boys had any education in what this black powder was capable of doing, they knew it was used to manufacture ammunition. And it was explosive, valuable, and in high demand for the war efforts out east. Someone from the North or South was going to make him a very rich man. That was all he needed to know. Still, though, not until the cave did he comprehend or appreciate its destructive nature.

"What's the plan, Pa?" Nick asked from the bottom of the ramp. Billy, Ty, and Michael huddled behind Nick.

Slade scratched his chin. "We's gonna trap that thing in the barn and blow its ass to smithereens."

"But, Pa," Nick said with a modicum of concern, "the barn took us all those years to build, remember?"

"Yeah," Slade said, the skin of his face hot with anger. The words that followed dripped with venom. "I remember. I also remember Julius, Walt, and Filmore helping to build it. I ain't come to this decision lightly, son, but I ain't gonna stand by waitin' for this thing to kill any more o' my boys. Michael said this thing was a ghost, but I ain't never heard o' no ghost leavin' footprints. That means this thing is real. But I ain't thinkin' this thing is natural either. I think we's bein' judged. This hell-spawn was sent to hunt us down, kill us dead, and take our souls to Hell. We got the means to blow a hole in the moon, if we's wantin'. And I aim to put this thing in a coffin the size of this here barn and blow its evil ass back to Hell or wherever it came from." He asked the others, "You with me?" They nodded. Slade asked Nick, "What about you, son? You with me?"

"It killed my brothers." He reached out and firmly squeezed his father's shoulder. Slade reciprocated.

"Fine. We'll send that three-toed spawn of Satan screaming back to Hell with its tail on fire," Slade said, smiling. In the back of his mind, a thought came to him out of the blue: Were they really going to war against Lucifer or some hellspawn? He wondered if it was even possible to kill something from Hell. His thoughts shifted to all that black powder he had hidden away, and for the first time in what seemed like ages, the hint of a smile found his craggy face.

* * * * *

The five of them worked together rolling barrels from the alcove to the barn. Slade figured six barrels, just like he'd stashed in the cave, ought to do the job. They carefully positioned the barrels on their bellies in the center of the barn. Slade removed the bung from the top of each barrel. Black powder trickled to the floor. Slade tilted each barrel to hasten the process. Content with the accumulation, he shoveled the black powder against the first five barrels. Slade rolled the sixth barrel to the back corner next to the ramp. A black squiggly line trailed after him. After rolling it back, creating a second line, he piled black powder against the sixth barrel. Slade returned to the rear corner and pulled a wood handle at the base of the wall. A trap door fell open under a workbench. It led to a roomy crawl space under the barn, separate from the underground tunnel. From there, it was a few crouched steps to another trap door leading outside the barn, which was hidden by overgrown shrubbery. The crawl space had been a handy addition. Slade thought back to when they'd built the barn and added the crawl space. He intentionally chose not to join it to the tunnel because, as he told his boys, "If law should find us cowering in our little hidey-hole, so be it. Better that than law finding our tunnels." Slade placed his lantern on the floor next to the trap door.

The others were waiting next to the half dozen barrels when another chorus of maniacal laughter drew their attention. It was close.

"I'll be the bait. I need you fellas to close them doors and throw the bar on the outside if it manages to find its way in here. I want that thing trapped in here with me. Once trapped, I need ya to run like hell. Don't be nowhere near this place when it blows, y'hear? But if you find yourselves bein' chased into the barn, you go straight for the trap door. No stopping and no looking back. You keep running. Head into Cheyenne."

The men shifted uneasily, staring aimlessly at their boots or the walls. They knew what this plan meant, and none of them liked it one bit.

"For now, stay in pairs and stay alert. I don't need any of you gettin' maimed or killed. You got me?"

Michael and Billy clomped down the ramp to the tunnel and cranked the ramp back up. Nick and Ty unbarred the barn doors, swinging one door inward. Nick nodded to his father before disappearing into the darkness with Ty at his side.

With his boys safely away, Slade waited, his revolver in hand. Minutes passed by, each one an eternity.

Someone called out for Slade. It was not the visitor Slade was expecting, and his body tensed. Slade let out a long, low whistle, as if to ask a question. He was answered with three rapid two-whistle bursts.

Slade contemplated shooting the sheriff. He cocked the revolver and holstered it. He wondered how many others were in the sheriff's posse. The last thing Slade needed was trouble from the law. Best to play it cool, remain smart, and keep his options open. He retreated toward the rear of the barn, near to the trap door. The black powder was out in the open. He could do nothing to hide it. There would be no point in denying it. Slade lifted the lantern from the floor with his non-shooting hand. His shooting hand rested against the side of his revolver.

The faint crunch of footsteps was followed by the silhouette of the sheriff. Even with a few lanterns burning brightly, the barn was immersed in shadow. In the dark, it might look like tilled earth, but the black powder carried an unmistakable odor.

"Slade," the sheriff called out in a deep, gravelly voice. "That you? It's the sheriff."

Slade saw the man. There was no denying who it was, but something did not click. It was his voice.

Slade answered, "What brings you out here this time o' night? I damn near shot you, thinking you's an intruder."

The sheriff took a single step past the threshold. "I came for you, Slade," came the gravelly reply.

Had the sheriff developed a cold over the past few hours? Turner's voice was far rougher than usual. Yet this man was the toughest, most stubborn son of a bitch Slade had ever known. He'd probably crawl all the way from Cheyenne in the middle of a blizzard with high fever, pneumonia, broken ribs, and two busted legs to arrest Slade. If it came to that, Turner was no fool. He would have come with overwhelming numbers.

"You alone?" Slade wondered.

"Yes. It is only me. Why are you here, alone?"

Slade noticed Turner was unarmed.

Something bit at the back of Slade's brain. Why was he here? If he was grieving over the death of his son, he sure didn't sound like it. He showed no emotion. The sheriff was calm and collected. Something very powerful was hunting them, and now the sheriff had showed up. The timing was extraordinary.

"My property, last I checked, Tillman. Couldn't sleep, so I come out to do some work," Slade said. But the curiosity was more than he could bear, so he added, "What's your excuse?"

The sheriff repeated in that gravelly voice, "Your property." His head tilted and jerked, studying Slade and the barn.

Slade gawked at the sheriff. Why had he let the name slide? Sheriff Turner took serious offense to stupidity and tomfoolery. Men dumb enough to test the sheriff felt the wrath of Turner. But Slade had just called the man *Tillman*, and it drew no reaction whatsoever. Alarms in Slade's mind thundered like cathedral bells on the Sabbath.

Turner had a great talent for playing mind games. There was no one better to squeeze a confession from a man with something to hide, but the sheriff was not up to his usual antics. And he was alone. Slade tried again, going full-tilt buck wild.

Slade said, "My property. Signed and sealed by you, my best friend, Mr. Sheriff Tillman, at the courthouse some hunnerd years ago. It was a birthday present from the Pope himself."

The sheriff gurgled out raspy laughter while turning to go back outside. He pulled the barn door with him. Slade heard the exterior beam ram home, locking him in the barn. The laughter morphed into something sinister, something more maniacal.

"Hey!" Slade bellowed weakly. The stark realization was as powerful as the kick one deserves when standing behind a mule and pulling its tail. It was already too late — Slade had pulled the mule's tail, and now he would get kicked.

Slade knew now that this wasn't Sheriff Turner. He had already lost three boys tonight. He couldn't help feeling they were doomed, and there was not a damn thing he could do about it.

* * * * *

The sheriff-demon stepped away from the barn and looked directly at Nick. Glowing gold light glittered in its eyes. Nick chased after it, firing shot after shot at the creature until his weapon clicked empty. The creature laughed, racing off into the moonlit darkness with incredible speed, leaving Nick eating the dust it kicked up.

The demon sped across the field toward the archway. It transformed back into its hellish form when it received the first suggestive tug. It hissed in reply. It had not finished its deed and was not ready to return.

Something else garnered its attention, and it skidded to a stop in the soft dirt. The demon cocked its head, listening, waiting. Then it raced for the trees. A moment later, a rider atop a horse trotted up the path past the archway. The demon watched from the shadow of the trees as the rider moved toward the house. The demon followed, keeping its distance.

* * * * *

Nick reloaded his weapon and was about to return to the barn when he saw a horse casually trotting up the trail. Nick was not about to let this thing get away again. It was time to put an end to its miserable life. It was either going to be him or the creature. If he were going down, he would do so on his terms.

He ran toward it, hard and fast, weapon drawn. On the first shot, the horse reared up as it had in the field. Nick fired shot after shot. Its rider tumbled onto the ground. The horse-thing fell over, landing on the rider.

Eureka!

He slowed a few feet from the horse-creature, allowing his eyes a chance to adjust. There was no movement and no sound. He kept his revolver trained on the thing, even though he'd spent all his rounds. He inched closer still, assessing its legs. They were naturally angled like a horse's, not inverted as they'd witnessed in the field. His boot crunched in the rocky dirt, but the horse-thing did not stir. He tried to move with the same stealth his father employed, but he may as well have been stepping on every egg in a chicken coop. He jabbed the barrel into its flank. The creature remained dead-still. The door to the shed creaked opened, and Michael and Billy ran out. Ty ran up the path from the barn. They converged on the horse-thing, now lying on its side.

"What in tarnation is that?" Michael asked.

"It's the horse-ghost," Nick said with pride. "And I killed it! I killed it dead!"

Billy wanted a better look and hunched over the horse-ghost. He spotted a dainty, bloodied hand jutting out from beneath the creature. He covered his mouth in horror.

Michael asked, "What is it, Billy?"

Billy stumbled back a step. His face contorted in anguish as his mouth moved, though nothing came out.

"Billy?"

Twin tears ran down his cheeks, and his chin quivered. Michael circled the creature. He froze when he saw the bloody hand. "Oh, dear Lord," he gasped.

"What? Who?" Nick sputtered.

"Holy Christ in Heaven, Nick," Michael's voice came out in a shaky whisper. His eyes rose to meet his brother's gaze. "You just wasted Billy's gal from the saloon."

"I… I didn't mean," Nick stammered as Billy held her hand, blubbering. "I thought she was it — that thing." His eyes welled with tears. "Well! You all saw it! I ain't the only one who thought different."

Maniacal laughter pervaded the night. A shadow ripped across the field from beyond the house and crashed through one side of the shed. There was an angry screech of metal.

"That thing is going underground! We got to stop it!" Nick yelled. He was already sprinting toward the shed. "Ty, get Pa out of the barn."

Michael and Billy chased after Nick. Ty ran in the opposite direction, toward the barn.

The way into the shed was blocked by the secret wall, which had been ripped from its hinges.

They crawled in through the demon-made hole. They descended the stairs, ready to plug the demon full of lead.

* * * * *

"I failed you all." Slade wallowed in shame while sitting on one of the powder kegs. He held his revolver flat against the side of his head, finger on the trigger. He slapped the gun against his head. A tear trickled down his cheek. He did not even try to hide it.

"No, don't say that, Pa," Ty consoled.

"We're all gonna die because I was too slow, too stupid, and too scared to react," Slade said, his head drooping even lower. "That demon came to judge me, and I failed." His face sagged. "Damn it all."

Ty was speechless. He had hoped Slade would put everything right; he always did. Slade was not a cowardly man. Not by a long shot. Seeing him grieve, however, was unsettling. Ty stepped back, thinking it best to give Slade some space.

A tiny voice called from somewhere, capturing Ty's attention. Ty followed the sound to the rear corner of the barn. It came from the underground cellar. Just when he hunched over to listen more intently, a demon fist smashed through the trap-door, striking Ty in the chin. The powerful blow hit him square, and Ty fell unconscious onto the hay-covered trapdoor.

Slade spun around. Instead of helping his son,

he dropped his head once more, defeated.

* * * * *

"Quiet," Nick whispered sharply. "It's in here somewhere."

Billy reached for a hanging oil lantern. Nick admonished him, but Billy ignored Nick. When Nick reached to grab Billy, Billy dodged it, cut back around Michael, and ran deeper into the underground tunnel.

"Billy, you idiot! Get back here!" Nick scolded, as quietly as he could. Michael and Nick waited. When Billy screamed, the two men made haste into the dark tunnel with their revolvers drawn, using the light proffered by the hanging oil lamps. Halfway in, at the alcove, they found Billy lying on the ground, unconscious. The distinct odor of black powder hung heavily. Many of the barrels had been reduced to scrap. Black powder covered the ground. Nick motioned to Michael, and the two men continued down the chamber toward the secret entrance to the barn. Nick noticed that a few oil lanterns were unlit, and one was missing. They hesitated.

A silhouette stood next to the secret ramp. Nick stepped forward while Michael stepped back. Nick felt his heart hammer. Sweat trickled. His gun hand had never wavered like it did now. He inched forward until he was five beams away.

"You killed my brothers, you son of a bitch,

and now I'm gonna send you to hell."

The demon, which had its back to Nick, suddenly spun. With all the courage he could muster, with all the rage he could gather, Nick pointed his gun at the silhouette and pulled the trigger. The unloaded weapon clicked. It was empty. Nick had faced the demon, and the minion burst into a great ball of smoke.

The demon, with no direct killings, would be lauded in Hell. Not because of the deaths it caused without violating the covenant. It had come to test Slade, and it had one last parting gift, meaning the Test of Mettle had not yet concluded. The goal of demons this powerful was to win, to collect souls.

Its departure sent a powerful shockwave down the shaft. Nick was knocked backward several steps, but he maintained his balance. The damned thing up and disappeared on him. In that split second, Nick felt elation, which was slowly replaced by the woe of a fatal realization. The silhouetted creature disappeared, but it held up something, right up to the ceiling, something that scarcely made its outline visible in the dark tunnel, something that he should have observed. For a brief moment, the missing oil lamp, burning brightly, remained suspended in the air. Then it crashed to the hard ground. Nick watched in dread as the glass lamp shattered upon the layer of black powder covering the floor.

A mile away, Cheyenne shook from the explosion. Windows rattled all around town. A giant ball of yellow and orange flame mushroomed into the sky. The sheriff released his grasp on a drunkard he was working over. The drunkard crumpled to the ground when the sheriff let go of him and turned his attention toward the fireball crawling toward the moon. When the fireball faded, he growled a single word.

"Slade."

13 - AN 11:34 CHRISTMAS

December 24, 1953: Oslo, Norway

Twin cathedral bells reverberated against the delicate confines of his skull. Rolf forced one eyelid open. Next to his bed, an alarm clock danced on a beaten end table standing on four uneven legs. He raised himself a few centimeters, but his head screeched like a locomotive locking its brakes. He pulled the pillow over his head and willed the infernal clock to cease its ringing. As the clock danced toward the table's edge, Rolf watched from under the pillow with one eye half open. Would it make the jump off the high cliff? He watched with wicked fascination. A moment later, the ringing brought something else: heavy footsteps from elsewhere in his flat. The thumping grew louder and more urgent until a pair of creamy naked thighs stopped before the table, and a hand slammed down hard on the clock, putting an end to its cacophonous dance.

"It would be most kind of you to make an effort to turn the bloody thing off yourself. I know it's your place, but I live here too. You know I worked last night, so a little courtesy is expected."

The pale legs abruptly turned, and her footsteps thundered away. His head pounded in unison with their cadence. Rolf closed his eyes, praying for the relentless drumming in his head to cease. He drifted off until that same irritated voice chastened him.

"I really am not coming back there to pull your arse out of bed. Good day, Rolf."

Rolf opened his bloodshot eyes. The room was entirely too bright. The clock, perched at the cliff's edge, mocked him. It was alive and ticking. It would live another day.

Preferring to avoid her wrath, Rolf sat up and swung his gaunt legs over the edge of his bed. He removed the crud from the corners of his eyes and rubbed at his face and head. His right side throbbed with an unusual ache. He twisted his torso right then left, and his spine snapped and popped in response. He leaned forward to pluck the packet of cigarettes and matches from the end table. Rolf eyed the clock and gave it a simple nudge. The merry clock fell to the floor, and its relentless ticking ceased.

The enemy has been felled. Victory!

Something bumped his right buttock and rested there. Rolf ignored it and lit the end of a cigarette. He took a long drag and shook the matchstick to extinguish the flame. On the floor next to the toppled clock was an ashtray overflowing with cigarette butts and burnt matchsticks. He dropped the matchstick onto the pile and glanced at the bothersome clock. It no longer ticked. The thick glass cover had two cracks spanning the face, and the minute and hour hands abutted the side with the Roman numeral III. Drat! That portended a visit to the clockmaker.

He glared at the clock once more, then tossed the small box of matchsticks and the cigarette pack onto the end table. He savored the first pull for several seconds before exhaling a long plume of smoke, a protocol to commence his morning ritual. With the cigarette dangling from his lips, he rolled his neck in moon-shaped arcs and was awarded a pair of pops. He took another deep drag and exhaled once more.

Glancing at the object that had bumped him on his rear, he lifted the vodka bottle and gave it a jiggle, hoping to extract a few drops. He turned the bottle over, disappointed. Rolf placed it neatly at the end of an array of empty bottles that lined the floor like dominoes. He snorted at the idea of how many times he awoke sore next to his glass bed partners.

Dressed in nothing more than dull white underwear, he stood with the cigarette dangling from his mouth. Ash broke off, falling to the floor, while he stretched to another chorus of pops and snaps.

A cold front had passed through the city the night before and refrigerated his flat. Tiny dots rose from his skin all over his body. The cold ramped up the urgency to urinate a thousand-fold. Rolf up-graded his usual morning amble to the bathroom across the hall to a full trot. He flipped on the light switch, swung the door closed, dropped his underwear to the floor, and closed his eyes, bracing his hand against the wall. Everything absorbed the morning chill. The air. The wall. Even the floor's tile made him wiggle his toes. With the second morn-ing ritual completed, he flicked the cigarette stub into the bowl and flushed. *God, does everything have to be so loud?* He moved to the sink and turned the hot water dial. Glacial water dispensed hard and fast. Rolf splashed the frigid water onto his face. He pulled an aspirin bottle from a nearby shelf, tossed a few pills in his mouth, chewed them up, and took a swig from the tap as the water warmed.

Rolf straightened to gaze in the mirror. Water dripped from his chin, and the bitter taste of aspirin filled his mouth.

There she was.

His facial muscles slackened, and his head-ache melted away. She moved up behind him and placed a neatly manicured hand on his shoulder and rested her chin atop his other shoulder. Her lips stretched into a beautiful smile. Her straight brown hair, dangling at her shoulders, had a boyish yet chic charm that enhanced her European features. Her freckled cheekbones supplemented her sculpted face. And then there were her eyes, his favorite trait. Her eyes. Brimming with vitality and painted a deep oceanic hue. He could swim in them for days. Rolf returned her smile, but a pair of short arms grabbing his leg stole his attention.

Hi Daddy!

Rolf looked down.

No one was there. The little girl was gone. He returned his gaze to the mirror. Steam rose around a forlorn face. The woman with the dazzling smile and the dreamy eyes was no longer there.

The loneliness stained his insides as black ink does an inkwell. His mind went wild. He refused to believe he was going mad. They were here. Both of them stood right here, next to him. He saw them with his own two eyes. He felt their touch. He refused to believe this was the work of his imagination. He could feel the impressions on his shoulder and leg. No! He was not going mad. He looked for them, or a hint of them, from one end of the bathroom to the sink. Next to the bathtub sat a washtub and washboard. A bucket of clothespins and a bundled circle of line rested atop a small wooden stool. He strained his ears, pleading them to listen, to hear them, to sense them. All he heard was the rush of water from the sink.

He staggered back to the mirror, gripping the sides of the sink for balance. This torment punched into his abdomen like storm-driven waves. He involuntarily gagged. Bile threatened expulsion. His breathing came out in short and ragged bursts. He splashed shaky handfuls of hot water onto his face.

Again, they had left him.

Rolf broke down, sobbing into the rush of

flowing water. The shattered remains of his life swirled down the drain. He reluctantly gathered himself to regard the pitiful creature in the mirror. He hated what he saw. His hand swiped angrily at the condensation clinging to the mirror. Staring at him was a man with flush, bloodshot eyes that clashed with his light blue irises. The man in the mirror ran his fingers over sallow skin covered with gruff whiskers. He had not shaved in a few days and would face the wrath of his boss should he press his luck more. He lathered up a washcloth using a bar of soap he plucked from a dish on the bathtub. After he gave himself a standing bath and soaped the whiskers on his face, he pulled out a straight razor. He eased the blade up his neck and rinsed the razor clean under the hot water. He began to work the other side of his neck, but the shiny metal of the straight razor reflected an arc of soft yellow bathroom light onto his neck. He stared, bewildered at first, his hand unmoving. There was no conscious thought about consequences or the afterlife or any rational or irrational speculation. His hand steadied and swiped. Rolf felt the whisper of the blade along his neck as he would a breeze on a cool spring day. Blood dribbled down to his shoulder. As he watched the man in the mirror bleed, a surge of shame replaced the emptiness. The cut along his neck was superficial. He lined the razor up with the cut, but, this time, his hand trembled. Doubt festered in his mind. Determined, he gave his hand a good shake and returned the blade to the wound along his neck. The hand shook more fiercely now. His chin quivered, and his chest heaved. He firmed up his grasp on the razor until his fingers went white. The miserable sod stared helplessly at him.

After bathing in front of the sink, he inspected the bandage on his neck, touching it gingerly to ensure it adhered to the side of his neck. With a towel wrapped around his waist, he returned to his bedroom across the dry, creaky floorboards, his toes absorbing the cold with every step. The flat was dark and quiet, just the way he liked it, save for a steady snore coming from the bedroom down the hall. He reached his bedroom and closed the door so as not to disturb her. He pulled off his towel and flipped it onto his bed. Sunlight penetrated the room from behind the drawn window shade, permitting him to see — to his extreme delight — two stacks of neatly folded clothes on a desk. She must have set them there when she turned off the alarm clock or while he was in the bathroom.

"Bless her heart," he whispered. His lips, somehow, managed a feeble smile.

There was something special about the woman with whom he shared his flat. He'd met her while walking home one winter evening two years ago. It was a familiar route with familiar women. He took the time to greet each of them when he walked along this stretch. Whenever possible, he provided them with food, clothing, and medicine. Of the people in Norway who had lost their way, these seemed the most forgotten souls. Rolf showed them that at least one person cared. In return, he was often greeted with a barrage of hugs and kisses from the grateful women even when he had nothing to offer.

Except for her.

She was new and waited on the fringes of the women who circled Rolf. She watched the amount of loving attention lathered upon this man. There was something different about him. He held out an enormous tote bag for them, and they twittered in delight. Perhaps he was wealthy. After several more hugs and kisses, they wished him well and left her alone with him. She was dumbfounded. Why did they fail to secure his services? Where they failed, she would succeed. She stepped forward, rubbing her bare arms. She asked the man if he would like some company. Even if she did not display it, he could tell she was chilled to the bone, and her frame, even with only a meager shawl covering it, lacked sustenance. He asked about her needs, like food, clothing, or a place to stay. She answered him honestly. He asked her when she had taken to the streets. She said it wasn't long ago. Her eyes betrayed the type of guilt that erodes with experience and time. She opened up to Rolf about a great many things, not fully understanding why she allowed herself to be exposed. She recalled how the other women admired him. They knew him, trusted him. He carried himself as a well-mannered individual who dressed better than the regulars.

The woman was unable to stifle the shivers.

He offered to take her to a nearby café for all the food and drink she could stomach in return for her company and some friendly chat. She agreed. They conversed until the café owner shooed them out so he could close up for the night.

Feeling comfortable with his decision, Rolf offered the woman a place to stay for the night. He wished to resume their conversation at his flat — nothing more than talk. He was quite adamant about this and agreed to pay for her time. An odd request from a client, but it was close to Christmas, and this time of year had a funny way with people, especially in these postwar times. There was something unique about Rolf. He exuded a strong paternal charm, which might explain why all the girls hugged and kissed him, remained polite and respectful in his presence, and did not offer themselves.

Winter was a detriment for women of the night. There were far fewer paying customers out and about and even fewer willing to pay. Most of the women dressed down during the winter to attract more paying customers. You had to take what you could when the occasion arose, so she was told. If you were fortunate, you found yourself in a warm place, even if the gentleman caller was not as pleasant.

She accepted Rolf's offer, and they strolled to his flat.

That night, he learned she had been staying at a shelter she described as having the humanity of a polar bear and all the warmth of a polar bear's home. Though she befriended others at the shelter, it was difficult to trust anyone outright. In the short time she had prostituted, she witnessed ugly things: beatings, abuse, disease, even death. Rolf seemed genuinely interested in her story and delved deeper. The man asked her about her youth. She told him she grew up with parents who prided themselves on education. Her mother was a teacher, her father a professor. She had intended to follow in their footsteps, until the Nazis invaded her town. Her parents were captured and transported to a detention center. Amid the chaos, she escaped. A few others managed to free themselves, and they ran for weeks, hungry and homeless. She was dirty, and her clothes were tattered. It did not hinder men from wanting to have sex with her. At first, she was appalled, but her hunger and thirst were too much to bear, and she found herself selling her body to survive. She scraped by, having enough to put a little food in her stomach, be reasonably clothed, and maintain some humane level of hygiene. When the war ended, and the Germans left Norway, she trekked home. She hoped to find her parents and people she knew. Instead, she discovered her town had been destroyed. Her house — the home she'd known all her life — had been burned to the ground, like so many others. She never saw her parents again. With no money, no family, and no friends, she slogged to Oslo.

Lonely, hungry, and penniless, she befriended a woman who showed her another side of Oslo, a place she could live with others sharing the same plight. It wasn't savory work, but it was all that was available in the late forties. And she was forced to do whatever necessary to survive.

They stayed up until the sky changed colors. Rolf asked her if she would like to room with him, offering the spare bedroom in his flat. He had only a few simple rules. First, she was not to bring her work here. No friends. No clientele. *I want to make this point particularly clear*, he told her. *I understand your desire to earn a living. In these times, I respect that decision, though I don't agree with it. I am not your father, and therefore I am not judging you. Do your business elsewhere. Are we clear?*

She repressed the urge to laugh and dance. She resisted ripping her clothes off and taking this kind man right there, for his simple act of kindness. She answered with a whimpering nod. The jubilation that enveloped her made her incapable of speech. She shook hands with Rolf. Happy tears curved around the cheek of a jubilant smile. At that moment, she felt she was the luckiest girl in the world, like a fairytale princess, and pulled him into the tightest hug she'd ever bestowed on anyone, including her own father.

The flat had hot water, plumbing, and electricity. They had a small stove, a pantry, and simple cabinetry, but no refrigerator. In the bathroom, there was a washtub with a washboard next to a bathtub. A bucket of clothespins and clothesline sat neatly atop a small wooden stool.

Instead of rent, he asked her to keep his flat clean and launder his clothes. Most importantly, he wanted someone to converse with on occasion, as they'd done at the café two years ago. Rolf had stayed true to his word, and she to hers.

She confessed he had saved her life by allowing her to room with him. She was a survivor, sure, but to someone in her line of work, the odds of something terrible happening were not in her favor.

Rolf responded, "I guess we were both lucky, because it was my life that was spared that night." Though she pressed to know why, Rolf refused to expound.

The row of flats along the street Rolf resided on was palatial, though this was not necessarily a wealthy section of the city. While new buildings had been constructed following the war, many more were left in disrepair after the Germans were ousted from Norway in May of 1945. Parts of Norway lay in ruins. The zones under German control had, for the most part, been well maintained. But war was war, and the Second World War left scars throughout Europe.

Oslo had been overtaken in 1940, and its citizens had to live under the blanket of tyranny. The Germans did everything to force coexistence with the Norwegians. Freedom was lost to death's shadow wherever Nazis took occupancy. The Norwegians were predominately a people with blond hair and blue eyes, a compelling fit for the leaders of the self-proclaimed master race.

The Norwegians distanced themselves at every opportunity from anyone who resembled or spoke German. The Germans grew increasingly frustrated over these perpetual acts of defiance by the Norwegians. If a Norwegian refused to be seated next to a German soldier, the Nazis called it an act of betrayal. The Germans outlawed standing on buses and decreed its occupants sit next to their German compatriots before choosing open seating.

After the Germans abandoned Norway, the rebuilding started. So did the rehabilitation. Like so many Europeans, much had been taken from the Norwegians during the war. Loved ones were separated when fleeing, during imprisonment, or, unavoidably, by death.

Rolf found postwar employment with a newly created division in Oslo called the Department of Human Services. It was not just a job but a way of life for Rolf. He loved his work and did not need prodding to go out of his way to help people. It came naturally to him, which made him beloved by his colleagues and the community. Rolf had an aptitude for charm, as women in and outside of his workplace could attest. His flatmate would agree.

He lifted a folded shirt to his face and inhaled, taking in its fresh, clean smell before slipping it on and buttoning it up. He stopped short of the door at a picture hanging on the wall. It was the last remaining picture — a framed black-and-white photograph — of his family. A handsome man wearing a white shirt and black suit stood behind a woman wearing a colorful fancy dress, though it appeared as contrasting tones of gray. A little girl, wearing a white dress, wrapped her arms around her daddy's leg. Though none of them smiled for the photograph, Rolf remembered how happy they were to be together that day. He stifled a sob when he pressed the picture against his cheek. He kissed his wife and his daughter before returning it to its proper place.

Rolf snatched his long wool winter coat, slung over a chair, and he left the flat.

* * * * *

"Merry Christmas, Rolf," a familiar deep-pitched voice said.

"Uh, yeah, Merry Christmas," Rolf mumbled without looking up. He pretended to be focused on paperwork when he was actually hiding his face. Some things carried far greater pain than a vodka-induced headache.

Rolf's boss was stern but fair. The two got along well at work as well as on a personal level. In fact, he was as close to a friend as Rolf had ever had, even inviting Rolf over for family and holiday dinners. He had a terrific sense of humor and was as warm and charming a human being as Rolf had ever met. As pleasant as the man was, he unfurled a pretentious side from time to time. In Rolf's opinion, he took manners to another level. He was the type who waited for someone to say *please* or *thank you* or return a *hello* or *good morning*. He would linger with a look of exasperation upon his face until the demand was met. It came as no surprise that the man detested being ignored even more.

A throat cleared, and the ghostly images from this morning evaporated. Rolf practically leaped from his chair.

"Sorry, Mr. Jorgesson. Good morning, sir."

His boss spotted the bandage on Rolf's neck. An oval brown-red area stained the bandage.

"Good God, man! What happened to your neck?"

"Shaving accident," Rolf said flatly.

"Shaving accident? What did you use, an axe?" He guffawed. "May I make a suggestion? Use a razor instead, or visit a barber next time. I can't have my people looking like minced meat. Understood?"

"Yes, sir."

"So, do you know what today is?"

"Yes, sir. Christmas Eve."

"That is correct." The boss let his words hang in the air for a few seconds before turning his head toward the direction of his office. "Kari, sometime before Rolf has to shave again!"

A cheerful woman dressed in a brown and green outfit danced through the doorway, humming a Christmas melody along the way.

Rolf stared at his boss, wondering what she was about. Jorgesson shook his head and responded, "Elves," expecting that to explain everything. In her arms swayed a large garment box. She set the box on the tabletop in front of Rolf.

"Merry Christmas, Rolf!" Kari sang.

He responded flatly, "Merry Christmas."

She looked at him expectantly, bursting with unrequited energy, wringing her hands together, then rapidly clapping them. Rolf stared at her, then at the large white box, half expecting something to spring out of it. She was now hopping up and down while eagerly clapping her hands. His boss looked on, enjoying the moment.

"What's this?" Rolf finally asked.

Kari stopped clapping and bouncing. A look of confusion replaced the exuberance. She turned to Mr. Jorgesson to ask, "Did you tell him, sir?"

"I was getting to that," Jorgesson said. He rubbed at his chin pensively, believing it would suffuse the moment with dramatic flair. Kari began to happy-hop again. Rolf sighed.

Jorgesson surrendered the jovial route and said, "Look, Rolf, you are my most loyal employee. Hell, we're damn lucky to have had you here for so long. You were the very first employee of this office. Because we work for the city, our job is demanding. Our department is required to care for its citizens. They need us more than ever."

Rolf nodded slightly. Whenever the boss wanted something, he often started his declarations like this. Kari was ready to burst at the seams. Jorgesson looked from Rolf to Kari, then back to Rolf again. Deciding this needed a bit of delicacy, he said, "That will be all, Kari." With a final clap-clap-clap and an ear-to-ear smile, she tapped Rolf on the shoulder as she bounded off. She blew him a kiss before leaving the room, giggling.

Jorgesson leaned forward, his tone serious. "Let's cut to the chase. How long has it been? Nine years?"

Rolf cleared his throat. In a faint whisper, he replied, "Yes, sir." Rolf bit at his bottom lip and avoided direct eye contact.

Jorgesson could see that Rolf was in rough shape. He began to pace.

"Look, we're in the business of helping people. It's what we do. The department we work in is called the Department of Human Services for a reason. The war ended eight years ago, but for some, it feels like yesterday. That war will live with us until our final breath. It will always be a festering wound, like the one on the side of your scrawny neck. So this decision becomes quite simple." Jorgesson walked toward a door with an engraved plaque adhered to it, displaying his first and last name and his title, *Director*. He turned to Rolf. They were the only two people in the open office. "In addition to being my most valued employee, you are my most pained employee. This time of year, like every year, I see it in you. Your posture, your behavior, your inability to arrive on time. Although I admit you have dressed infinitely better the past few years."

Rolf normally volunteered his services on Christmas Eve so that everyone else could be at home with their families. The workday was usually peaceful and required little effort. This speech, today, was unusual. Normally Jorgesson arrived at work, spent a few hours chatting with Rolf, then demanded Rolf accompany him home because he refused to face his wife's cooking alone. After having ingested several dinners that led to unpleasant episodes of heartburn, Rolf knew Jorgesson was not joking.

"I know you are hurting. I don't know what I'd do if I lost my wife and children. Many people are hurting right now. They're cold and alone. Someone has to step up and give them a show of love and compassion. And one of the ways we can combat that pain is by being sympathetic. You of all people should know the pain they feel. I think you would make a fine sympathy man. You are already kind and compassionate. If you are my star employee, then I think it is time for you to shine."

Rolf shut his eyes, took a long healthy breath, and exhaled. He asked, "What do you need me to do, sir?"

"That's the spirit, ol' boy! Karl Svendenson, as you know, had a little accident. He learned that ice is slippery. We are in a tight spot because, every year, he dresses up as Kris Kringle for the children at the City Orphanage. We can't have Karl limping around with a cast on his leg, nor can we push him around in a wheelchair. Could you imagine what those poor kids would think if Santa Claus was hurt? Stubborn as Karl is, he tried pulling those baggy slacks over his casted leg even after the doc told him to rest."

The point did not drive home until Rolf saw

the look on his boss's face. Rolf glanced down to the white box, then back to his boss.

"You want *me* to be Kris Kringle this year?"

"Yes. That's the job."

Rolf scanned the room, wishing that some-one, anyone, would spring from their hiding place and nominate themselves for the task.

"Oh, Mr. Jorgesson. I appreciate the gesture, but I'm no Kris Kringle. Look at me."

It was true. Rolf was tall and lacked the sub-stantive belly to fill the suit. He was twig-skinny.

"Fake it," Mr. Jorgesson said.

"Fake it?" Rolf answered incredulously. "How does one fake being plump?"

"Try eating something, and be sure to eat a lot of it. Besides, you could use a little meat on your bones."

Jorgesson stepped into his office. "Oh, before I forget, be there at midnight tonight. Directions are in the box. Kari will be in her elf costume with a giant bag of goodies. All you have to do is show up, hand out a few toys, and be happy. The children will be waiting for you. It's tradition. So don't be late. And for God's sake, smile. Better yet, make a grand entrance. I don't know how. Just give those kids something to be excited about."

Jorgesson closed the office door, leaving Rolf alone with his thoughts and the garment box. He opened the box and inspected the suit at the end of his outstretched arms. Grand entrance in this? How was he supposed to make a grand entrance? He picked up the baggy slacks, shaking his head. Well, he thought, at midnight he would enter the orphanage, yell out Merry Christmas, and his pants would drop to his ankles. He grimaced at the imagery and concluded that he needed to visit a tailor for alterations, provided he could find one open on Christmas Eve.

* * * * *

At four in the afternoon the sky remained clear. The air was hungry with cold and bit at the tip of his nose. Rolf was glad to find a shop open and gladder still to leave the frigid city streets for a spell. A little bell mounted above the door jingled as Rolf entered the shop. The attendant sat on a chair at the front counter reading a newspaper and smoking a pipe. The air was thick with sweet smoke. Rolf found it to have a mellow, pleasant aroma, but some customers didn't share the same sentiment when retrieving clothing smelling smoky. Rolf explained what he needed and paid a hefty amount to the attendant in advance to have the alterations rushed.

Sixty minutes later, the bell above the door jingled, and Rolf was outside feeding his nose to the hungry afternoon air, with the tailored outfit stashed in the white garment box. His gut writhed like a pit of snakes, and he wanted nothing more than to head home to drink away his pain. Rolf scanned the unfamiliar street. Few people ventured out, but he noticed a small group leaving an establishment down the street from the tailor. His parched lips curled into a thin smile.

Rolf plopped into a chair at a table furthest from the entrance and from anyone else. He leaned the box against a table leg. A cheery, middle-aged waitress stepped up to take his order.

* * * * *

Having no car of his own, Rolf had to rely on his legs or public transportation. He stumbled off a bus, staggered a few blocks, boarded a second bus, then managed the remaining distance to his flat on vodka-soaked legs, all the while hefting the garment box. His stomach growled. He looked down at his belly. It was numb, but so was everything else. And that was all the satisfaction he needed.

He fetched the key from his pocket and dropped it. His fingers made several attempts to scoop it up, but the lack of coordination caused by the lack of sobriety combined to make him incapable of the simple task. He wobbled and lost control of the garment box. He cursed, attempting to get his fingers to cooperate, but he leaned forward too far, and gravity carried him over like a falling tree. Rolf smacked the thick wooden door with his cheek, sliding awkwardly to the floor. He needed a minute to shake off the grogginess before successfully retrieving the key.

Rolf stood up and tipped forward against the door. He attempted to work the key into the lock, but then the door opened. His neighbors, a married couple, holding gift-wrapped packages, shuffled out of the way as Rolf fell past them. The man rested his packages on the floor and helped Rolf to his feet. Realizing the condition Rolf was in, the man picked up the garment box and helped Rolf to his flat. Rolf thanked the man, whose name he couldn't remember. His right hand searched his pockets for his key before he realized the key was in his left hand. He searched for the garment box and found it leaning against the door jamb. Despite the numbing effects of the vodka, he rubbed his groggy head, and the key slipped out of his hand again. He cursed himself and retrieved the key, supporting his weight by bracing his free hand against the door. He carefully guided the key into the lock and unlocked the door. He entered the flat, closing the door behind him, then realized the garment box was outside his flat. He staggered out to retrieve it. He placed the box against the wall inside before locking the door.

His roommate stood nearby with her arms crossed. "Oh, look at you. Aren't you a sight?"

Ignoring her, he picked up the box; a red arm from the suit dangled out of it. He swayed past her and into the bathroom, slamming the door shut behind him. She continued to criticize him from the other side of the door. He cranked the cold water dial to mute her. Staring into the mirror, he found the other man staring back. His eyes were droopy, bloodshot, and empty. His face appeared drawn, and his hair needed combing. The man in the mirror abruptly burped in his face, and Rolf jerked his head back in disgust. After waving his hand to clear the air, he buried his face into the sink and hit it with handfuls of cold water. He glowered at the man in the mirror.

An image of his wife replaced his reflection and abruptly disappeared. He flinched. There was another flash — another mental image of his wife and her amazing smile — and then nothing. A flash — his little girl, excitement in her expressive features, running to him as he arrived home from work. The visual disappeared. He squeezed his eyes closed. *No, please*, he begged. Another flashback. In this one, he watched his little girl hug a freshly un-wrapped doll on Christmas. More images displayed in the mirror. Repressed memories blew past his al-cohol-induced haze, memories he buried long ago. He watched another memory appear. Gone. Then another. Gone. His wife lifted his hand, twirled, and wrapped herself in his arms. Gone. An air-raid siren in the middle of the night. Gone. His daughter sucked her thumb, her face tired and dirty, her hair a mess. Gone.

Then the memories he'd repressed below all others played in the mirror.

Mass confusion. Dark. Cold. Panicked people running in every direction. Screaming. Crying. Someone trips and gets trampled. In the chaos, he loses his wife and daughter. He calls for them. Their names are drowned out by the hysteria that has seized the town.

Gone.

Rolf peers into the night sky at the buzzing sound of warplanes.

Gone.

Explosions rip through the city. One after another. Buildings shred like bits of paper.

Gone.

He searches until he comes across a dirty, tattered doll on the ground. His daughter's doll. It gives him hope they're near. He sees them. They stand amid a small group of townspeople he recognizes. He calls out as loud as he can. His wife hears him. She searches until their eyes meet. His daughter holds her mother's hand. He fees relief — they are safe. His wife smiles, beckons him over. His daughter cries out for her daddy. A white flash. A deafening explosion. It all ends in a single scream — his scream — as he's thrown back by the blast wave.

He sobbed into handful after handful of cold water. "Please stop, please stop, please stop."

There was one more image. *The* image.

"No," he choked out. "Please. No."

The final flashback appeared in the mirror. He stares down at two burned, bloodied bodies lying in smoking rubble. Somehow, they've died together. Rolf stands over them; the doll slips from his fingers, landing where his daughter's leg should be.

Eyes wide, Rolf backed away from the sink, slamming hard against the bathroom wall.

"No, no, no, no, no," he said, and shook his head. Rolf slid down to the floor. He cried even after the tears ceased to trickle.

There was a soft tap upon the door.

"I'm okay," he said, wiping his face. "I'll be right out."

He stood up and looked into the sink, purposely avoiding eye contact with the man in the mirror. He wiped his nose with his arm. The water was still running. He splashed his face once more and turned the water off. He reached for a hand towel and dabbed his face dry.

A gentle knock accompanied a soft, concerned voice. "Rolf, come out, please."

He unlocked the door. Before he had a chance to open the door, she burst in. She evaluated him head to toe. Satisfied that he was in no immediate danger, she pulled him into a hug so tight it stole the wind from his lungs. He returned the hug but felt her body shake. It took a moment before Rolf realized she was weeping.

"Hey, what's wrong?" he asked her.

"I thought I lost you." Her words were almost incomprehensible, and her embrace tightened.

Not understanding, he responded, "Lost me?"

"I thought you were going to do it."

He was at a loss. "Do what? What do you mean?" The words hissed out. Rolf tried to wriggle himself free before she squeezed the life out of him. She relented, and her arms slackened. She backed away, but when their eyes met, she launched into him, reapplying her death grip. He squirmed, trying to catch his breath.

"Let go," he insisted.

Reluctantly, she released him. Her eyes sagged, and Rolf lifted her chin to look into her tear-stained eyes. There was an inconceivable amount of anguish tucked behind those pretty blue eyes. The man in the mirror bore a similar pain.

"I'm okay," he said. "Why are you crying?"

She gave his chest a hard shove, and her eyes flared with anger.

"You are the only friend — the only family — I have in the entire world. I..." She swallowed the lump in her throat. "I don't know what I'd do without you. You are my guardian angel."

She swiped at her nose and cheeks, using her shirt sleeves.

She continued, "I stopped working on the street last year. I got a job. A real, paying job working nights. I never said anything because I wasn't sure how to tell you. You got bad this year. You stopped talking to me. I was so proud of myself and still tried to make you happy. I wanted to tell you, but every time I tried, you were drunk, passed out, or needed to be left alone. You shut me out, you bastard. You shut me out."

He was unprepared for the sharp, sobering slap she gave him. He rubbed his cheek. When she raised her hand a second time, Rolf flinched, but she lowered her hand.

"Then I got up this morning after you left for work and found your razor in the sink. I saw bloody handprints on the mirror and the sink. There was blood everywhere: on the wall, on the floor, on your razor. I didn't know what to do. I know you've been having a hard time. It's been a rough year. But I never thought you would..." She gazed at the bandage on his neck. Gathering her will, she finished calmly, "Then you came home and locked yourself in the bathroom. You wouldn't answer me when I called out to you. I thought this was it. I thought you were going to leave me."

He was dumbfounded, because she was right. He considered what to do or say next. Taking his silence as another attempt to avoid confrontation, she cocked back her hand to slap him as hard as she could, but he stepped forward and hugged her. She punished his back and arms, screaming curses at him. He pulled her in more tightly, until she wrapped her weary arms around him.

"You bastard," she cried.

Rolf closed his eyes. She was right.

"I'm... I'm sorry."

She ripped herself from his embrace and shoved him back.

"You bastard," she said coolly. Her bedroom door slammed shut, and he stood alone once more.

Rolf's head drooped, and his eyes spied the garment box on the floor. The white beard hung out from one corner. He glanced down the gloomy hallway at her bedroom door before quietly gathering the bulky white box and retreating to his bedroom, closing the door gently behind him.

* * * * *

He sat on a wood chair, staring out a window with his face pressed against the pane of glass. If only he could will the pain away. Rolf closed his eyes.

Rolf jerked awake, his face pressed against the window. It was dark outside. He shot up and switched on the bedroom light, kicking over empty vodka bottles in the process. He pulled a dresser drawer open, fumbling around for his watch. He checked the time and sighed in relief.

He finished dressing, worked the kinks out of his beard, and gave his watch a cursory glance. 11:08. He needed to hurry, and reluctantly placed the watch in his dresser. He considered wearing it but questioned whether it would diminish the costume's authenticity.

The building the orphanage was housed in was once a hospital, but, after the war, moving trucks came, loaded up all of the hospital's medical gear, and relocated it further inland. The building was located on the fringe of the docks, five kilometers away. The buses surely would have ended their service for the day, meaning he had to leg it out; maybe even run, given the time.

Rolf pulled on his long wool coat as he left the scolding silence of the flat. He stared with guilty awe at the quaint table outside the kitchen. The table sported a pair of shiny dinner plates, silverware, a bottle of unopened red wine, and a fully cooked dinner, presumably cold by now. A small wrapped gift box rested on top of one of the dinner plates. A red bow with gold trim completed the decoration. Rolf picked it up as if it were an injured butterfly. He cupped it in his hands, unable to find the words. His stomach twisted in an uncomfortable knot. The sight of it all was just beautiful, and it smelled lovely. He had not smelled or seen much of anything when he'd arrived home earlier. His inebriated state had undoubtedly upset her. She must have spent the entire day shopping and preparing and cooking, even after what she witnessed in the bathroom. He picked up the little wrapped box with its pretty red bow. Tears formed around his eyes. He eased it down onto the plate.

Bless her heart, he thought, though his own heart agonized over what he had been putting her through. He could see it was just eating at her. Damn it! It wasn't supposed to be like this. The war took everything from him.

He thought back to when she had saved him two years ago. He held that same razor against his wrist. Dropping it, he grabbed a bag filled with warm clothes, blankets, and toiletries, and went for a long walk that night. If he'd lingered another second, his fate would have been the blade. It was on that night, during that walk, when he met her. They talked. She was sweet and smart and not typical of those he met working the street. He thought it over while they spoke in the café, and he took a chance, asking her to stay with him. If he hadn't, he surely would have ended his life that night or the next. She had given him a gift that night: time. She had taken away his loneliness, replacing it with hope. This year, though, the walls he built had begun to crumble. Hope gave in to despair. He glanced at the table once more, his gut roiling with guilt.

Rolf scribbled a note and left it on the table next to his plate. He *wanted* to talk to her. She needed to hear his story — the whole story, if she would allow him. He may have pushed her to the brink, knowing deep down he had hurt her. He had to make things right before it was too late.

Rolf moved briskly south along the sidewalk of the amply lit boulevard. Improved lighting had been an essential focus for the city leading up to the Winter Olympics, which were held a year ago. It aided Rolf greatly. With the streets empty of traffic, Rolf half jogged across an empty intersection, moving efficiently toward the docks. The long wool coat and the St. Nick holiday suit kept him warm. The tailor had done a magnificent job with the measurements on short notice. Neither constrained his movement whatsoever. It felt as if it were a second skin, oddly enough, even at an increased pace. He briskly passed many shops selling wares of all types, only to stop at a store that sold and repaired clocks and watches. The store was closed, and the sales floor was dark. The window displayed new and refurbished clocks and watches. He needed to have his clock repaired or replaced. The streetlight reflected off the glass window of the storefront, making it impossible to see any of the timepieces, so Rolf cupped his hands around his eyes and leaned against the glass. He spotted a decorative table clock nearby displaying the current time.

11:34.

He was only halfway there and needed to hurry. His legs were tiring, his chest burned from the cold, and he yearned for a cigarette. He reached an alleyway and pulled a cigarette from his pack and a matchbox from his pocket. He stroked the match, but it blew out before it reached the end of the cigarette. The bay winds usually picked up nearer the waterfront warehouses and docks. He slipped into a darkened alley, using the buildings to shield himself from the confounding wind.

Heavy breathing made it a challenge to keep the cigarette dangling from his mouth while he lit the second matchstick. A sharp metallic *clang* somewhere down the alley caused Rolf to startle, and he dropped the lit match. The streetlights did not penetrate the alley. A half-moon floated in a starry sky. Like the streetlights, the moon and stars were useless here. His skin prickled as he heard the sound of heavy, raspy breathing. Whatever it was, it sounded big and scary. His mind toggled through a list of threatening four-legged animals. Maybe the animal was feral and hungry. Maybe it was rabid. The screech of metal made his hair stand straight. It generated several sparks.

Rolf took a step back.

Then another.

His free hand tried to reclaim the cigarette from his mouth, his eyes never moving from the depths of the alley in front of him.

He took a clumsy third step backward and bumped into a stack of empty crates. The crates threatened to topple over. He tried to secure them and lost his cigarette in the process. There was another metallic scraping sound, nearer this time, and the clatter it created echoed in the narrow alley. Rolf rushed out of the alley and down the boulevard. The last time he'd found himself running was during the war, and he did not care to trigger any more flashbacks to unsettle him further.

Rolf reached a railroad crossing, marking the end of the city and the beginning of the warehouse district. The city lights were now at his back. The air smelled of sea and left a briny taste in his mouth. To his left, strings of barren coal cars sat idle in the rail yard along lengthy stretches of track. He crossed several sets of tracks, checking both ways as he went. The rail yards were busy all hours of the day. He had no idea what to expect on Christmas Eve, but he felt he should remain alert. Halfway across, he stopped. Echoing from somewhere in the rail yard came the sound of screeching metal. It was far more savage than what he'd heard in the alley. Swallowing hard, he finished crossing the railroad tracks and ran until he reached the outer warehouses. From here, he was only two or three blocks from the orphanage. The lighting here was sparse, a mere fraction of the central city avenues.

He leaned back against the metal wall of a warehouse. With his chest ready to explode, Rolf worked to control his breathing. He kept watch of the road from either direction. Thinking back to the alley, that could not possibly have been an animal. Someone was surely toying with him. Maybe this was some kind of mindless prank. It seemed like an awful thing to do to someone on the eve of Christmas.

The wind tended to be fiercer around the warehouses. Even donning many layers, Rolf felt the effects of the windchill. It probably did him no favors to lean against a cold metal wall.

Rolf wondered what time it was, then chastised himself for not wearing his watch. He could have simply taken it off and hid it away in a pocket. With a renewed sense of urgency and feeling a bit more secure, Rolf pushed off the wall. Whoever was fooling with him was gone now. He hoped he was not late. Mr. Jorgesson, friend or not, had zero tolerance for failure. Rolf started for the orphanage.

A window over his right shoulder shattered. Rolf threw an arm up to shield himself from the shower of sharp glass. He peered down at the glittering pieces. If the glass was on the *outside*, then whoever had chased after him was *inside* the warehouse. He recalled the metal screech as he'd crossed the tracks. Something must have broken into the warehouse. *Something*. Not someone, he was reasonably sure.

"What do you want?" Rolf demanded, his

voice resonating a bit higher than he wanted.

In response came a raspy laugh from inside the warehouse. The laughing heightened in intensity until it reached a maniacal pitch. A blunt object struck the inside wall of the warehouse where Rolf had leaned moments ago. The wall appeared disfigured. Whatever hit the metal wall left a protruding dent the size of a milk crate and a smile-shaped perforation under it. Needing no further encouragement, Rolf ran down the street.

The black boots Rolf wore grew heavier and clomped louder on the pavement with each step. Ahead on the right was the side street leading to the orphanage. On the corner was the burned husk of a former supply building. Next to the charred building was a razed dirt field followed by a three-story L-shaped building that once served as a hospital. An unilluminated white cross remained on its façade. The short street ended in a roundabout, which formerly served as an ambulatory entrance. No sidewalks lined the street. A few cars were parked along the front of the old hospital. Two of them belonged to the city police department. Rolf felt a surge of elation.

The side street remained dark despite the efforts of the half-moon. There were no functioning outdoor lights to help with visibility.

Rolf reached the first parked car. There was a pattering of footsteps and raspy breathing racing up from behind him. Whatever it was moved incredibly fast, far too fast for a human. He was too late to react. The impact to his lower back sent him tumbling head over heels into the dirt field along the cobbled road. The thick, cushioned layers he wore did little to absorb the impact of the assault. Rolf groaned at the first pulse of pain. His back took the brunt of the wicked blow. He pushed the discomfort aside, shoved himself up from the pavement, and slapped pebbles and dirt from his palms. Whatever had struck him was around here somewhere. He examined the open field, but couldn't make out anything. His gaze stopped where the cars closest to the hospital were parked. He thought he saw something. Craning his neck, he could not be entirely sure, but he thought he spotted a pair of glowing red eyes through a dirty set of car windows. He blinked several times, but the glowing red eyes were no longer there. This was not a *he* or a *she*. This was an *it*, and *it* was hunting him.

Rolf began to walk back toward the intersection. Slowly, carefully. His back throbbed. Every few steps he turned his head to watch the road behind him. He spotted movement, but it was still fuzzy. He was out of breath, easy prey. Why was it waiting? Was this some cat-and-mouse game?

Little did Rolf know that the demon felt a sharp slap after being sighted. It came very close to being jettisoned back to Hell. The human glimpsed its eyes but hadn't fulfilled the requirement, as agreed upon by Jesus and Lucifer, of facing his demon.

By the time Rolf reached the supply building

at the end of the block, the nightmarish pattering was coming hard and fast. He made a sudden turn past the double-doored entrance and into the building. The demon whizzed past, barely missing Rolf. The right door had been boarded up and nailed shut.

The two-story supply building had suffered a devastating fire. It was missing the floors and ceilings that separated each floor, and the roof was gone. Warped beams strayed out from the main framework like burned and twisted fingers. The sky was visible, the moon starting to peek over one of the walls. The aisles were extra wide to accommodate a forklift. Moonlight made navigation through the charred building precarious, and doubly so with the soot and debris covering the floor. The wind whistled through the building, causing the unstable structure to creak. Whatever had been stored here during the time of the fire remained in blackened pallets and crates.

Rolf ran over and through the debris, passing row after row, before ducking behind a crate on his right. He could see through some gaping holes in the container. The building's front doors exploded inward. Rolf tensed as the building's emptiness came to life. Soot, charred wood, and shadows all seemed to flicker. An unearthly growl appeared to unsettle the structure, and it began to creak.

The demon went to work. Objects were being pitched in all directions. Debris smashed into the crate Rolf used as a shield. He sucked in a breath, but with it came the dust and soot that filled the air, making him cough. Rolf's eyes went wide as he slapped his hands over his mouth. The frenzy of activity ceased. Several seconds passed. Rolf heard a snuffle. Debris clattered and shifted as the demon moved deeper into the supply building. It was getting closer. The clattering stopped. Nothing happened for several seconds. Rolf guessed it could not have been more than five meters away.

He inspected his surroundings and the structure in front of him. Rolf was pinned in a dead-end elbow. Behind him was the wall of the structure. He hid behind a three-meter-tall shelving unit packed with the charred remains of various-sized crates. Glimpsing a gap between the wall and an adjacent shelving unit, Rolf dashed into the gap. Raspy breathing chased him, heading down the main aisle parallel to Rolf.

The end of a fallen steel beam blocked the gap, but it created a ramp to the top of the shelving unit. Rolf ran up the beam to the top of the unit, U-turned, and ran back toward the front of the warehouse, jumping the narrow gaps between the shelving units. Following Rolf's noisy retreat, the demon reversed direction and chased Rolf rancorously over the shifting mounds of fallen debris littering the floor. The stressed unit Rolf stood upon creaked and groaned, giving him a reason to apply the brakes. Rolf waited until he heard raspy breathing below. The creature, sensing it had the upper hand in this Test of Mettle, launched into maniacal laughter.

Rolf desperately needed to know where the

creature was. He wanted to face the thing with his own eyes, not be cut down by some invisible enemy. He worked up the nerve to step up to the edge to peek down at his assailant. The structure jerked after a resounding crack. Rolf lost his balance and fell onto his back. The storage unit swayed as another support gave way. The brittle unit shuddered and tilted toward the central aisle, as the remaining braces failed. The unit lurched. Rolf had a split-second to grab the side that ran near the wall and pull himself over the edge just before the structure toppled over. The structure, charred crates, and ceiling and roofing debris fell over. The demon shrieked. The fallen debris crashed into the main supports of the storage unit across the aisle. It collapsed into the aisle, further burying the demon under an unimaginable amount of weight.

Rolf had squeezed his eyes shut, believing he would be crushed, impaled, or worse. When he realized he was alive, he climbed out of the remains of the smashed, fire-ravaged crate, grateful for having no injury more severe than having the wind knocked out of him from the three-meter fall. The crate he fell through cushioned his fall, saving his life, he figured. Having a long, thick wool coat over a plush Kris Kringle suit probably helped lessen the impact.

Soot drifted in the air, making it difficult to breathe. Rolf covered his mouth with the lapels of his wool coat. The wind hampered visibility by swirling the soot around.

There was only one way out.

Rolf climbed the pile of debris that littered the central aisle, stepping over jagged shards of wood and twisted metal. He turned left at one of the support beams that jutted out of the pile, but his long coat became ensnared. He flapped it, trying to get free. It held fast. He gave it a gentle tug, enough to prevent it from being damaged. It would not budge. He tried another firm shake. Nothing.

As he reached again to untangle his coat, the demon grabbed his arm from under the coat. The creature snarled, and the debris shuddered, causing a wooden joist to slide into the creature's arm. It howled and let go of Rolf's arm.

As Rolf retreated, the demon snatched the coat once more. Rolf wiggled himself free of the wool coat. He bounded from the debris pile, tripped, rolled across the blackened floor, and popped up to his feet. Rolf fled the crippled building, sprinting past the field and the police cars.

There was an unearthly growl followed by the steady crashing of debris as the determined demon was hell-bent on tearing, ripping, and thrashing its way through everything. The unstable building could take no more, and it collapsed onto the enraged demon, curtailing its howl.

Rolf whipped the orphanage door open. A third of the ceiling lights were lit, offering ample light for him to see a sign on a wall at the bottom of a stairway that read CITY ORPHANAGE. An arrow pointed up. Rolf ascended the stairs two at a time.

When he reached the top of the stairs, he heard the creature enter the hospital. It smashed through the doors, sending glass and debris skittering down the hall.

Rolf reached the second floor, and his boots thundered down the short hallway. The demon reached the stairwell and was closing fast.

As Rolf approached the crook in the L-shaped floor, he screamed as loud as his soot-covered lungs would allow, "Police! Police!"

Pattering echoed in the hall. There was nothing left to do. Rolf rounded to face his demon.

Hearing the desperate cry for help, two police officers, the orphanage staff, and dozens of children bounded from their places in the ward and hurried to the main hall. They stopped dead in their tracks as they witnessed a burst of opaque vapor at the end of the hall. They watched with curious intent, at first, as the cloud filled the hallway, then with awe as it dissipated. To their delight, there stood a figure clad in red and white with a long white beard, covered with soot from his head to his black boots. The sight they witnessed was as magical as a fairy tale.

"It's Kris Kringle!" one of the little boys shouted.

All of the kids raced to the bearded man in the holiday suit, bringing with them sincere smiles stretching from earlobe to earlobe. Behind them, also in awe, were the policemen and orphanage staff members. And behind them was Kari, the elf. Her hands covered her mouth, overwhelmed by the joy she felt at Rolf's grand entrance. She slipped behind a counter at an old nurses' station, picked up a great red sack, and made her way to Rolf, squeezing through the crowd of children cheering with vivacious enthusiasm.

"Wow! That was some entrance!" she exclaimed, bouncing up and down.

Rolf had been rendered mute. He stared down the hall behind him in disbelief. There was nothing there. He tried to describe what happened. All eyes were on him, watching him curiously.

The demon had returned to Hell when he faced it; Rolf faced his demon but never saw it. Clueless over what had transpired, Rolf was nonetheless the victor in his Test of Mettle. The demon returned to its domain, leaving behind nothing more than an innocuous vapor cloud.

Some of the children began to giggle at the way Kris Kringle stuttered. Rolf turned his attention toward them. The policemen. The orphanage director. The giggling children. They all watched and waited. The only thing he could manage was, "Ho, ho, ho?"

The children erupted into a gleeful cheer and surged forward. The orphanage director waded through them and gave Rolf a fervent handshake.

"Wow! That was one of the most beautiful things I have ever witnessed. I've never seen anything like it," she said, winking at him. "Thanks, Mr. Kringle."

"It's a Christmas miracle," one of the little girls

said. She stepped forward and grabbed Rolf's leg. His eyes slammed shut, his face contorted in a wince, hidden by his sooty beard.

This was not lost on the director, who placed a hand on his shoulder and asked, "Is everything okay?"

He eased his eyelids open, daring himself to look down. He was met with beautiful innocence. The eyes that looked up sparkled with the promise of life. More importantly, she did not disappear inside a flashback. There she was, eyes twinkling, giggling with joy. It melted his heart, and he took a mental photograph of the moment. The hand on his shoulder gave a gentle squeeze, and he turned to the director, who smiled at him with a mix of concern and amusement.

At once, he felt at ease. His muscles lost their tension. A torrent of genuine peace erased the horrors that had been trapped within him for the past decade; they dissipated like the demon cloud. A flow of soul-consuming warmth filled him now. A tear trickled down his cheek and into his beard.

"Kris?" said Kari, who was also watching with concern.

Kris Kringle smiled. "Ho! Ho! Ho! Merry Christmas to all the little boys and girls. I apologize. The journey here was incredible. I thought I was not going to make it. It's a wee bit cold outside, as you can imagine. I just needed a moment to thaw out." He looked at the little girl grabbing his leg. "You think it's cold on the ground outside? Try flying. The air up there is freezing."

"Wow!" one of the young boys exclaimed. "He can fly?"

One of the older boys answered, "Yeah, he has flying reindeer and a magical sleigh."

"That's right," Kris Kringle said. "But what is important is that I arrived here safe and sound." He looked down at the little smiling girl. "And there is no other place on earth I wish to be right now."

"Why are you covered in that black stuff?" asked the curious girl clutching his leg.

Rolf peered down.

"Because those crazy reindeer tried to park on the roof of that warehouse next door. Well, those silly reindeer gave us a rough landing. Instead of coming from the roof, I had to run across the field and up the stairs to get here in time for all you good little boys and girls."

The children cheered. The staff members and police officers stood outside the excited circle of boys and girls as Kari handed Kris Kringle presents from the sack, presents he, in turn, handed out to the excited children. The children proudly carried the packages wrapped in cheerful colors of gold, green, and red, each finished with a bright red felt bow. They showed each other their gifts before tearing into them. The police officers laughed, patted the jolly man on the shoulder, and shook hands with Kris Kringle and Kari the elf for a job well done.

With everyone distracted, the orphanage director stepped away and removed her glasses to wipe the tears from her eyes. After composing herself, she returned the glasses to their proper place. She blinked a few times and was rendered aphonic. Down the hallway in the direction of the stairs were two sets of gray footprints. One matched the boots worn by Kris Kringle. The second set, which appeared to be heading in the same direction, had three toes, and abruptly ended a short distance from where she stood.

ACT 3: A SECRET ORGANIZATION

14 - HOME

December 11, 2016: Samedan, Switzerland

T he pilot attempted to drum up a little small talk during the flight, but the passenger, an Englishman who introduced himself as the Executive, kept to himself, leaving the pilot to do all the talking. The pilot had introduced himself as Samuel and spoke with a thick European accent.

The Executive stared straight ahead, deep in thought, his hands relaxed on the armrests in the cockpit. He paid little attention to Samuel, but the pilot was relentless. He understood why Samuel had come highly recommended. The man would not stop talking, and his smile never diminished. The Executive understood the angle. Samuel intended to keep the minds of his passengers busy — have them tell him their stories, or make them listen to his stories, of which he had an infinite supply. Keeping them engaged made them forget things like turbulence and the proximity of the Swiss mountaintops.

The Executive needed no soothing words, for he had flown from one end of the world to the other multiple times. He had endured all sorts of conditions in all kinds of aircraft. Nothing about flying bothered him.

They cruised near jagged mountain peaks that felt close enough to graze your fingertips against if you stuck your arm out far enough. Mountains zipped by one after another, each one as magnificent as the last. The private jet bounced harshly before suddenly tilting to one side. Samuel stole a glance at the Executive, who, given his composure, might as well have been asleep the entire flight, and he laughed after finishing his story.

"Smashing fun, I'm sure." It was the first time the Executive spoke during the flight. "How much longer until we touch down?"

Samuel answered with another smile. "We have arrived."

Samuel flipped a switch on the dashboard and began to speak in another language. The radio crackled, and there was a reply in the same language. The pilot acknowledged, and the plane started its descent.

"We have begun our descent to Engadin Airport in Samedan, Switzerland, sir." The Executive said nothing, staring forward while furtively working his bottom jaw to help with the pressure in his ears. Samuel added, "There is some great skiing south of here. St. Moritz. Popular place. Good resort area." The Executive wanted to ask a question, but the pilot was already into a short story about a famous actress who took her little dog skiing and said her dog skied better than her second husband. Samuel didn't see what was hidden behind the eyes of the Executive at that moment. The Executive returned his attention to the airstrip in the distance, his hand squeezing the ornamental handle atop the cane resting between his legs until his fingers hurt.

* * * * *

The Executive took his time stepping down to the tarmac. A man and a woman waited alongside an SUV.

"Ah, Pyotr, Neisha, it is good to see you."

The Executive limped toward them, using the cane for support.

Neisha trotted up to him and gave the man a long, tight hug, resting her chin on his shoulder, hiding the tears that welled up.

The Executive returned the hug in earnest, whispering into her ear, "Everything is good now. I promise." Her grip tightened before she let go. The Executive gazed into her soft brown eyes, giving her shoulder a reassuring squeeze. "Truly, the worst is behind us. Now, we must move forward. We have much to do."

Pyotr lifted his hand, and the Executive gave it a good, firm shake.

"Welcome home, sir," Pyotr said. "We missed you."

The Executive responded, "Damn glad to see you, boy."

"You gave us a real scare there," Pyotr said.

The Executive nodded. "There were days — weeks even — when I didn't think I'd ever see this place again."

Pyotr recalled all too well. He'd been there when the Executive was shot, clamping down on his leg to stanch the bleeding. They had taken a team of men, which included a field operative, into a near massacre. The remains of field operative Chad Manning painted the interior of a third-story apartment. A sniper killed Harvey Mitchell, a citizen they attempted to rescue and owner of a critical piece of evidence they hoped might lead to a resolution of the cosmic puzzle they had worked so hard to piece together. Pyotr and the soldiers he commanded were trained professionals. Failure was never an option, not in this division. Not with a group of guys who took tours to Hell and back in places like Afghanistan and Iraq in the mid- to late 2000s. They'd all chewed the same sand together. Though they remained optimistic over the Executive's recovery, the weight of guilt left an implicit stigma on the team.

Shaking the memory of that day nearly one year ago, Pyotr opened the rear passenger door and tried his cheerful voice. "Well, come on, then. Hurry it up, old man. We have much to do."

The Executive regarded him for a moment, then his steely demeanor melted into a wry smile. "Let's," he said. After he climbed in, Pyotr closed the passenger door. His hand gripped the door handle for a moment. It felt like his insides had passed through a wood chipper.

* * * * *

They traveled on a smooth, winding highway through a mountainous panorama brimming
with snow-covered larches, inspiration for starving artists hungering for that magical moment that
could forever sate their creative imaginations. They
turned at a path visible only because of the twin
tire tracks in the snow. The vehicle stopped at an inconspicuous wood cabin. A bland metal warehouse
shaded by more of the conifer trees that painted the
landscape stood thirty meters away. The warehouse
stored snowmobiles and other privately owned utility vehicles. Neisha and Pyotr assisted the Executive
into a snowcat, a vehicle designed with articulating
tracks to travel on snow. They followed a track along
the shadowy base of a steep mountain until they
reached a benign five-way intersection. They veered
to the second-leftmost trail and followed the winding ruts until they reached a vale sparsely populated
by trees. In the distance stood several cabins. At first
glance, they presented as nothing more than a se-
cluded resort, one of those posh, ridiculously expen-
sive places hosting those with an absurd wealth.

Each cabin accommodated up to twenty
people. They drove past the cabins to a spacious
two-story wood structure whose façade gave the
impression that it was the main lodge. The back of
the lodge was built right up to the side of the moun-

tain. The powerful vehicle followed an exterior loop passing by the lodge, then circled to the front of the building. Pyotr and Neisha hopped out before assisting the Executive down from the vehicle. The Executive scanned the property, filling his lungs with the fresh, cold mountain air, taking it all in. He mentally checked off the last item from a year-old list of goals: go home.

His cane ticked up the concrete steps to the main entrance. Neisha and Pyotr followed after the limping man.

There was no shortage of trophy animal heads covering the walls. Lacquered wood furniture and side tables in the vast lobby, huddled near a small wood-burning fireplace mortared together by mountain stone, delivered a cozy atmosphere. A carpeted, crisscrossing staircase added to the elegance of the lobby.

Members of the organization gathered in the lobby to witness the return of the Executive. They offered their praise and well-wishes as he limped past them. In a show of strength, he climbed the stairs, with Neisha and Pyotr trailing. He reached the top, breathing hard. The lobby erupted in applause, and he expressed his thanks with a wave.

When they quieted, he addressed them from the balcony: "You are too kind. I'll keep this brief. This day has arrived, and I thank each one of you for staying the course, for staying disciplined, for not losing hope when you could have easily surrendered. Our conviction to the cause has given us proof we were right all along. Soon, I will share with you an important clue, one I have been searching for since long before this covert organization was established. We will meet soon. Let's all get back to business."

The Executive turned and walked away as the team extended another round of applause. His cane tapped down a long, dim hallway, at the end of which was a magnificent door. With all of its strange and intricate carvings, the door looked like it came from some faraway place like Narnia. The door handle was of braided steel, and onyx in color. The Executive pushed the door open with his cane. The door was several inches thick and held in place by a trio of heavy-duty iron hinges. The well-lubricated hinges allowed the massive door to open smoothly into a modern office. Following the trio was a woman carrying a small silver tray with a cappuccino and biscotti. She set it on an impressive mahogany desk.

"Ramone, how nice to see you again."

The slight woman was dressed in business attire: a white button-down shirt, black skirt, nude stockings, and black pumps. Light as a feather, she floated around the imposing desk and hugged the Executive hard enough to force the air from his lungs. Neisha and Pyotr enjoyed the moment while the Executive stared at them helplessly.

"Welcome back, sir," Ramone said, releasing the Executive.

Ramone was the lone secretary in his organization, and the woman was trusted unconditionally. She coiled like a viper when anyone — including him — crossed her. If she ordered breakfast delivery to his office at four in the afternoon, she did so with a sweet, flowery tone. A follow-up phone call at 4:02 inquiring about the status of the afternoon breakfast carried an inflection of serious business. She was never rude, but she was an expert admonisher of those who failed to get the job done. She had the Executive's back in a way no one else did.

After the hug, she did something she had never done before — she kissed him on the cheek. Then she retreated from the room, closing the massive door on her way out.

The Executive plopped into a tall leather chair behind his desk. Neisha and Pyotr tried — and failed — to stifle their sniggering. The Executive held his hands up in a show of asking what was so funny.

Neisha asked, "Do you and Ramone shop at the same store for lipstick?"

Pyotr had to turn away.

The Executive stared dumbfounded for a moment before it finally clicked. He leaned forward to stare into the mirrored surface of the serving tray and discovered a set of lavender lips imprinted on his cheek. Sighing, he wiped the lipstick from his cheek with a linen napkin.

After composing himself, Pyotr said, "Welcome home, sir."

He was home, as healthy as he could be, surrounded by people he knew and trusted. There was a camaraderie that extended beyond employment, beyond even cordial friendship. The three shared a kinship like family. Despite his usual steely exterior, the Executive allowed himself to enjoy the moment. He sipped his cappuccino. It was perfect, just as he remembered it. He let out a contented sigh, a small, satisfied smile creeping across his face.

"Yes, yes." Something weighed on his mind, and his steel-gray eyes met theirs, melting away the mirth. "To both of you. I would not be alive today if not for both of you. I spent hours preparing for this moment, trying to conjure the right words." He sat quietly for a moment before finishing. "Thank you, from the bottom of my heart." The two beamed at him. Before things grew entirely too sappy, he followed it up with, "Time to get back to work. We have a world to save."

Taking the cue, Neisha and Pyotr nodded and exited the office.

The Executive leaned back in his chair and sipped his cappuccino.

He was back.

15 - THE BOX

December 14, 2016: Samedan, Switzerland

T he Executive rested against his cane atop the stage as all fifty-two people under his employ entered the auditorium. The cavernous room, designed to seat over two hundred, had been carved out of the mountain adjacent to the main lodge. It remained a constant sixty-seven degrees year-round and required minor attention to control the humidity.

When everyone had assembled near the stage, the Executive began his presentation.

"It has been a rough year for us," he said. "Many of you were left in limbo. I imagine most of you pondered your future. Would our organization reach a premature conclusion? What would you do if it did? Where would you go from here? I would have been as stressed as you if our roles were reversed, and for that, I sincerely apologize. We lost no one during that time. I tip my hat to every single one of you for sticking it out.

"Over the past year, some of you took to questioning the agents in Philadelphia. You are all passionate, and I am sure your hearts were in the right place, though some chose to blame the fine men and women who stood at my side. This has created disharmony in the ranks. Giving the soldiers who stood beside me — who saved my life — another reason to assume unwarranted guilt. I take full responsibility for the past year. Every directive in Philadelphia was my call, and our agents followed the operation perfectly. Our agents are the reason we continue to function today. Their quick thinking in the line of fire is why I am still alive and why our operation stayed afloat in my absence."

The Executive allowed his words to sink in. Then he crossed the stage and eased himself onto a simple conference chair. Next to the chair was a small table with a bottle of water. He rested his cane on the floor next to the chair. He uncapped the water, took a long drink, and returned the bottle to the table.

"I died three times and was resuscitated each time. After being stabilized, I endured multiple surgeries on my leg. Amputation was mentioned more times than I care to recount, but I am alive, and with my leg intact."

They all stood and applauded. It carried on for many moments. The Executive obliged them, partly because there was a collective need to feel good.

After it quieted down, he continued. "The vast majority of you receive bits and pieces about what we work to achieve, what our endgame truly is. You have worked admirably under the guise of our objective, which is to save the world. For decades we have been piecing together the greatest puzzle. A puzzle from long before the birth of this organization, and long before any of us were born. We can thank a pair of archaeologists commissioned by my great-grandfather for bringing this great puzzle to our attention. They discovered the first puzzle piece in 1933. Since their discovery, we found little more to help us, until our mission in Philadelphia one year ago."

The lights in the auditorium dimmed. A curved white wall along the back of the stage illuminated. It shifted to a picture of a desert city surrounded by a stone wall. Within the walls were several buildings constructed of sand and stone.

"Here is the puzzle as we know it today," the Executive said. "We begin our journey here, in the city of Golgotha. It is widely believed to be where Jesus was crucified. I am here to tell you that the Son of God was real, and He died on a crucifix. Many have wondered why our organization is called 11:34. It is most unusual, until you realize that this was the exact time of Jesus's death."

There were a few murmurs from the audience. The Executive pressed on.

"There is a Christian prayer called the Apostles' Creed, which mentions that Jesus died, descended into Hell, and on the third day, He rose again. Christians call this event Easter Sunday."

Pictures depicting Hell floated by one after the

other until stopping on an ominous drawing of Lucifer.

"The most obvious question is: Why did Jesus go to Hell? He is the Son of God, after all. Wouldn't someone of His stature simply walk past the Pearly Gates, and into Heaven, where He would sit at the righthand side of the Lord? But Jesus did not do that. He went to Hell, spending three days there. What purpose did Jesus have important enough to spend three days in Hell for? Think about that for a moment."

There was a quiet hum of electronics overhead and onstage.

"I have the answer to that question."

This statement drew murmurs from the audience, and the picture on the wall changed to a canned JPEG image of a thick contract. The word CONTRACT in bold was centered at the top of the document.

"For millennia, scribes documented the existence of man. The Holy Bible includes stories of man receiving gifts from God and then finding ways to repay Him with disrespect. We have had the back of our hands slapped many times for our transgressions in the form of famine, plagues, insects, and floods. Oh, our freethinking monkey brains! Growing restless, God sent us a man purportedly born of a sexless act by a woman named Mary from Nazareth. It was the greatest gift of all. Jesus cured the afflicted, fed the starving, helped the weak. You've all heard the stories, but here is the one that matters most. We crucified Jesus. We killed off the greatest gift given to us. We snubbed our noses at God, and He was so pissed off, we came this close to being smitten from existence two thousand years ago."

The Executive took a sip of water. The slide changed to a cartoon image of the devil, its long tail ending in a spade.

"Ready for another piece of the puzzle? Lucifer saved us."

This revelation drew even more murmurs than before.

"Shocking, huh? I hate to admit it, but it's true. The devil himself came to our rescue. He had an idea, one that preempted our smiting with a meeting in Hell with Jesus. It seems Lucy had an idea for God to step aside and place the fate of man into the hands of Jesus. What irony! Who better to determine if we live or die than the very man we killed? It was not only clever but poetic. In those three days, Jesus and Lucifer hashed out the Contract, an agreement between Heaven and Hell. Instead of smiting us, they gave us yet another chance, but this time, the gift we received came with a big red bow and a huge fucking detonator."

The screen displayed old footage of an atomic bomb's blinding detonation. The audio taken from its blast had intentionally been turned up several decibels for effect. Clouds scattered away as the radioactive fireball mushroomed into the sky while its blast wave leveled a fake community of houses, automobiles, and dummies, incinerating everything in its wake.

"Next puzzle piece."

The screen displayed a black-and-white drawing of a medieval structure standing next to a river. Riders on horseback approached the structure.

"Sometime in the seventeenth century, a group of bishops rode along a path next to a river far from the Vatican, where they were traveling. They found something called the Repository. We know that the Repository is a high-ranking angel — an immortal — who can transform into any structure, anywhere, at any time. There are only three known sightings of the Repository in our history. This was the first known sighting.

"It was cold and raining. The bishops tethered their horses and went inside. Next slide." The next slide displayed the assumed layout of the Repository. "There is a great antechamber inside the Repository. At the rear of this room is a long, narrow hallway leading to a holy chamber — a library of sorts. Strange symbols cover the walls of the antechamber and the long hallway."

Several images of symbolic languages appeared one after the next, the last displaying hieroglyphs.

"I assume some of you recognize hieroglyphs. Well, we can add one more language to the list. It's Angelic, and one who looks upon the symbols hears the translation of the symbols in their mind — like telepathy in a sense, but the voice they hear is their own.

"The bishops strolled down the hallway toward the library. The symbols along the walls near the antechamber spoke a warning not to cross the Great Seal marking the entrance of the holy chamber, which houses and protects the very contract agreed upon by Jesus and Lucifer. The bishops heeded the warning, save for one senior bishop. Call it bravado, or ego, or whatever you want. While the others called the place a miracle and a gift from God, the senior bishop declared any structure containing magical tricks to be the work of the devil, and so he strutted down the hall, crossed the seal, and entered the holy chamber. The ground quaked when the Final Sin was committed."

The Executive took another drink of water.

"There were rows and rows of empty shelving units used to store scrolls in the holy chamber. In the center of the room, past the Great Seal, and between a pair of golden sconces, was a podium containing the Contract. When the senior bishop read that parchment, only then did he realize his catastrophic mistake. He ran from the Repository. Outside, the bishops huddled under trees in a vain attempt to remain dry. In the morning, when they awoke, the Repository had disappeared. Remember, the Repository is an angel that can appear anywhere, any place, and any time, and it decided it was time to move on."

He took another sip.

"The shelves within the antechamber began to fill from that day forward with written encounters of something called the Test of Mettle. It is documented in the Contract, and was repeated by the symbols in the great hall. For the next thousand years, humanity will be tested by Lucifer's minions. Each encounter begins at 11:34 at night, the time of Jesus's death. If the man being tested loses, then his soul is forfeited to the demon. If the man being tested wins, then he keeps his soul and can never be tested again. This is one of the ground rules agreed upon by Jesus and Lucifer.

"The Test of Mettle carries a more considerable significance than I currently understand. We know that it is a test within a test. We have a millennium — one thousand years — to end the Test of Mettle and fix what we broke.

"We have been reprimanded by God for our sinful nature, but humanity has never had to atone for our transgressions. We merely carried on. This time, however, it is different. We *need* to fix this, or we lose our very existence. If we fail, after a millennium Jesus hands the keys over to Lucifer. Lucifer will unleash his minions among us. We will be tortured for all eternity, wishing for death, begging for it, but never feeling its embrace."

A hand went up. The Executive pointed to a man as he took another sip. The man stood up.

"What do we need to do to end the Test of Mettle? And why not tell the world about it? Surely, we can fix this faster with millions at our side instead of, what, fifty of us?" He sat down.

The Executive placed the water bottle on the table. He used his cane to stand, then limped to the front of the stage to face the man in the second row.

"Both good questions. To answer the first, we have no worldly idea of how to end the Test of Mettle. To answer the second, and this goes to everyone present, you are not, under any circumstances, to speak of any of this to anyone outside our organization. I would hate to have to hunt you down and end your life, but that is the penalty for treason in this organization. You all knew that coming in. I will answer your question with a question." Staring directly at the man, he asked, "What do you think would happen if an asteroid or comet hurtled toward our planet? How would the public react?"

The man considered the question. "Panic?"

The Executive exclaimed, "Yes, there would be unrest on an epic scale." Then evenly, he said, "What would happen if an incurable plague spread across our planet? What would happen if the magnetic field failed, or if Earth's atmosphere collapsed? In hours — not days — chaos would ensue. The world would be lost to chaos. Panic would plant a fatal foothold across the Internet. Economies would crash. Social systems would fall. All forms of transportation and communication would fail. People would die by the billions from starvation, thirst, disease, and each other. The aftermath would set humanity back tens of thousands of years. It would become survival of the fittest. There would be no order and no civility. Humans might cause their very own extinction before the thousand years is up. Confirmed knowledge of the Apocalypse would be a planet killer."

The Executive drank the last of the water and set the empty bottle on the table.

"That said, we need to do our jobs, preserve order, and, above all, maintain secrecy. With six billion sets of eyes glued to instant forms of communication, we must also understand that our window to get this done is narrowing. When — not if — society learns the truth, if demons are captured on video, it could trigger a cataclysm. We may have days or months or years. On the bigger clock, we have six hundred years before Lucifer takes over. I don't think we have a snowball's chance in Hell of reaching that milestone if society implodes."

The man in the audience nodded. No further hands went up.

"As I said, we know the Repository was located on at least three occasions. The bishops found the Repository first in the 1600s. Exactly when, we do not know. I believe there is a strong probability the Vatican knows what the bishops learned. Keep in mind that the Church has a violent and bloody history." Several gory images depicting violent acts flashed onto the screen. "Something like this might be kept secret. Maybe they, like us, quietly search for answers, knowing the risks of blabbing it to the world. The Church has always had a greater obligation to humanity. Conversely, watching and waiting for humanity to fall to Lucifer is counterproductive to their laws and beliefs. Given the history of the Church, I implore you all to be on your guard at all times. Something about this does not sit well with me. As I have stated, this is the one thing that remains a dangerous unknown, and I cannot overstate the fact that the Church has a dark history."

The screen went black for a moment.

"Getting back to the Repository, the second sighting occurred in 1933. It was discovered by a pair of archaeologists under the employ of my great-grandfather. They sought power and glory, something I believe was a line in one of the Indiana Jones movies. This turned out to be an ironic twist to what they'd hoped would be their dearly sought-after concept of power and glory. They were unearthing clay pots at a small dig in Cairo, Egypt. By some random accident, they stumbled across the Repository buried in the sand along a relatively deserted road, but one they frequently traveled. It took on the shape of an upside-down pyramid. They entered the antechamber and found all the things I told you, with a couple of exceptions. This time, the symbols in the great hall included the story of the bishops. They found the Contract, exactly as I described. The one major difference this time was that the shelves carried scrolls. Hundreds, maybe thousands, of scrolls, each telling the story of a Test of Mettle. They read some of the scrolls. They left and returned the next day, only to find the Repository gone. They told the story of their adventure to my great-grand-father. He believed their every word, and he made them vow never to tell another soul about their discovery. Besides, who would believe them?"

The screen now showed a sad, worn-down building. Pyotr carried a box across the stage. A stage light shined down where they stood. He turned toward the audience, holding the box in front of him. Blood, from the assassination of Harvey Mitchell, stained the box.

"Pyotr holds the very box we retrieved from the mission that nearly ended my life and cost Harvey Mitchell his life last year," the Executive said. "We spent the past three days studying its contents." The picture on the screen changed. It displayed an image of the empty bloodstained box, next to several photographs and a journal. After a moment, it transitioned to showing each photograph. "Harvey's father was a journalist back in the seventies. He was a solid writer with an amateur eye for photographing the dramatic. He had been assigned to do an inner-city story in Philadelphia. He photographed several abandoned buildings, as you can see, run-down and ready for the wrecking ball." The screen displayed a single photograph, then transitioned to several more of the building from different vantage points. The building appeared as derelict as the ones in the background. This building, however, stood in the middle of a neglected field comprised of weeds, broken glass, and other detritus. There was no sidewalk leading to it. No electrical boxes or power lines connected it to the grid. It was as out of place as an ocean tanker in a cornfield. "It struck a chord, and the amateur photographer with an eye for the dramatic took twenty-two pictures. He took his time photographing the building; you can see the change of day from the subtle shift of the building's shadow. Take note that there is no door at the building's main entrance. It appears to be pitch-black inside."

Another series of photographs clicked onto the screen; they were completely black.

"These are all of the photographs he took inside the Repository. Not a single one of them developed, every one a mystery. After each photograph, Harvey's father documented when he took the picture and what was special about it. He inventoried what he witnessed and photographed, what he read, everything. Apparently, ink works in the Repository, because his journal was not affected while he jotted his experiences inside the structure. Film, on the other hand, did not fare as well.

"He wrote about the symbols that spoke in his head, the story of the bishops, and a possible solution to this great mystery. I assume he was so overwhelmed by his discovery that he neglected to take the time to note the solution itself. He read the Contract and a few scrolls, taking several photographs of them until he ran out of film."

The wall changed to one final photograph. It was of the same field, taken from the same position as his first photograph of the derelict building. Except, there was no building.

"The sun had set after he left. He returned the next day. There were no signs of the building, no evidence that a building had ever been there. The Repository, he knew from reading the symbols the day before, had moved on. He returned home to develop his film. He worked through the night and into the following morning. With most of the photographs going black, he feared he had chemical or light contamination. He cleaned his room, restocked his trays with the required chemicals, and made sure no light of any kind seeped in. He tried again, and all the pictures he'd snapped inside the Repository were black. He tested his camera, thinking the worst. He shot a few photographs in his apartment. As you can see on the screen, they had developed perfectly."

The lights in the auditorium turned on, dim at first, allowing eyes to adjust to the growing brightness.

"In conclusion, folks, we have a singular mission. We must find the Repository. It's a needle in a haystack, I realize, but the Repository holds the key. The journal in that box said the Repository told Mr. Mitchell there was a way to end the Test of Mettle. To save the world, we must find the Repository."

16 - TRAITOR

December 14, 2016: Samedan, Switzerland

An hour later, a small team huddled in the Executive's vast office. It included the field team from Philadelphia. Both members of surveillance joined them. The Executive sat in his chair behind his desk with his fingers steepled, allowing them time to settle down. He clicked a mouse button, and a magnetic bolt locked his office door. Another click. The office went dark. Another click and a presentation screen lowered. A final click and the screen displayed a high-resolution satellite image of the apartments lining the avenue where Harvey Mitchell had lived. On the right side of the street, circled in red, was Harvey's apartment building.

"The details of this meeting are not to leave this room," said the Executive. "I wanted to share something about our operation in Philadelphia. While I rehabilitated, something nagged at me until I formulated a theory.

"This is the apartment where the late Harvey

Mitchell resided."

Click. The image on the wall changed to another satellite image. Another building, one they recognized from the mission, was circled in red.

"The apartment you see here is where field operative Chad Manning took temporary residence."

Click. An official police report was displayed.

"The police found the body and classified Mr. Manning's death as a homicide. What I find interesting is the date of the report."

Typed in the date field was *20/12/2015*.

One of the soldiers spoke up. "That was the day of the operation."

"Yes," the Executive drawled. With an inquisitive tone, he asked, "Does anyone find it odd that the police were called the same day of the operation? No one from our organization called it in. I checked. So who made the call? It was not a neighbor or the apartment manager. The tip, as it turns out, was anonymously phoned in."

He paused for a moment before clicking to the next slide. It was a third satellite photograph. This one displayed a high overhead shot of the distance between the two apartment buildings. Both buildings were circled in red, and a short red line linked the two circles.

"I am guessing Mr. Manning had less than a day to locate a place to live, and he successfully found a flat only a few blocks away. The landlord, a Mr. Jerry Irving, required three months' rent up front. What was odd was the fact Mr. Irving was unaware Mr. Manning had taken residence in the apartment. He received no payment. If he had found the remains of Chad Manning, for insurance purposes he would have needed to file a claim. Therefore, it's highly unlikely he made the anonymous phone call. When I spoke with Mr. Irving, he admitted he had trouble placing tenants in the building. The building was empty and had remained unchecked for some time."

The Executive pushed his chair back, and, with the help of his cane, he stood up. Everyone turned to their attention to him.

"Because we were forced to move forward with the operation, we never had time to install and test body cameras," he said. "Alpha Team, once again, take me through what happened after you arrived at Mr. Manning's apartment building."

Jerome Tate, a burly black man with a barrel for a chest and massive biceps, stood. His posture was military-rigid. His deep voice nearly hid the Carolinian twang. "Sir," he said, "upon arriving on location, we headed down a short alley single-file. We arrived at the rear of the property and entered through a latched, but unlocked, metal gate. We went up three flights of stairs until we reached Agent Manning's apartment entrance. We entered three-two-seven-five on an electronic keypad as instructed. The door unlocked, enabling us ingress."

"Thank you, Mr. Tate." The big man sat down. "The landlord was unable to access the apartment with three-two-seven-five because he did not program it. I traded the number to him for the one he'd programmed into the keypad. That number was twenty-twenty. He is quite a fan of the Philadelphia Phillies, an American baseball team. The number twenty belonged to a Hall of Fame player by the name of Mike Schmidt. He admitted to me that he used twenty-twenty as the default keycode for all of his unrented flats."

The Executive tapped the spacebar on his keyboard. The slide changed, and an image of Chad Manning and his profile covered the wall.

"Someway, somehow, Mr. Manning found a way to reprogram the keypad, which is not entirely unusual for our field agents. We gather intelligence ahead of time to avoid as many difficulties as we can. We provided no such intel to Mr. Manning. Therefore, it was rather unusual that, in just a few hours, he conveniently located a flat and somehow managed to reprogram its security keypad.

"Mr. Tate, would you kindly read Agent Manning's birthdate?"

"March 2, 1975, sir."

"Thank you, Mr. Tate," the Executive said. "Does anyone see it yet?"

Jerome answered immediately, "It is the same as the access code: three-two-seven-five."

"All coincidence, I'm sure," said the Executive with little conviction. He clicked the spacebar. The slide changed. "Until this." It was one of the photographs of the crime scene taken by the police department. A body lay on its back. The body wore winter clothes: boots, coat, gloves. Its head was crushed to a pulp. Brain matter, blood, bone, and hair created a thick soupy puddle on the floor. Bloody boot prints could be seen going in every direction. The same boot prints were on a back wall in the photo. "Here is what I find interesting. We determined the size of the boots worn by the victim and those used by the alleged murderer. The victim had size eleven-wide. Manning wore size thirteen-regular."

Another click and, in red digital font, the final slide displayed *11:34*, the name of the organization.

"We followed up with the morgue and learned that the body was cremated the same day. The director, a middle-aged woman named Lydia Benita, fifty-two, was unable to provide a reasonable explanation of who authorized the cremation that day. Ms. Benita began her directorship seven months ago. She said her department had an unusual bout with employee turnover before her employment, and she is the longest-tenured employee in her department."

He reached down and clicked his mouse twice. The projector turned off, and the office lights switched on.

"If Agent Manning is alive, he has remained off the radar since the operation. The suggestion that Agent Manning is somehow involved is circumstantial."

It went quiet for a spell before Pyotr stood. "Why is it that Harvey remained alive, and the box remained untouched in his closet?"

The Executive answered, "A good question, indeed. The box would have been an easy in-and-out job. I guess there was not enough time to recover it. Or, maybe it was because I never mentioned the box to anyone — not even Pytor or Neisha — until the day of the operation. Up to then, I had discussed only our target, Harvey Mitchell, with our team in the short time leading up to his extraction. Right after I mentioned Harvey Mitchell's name in our mission meeting, an assassination attempt was made on his life. Someone had tried to run him down. I suspect Mr. Manning is a double agent. Someone got to him, perhaps a secret group with knowledge of the Apocalypse. If this is true, we need to be very cautious going forward. Chances are Mr. Manning presented them with inside intel: our location, our organization, our missions. I have been out of touch for the past year, and, perhaps, I have been naïve to think we could not be compromised. We must double our security efforts. Anyone committing treason will be executed on the spot."

The projector fan whirred.

The Executive added, "Manning had a short window to execute an elaborate plan to take out Harvey and then fake his death. When we suddenly moved up the timetable for extraction, we offered him no chance to carry out his intended plan. He had only enough time to find a suitable sniper's nest, kill Harvey, and take his exit. Thankfully, we had possession of the box."

The Executive reached into his pocket and removed a clear plastic bag containing a deformed bul-

let. He held it up for all to see. His face darkened.
The dam that held back the rage he had accumulated
over the past twelve months burst. "This is what
fueled me all these months. We have fifteen people
who could have pulled off that hit with a single shot
from that rooftop in Philadelphia. Eight of them are
in this room, four others are on-site, and two were
in other parts of the world at the time. That makes
fourteen. Chad Manning worked in Special Forces
and had been a certified sniper. He is number fifteen." Spittle flew from his face when he uttered
those final words. The Executive pulled out a handkerchief and wiped his mouth, then eased himself
into his chair. "We will deal with Chad Manning in
due time, but we have more pressing matters — like
locating the Repository."

Pyotr said, "Maybe there are others like Harvey's father out there. Maybe one of them has the key
to putting an end to the Tests of Mettle."

The Executive considered that for a moment.
"True. Good point." He turned to the two surveillance guys. "I need you to scan the Internet. Dig
deep. Drum up everything you can. We need to find
anyone who might have an inkling of knowledge."

Pyotr added, "If someone was able to infiltrate
and turn Mr. Manning against us, apply substantial
resources in short order, and somehow have Manning's body double cremated in no time, then we can
assume we share the water with a wicked big fish."

The Executive nodded. "It is possible they
want the Apocalypse to occur. Money, power, and

a desire to see the world brought to an end. That should scare every single one of us to the core. We must work hard, move fast, and remain vigilant at all times. I have a feeling we are in for quite a battle."

ACKNOWLEDGE-MENTS

I want to thank my wife, Melissa, who is my rock, my hero, my inspiration. Thank you Larry Brooks, Tony Scott, and Tina and Renan Alfaro for your eternal optimism and for never losing faith in me. And a special thanks to friends and family for the unimaginable amount of support you've provided me. Lastly, I want to give a socially distant high five to the crew at Write by Night for the fantastic work they did in making my dream to be a published author come true.

ABOUT THE AUTHOR

M J Del Conte

MJ DelConte is a member
of the Wisconsin Writers
Association. He earned a
degree in Web Technolo-
gies from New England
Institute of Technology,
attended Florida Culinary
Institute, and honed his

writing skills at Gotham Writers Workshop in New
York. He currently resides in Madison, Wisconsin,
with his wife, Melissa, and two daughters.

A FAVOR

Because you purchased this work, I wish to say thank you.

Independent authors like myself work extremely hard to put out a quality product for our readers. We are responsibile for editing, proofing, book covers, advertising and marketing, websites, and so much more. As you can imagine, it takes quite a bit of time and personal resources to produce this simple little bundle of entertainment.

That brings me to the favor I wish to ask of you. If you enjoyed this novel, or any of the books I produce, I humbly ask that you provide a positive review from where you made your purchase. Word-of-mouth advertising is free, and it travels far and wide.

Finally, to stay up-to-date on all the updates and goodies, visit my website to subscribe to my newsletter at www.mjdelconte.com.

Be well. Be safe. Be blessed.

Made in the USA
Coppell, TX
25 June 2021